THE IRIS FAN

THE IRIS FAN

Laura Joh Rowland

MINOTAUR BOOKS
NEW YORK

THE IRIS FAN. Copyright © 2014 by Laura Joh Rowland. All rights reserved. Printed in the United States of America. For information, address St. Martin's Press, 175 Fifth Avenue, New York, N.Y. 10010.

www.minotaurbooks.com

Library of Congress Cataloging-in-Publication Data

Rowland, Laura Joh.
    The iris fan / Laura Joh Rowland.—First edition.
        pages   cm (Sano Ichiro novels; 18)
    "A novel of feudal Japan."
    ISBN 978-1-250-04706-9 (hardcover)
    ISBN 978-1-4668-4743-9 (e-book)
1. Sano, Ichiro (Fictitious character)—Fiction.   2. Samurai—Fiction.
3. Japan—History—18th century—Fiction.   I. Title.
    PS3568.O934I75 2014
    813'.54—dc23

                                                    2014027065

Minotaur books may be purchased for educational, business, or promotional use. For information on bulk purchases, please contact the Macmillan Corporate and Premium Sales Department at 1-800-221-7945, extension 5442, or write to specialmarkets@macmillan.com.

First Edition: December 2014

10 9 8 7 6 5 4 3 2 1

菖蒲

Edo, Month 1, Hoei Year 6

(Tokyo, February 1709)

Prologue

SLOW, HISSING BREATHS expanded and contracted the air in a chamber as dark as the bottom of a crypt. Wind shook the shutters. Sleet pattered onto the tile roof. In the corridor outside the chamber, the floor creaked under stealthy footsteps. The shimmering yellow glow of an oil lamp diffused across the room's lattice-and-paper wall. The footsteps halted outside the room; the door slid open as quietly as a whisper. A hand draped in the sleeve of a black kimono held the lamp across the threshold. The flame illuminated a futon, covered with a gold brocade satin quilt, in which two human shapes slumbered.

The quilt rose and fell with their breathing. The black-robed figure hovered at the threshold, then tiptoed, on feet clad in split-toed socks, into the bedchamber. The hem of its silk kimono slithered across the tatami floor. Its breathing was shallow, ragged with anxiety. It paused by the bed, holding the light over the two sleepers, whose gentle, rhythmic respirations continued. Then it crept to the one on the left, nearest the door. Kneeling, it set the lamp on the bedside table without a sound. In the dim light from the flame, a hand slowly, carefully, drew back the quilt.

Underneath, a man lay on his stomach, his head turned away from the intruder. He wore a white nightcap over his hair; his body was naked. The intruder contemplated his thin back, his protruding ribs and spine, his scrawny limbs. Red blotches covered his sallow, sweaty skin. He coughed in his sleep; he didn't wake.

The intruder sat back on its heels. Its ragged breaths quickened as its hand withdrew from beneath its sash a long, thin object with a sharp, gleaming metal end. The intruder glanced over its shoulder toward the door.

The corridor was silent, still.

Sleet bombarded the roof with a noise like raining arrowheads.

The wind moaned.

The intruder sucked in a deep, tremulous gasp, raised the weapon high above the sleeping man, and brought it slashing down.

1

"IT'S A BAD night for a trip to the pleasure quarter," Detective Marume said.

"It's a good night when we're following up on the first lead we've had in this investigation in more than four years," Sano said.

They rode their horses along the Dike of Japan, the long causeway above the rice fields northeast of Edo. Metal lanterns swung from poles attached to their backs. On this winter night just after the New Year, they had the road to Yoshiwara to themselves. Their cloaks were drenched by sleet that lashed and stung their faces. Ice coated their metal helmets. Cold wind seeped through the heavy padding in Sano's cloak, under his armor tunic and his kimono. As sleet turned to snow, a veil of white crystals obscured the distance.

"How did you get us assigned to patrol the dike tonight?" Marume asked.

"I didn't even have to try. You know the captain likes giving the worst assignments to the shogun's disgraced former chamberlain and second-in-command." Bitterness edged Sano's wry tone.

In four years he'd been demoted four times, from chamberlain down to patrol guard, the Tokugawa regime's lowest rank. His son, Masahiro, aged seventeen, was also a patrol guard, with no prospects for advancement, and their family had been evicted from their estate inside Edo Castle. It was a great humiliation for Sano, but he was lucky to have a position at all. For more than four years he'd been pursuing a forbidden investigation, a thankless mission of honor.

Marume laughed. "He did us a favor without knowing it." The big samurai relished humor in any situation. "How do you know our new suspects are in Yoshiwara tonight?"

"An informer." Sano had bribed a servant of Lord Tokugawa Ienobu, the shogun's nephew and designated heir to the dictatorship.

Ahead, Yoshiwara rose up from the rice fields, a city unto itself, the only place in Edo where prostitution was legal. Lights within its high walls made the falling snow above it glow like a halo. Sano and Marume rode across the moat to the gate where two sentries occupied a guardhouse. Moat, gate, and sentries were there to prevent troublemakers from entering the pleasure quarter and unhappy courtesans from escaping. The sentries opened the gate; Sano and Marume rode in.

Naka-no-chō, the long main street that extended between rows of brothels, was almost empty. A few drunks stumbled to and fro. Snow frosted the tile roofs of the brothels; icicles grew between the red lanterns that hung from the eaves. Storm shutters covered the window cages where courtesans usually sat on display. Sano heard faint music played on samisens, flutes, and drums.

"The cold is keeping the customers at home," Marume said.

"Or the measles epidemic is."

The epidemic had been raging across the country since autumn. It had come to Japan via Chinese priests visiting Nagasaki, the only place where foreigners were allowed. In Nagasaki some ten thousand people had died. Hundreds of people in Edo were sick. The disease was often but not invariably fatal. Here in Yoshiwara, as well as in town, incense burned outside doors to chase away the evil spirits of disease, and citizens feared contagion.

"Speaking of measles, how is the shogun?" Marume asked. The shogun had come down with the measles just before the New Year.

"I hear he's recovering, but I haven't seen for myself," Sano said. He'd been banned from court four years ago. That had been his punishment after the shogun had ordered him to stop the investigation and he'd disobeyed. Sano had continued pursuing it for the good of the regime, to the detriment of his own career and domestic peace.

He and his wife, Reiko, were seriously at odds over his actions. Long hours of patrol duty were a blessing for a man who didn't want to go home.

"So it looks like the shogun isn't going to die," Marume said with relief.

"Yes, but he's badly weakened. His health has always been frail, and he's sixty-three. Lord Ienobu is going to inherit the dictatorship sooner rather than later."

That was why this new lead was so crucial.

Sano and Marume turned their horses down one of the narrow lanes that crossed Naka-no-chō and stopped outside a small brothel. Laughter burst upon them as they peered through the window whose shutters were cracked open to clear out the smoke from charcoal braziers and tobacco pipes. A party occupied a room bright with lanterns. Young women as colorful as butterflies in their gay kimonos, their faces heavily made up and their hair spangled with ornaments, flirted with four samurai and plied them with sake.

"Who's who?" Marume asked.

"The old fellow at the head of the table is Manabe Akira, Lord Ienobu's chief retainer."

Manabe, in his late fifties, had a gray topknot and wore gray robes. His shaved crown and face were brown and shiny like an iron war mask from martial arts practice in the sun. He'd been a top swordsman in his day. When a courtesan teased him, he responded with grunts.

"A real sociable type," Marume said.

"The men seated with their backs to us are Setsubara Ihei and Ono Jozan," Sano said. They were big and muscular, their kimonos fashionable with garish patterns, their black topknots slick with oil. They raised their cups in a toast. "They're Manabe's aides."

"The one across from them must have been a kid at the time of the murder."

"Kuzawa Daimon, age nineteen. He's a guard."

Kuzawa was as big and strong as Manabe's aides, and dressed like them, but his face and body had the softer look of youth. A courtesan stroked his beefy arm while telling him a joke. He laughed uproariously.

"Why do you think it's these men who killed the shogun's son?" Marume asked.

"Yoshisato wasn't the shogun's son," Sano reminded him.

"I know. It's just easier to call him 'the shogun's son' than 'the cuckoo's egg that Chamberlain Yanagisawa foisted off on the shogun.'"

Six years ago, Yanagisawa had put Yoshisato, his own son, in line to inherit the dictatorship by proclaiming that Yoshisato was really the shogun's secret, long-lost son and he himself was only Yoshisato's adoptive father. Sano had tried to debunk the story and failed. The shogun believed it. So did enough top government officials and *daimyo*—the feudal lords who ruled the provinces. The shogun had named Yoshisato as his successor, and Yanagisawa had been set to rule Japan through him and gain absolute power. But two years later, a fire set in the heir's residence had killed Yoshisato.

Sano began the answer to Marume's question. "Yoshisato's death cleared the way for Lord Ienobu to succeed the shogun, and we know Ienobu is responsible for the arson."

"The woman who set the fire said he put her up to it, but she died right after confessing." Marume watched Manabe puff on his pipe. "You think he helped Lord Ienobu set up Yoshisato's murder?"

"Yes. My informer says that shortly before the fire started, Manabe and the other three left Ienobu's estate. They didn't come back until the next day. They're the only people from the estate who were unaccounted for at the time of the murder."

"But what part did they play in it?"

"That's what we're going to find out. And then we'll have proof that Lord Ienobu is guilty of at least one murder."

Sano already knew that Ienobu was responsible for the murder of the shogun's daughter. The culprit in that crime, also unfortunately dead, had implicated Ienobu. Sano wanted the proof as urgently as a starving man salivates for food. It wasn't just duty that compelled him to deliver Ienobu to justice and prevent a murderer from becoming the next shogun. Sano had liked Yoshisato even though he was Yanagisawa's son and

Yanagisawa was Sano's longtime enemy. Sano wanted to avenge Yoshisato's death, and he had another, even more personal motive for bringing Lord Ienobu down. Ienobu was the one who'd demoted Sano, as punishment for telling the shogun that Ienobu had murdered Yoshisato. The shogun didn't want to believe that his nephew and heir had murdered the man he thought was his son. He kept Sano in the regime, but Lord Ienobu constantly found ways to make life miserable for Sano.

Manabe spoke in a gruff, peremptory voice to his subordinates. All four men drained their sake cups and headed for the door. Sano and Marume backed their horses into an alley, watched the men emerge from the brothel, then exited the gate behind them. Across the moat, the men retrieved their horses from a stable and attached lanterns on poles to their backs. They didn't notice Sano and Marume trailing them as they rode along the dike; patrol guards were ubiquitous, invisible. All Sano could see of them was their lights like swinging stars in the darkness. He was fifty years old, and his night vision was poor.

A glow in the distance signaled that they were nearing Edo. Sano and Marume spurred their horses to a gallop. "Stop!" Sano called as he and Marume caught up with their quarries.

The four men looked over their shoulders. Their lanterns threw arcing beams across the road. They reached for their swords as they turned their horses around, their expressions wary as they squinted through the snowflakes. Recognition appeared on Manabe's hard, shiny face.

"Sano-*san*." His gruff voice rasped with disapproval. "What do you want?"

At long last Sano was about to solve Yoshisato's murder and defeat Lord Ienobu. Apprehension coiled within his excitement: This was his one chance, a big risk. "To talk with you four." Beside him, Marume put his hand to his sword.

"You're supposed to stay away from us and everybody else in Lord Ienobu's retinue," Setsubara said. With his strong jaws, prominent nose, and sharp cheekbones, he was a caricature of masculinity.

"Those are Lord Ienobu's orders, and you know it." Ono's lumpy features reminded Sano of a bitter melon.

Even as his heart raced, Sano spoke calmly. "When you hear what I have to say, you'll be glad I disregarded those orders." He eyed Kuzawa. The young samurai looked nervous; he hadn't learned to hide his emotions.

"When Lord Ienobu hears that you've disobeyed him, he'll have your head." Manabe jerked his chin at the other men. They all started to turn their horses.

Sano said quickly, "You four left his estate shortly before the fire in the heir's residence started. Isn't that an interesting coincidence?"

The four men went still. Sano focused on Kuzawa, whose eyes were wide, stricken. Seeing that he was right about the four men, Sano felt a rush of exhilaration.

"We went night fishing on the river," Manabe said in annoyance.

"Did you catch a big one?" Detective Marume asked scornfully.

"We can vouch for each other," Ono said.

"Meaning, no one else can," Sano said. "You weren't fishing. You were up to your necks in Yoshisato's murder."

Manabe uttered a disgusted sound. Setsubara and Ono shook their heads, as if pitying Sano's foolishness. Detective Marume laughed and pointed at Kuzawa, who looked scared enough to wet his trousers. "Whoops, your young friend as good as admitted you're guilty."

Kuzawa ducked his head. Manabe said to Sano, "You can't prove anything."

"You're wrong. I have evidence," Sano bluffed.

"What evidence?" Ono asked disdainfully.

"The shogun will be first to know."

"You won't be able to tell him anything." Contempt didn't quite mask Setsubara's worry. "You're banned from court."

"I'll make sure the information is shouted by every news seller in Edo," Sano said. "Soon it will be on the tongue of every samurai at the castle. It will reach the shogun eventually. He'll know you're as guilty as the woman who set the fire."

"And then he'll have your heads," Marume added.

Kuzawa gulped. Setsubara and Ono glared at him, but they looked scared, too. Manabe's hand tightened on his sword.

"If you're thinking of killing us to shut us up, forget it," Sano said.

"Other people know. If anything happens to us, they'll make the evidence public. You're going down for treason."

The penalty for treason was death. The three subordinates looked anxiously to Manabe; he scowled. Sano urged his horse forward, advancing on them. "But it doesn't have to be that way, if you confess that you arranged Yoshisato's murder on orders from Lord Ienobu."

The four men looked stunned as they realized what Sano was after. Detective Marume clarified, "He doesn't want your fat rear ends. He wants Lord Ienobu's skinny one."

"Give me Lord Ienobu, and I'll see that you're pardoned," Sano said.

He knew he was asking a lot from them. They owed their master their complete loyalty. That was Bushido, the Way of the Warrior, the samurai code of honor. And although the shogun was the lord over everyone in Japan, their ties to Ienobu were closer; they were his personal retainers. Anger darkened their faces as they comprehended that Sano was making them choose between dooming themselves and betraying Lord Ienobu, the ultimate sin.

Manabe spoke through clenched teeth. "We will not submit to blackmail. We will not help you destroy our master." The other men nodded.

Sano had to break them, or heaven help him. "Fine. Be good samurai. But don't expect Lord Ienobu to protect you when it comes out that you were involved in Yoshisato's murder."

"He'll let you take the entire blame rather than admit you acted on his orders and be put to death along with you," Detective Marume said.

That was Bushido, too: Loyalty didn't cut both ways. Emotions flickered across their faces as the four men stared down Sano and Marume. Sano detected fear, confusion, and something oddly sly in their expressions. The wind keened. The lantern's flames hissed as snowflakes hit them. In the instant that Sano realized what was going to happen, the four men drew their swords and charged.

Sano and Marume barely had time to draw their own weapons before the men were upon them. Horses collided, whinnied, and reared. Sano lashed out. His sword cleaved falling snowflakes. The lanterns attached to his back and the other men's swung crazily. He glimpsed his opponents in flashes—a red embossed breastplate; a chain-mailed arm;

Ono's snarling face. Everything was dark except where the light momentarily touched. Sano's poor night vision put him at a serious disadvantage. His opponents flew at him out of nowhere. A blade struck his helmet, and the metallic clang shuddered his skull. He dodged and swung frantically. This was his first battle in more than four years. He practiced martial arts every morning, but real combat was different, not bound by rules, chaotic. And although Sano had won battles in which he was hugely outnumbered, he was older now. Maybe he could beat Manabe, but he couldn't outmatch the three younger samurai whose vision was sharper, reflexes quicker, and stamina greater.

Marume yelled. Lights swung. In their path appeared a brief image of Marume covered with blood, arms thrown out, falling. Sano was horrified, and not just because Marume was his only ally tonight and among the few retainers he had left; he'd discharged the others when he was demoted and his government stipend reduced. Marume had been his friend for twenty years. Heedless of his own safety, Sano leapt off his mount. He faltered through the tumult of hooves pounding and blades slicing at him, desperate to save Marume.

Marume staggered up from the ground. "I'm all right! My horse was cut."

The other men jumped off their horses. Kuzawa grabbed Sano from behind. Sano struggled, but he couldn't break the young man's grip. Setsubara and Ono wrestled Marume to the ground. His face red with horse blood, Marume shouted curses. Setsubara and Ono bound his wrists. Kuzawa tied Sano's wrists so tight that the rope cut into his flesh. Sano glared helplessly at Manabe.

"Four against two—are you really that stupid?" Manabe scoffed. He told his men, "We'll take them to Lord Ienobu. He'll want to deal with them personally."

The men boosted Sano and Marume onto Sano's horse, knotted rope around them so they couldn't escape, and confiscated the swords they'd dropped.

"You think you know so much, but you don't know anything," Manabe said with a pitying look at Sano. "You're going to wish you'd minded your own business."

2

ESCORTED BY IENOBU'S men, Sano entered Edo some three hours before midnight. He was glad of the bad weather; there was no one around to see him and Marume tied onto his horse like captured criminals and to throw stones.

Edo, home to a million citizens, still showed the effects from the eruption of Mount Fuji two years ago. The sky had rained sand and pebbles all night and by morning the city was ankle-deep in ash. Houses built since the great earthquake five years ago were grimy with ash that the wind still blew in from the mountains. The ash turned the wet snow on the streets and the tile roofs gray.

The castle occupied a hill that rose above the city, its buildings constructed on ascending tiers up to the peak. Lights shone from the windows of covered corridors atop the retaining walls around each tier. Snowflakes scintillated in the lights and swirled around the guard towers. The castle looked like hazy rings of golden stars between layers of darkness. Sano had once lived there but hadn't been inside since he'd been banned from court. When they reached the moat, Manabe's men untied Sano and Marume. They left Marume to ride home and marched Sano up to the gate. Sano looked back on twenty years of some difficult but mostly good times inside this fortress. Here he'd brought Reiko as his bride and they'd fallen in love. Both their children had been born here. He'd risen from the shogun's chief investigator to chamberlain and second-in-command.

This wasn't like coming home. It was like entering the enemy camp. The good times were over, his family life in shambles.

Sentries opened the gate. Manabe walked Sano up through stone-walled passages to the shogun's heir's residence in the western fortress, on the tier of the hill just below the palace at the peak. The building had white-plastered, half-timbered walls, wings connected by corridors, and a curved tile roof. Icicles on pine trees outside dripped water on snow-glazed grass. Flames burned in stone lanterns along the gravel path. Here Yoshisato had died in the fire that had burned down the residence more than four years ago. Rebuilt, it was now home to Lord Ienobu.

Manabe's three henchmen guarded Sano in the courtyard while Manabe went to notify Lord Ienobu. Soon Manabe escorted Sano into the reception chamber, a long room with a lattice-and-paper wall on one side and wooden sliding exterior doors opposite. Two men sat on a dais furnished with gold-inlaid metal lanterns and satin brocade cushions, backed by a mural that depicted a garden of brilliant red and orange peonies on a gold background.

"Here we go again, Sano-*san*," Lord Ienobu said. "You keep disobeying my orders and getting caught." With his stunted figure, jutting elbows, and the hump on his back, dressed in a green and gold kimono, he blended into the mural behind him—a cricket amid the flowers. He looked much older than his forty-eight years. His upper teeth protruded above a tiny lower jaw; his deformities stemmed from a hereditary, painful bone condition. "When are you going to learn your lesson?" His tight, raspy voice sounded squeezed out of him, like a cricket's chirp. In the two years since Sano had last seen him, he'd gained weight, as if fattened by a rich diet of power. Maybe he looked more like a maggot, Sano thought. "Are you getting slow on the uptake in your old age?"

Manabe pushed Sano to his knees. Charcoal braziers under the tatami floor breathed heat through iron grilles, but Sano, chilled to the bone, took no comfort from it. Angry at the futility of his own stubbornness as well as at Ienobu for mocking and punishing him, Sano said, "When are you going to stop denying that you're responsible for Yoshisato's death? Do you really think you can get away with it forever?"

14

Ienobu grimaced in impatience. "I am not responsible. That woman Korika set the fire."

"She said in her dying confession that you put her up to it," Sano said.

Chamberlain Yanagisawa, the other man on the dais, responded in a suave voice, "And who heard this dying confession?"

"My wife," Sano said. His temper boiled at the challenge from Yanagisawa.

They'd been enemies for twenty years. From the outset Yanagisawa had viewed Sano as his rival for political power, and he'd developed an extreme hatred toward Sano. Sano's own antagonism toward Yanagisawa stemmed from Yanagisawa's attacks on him and his family. Their feud had escalated when Yanagisawa had tried to pass his son off as the shogun's son. It was a fraud that Sano couldn't let slide even though the shogun had accepted Yoshisato, the cuckoo's egg. Not only would Yanagisawa's gaining control over the regime mean doom for Sano, it was a crime against the lord that Sano was duty-bound to serve. Bushido demanded that Sano redress it no matter that Yoshisato was dead. And now Yanagisawa was committing yet another breach of honor by allying with Ienobu, the man responsible for the murders of both Yoshisato and the shogun's daughter.

Sano couldn't figure out why.

"Oh, well, then." Yanagisawa's look said that of course a wife would lie to support her husband.

Sano studied Yanagisawa, whom he hadn't seen in four years. At age fifty-one, Yanagisawa exemplified how handsome a man can remain as he gets older. Red and bronze satin robes infused color into his skin, still firm over strongly modeled bones. Silver threads in his glossy black hair enhanced his masculine beauty. But his eyes, which had once gleamed as if made of liquid darkness, were now dry and hot like stones baked in a fire. Viewing him and Lord Ienobu side by side, Sano had the odd sense that Ienobu thrived by sucking Yanagisawa's marrow.

"Why are you so quick to believe he's innocent?" Sano pointed at Ienobu. "He had the best motive for Yoshisato's murder. It cleared the way for him to become the next shogun."

"So you told me more than four years ago," Yanagisawa said with a tired air. "So you've been saying ever since, to anyone who'll listen."

"May I remind you again, there's no evidence that anyone besides Korika was involved in the arson," Lord Ienobu said.

"How did she get to the heir's residence, set it on fire, and leave without being caught?" Sano demanded. "The residence was heavily guarded. And there's new evidence that she had help." He explained about Manabe and the other men. "I think they killed Yoshisato's guards. That's why Korika wasn't caught."

"My men have an alibi," Ienobu said.

"Your men are one another's alibi. There's nothing else to prove they weren't at the heir's residence murdering Yoshisato."

"There's nothing to prove they were, either," Ienobu said

"I say Manabe and his henchmen killed Yoshisato as well as the guards, and the fire only disguised the real cause of their deaths."

Yanagisawa shook his head sadly. "You've come up with some wild stories in the past, but this time you've gone completely insane."

"Me? That's the coal calling the ink black! You're the one who wanted to put Yoshisato at the head of the regime. You're the one who lost your chance to rule Japan when Yoshisato died. Lord Ienobu was Yoshisato's rival and your enemy, yet you joined forces with him when Yoshisato's ashes were barely cold!" Perplexed, Sano said, "Why?"

The arid heat in Yanagisawa's eyes flared, as if with anger smoldering beneath his calm façade. "I've let bygones be bygones. You really should try it. It would make your life easier."

"How could you? I know you cared about Yoshisato. I saw how upset you were when you saw his burned corpse." Yanagisawa grimaced, as if more vexed at Sano for bringing up trivia than grieved by the loss of his son. Lord Ienobu watched them complacently. "It wasn't just because you'd lost your political pawn. You loved him." A father himself, Sano recognized paternal love when he saw it. And Sano had contended with Yanagisawa for so long that they were almost mystically attuned to each other. "You were devastated that Yoshisato was gone. How could you sell him out by allying with his enemy?"

"Lord Ienobu and I were enemies, yes," Yanagisawa said smoothly, "but we decided it would be best for both of us if we teamed up."

"You mean you decided to hitch your cart to the shogun's new heir."

"If you cooperated with Lord Ienobu instead of beating your head against a stone wall," Yanagisawa said, "you would be better off. And so would your family."

His family was the only reason Sano regretted opposing Ienobu. They'd suffered badly on account of it.

"You really should have accepted the deal I offered you," Lord Ienobu said.

Several times he'd offered Sano respectable posts in the regime in exchange for ceasing the campaign to prove him guilty of Yoshisato's murder and knock him out of line for the succession. Sano had turned Ienobu down flat. It was a point of contention between Sano and Reiko.

Angry at Yanagisawa and determined to shake some sense into him, Sano asked, "Don't you want to avenge Yoshisato's death? Why won't you help me bring his murderer to justice? You owe it to the shogun, if not to Yoshisato or yourself. You're a miserable excuse for a samurai!"

"False accusations against Lord Ienobu didn't get me on your side. Insults certainly won't." The hostility in Yanagisawa's eyes said he hadn't forgotten their two decades of bad blood. Maybe the bad blood was enough to make him think Ienobu was innocent rather than believe anything Sano said, but Sano sensed something terribly off about Yanagisawa.

"What's wrong with you?" Sano asked in honest, concerned bewilderment.

Lord Ienobu raised a hand. "Sano-*san*, you've used up your last chance to stop your ridiculous investigation. I'm going to put an end to it once and for all."

"How? You'll kick me out of the regime?" Sano laughed scornfully. "If you could, you already would have. The fact that I'm still here must mean the shogun either still has some affection for me or he isn't sure I'm wrong about you. You can demote me to cleaning toilets, but I'll prove you're guilty of murder and treason."

Lord Ienobu grinned; his lips peeled back from his protruding teeth. "Things have changed. I've been appointed Acting Shogun. Until His Excellency recovers from the measles, I have the power to do as I like."

Sano was too shocked to hide his dismay. "Appointed by whom?"

Yanagisawa smiled, sharing Ienobu's triumph. "The Council of Elders." The four old men on the Council comprised Japan's principal governing body and the shogun's top advisors. "They decided Lord Ienobu should take charge temporarily."

"When did this happen?"

"Today."

The lower Sano fell, the longer it took news to trickle down to him. He'd unwittingly made a bad mistake by going after Manabe and his henchmen tonight, when the stakes had just risen drastically. A cold, dreadful hollow formed in Sano's gut. He'd been courting disaster for more than four years, and now it was here.

Lord Ienobu opened his mouth to pronounce the words that would make Sano a *rōnin*—masterless samurai—and strip him of his livelihood and his place in society. Thrown out on the streets, his family would starve and Sano would forever lose his chance to bring Lord Ienobu to justice. Yanagisawa wore a strange smile—glee mixed with pain. Before Ienobu could speak or Sano could protest, Manabe rushed into the room.

"Excuse me, my lord. There's an emergency in the palace. The shogun has been stabbed!"

3

SHOCKED SILENCE GREETED the news that Sano couldn't believe. Security in the palace was the tightest in Japan. How could someone have stabbed the shogun? Sano's shock turned to horror, and not just because his lord, the reason for a samurai's existence, had been attacked. If the shogun was dead, then Lord Ienobu was the new dictator. Sano wouldn't just lose his place in the regime and his samurai status, Lord Ienobu would put Sano and his family to death before the funeral rites for the old shogun were over.

Ienobu gaped. Elation visibly rose up in him like gas bubbles in stagnant pond water as he saw his dream of ruling Japan within reach.

Yanagisawa looked like he'd been shot. His handsome face was pale, drained of blood. Sano frowned in surprise. After supporting Ienobu for more than four years, Yanagisawa should be thrilled by the news of the stabbing, but he obviously wasn't. He didn't even seem glad that Ienobu's rise to power would mean the end of Sano. His stricken eyes focused inward.

"Is my uncle . . . ?" Lord Ienobu's voice trailed off as if he dared not speak the word. He held it in his mouth like a child savoring a piece of candy.

"Dead?" Manabe said. "No. But he's seriously injured."

An avalanche of relief overwhelmed Sano.

"What happened?" Yanagisawa spoke in a strange, toneless voice.

Manabe shook his head. Lord Ienobu said, "We'd better go to the palace and find out." He scuttled out the door faster than Sano had ever seen him move.

Yanagisawa hurried after him; Sano followed. Manabe stuck close behind Sano, in case Sano should decide to bolt. The night echoed with yells as troops stationed throughout the castle spread the news. Ienobu's hunched figure led the rush along the dim passage up the hill through falling snow. The palace compound was lit up as if for an unholy festival. Soldiers stood around the tile-roofed, half-timbered building. Their lanterns and torches splayed yellow light on the snowy grass, shrubs, and paths. Their silence was eerie, their anxiety palpable.

"Let us through!" Yanagisawa said.

He and Lord Ienobu, Sano, and Manabe sped into the palace, through a maze of corridors where frightened servants huddled and more troops stood guard. Sentries admitted them to the shogun's private quarters. Moans filled the passage along which Sano and his companions raced. The paper wall of the shogun's bedchamber was bright with lights behind it. The lattice crisscrossed the moving shadows of people inside. The sliding door was open; the moans issued from it. Lord Ienobu and Yanagisawa bumped against each other in their hurry to enter. When Sano crossed the threshold, the smells hit him—diarrhea and the salty sweet, iron odor of blood. The shogun lay facedown and naked on the futon with two deep, ragged, bleeding cuts between his ribs and two lower ones on either side of his spine. The white sheet under him and the quilt at the foot of the bed were red with blood and foul with excrement released from his bowels. The chief palace physician—an elderly man dressed in the long, dark blue coat of his profession—hovered by a medicine chest. Two male servants were trying to remove the soiled sheet. As they pulled on it and lifted the shogun, he screamed.

"Stop! It hurts!"

Alarmed by the shogun's injuries, Sano was also amazed at how much the shogun had aged since he'd last seen him four years ago. His hair was all gray, his body spindly. Lord Ienobu struggled to hide his disappointment—he must have hoped the shogun would be dead by now. Yanagisawa swallowed hard as he beheld the lord whose lover he'd been when he was young, whose patronage had raised him from a lowly vassal to the heights of political power.

The other person in the room was Captain Hosono of the palace's night guard, a samurai about forty years old. He stood in a corner, his usually pleasant face terror-stricken because the attack had occurred on his watch.

"If you won't let the servants make your bed clean, we'll have to move you to another room," the physician told the shogun.

"No! I can't bear to be moved. Give me some more opium!" the shogun begged.

"I've already given you the maximum dose," the physician said.

The shogun screamed while the servants eased the sheet from under him and covered the stained mattress with fresh sheets. One carried out the soiled bedding; the others washed the shogun. The physician dabbed his wounds with a pungent herbal solution. The shogun moaned, his frail body tense with pain. The measles rash was bright red against the white pallor of his skin. Afraid of contagion, Lord Ienobu and Yanagisawa stood near the door by Sano.

"Uncle, how are you?" Ienobu asked with exaggerated concern.

"Can't you see? Or are you blind as well as ugly?" The shogun had once been a meek, timid man, afraid to speak his mind and offend. It wasn't just pain that made him rude now. He'd turned over a new leaf several years ago. "Ouch, you're hurting me!"

"I'm being as gentle as I can," the physician said. "I have to clean your wounds."

"Fie upon the whole medical profession! You're nothing but a bunch of quacks!"

"What happened?" Lord Ienobu asked Captain Hosono.

"His Excellency was in bed. Somebody sneaked in and stabbed him."

"Who was it, Your Excellency?" Yanagisawa's voice was tight, as if he were trying not to retch.

"I didn't see. I was asleep." As the doctor cleaned another wound, the shogun shrieked, "Damn you!"

Sano shifted his mind from its focus on Yoshisato's murder to the attack on the shogun. It felt like pushing a cart and trying to turn its wheels out of deep ruts they'd been rolling in for more than four years.

"Where were His Excellency's bodyguards?" Lord Ienobu asked.

"He sent them away," Captain Hosono said. "He had a concubine with him."

Sano had heard that the shogun had become impotent and any distraction, such as people outside his chamber, prevented him from performing sexually. "Where is the concubine?"

Captain Hosono looked surprised that Sano was present after he'd been banned from court. "In here." He opened the wooden sliding door between the bedchamber and the adjacent room, the shogun's study.

A small boy who'd been kneeling on the tatami, his ear pressed against the door, fell into the chamber and scrambled to his feet. He looked about nine years old. The shogun preferred sex with males, especially children and adolescents; he rarely slept with women. That was one reason Sano didn't believe Yoshisato was his son. Sano also had doubts about whether the shogun had actually fathered his daughter.

"Eavesdropping, were you?" Captain Hosono said to the boy.

The boy nodded sheepishly. A white blanket wrapped around his body slipped to reveal bare, thin shoulders. He pulled it up and brushed back his tousled hair. His innocent face was as delicate and lovely as a girl's.

Sano felt sorry for him. He was the shogun's sexual toy, he'd been sharing a bed with the shogun at the risk of catching measles, and he'd been present during a violent attack. Sano went to him and said, "What's your name?"

"Dengoro," the boy said in a clear, sweet voice.

"Dengoro, can you tell me who stabbed His Excellency?"

The boy shook his head. Encouraged by Sano's friendly manner, he said, "I was asleep. I woke up when His Excellency started screaming. Somebody ran out of the room."

"Can you describe the person?"

"No. It was too dark to see."

The physician prepared to stitch the shogun's cuts with a long needle. Sano dismissed the boy. The shogun panted and shivered. Yanagisawa and Lord Ienobu regarded him with frowning speculation. Sano asked Captain Hosono, "Who was first on the scene?"

"His Excellency's valet. He called the bodyguards." Hosono anticipated Sano's next question. "He didn't see anything, either. The attacker was already gone."

Sano persisted even though he was just a patrol guard and this wasn't his case to solve. "Were any clues found?"

"The weapon." Captain Hosono walked to the bedside table, picked up a long, narrow object wrapped in a white cloth, and handed it to Sano. "It was lying by the bed. I thought I'd better wrap it up for safe-keeping."

Sano uncovered a large, folded fan with ribs that came to long points at one end and a green silk tassel attached by a braided green cord at the other. The points were red, bloodstained. Sano unfolded the fan, displaying an arc of heavy gold rice paper painted with blue irises on leafy green stalks. Irises symbolized boldness, courage, and power. Perhaps they'd served as a talisman for the would-be assassin.

"How could a fan do that?" Ienobu pointed his crooked finger at the shogun's back. The doctor threaded the needle with a long horse tail hair.

The fan felt abnormally heavy in Sano's hand. "The ribs are made of iron. They're sharpened at the ends." This was no ordinary fan used to create cooling breezes in summer. It was a weapon of the kind used for self-defense, often by merchants, peasants, or women. The law permitted only samurai to carry swords.

The physician applied a numbing potion to the edges of a cut between the shogun's ribs. When he inserted the needle, the shogun moaned, but quietly: The opium was taking effect. "Nephew, come here." The shogun extended his trembling hand toward Lord Ienobu.

Ienobu hesitated, reluctant to go near the shogun, fearful of measles, but he didn't dare refuse, lest the shogun get angry and disinherit him. As he knelt beside the bed, the shogun gripped his hand tightly; he winced. The doctor stitched. Ienobu averted his face as the needle went in and out of flesh. Sano contemplated the whimpering shogun. Although Bushido decreed that a samurai should feel nothing but respect and loyalty toward

his lord, at times Sano had hated the shogun for his selfishness, unfairness, and cruelty. But now the lord he'd served for twenty years was a
suffering old man. Sano felt the same outrage as he did on behalf of any
helpless victim of a crime. His spirit clamored to avenge the attack on
his lord.

The physician knotted and cut the last thread, slathered healing balm
on the stitched cuts, bandaged them, and covered the shogun with a clean
quilt. Yanagisawa said to him, "May I have a word?" and drew him out to
the corridor.

Lord Ienobu started to follow, but the shogun clutched his hand. "Stay
with me, Nephew."

Ienobu shot Yanagisawa a warning glance. Sano became aware that
something was different between his two enemies since they'd heard
about the attack on the shogun. The political game board was rearrang-
ing, the players in transit to new positions. The crisis had created new
opportunities as well as troubles, and not the least for Sano himself.

Now the shogun noticed Sano. The pupils of his eyes were dilated by
the opium; he smiled groggily, as if he'd forgotten he'd banned Sano from
court and he was welcoming a dear, long-lost friend. "You stay, too,
Sano-*san*."

4

IN THE CORRIDOR, Yanagisawa quietly asked the physician, "What's the prognosis?"

"His Excellency may have internal hemorrhaging. His wounds may fester. There's a danger of permanent damage to his organs—"

"Don't tell me what might happen!" Anxiety raised Yanagisawa's voice, and he struggled to control himself. He didn't want Sano to hear him, guess how much he didn't want the shogun to die, and wonder why. He couldn't let Ienobu know how desperately afraid he was. "Tell me if he's going to survive."

The physician hesitated, clearly reluctant to be negative lest he bring bad luck to the shogun, yet not wanting to hold out false promise. "That he's still alive is a good sign, but his condition is very serious."

Dread sank Yanagisawa's heart. If the shogun died, it would mean the end of Yanagisawa's alliance with Lord Ienobu, the end of his ambition to rule Japan someday, the end of his life. But that wasn't the worst. The shogun's death would also mean the end of Yanagisawa's hopes of saving the only person in the world he loved.

"If you'll excuse me," the physician said, "I must tend to my patient."

Yanagisawa stood alone in the corridor, remembering his shock at the news he'd received the day after Yoshisato's funeral. He'd been standing outside the palace, with the smell of smoke and burned flesh in the air, when Lord Ienobu spoke the words that turned the world upside down.

"Yoshisato is alive. He didn't die in that fire."

At first Yanagisawa hadn't believed it. Then Ienobu had explained. *"I told Korika that if she set a fire that night, she wouldn't be caught. I arranged for the castle guards to be absent from their posts. Korika went to the heir's residence. Five of my men got there first. They killed Yoshisato's personal bodyguards, tied up Yoshisato, and drugged him. Korika set the fire, and ran away. Before the house burned down, my men dragged the dead bodyguards inside. They killed one of their comrades and left his corpse in Yoshisato's chamber. Then they carried Yoshisato out of the castle in a trunk."*

"Why would you save Yoshisato?" Yanagisawa demanded. *"If he's alive, he's the shogun's first choice for an heir."*

"I have enemies who don't want me to be the next shogun," Ienobu said. *"I need you to help me neutralize them. When I'm shogun, you can have Yoshisato back."*

Then Lord Ienobu had produced a letter written by Yoshisato, that had demolished all Yanagisawa's doubts about whether Ienobu was telling the truth.

"Where is he?" Yanagisawa demanded.

"In a guarded, secret place," Ienobu said. *"Breathe a word of this conversation to anyone, and you'll never see him again."*

"I'll kill you!"

"If anything bad happens to me, or if you refuse to support me as the next shogun, Yoshisato dies for real."

Yanagisawa had known that Ienobu meant to string him along until Ienobu was shogun; then Ienobu would kill Yoshisato. The only way for Yanagisawa to save Yoshisato was to find him before the current shogun died and Ienobu didn't need a hostage anymore. The only way for Yanagisawa and Yoshisato to rule Japan was to destroy Ienobu before he took over the dictatorship. For more than four years he'd been searching for Yoshisato. He had spies secretly combing Japan while he acted the role of Ienobu's vigilant ally. He'd exiled some of Ienobu's enemies within the government to faraway islands, demoted others or dispatched them to posts in the provinces. That had brought other men hostile to Ienobu into line. Although Yanagisawa longed to join forces with Sano to prove Ienobu was a traitor, he pretended to believe Ienobu was innocent. His son's life depended on his charade.

But every clue to Yoshisato's whereabouts had led to a dead end, and if the shogun died, Ienobu would become dictator. He would put Yoshisato—and Yanagisawa—to death. Panic beset Yanagisawa like a horde of shouting madmen pummeling him. How could he save Yoshisato? He might have only days, hours, or moments left in which to do it.

The instincts that had served him well during three decades in politics gave Yanagisawa the first piece of his emergency strategy: He must keep the shogun alive, keep Sano under control, and keep Ienobu from gaining any further advantage.

SANO KNELT ON the left side of the bed. The shogun lay facing toward Ienobu on his right. The doctor knelt at the foot of the bed, Captain Hosono by the wall. The air still stank of blood and feces. The servants stirred the charcoal braziers set in the floor, fanning up heat to keep the shogun warm. Sano wished he could fling open the exterior doors and let in the cold, fresh wind. It might sweep the shock and confusion from his mind and help him think clearly.

The shogun trembled, then went still, then trembled, at irregular intervals. His hand clung to Lord Ienobu's. Ienobu wore the proper, concerned expression, but Sano could almost see his ill will flowing like black poison from his heart, through a vein in his arm, and into the shogun. Sano wanted to tear their hands apart.

Yanagisawa returned, bringing two guards. He knelt beside the doctor and studied the shogun. "Why is he shaking?"

"He's in shock," the physician said.

"Then do something." Yanagisawa's concern, unlike Ienobu's, seemed genuine.

"I gave him medicine. There's nothing more I can do for him at present."

"Well, I've arranged extra security for him." Yanagisawa announced, "He'll have two bodyguards, specially chosen by me, with him at all times." He indicated the men he'd brought—loyal, trustworthy, longtime Tokugawa retainers. "No one is allowed to be alone with His Excellency."

Although Sano knew that Yanagisawa was an expert actor, he had a strong sense that Yanagisawa truly didn't want somebody to finish off the shogun. When Lord Ienobu bent a quizzical gaze on him, Yanagisawa responded with a bland look. Sano recognized that look; it masked all manner of evil intentions. Why were Yanagisawa and Ienobu suddenly at odds?

As if he thought his own concern for the shogun might seem lacking, Lord Ienobu said, "Is there anything you want, Uncle?"

"Yes." The shogun's voice was faint, sleepy, but tinged with anger. "I want to know who did this to me."

Opportunity beckoned Sano, as clear, bright, and many-faceted as a crystal. "I'll find out, Your Excellency."

The shogun started to turn toward Sano. Alarm bulged Ienobu's eyes; he gripped the shogun's hand tighter. "No, Uncle, let me handle it."

Sano understood why Ienobu didn't want him to investigate the stabbing: Here was his new chance to bring Ienobu down.

"Leave us for a moment," Yanagisawa told the physician, Captain Hosono, the guards, and the servants. He obviously didn't want them blatting all over town about the argument that was about to begin.

Another fit of trembling seized the shogun, then subsided. Dazed from the opium, he squinted at Ienobu, then Sano.

"Lord Ienobu shouldn't be in charge of the investigation," Sano said.

Ienobu started to protest. Yanagisawa leaned forward; the fire in his eyes intensified. Sano recognized that look, too: Yanagisawa was scouting the situation for an advantage for himself. The shogun interrupted Ienobu. "Why not?"

Sano couldn't say, *Because I think he sent the assassin to kill you.* He'd learned the hard way that it was dangerous to accuse the shogun's heir of murder and treason. If he accused Lord Ienobu again, and the shogun again didn't believe him, the result would be death for him instead of another demotion. "Because he has no experience with investigating crimes."

Yanagisawa said, "Whereas you've investigated crimes for twenty years." Although his scornful tone denigrated Sano's expertise, he'd also pointed it up.

"That is true," the shogun murmured.

Ienobu hurried to object. "But, Uncle, you banned Sano-*san* from court."

"Your Excellency can bring me back," Sano said. "It's your prerogative to have the attempt on your life investigated by the man you've always trusted to solve crimes for you."

The shogun twisted himself toward Sano. Ienobu clutched the shogun's hand so hard that his own knuckles turned white. "Uncle, you appointed me Acting Shogun so you wouldn't have to deal with difficult business while you're ill."

"Your Excellency can revoke the appointment," Sano said.

Worry crinkled the red, measled skin on the shogun's forehead. His eyelids drooped, then fluttered open. Where once he would have gladly let the matter be taken out of his hands so that he could sleep, now he struggled to stay awake because he wanted to make up his own mind.

"Sano-*san* and Lord Ienobu have both raised valid points, Your Excellency," Yanagisawa said. "I suggest a compromise."

If Sano hadn't already suspected that something was off about Yanagisawa, these words would have alerted him as loudly as if a gong had been struck beside his ear. Compromise was an alien concept to Yanagisawa.

"What sort of compromise?" The shogun reverted to his thirty-year habit of relying on Yanagisawa's counsel.

"Sano-*san* conducts the investigation. Lord Ienobu and I supervise." Yanagisawa sounded as if this were the happiest, most reasonable answer. "We'll have the benefit of his expertise while making sure he doesn't step out of line."

"Very well," the shogun said with a tremulous sigh. "Nephew, let go of me, you're crushing my fingers."

Ienobu released the shogun. Holding his own hand in midair, afraid it was contaminated with measles, he glared at Yanagisawa. Sano saw the division between them as clearly as if it were a line drawn with the shogun's blood.

With immense, groaning effort, the shogun turned himself on his other side and faced Sano. Sano hurried to say, "Your Excellency, in order for me to do my job properly, I must beg you to restore me to my original rank of chief investigator. And appoint my son as my assistant. And order my swords returned."

"Done," the shogun murmured.

Sano exhaled. In these few moments, his fortunes had reversed. His detective instincts and warrior spirit rose up in him like a rejuvenating tide. This was the most important case of his career, and the battle he'd been fighting for more than four years was shifting into a new, decisive phase. This was his chance to make things right for the regime, for his family.

Yanagisawa regarded him with opaque serenity. Ienobu gawped at him in outrage. Sano didn't know how far he could rely on Yanagisawa; his old enemy's motives remained a mystery. But he could count on Ienobu to retaliate.

5

SNOW FELL ON the *banchō*, the district where low-ranking Tokugawa vassals resided in small estates crammed together and surrounded by live bamboo fences. The bare stalks and dried leaves rattled in the wind. At an hour past midnight, the maze of dirt roads was deserted. Nailed to a rough wooden gate at one estate was a brass medallion of a flying crane—Sano's clan insignia. Inside the house, a girl tiptoed down the passage. She carried a candle that illuminated her round, pretty face. Her eyes had an eager glow; her soft lips smiled. A green-and-white-flowered nightdress clothed a short figure that was womanly for her fourteen years.

Taeko trembled with anticipation. She stepped carefully, avoiding the spots where the floor creaked. She mustn't awaken the family.

A tall samurai youth dressed in a dark kimono crept around the corner. The candlelight touched his handsome, alert face. Taeko's heart leapt. No matter that their families were old friends and they lived in the same house, the sight of Masahiro always thrilled her. She'd loved him since she'd been little and looked up to him and followed him around. Three years her senior, he'd played with her and teased her like a big brother would. Now his face lit with the same joy she felt. He grabbed her hand, blew out the candle, and pulled her into a storage room full of unused household furnishings. Taeko dropped the candle as Masahiro drew her down onto a pile of quilts spread on the floor. He shut the door while they passionately embraced.

Even though they'd been lovers since last autumn, Taeko could hardly believe this was happening. For a long time she and Masahiro had been best friends, and it had seemed he would be content with that forever—until that golden day when he'd looked at her, a new expression had come into his eyes, and it was as easy as that. Now his hands fumbled opened her robe; he caressed her breasts. Taeko cooed with delight.

"Shh!" Masahiro said.

The house was so small, any noise could wake someone. Containing her excitement, Taeko reached under Masahiro's robe and grasped his erect penis. He stifled a moan. Taeko wished she could see him naked in the light, touch him all over his body, and admire him, but they had to make love in a hurry, under the cover of darkness. Masahiro touched her between her legs. More than ready, she flopped back on the quilts, and he climbed on her. When he entered her, they both gasped with pleasure.

The first two times, it had hurt, and she'd bled. The third time she'd experienced an incredible, wonderful feeling. Now, as Masahiro began to thrust, she held him tight while she soared toward rapture.

Masahiro started to withdraw.

"No!" she whispered, holding him tighter. "Stay!"

"I can't hold off any longer."

"It's all right!"

He groaned, thrusting faster. His body tensed; he shuddered and panted. Taeko screamed as the ecstasy rocked her like waves from the sea.

A little girl's voice called from down the corridor, "Mama!"

A woman's drowsy voice answered. "What?"

"I heard somebody scream. And Taeko is gone."

"Oh, no," Masahiro groaned.

Quick footsteps approached. As Taeko and Masahiro disentangled themselves, the door to their hideaway opened. Light poured in from a lantern held by Taeko's mother. Astonishment opened her eyes and mouth wide. Masahiro covered his penis with his hands. Taeko pulled her robe closed.

"Taeko! Masahiro! What are you doing?" The surprise on Midori's plump face changed to dismay. She grabbed Taeko's arm, yelled, "Get up!" and dragged her out of the room.

The children came running—Masahiro's nine-year-old sister, Akiko; Taeko's eleven-year-old brother, Tatsuo, and six-year-old sister, Chiyoko. Then came a small, lithe, beautiful woman wearing a teal silk night kimono, her hair in long black braids, her expression anxious. It was Reiko, Masahiro's mother.

"What's wrong?" she asked.

MIDORI GLARED AT Taeko, who hung her head. Masahiro, standing in the doorway of the storeroom, hunched his shoulders, rubbed his shaved crown, and avoided Reiko's eyes. Although a man of seventeen, a patrol guard in the Tokugawa army, he acted as if he were still a child and Reiko had caught him misbehaving.

"Oh." Enlightenment dawned; Reiko's heart sank.

"Your son was having sex with my daughter." Midori grabbed Taeko by the shoulders and demanded, "How long has this been going on?"

"Since last fall," Taeko said in a weak, frightened voice.

Midori shook Taeko, then flung her away. "I told you never to let a man touch you! You could get pregnant!"

Reiko said, "Akiko, Tatsuo, Chiyoko—go back to bed."

"But, Mama, I want to hear," Akiko said.

She was always curious, always challenging authority. Reiko had herself to thank for that. As a child she'd been the same way. But the business at hand wasn't for children. "Go!" Reiko said. "Take Tatsuo and Chiyoko with you!"

Akiko's expression turned sullen. "Yes, Mama." She reluctantly accompanied the other children to their bedchamber.

Reiko sighed, aware of the hurt beneath Akiko's sullenness. It seemed that she was always pushing Akiko away or abandoning her in some fashion. When Akiko wanted Reiko to play with her, Reiko was busy. When Reiko went somewhere, Akiko wanted to come, but Reiko told her to stay home. There were always good reasons, but Akiko was too young to understand. She obviously believed Reiko didn't want her or love her, although it wasn't true. Their relationship had grown more difficult as the years passed and the number of perceived slights mounted up. Reiko thought their troubles stemmed from a terrible experience she'd had while pregnant with Akiko. It probably hadn't helped when Masahiro had been kidnapped and Reiko had gone off with Sano to rescue him while leaving Akiko, then an infant, behind. On some level Akiko hadn't forgotten or forgiven her mother. Reiko needed to fix her relationship with Akiko, but this wasn't the time. She and Midori turned their attention to Taeko and Masahiro.

Taeko whispered, "We're in love."

"Yes," Masahiro spoke up, moving close to her. "We want to get married." They smiled fondly at each other.

In hindsight Reiko understood why they'd gotten so serious. The house was small, Masahiro and Taeko were constantly together, and they didn't have other friends. Shunned by their peers because their fathers were in disgrace, they'd turned to each other for companionship. And Masahiro was unhappy because he'd been a patrol guard for two years since he'd attained manhood at age fifteen, and it looked as if he would be forever. It was a bitter blow for an intelligent, ambitious young man whose peers were marrying, having families, and getting ahead. Stuck in a prolonged, unnatural childhood, he was bored and frustrated as well as virile.

Midori brandished her lantern at Masahiro, as if to strike him. "You know you're not going to marry her! You seduced her by tricking her into thinking you are!"

Anxious to prevent a scuffle and a fire, Reiko grabbed the lantern from Midori and hung it on the wall. Taeko looked at Masahiro with fearful uncertainty. Masahiro said angrily, "Yes, I am!"

Reiko hated to disappoint them, but she said, "Masahiro, you can't. We've talked about this."

"Oh, yes, I'm supposed to marry into some rich, high-ranking clan that can help us financially and politically. But I've been betrothed four times. Every time, the other clan has backed out because Father keeps getting demoted."

"I'm sorry." Reiko hated that Sano's problems with Lord Ienobu, Chamberlain Yanagisawa, and the shogun had affected Masahiro's future.

"I'm not," Masahiro declared. "Father and I will keep fighting Lord Ienobu. We're not giving up."

He was fiercely loyal to Sano, but Reiko took issue with their quest to prove Ienobu was a murderer. The cost to their family was so high. She, too, hated Lord Ienobu and the fact that he'd gotten away with two murders, but she'd begged Sano to take the deal he'd offered. She was a mother, and honor mattered less to her than her children's welfare. But Sano had refused. Lord Ienobu had gotten fed up with Sano, rescinded the offer, and banned Sano from court. Reiko was angry at Sano for being such a stickler for Bushido. Sano was angry at her for asking him to sacrifice honor for peace. They fought about every little thing—when they spoke at all.

"No important clan will have me as a son-in-law," Masahiro said, "but I don't care. I'm glad." He put his arm around Taeko. "I can marry anybody I want."

"Anybody except her," Midori retorted. "Because her father is a traitor."

Taeko's father, Hirata, had been Sano's chief retainer for almost twenty years. He was a mystic martial artist, one of the best fighters in Japan. Six years ago he'd joined a secret society of fellow mystic martial artists and later confessed to Sano that they'd lured him into a plot against the Tokugawa regime. The exact nature of the plot was known only to them, but Sano had reported Hirata to the shogun. It was his duty, no matter that Sano was in disfavor himself or that his family and Hirata's were close friends. That was Bushido. Now Hirata had been missing for more than four years, the army was searching for him and his comrades, and there was a warrant for their arrest and execution. Anyone who married into his family would be deemed parties to his treason and share his punishment. That was Tokugawa law. Reiko thought Sano was being too hard on Hirata at the expense of Midori, the children, and twenty years of friendship. Sano thought Reiko was too lenient toward a traitor because she, as a woman, didn't understand duty. And now Masahiro was involved with Taeko! Reiko saw Hirata's family bearing the brunt of her men's actions. She grew even angrier at Sano on account of her friends.

Midori pulled Taeko away from Masahiro. "We're leaving."

"I don't want to!"

"You can't stay in the same house with him."

Midori and her children had lived with Sano's family since Hirata had disappeared. Back then, Sano had still had friends in the government, and he'd convinced them to make Hirata's wife and children his wards. They'd initially been hostages kept under house arrest—bait to lure Hirata so that he could be captured. Because years had passed and Hirata hadn't shown up, they were now free to move about as they pleased. Sano fed, sheltered, and protected them as best he could. All the more reason that Reiko thought Sano should have accepted Lord Ienobu's deal—he might have worked out a pardon for Hirata.

"But where will you go?" Reiko asked in alarm.

Woe filled Midori's expression as she remembered that her family had disowned her and Hirata's family had disowned him. Anyone who aided them risked being named parties to treason and executed. "I don't know. I'll find someplace."

"It's the middle of the night," Reiko said. "Wait, we'll work things out somehow."

"Wait for how long? Until Masahiro gets Taeko with child? Is that what you want?"

"Of course not." The last thing they needed was an illegitimate pregnancy. Reiko felt a stab of sorrow at the idea of a baby. She'd had a stillbirth four years ago. A part of her had never stopped mourning, although she tried not to let it show. Any little thing—the sight of a baby or a pregnant woman—could evoke painful memories of the circumstances of the stillbirth, which had been almost as traumatic as the baby's death. And there had never been time to recover. Reiko was too busy, in charge at home while Sano and Masahiro were working. With fewer servants than when they'd lived at Edo Castle, she did housework, took care of Akiko, and helped Midori with her children. Now, while trying to cope with the problem of Masahiro and Taeko, she felt the empty ache inside her and fought tears.

"How could you let your son seduce my daughter?" Midori burst out. "Why didn't you control him?"

"How could I?" Reiko spread her hands. "He's a grown man."

When samurai boys turned fifteen, they acquired all the duties and freedom of adults. Masahiro, like other honorable young men, respected his parents' wishes, but if Reiko had told him to leave Taeko alone, he probably wouldn't have listened. He could be just as stubborn as Sano—or herself.

"He lives under your roof," Midori said. "You and your husband are responsible for what goes on here. How could you let this happen? Haven't you hurt us enough already?" She was furious at Sano for reporting Hirata, Reiko knew. Midori had begged Sano to give Hirata another chance, even though Sano had already given Hirata many chances. "I hate you all!" Midori cried.

Reiko also knew that although Midori blamed Sano's family for the fact that hers was homeless and disgraced, Midori blamed and hated Hirata—the husband who'd abandoned her and her children—most of all. "I'm sorry," was all Reiko could say.

Midori's anger dissolved into misery. "You've taken care of us when nobody else would and look how I'm acting! I don't deserve your kindness. I just don't know what to do!"

Taeko and Masahiro looked shaken; they realized how much worse they'd made a bad situation. Reiko took Midori in her arms and patted her back. She felt just as helpless; she didn't know what to do, either. Along with the baby she'd lost her confidence, resourcefulness, and bold, adventurous spirit. She felt overwhelmed and afraid all the time, and now she was in charge during this new crisis.

"I'll make sure that Masahiro and Taeko are never alone together again. All right?" Reiko aimed a stern glance at the couple.

Midori nodded, weeping against Reiko's shoulder. Reiko understood that this was just a temporary solution to one problem. The bigger problem was Hirata. Only heaven knew what had become of him or what would happen when he was caught.

Every problem that both families had stemmed directly from Sano's stubborn commitment to honor.

6

Month 4, Hoei Year 2
(April 1705)

A TRILL OF birdsong pierced the black silence in which he floated. Falling water splashed in the distance, a cool breeze swept his skin, and wind chimes tinkled.

Hirata opened his eyes to soft, pale light. He was lying on a futon, alone in a small room. Through the open doors he saw a veranda with red railings and wooded hills veiled with fog. Twisted pines clung to rocky cliffs above a waterfall that cascaded like a spill of liquid silver. The breeze tinkled brass wind chimes hanging from the eaves. A red bird perched on the railing and trilled. The view had a serene, unearthly beauty.

Hirata had never seen it before, nor this room.

Confused, he kicked off the white quilt tangled around his legs. He was naked. Although his mind was fully alert, he couldn't recall what he'd been doing before he fell asleep. He jumped out of bed. A white cotton kimono lay folded on the tatami.

Who had left it there? Whose house was this?

Hirata put on the kimono, then ran outside. The red bird flew away. The veranda jutted over empty space. On hills that sloped down to a valley were dark pines and trees with pink and white blossoms. Hirata searched for familiar landmarks and found none. He leaned over the railing and peered upward. The house was part of a temple built on a cliff. The tiers and spire of a pagoda rose above the curved roofs of other buildings.

What temple? How had he come to be here?

Into his mind seeped a dim memory of flashing blades, a sword battle with . . . *Tahara and Kitano.*

The rusty floodgate between past and present creaked open. He'd tried to kill Tahara and Kitano, to shut down the secret society and end its treasonous scheme. Details of the battle were hazy, but he knew he'd lost.

"Then why am I still alive?" Hirata said aloud.

Birdsong echoed across the valley. Hirata remembered lying strapped to a table in a cave while Tahara and Kitano chanted a spell, pressed a leather mask over his face, and fed fluid through a metal tube into a vein in his arm—some bizarre, unheard-of medical procedure. The smell of sweet chemicals was the last thing Hirata remembered.

What had they done?

Hirata flung open his robe and examined his body. It looked normal, with the long, puckered, familiar old scar on his left thigh. He pushed up his sleeves. On his left forearm was a small, round discoloration where the tube had pierced. He felt fine, but his eyes couldn't tell him if he still had his martial arts skills, his supernatural powers.

Merciful gods, had they taken those away?

Hirata drew deep, slow breaths. Meditation aligned and amplified the mental, spiritual, and physical energies in him. Power flowed through nerves and muscles. He pointed his finger at the wind chimes. Each slender brass cylinder began to spin, one after another, on its string. Hirata exhaled with relief. Then he felt the pulse of an aura, the energy that all living things emitted. His trained senses identified its source as human. Each human had a unique aura that signaled his personality, health, and emotions. This one was a strong, booming, familiar cadence that struck fear into his heart. Reaching instinctively for his sword, forgetting that he was unarmed, Hirata whirled.

Two samurai, dressed in white martial arts practice jackets and trousers, strolled out onto the veranda. Their conjoined aura dissipated. They, unlike other creatures, could turn it on and off. They weren't armed, either. They didn't need weapons to kill.

"Somebody's up and around," said Tahara, in his voice that was both smooth and rough, like water flowing over jagged rocks. His deep black eyes twinkled. His left eyebrow arched higher than his right, lending his strong, regular features a rakish charm.

"It's about time." Kitano's mouth moved, but the rest of his face was an immobile mesh of scars. Cuts sustained during a long-ago battle had severed his facial nerves. He was in his fifties, with gray hair and a robust physique that seemed impervious to aging.

"Where am I?" Hirata demanded.

"At the Sky Mountain Temple in Chikuzen Province," Tahara said.

He and Kitano studied Hirata with an intense, eager interest. Hirata realized that someone was missing. "Where's Deguchi?"

Deguchi was a Buddhist priest, the fourth member of the society. "Don't you remember?" Kitano sounded concerned.

Now Hirata did. Deguchi had fought on his side in the battle against Kitano and Tahara. Memory served up an image of Deguchi's dead, broken body. Hirata's heart sank.

Tahara smiled as if relieved that Hirata's wits were intact. Kitano's eyes crinkled in his paralyzed face. Hirata also remembered that they'd all been injured during the battle, but the other men seemed as fit as himself. "How long was I unconscious?"

"Oh, about a year," Tahara said.

"A year?" Hirata was horrified. "What's happened to my wife and children? And Sano?"

"Damned if we know," Kitano said. "We haven't been back to Edo in all that time."

"We've been on the run," Tahara said with a spark of anger. "After you told Sano about our society, he reported us to the shogun. There've been troops hunting us. We've had to keep a low profile, which means no contact with anyone in Edo. And it's no easy task, lugging an unconscious man all over Japan. You should thank us for keeping you safe."

" 'Safe'? You ruined my life!" Because of them he'd lost his family, his relationship with his master, and his honor. "What did you do to me while I was unconscious?"

"We healed you," Kitano said. "We gave you plenty of good food and exercise. We kept you in good shape."

They'd used their mystical powers to manipulate his body. Hirata pictured himself eating, practicing martial arts, and going through the motions of daily living like a sleepwalker. He shuddered. "What else?"

They watched him; they seemed to be waiting for something. Then Tahara spoke in a tentative voice. "General Otani? Are you there?"

General Otani was a samurai who'd fought in the Battle of Sekigahara more than a century ago. His side had lost to Tokugawa Ieyasu, who'd unified the warring factions of Japan, founded the Tokugawa regime, and become its first shogun. General Otani had died on the battlefield. Tahara, Kitano, and Deguchi had stolen an ancient book of magic and learned a spell to summon his ghost. The ghost had granted them, and Hirata, supernatural powers in exchange for services. General Otani had one goal—destroying the Tokugawa regime and avenging his defeat at Sekigahara. He couldn't do it alone; he was disembodied energy. He needed human help, and he could only be seen by and interact with the secret society members while they were in a mystical trance.

Sudden terror gripped Hirata. "Are we in a trance? Is that what this is?" He looked around for General Otani, whose powers were limitless, his wrath deadly.

"No," Kitano said. "This is the real world."

"Then how—?"

"General Otani?" Tahara repeated, louder.

Hirata experienced a strange, zinging sensation, like a current of extra life force speeding along his nerves. The blood in his veins and organs swelled. Heat flushed him. He felt a jolt in his brain. A part of him that he hadn't known was still unconscious snapped alert. His lungs drew a deep, involuntary breath. His arms and legs stretched and flexed of their own accord. He couldn't control his movements! He opened his mouth to yell, "What are you doing to me? Stop!" Instead he said, "I am here."

His voice was deeper than normal, with a strange yet familiar accent. Tahara said to Kitano, "It worked!" They hooted with laughter and slapped each other's backs.

"What worked?" Hirata was relieved that this time he'd said what he meant to say, yet terrified by what had just happened.

"The spell for possession," Kitano said. "We've been working it on you for six months."

"General Otani isn't just a disembodied spirit anymore," Tahara said. "He's inside you!"

An alien presence bloomed in Hirata's mind, like a carnivorous flower that preyed on his mental faculties. General Otani spoke in his thoughts: *You and I share your body.*

This was the terrible purpose for which General Otani had ultimately wanted Hirata—to give the ghost a human form. Hirata cried, "No! I don't want you! Get out of me!"

"The spell is permanent," Kitano said.

Tahara shrugged and smiled. "Sorry."

Their attitude compounded the rage Hirata felt toward them for luring him into treason. "Why does Otani have to possess *me*? Why not one of you?"

"He thought you would be the easiest to take over," Tahara said.

Hirata clawed at his chest, yelling, "Get out!" His nails raked bloody tracks on his skin.

You can't get rid of me, General Otani said inside his head. His arm muscles stiffened, jerking his hands away from his body.

Hirata lunged toward the veranda railing. "Leave, or I'll jump!"

A fear that wasn't entirely his own stabbed his gut. Hirata realized that General Otani shared his mortality as well as his body. He tried to climb over the railing, but his legs wouldn't cooperate. He staggered toward the wall of the building and beat his head against it. Otani's voice in his head howled at the pain. Hirata's back arched, and he fell to the veranda. His arms and legs curled to his chest. He struggled with all his might, but he was as immobilized as if wrapped in chains.

"No use fighting," Kitano said.

"He's got you good," Tahara said.

"You should listen to your friends," General Otani said aloud. His voice was breathless as it emerged from Hirata; the struggle had tired him. "Stand up, or must I force you?"

The chains loosened. Hirata stood, conceding defeat, but he'd learned that the ghost had physical limitations now that it was in him. He would play along until he figured out how to expel it and be his normal self again.

It won't work.

Hirata's breath caught. General Otani said, *I can hear your thoughts. You can't hide anything from me.* Hirata's lips moved as General Otani spoke aloud: "We are going back to Edo."

"Good, I'm ready for some action," Tahara said.

"It's too quiet here," Kitano said.

"You two are not coming with us," General Otani said through Hirata.

The other men looked surprised. "Why not?" Kitano asked.

"I have no further use for you."

They apparently hadn't realized that after they gave Otani a human body, he would be independent. "We've served you for years." Tahara's voice rose with indignation. "You can't just ditch us."

"Watch me."

Propelled by the ghost, Hirata moved toward the door to the bedchamber. Tahara and Kitano stepped in front of it. "We gave up everything to help you destroy the Tokugawa regime," Kitano said. "We're fugitives because of you. We're not letting you walk away."

"I've rewarded you handsomely for your service. You have mystical powers that you could not otherwise have attained." Hirata tried to bite his tongue to stop Otani from speaking, but he couldn't. "Our collaboration is over."

"If it's over, then we'll send you back where you came from," Tahara retorted.

He and Kitano began chanting words in archaic Chinese that Hirata couldn't understand. Inside him, General Otani's spirit recoiled with fear from the spell that would permanently banish him to the netherworld of the dead. Hirata's mouth opened. From his depths came a shout so loud that he thought his head would explode. Tahara and Kitano choked and staggered, mouths agape, while the force that Otani had summoned from Hirata blasted down their throats. They jerked and twisted like hanged men suspended from gallows, then fell to the floor. Flames burst from their mouths and eyes. They writhed, screamed in agony, then lay still. In the sudden quiet, the waterfall murmured.

Hirata fell to his knees, crying, "Tahara-*san*! Kitano-*san*!"

Their eyes were burned black as coals; their mouths leaked wisps of smoke. Hirata remembered how much he'd hated them, how he'd wanted desperately to kill them. He'd thought that if they were gone, he could reunite with his family, reconcile with Sano, and regain his honor. Now he desperately wished for the power to bring them back to life. They were the only people in the world who could have saved him, and the Tokugawa regime, from General Otani.

It is time to go.

Hirata's muscles jerked him upright. He and the ghost inside him walked out of the temple, down a mountain path, toward the road to Edo.

7

Month 1, Hoei Year 6
(Edo, February 1709)

"HAS ANYONE STARTED a search for the attacker?" Sano asked Captain Hosono.

"Not yet. But the sentries reported that no one has left the palace since His Excellency was stabbed, and all the exits are sealed now."

"So he's still inside. He can't go anywhere." Sano knew that wouldn't necessarily make catching the attacker easy. There were hundreds of people in the palace, any one of whom could be the culprit. The first order of business was examining the crime scene for clues that would focus the search.

Sano looked around the chamber. The shogun was deep in opium-induced sleep, his breathing harsh and labored. The physician and guards sat by the bed. Lord Ienobu and Chamberlain Yanagisawa hovered warily near Sano. Sano unhooked a lantern from its stand and moved it in a slow arc as he walked, sweeping its light across the floor. He bumped into Ienobu, turned, and came up against Yanagisawa.

"Would you mind not breathing down my neck?"

"We're supervising your investigation," Yanagisawa said.

"Supervise it from over there." Sano pointed at a corner he'd already searched.

"Sano-*san*, I'd like a word outside with you," Ienobu said. "Then I'll leave you to your work."

Anything to get Ienobu off his back. Sano replaced the lantern, then followed Ienobu and Yanagisawa to the corridor. Ienobu said in a vehement whisper, "I didn't do it!"

"I don't believe you," Sano said.

"Keep your voice down," Yanagisawa murmured. "You'll wake the shogun."

"When he was stabbed, I was with you," Ienobu insisted.

That Sano himself was the alibi for the man he thought responsible for the attack! "You'd have sent someone else to do your dirty work. There must be an incompetent assassin with your money in his pocket. You'll have to ask for a refund."

"I didn't hire an assassin!" Distraught as well as angry, Ienobu said, "Just ask Yanagisawa-*san*. He's privy to all my affairs."

The day the secretive, cautious Ienobu let anyone in on all his affairs would be the day whales flew. Sano turned his skeptical gaze to Yanagisawa.

A beat passed. Yanagisawa said, "Lord Ienobu is telling the truth."

Lord Ienobu frowned because Yanagisawa hadn't spoken up for him fast enough. Sano was all the more puzzled. Was Yanagisawa trying to encourage Sano's suspicions? If so, why?

"Did *you* send the assassin?" Sano asked.

"No," Yanagisawa said calmly.

"What's going on between you two?"

"Don't try to change the subject," Ienobu snapped. "And don't try to pin another crime on me. It didn't work last time. It won't this time."

"Both the shogun's children were murdered and now there's been an attempt on his life," Sano said. "The two people who confessed to killing Yoshisato and Tsuruhime are dead. They couldn't have stabbed the shogun. But you're still around."

Ienobu sputtered. "That's ridiculous logic! Everybody else in Japan is still around, too. You might as well say they're all guilty."

"The two confessions implicated you, not everybody else in Japan,"

Sano said. "You were my primary suspect for those murders. You're my primary suspect this time."

"And you think you can use your investigation to frame me and get me this time?" Scornful anger twisted Ienobu's face. "Well, think again. You're going to prove I'm innocent."

"How so?" Sano said, offended that Ienobu would ask him to conduct a dishonest investigation, get Ienobu off the hook, and subvert justice.

"I don't care. Just do it." Ienobu jabbed Sano's chest with his finger.

Sano pushed the finger away. "I don't take orders from you."

"I'm Acting Shogun. You'll do as I say." Ienobu's bulging eyes gleamed with vengefulness. "Or I'll have you and your family put to death."

Being thrown out of the regime and made a *rōnin* was trivial in comparison to the threat that Lord Ienobu had kept in reserve for a special occasion like this. Sano knew that Ienobu could kill him, his wife, and his children without asking for the shogun's permission and worry about the consequences later, but even as fear knotted his stomach, he said, "Go ahead, kill me. That should convince the shogun that you're afraid of my investigation because you're responsible for the attack."

Angrily aware that Sano had a point, Ienobu scowled. Yanagisawa said, "Lord Ienobu, why not let Sano-*san* do a proper, thorough investigation? You've nothing to hide." A dubious note in his voice suggested the opposite. "Let him find the real culprit, and your innocence will be proven."

Ienobu turned on Yanagisawa, who'd pretended to uphold his claim of innocence while virtually proclaiming that he was guilty. Sano was stunned because Yanagisawa apparently wanted him alive, after years of trying to destroy him.

"Very well." The black look Ienobu gave Sano and Yanagisawa said the matter was far from settled.

Sano led the way back inside the shogun's bedchamber. His knees felt shaky; he'd walked away from a battle he'd expected to lose, and onto very thin ice. This was his most important case ever—the attempted murder of his lord. Bushido required him to find the truth, to exact blood for blood. Yet it might not be Ienobu's blood. He hadn't one scrap of evidence against Ienobu, and Ienobu could still make good on his threat.

For now Sano concentrated on solving the crime, his first priority. He would worry about Ienobu—and wonder about Yanagisawa—later. He fetched the lantern, resumed inspecting the floor, and found a dark patch on the tatami, near the wooden sliding door between the bed-chamber and the shogun's study. He crouched.

"What is it?" Ienobu's tone was half eager, half frightened.

The patch gleamed red. "Blood." It was irregularly shaped, and wider at the end nearer the door. Sano noted the distinctive marks made by toes and heel. "It's a footprint."

YANAGISAWA WATCHED SANO open the sliding door and carry the lantern into the shogun's study. More footprints led past the niche that contained a desk on a platform, to the lattice-and-paper wall that divided the room from the corridor. They grew fainter with each step.

"The attacker escaped through here." Sano slid the partition aside and walked into the corridor. Tracking the bloodstains along the palace's maze of corridors, he gathered an entourage of curious guards, servants, and officials. Yanagisawa and Lord Ienobu walked together behind the parade.

"What do you think you're doing?" Ienobu demanded in a furious whisper.

"I'm trying to help Sano find out who stabbed your uncle."

"Don't feed me that tripe! You as good as told Sano that I'm guilty and dug my grave!"

Yanagisawa smiled at the fear he saw beneath Ienobu's anger. He'd lived in fear since Ienobu had kidnapped Yoshisato and it felt good to have the shoe on the other foot.

"You're playing a dangerous game," Ienobu said.

"Dangerous for whom? *I'm* not the primary suspect in this crime."

Ienobu shook his finger in Yanagisawa's face. "Hold up your end of our deal or you'll never see Yoshisato again."

"Our deal is off. I'm going to help Sano convict you of conspiring to assassinate the shogun."

"Do you really think I did?" Ienobu's air of wounded innocence stank like old fish.

"It doesn't matter what I think," Yanagisawa said. "What matters is whether the shogun believes you're guilty, and when I'm done with you, he will. You won't live to inherit the dictatorship."

"Don't forget, I have Yoshisato. Step out of line again, and he'll be as dead as everybody else thinks he is."

Yanagisawa swallowed the panic that always clutched his heart whenever he thought of his beloved son at the mercy of Ienobu's henchmen. "You've only got him until I find him."

"I suspect you've been looking for him all these years. You haven't found him yet."

Every trail had gone cold, and there had been no new leads for fifteen months, but Yanagisawa said, "I feel my luck changing."

Ienobu chuckled, a sound like the rattle of a snake. "Your time is running out. The shogun is going to die." He didn't have to say, *When I take over the regime, I won't need to keep your son—or you—alive any longer.*

"Maybe the shogun will make a miraculous recovery and my searchers are rescuing Yoshisato even as we speak." Yanagisawa added with sly humor, "I feel your luck changing, too."

"Are you really willing to gamble that you can find Yoshisato, or destroy me, before the shogun dies and before I can send out my orders to have Yoshisato killed?"

Yanagisawa answered with passion, a substitute for certainty. "*Yes.*"

The parade slowed. Yanagisawa heard Sano say, "The footprints stop here."

Over the heads of the men in front of him Yanagisawa saw a massive oak door banded in iron and decorated with carved flowers. It sealed the door to the Large Interior, the private section of the palace where the shogun's wife, female concubines, their attendants and maids lived. A murmur swept through the crowd.

"A *woman* stabbed the shogun?"

"HERE'S YOUR NEW chaperone," Midori said.

Taeko's heart sank as she beheld the plain young maid named Umeko, whose sharp eyes missed nothing.

"How am I supposed to keep her away from Masahiro, along with all my other work?" Umeko said in her nasal, insolent voice.

Taeko missed the old days, before they got so poor, when their servants were polite. Now they had servants like Umeko that richer folks wouldn't put up with.

"Taeko will help you do your work." Midori glowered at Taeko. "Cleaning house will keep you too busy to get in trouble."

Umeko led Taeko into the bedchamber; the younger children were asleep there. She laid bedding in front of the door and tucked herself in. "I'm a light sleeper. Don't bother trying to sneak out."

Taeko crawled into her own bed and lay awake and miserable in the dark. She'd been so happy in love with Masahiro that she hadn't thought about the future. She couldn't bear to be separated from him, and if they couldn't marry, all was lost.

"Taeko?" whispered Masahiro, kneeling outside the chamber on the other side of the paper wall.

"What are you doing here?" Taeko whispered, glad to have him near her yet afraid Umeko would catch them.

"I wanted to tell you, I'm sorry for what happened." Masahiro expelled a mournful breath. "I shouldn't have started this."

"It's not your fault. I wanted it as much as you did." This was such a bold, unfeminine thing to say, Taeko's face burned.

"But I'm older. I should have kept things under control."

Glum silence stretched between them. Taeko whispered, "What are we going to do?"

"I'll think of something." But Masahiro sounded as forlorn as she felt.

Taeko thought of the times when matchmakers had brought proposals from clans that wanted to wed their daughters to Masahiro. Each time she'd prayed that the marriage would fall through. Each time one had, she'd secretly rejoiced, but now she was scared.

"You won't marry someone else, will you?" Her voice came out loud and shrill.

"Shh! Don't worry. It's like I said: Nobody else wants me."

"But if somebody did . . . ?"

"I'll never marry anybody but you." Masahiro spoke with impatience and tenderness.

Hearing him say it pleased Taeko but didn't relieve her fear. She knew how much he loved, respected, and felt a duty toward his parents. If a match were arranged for him, would he be able to say no? "We should run away and get married!"

He shifted position; she sensed his surprise. "You mean, leave Edo?"

"Why not?" Taeko hurried to justify the drastic action. "Our families will never let us be together. It's the only way."

"What about my post?"

Unhappy because he sounded so reluctant, Taeko said, "You're just a patrol guard. That's nothing to give up."

"Nothing except my honor!" The heat of his anger burned through the paper wall. "If I leave the shogun's service, I'll be a deserter and a *rōnin*."

Taeko had heard about Bushido all her life, but she didn't understand why Masahiro and his father cared so much about it, when it only seemed to get them in trouble. She'd heard Reiko and Sano arguing about it. Their arguments frightened Taeko. With her father gone and her mother often cross and mean, she looked to Sano and Reiko as parents. If they couldn't get along, there was no security. It frightened her that now she and Masahiro were arguing about the same thing.

"What's so bad about being a masterless samurai?" Taeko thought it couldn't be worse than being poor and looked down on. "At least you can do what you want."

"It's the biggest disgrace there is! Besides that, what would we live on?"

"You could teach martial arts, like your father did before he got into the government."

"That would be a giant step backward for our family!"

"Maybe I could sell my paintings." Taeko had always loved painting. She painted even though her mother told her it wasn't for girls. Her work looked as good as many of the paintings in the shops. To be an artist was her cherished dream.

To be Masahiro's wife was her most urgent wish.

"Oh, sure," Masahiro said flatly. "We'd starve." Although he'd admired her paintings, he obviously didn't think they were worth much. "And don't you see, if we ran away, we'd be dropping out of the samurai class? We'd never see our families again."

Taeko hadn't thought that far. The idea of never seeing her mother, brother, or sister again was disturbing, but she said, "We would have each other."

His robes rustled as Masahiro stirred uncomfortably. Desperate, Taeko said, "I thought you loved me." It seemed that there were limitations to his love.

"I do." Masahiro sounded more impatient than passionate.

"Then let's run away together and get married!"

Masahiro was speechless for a long, tense moment. Taeko heard him draw, hold, then release his breath. "You never seemed to care about getting married. Why are you talking like this all of a sudden?"

The sound of heavy footsteps in the corridor spared Taeko the necessity of answering. Detective Marume called, "Lady Reiko!"

"Why are you home so early?" came Reiko's surprised voice. "Where's my husband?"

"Sano-*san* is at the palace. The shogun was stabbed tonight. He's not dead, but he's badly wounded."

Reiko exclaimed. Masahiro muttered under his breath. Taeko could tell that he was upset by the news but glad for the interruption.

"Why is there blood all over you?" Reiko asked.

"Long story, later," Marume said. "I'm heading to the palace to find out what's happening there, as soon as I wash up."

Masahiro jumped to his feet and called, "I'm going, too!" He whispered to Taeko, "I have to help my father. Don't worry. Someday, somehow, we'll be married. I promise." Then he ran off.

UNDER THE DARK sky, Hirata skimmed across the snow-frosted tile roofs of mansions where Edo's richest businessmen lived in the Nihonbashi merchant district. He jumped from one to the next like a cat, effortlessly clearing the wide distances and landing without a sound. His body's trained muscles absorbed the impact and dissipated it in heat that melted the snowflakes falling around him. A humorless smile twisted his mouth as he thought that anyone who saw him would think he was alone.

"Where are we going?" he asked.

To steal money for Lord Ienobu, the voice of General Otani said in his mind.

Since Tahara and Kitano had worked the possession spell on him three and a half years ago, Hirata had stolen millions of *koban* from merchants, *daimyo,* and gangsters and delivered it to Ienobu. Hirata wondered what Ienobu thought about the money that showed up on his doorstep. He didn't know that Hirata and General Otani were working for him. No one knew Hirata was back in Edo. He wore his hair cropped short instead of in a topknot with a shaved crown, and he lived under a false name in a slum, where the neighbors thought he was a peasant from the countryside and the army wouldn't think to look for him. Burglary was only one of the illegal services into which General Otani had pressed Hirata. It wasn't the worst. Each additional day that Hirata had to serve Lord Ienobu's interests, he despised it more.

"Lord Ienobu has the whole Tokugawa treasury at his disposal. Why does he need more money?"

Lord Ienobu has plans.

"What kind of plans?"

You will find out soon enough.

That was what General Otani always said. Hirata frowned in irritation.

If you dislike the same answer, then stop asking the same question.

Hirata especially hated that General Otani could read his thoughts but he couldn't read Otani's. The ghost hid them in a part of Hirata's mind that Hirata couldn't access no matter how hard he tried; it was like pounding on a locked door.

"I've been your slave for three and a half years," Hirata said. "The least you owe me is an explanation for why we're stealing money for Ienobu and why you want him to be the next shogun. How is that supposed to destroy the Tokugawa regime?"

Not now.

"Then let me see Sano-*san*." Hirata wanted desperately to tell Sano what had happened to him. Even though Sano knew he was a traitor and had set the army on him, Hirata clung to the hope that a face-to-face talk would somehow set things right. And he missed Sano, his beloved friend as well as master.

No.

"I want to see my wife and children." Hirata felt terrible about abandoning Midori, Taeko, Tatsuo, and Chiyoko. He hadn't realized how much he loved them until he'd lost them. Midori probably hated him, the children had probably forgotten him, but he had to make it up to them, too.

You will see them when the time is right.

"You've been saying that ever since we came back to Edo three and a half years ago, and the time is never right, according to you." Hirata halted his steps. "I'm going to see them now."

His leg muscles jerked as the ghost overrode his will. He resisted, but the ghost jumped him onto the next rooftop. He cursed in frustration. "You can't keep me away from Sano or my family forever!"

I can do with you what I like.

"I can make it hard for you!"

They'd had many arguments, and Otani always won, but it took a toll on him, too. Hirata's body was their mutual home, their battleground. *Shut up.* A blinding stab of pain in his head quelled Hirata's resistance. *Here we are.*

Propelled by the ghost, Hirata crept down the sloped roof of a mansion. Below, in the courtyard, were two storehouses with tile roofs, thick plaster walls, and ironclad doors. Outside the doors stood two men— samurai mercenaries guarding the householder's wealth. Hirata jumped down to the courtyard. Sensing the movement, the guards turned; they reached for their swords. Hirata projected bursts of mental energy at them, and they fell unconscious to the ground. He opened the door of a storehouse with a hard yank that broke the lock. His keen night vision perceived iron trunks of coins inside.

As he moved to pick up a trunk, General Otani said, *Stop. We're going to the palace. The shogun has been stabbed.*

"He's dead?" Terror and hope filled Hirata as the ghost maneuvered him toward the gate. If the shogun was dead, Ienobu was the new dictator and it was the beginning of the end of the Tokugawa regime. General Otani wouldn't need Hirata anymore.

No. He's seriously wounded but alive.

Hirata had never understood how General Otani knew things that he himself didn't. Relieved because the end wasn't yet at hand, and disappointed because General Otani still needed him, Hirata asked, "Why are we going to the palace? To finish off the shogun?"

He'd once asked why General Otani didn't just make him kill the shogun so Lord Ienobu could inherit the dictatorship. Otani had replied, *Because the shogun must die a natural death.* Hirata supposed that was so there would be no complications afterward. He'd always been glad he didn't have to add "murder of my lord" to the list of his sins. That would be the ultimate disgrace. Now it seemed that Otani couldn't always foresee the future and step in fast enough to bend the course of events to his needs. He hadn't expected, or been able to prevent, the stabbing.

"Who stabbed the shogun?" Hirata asked.

That is yet to be discovered.

It also seemed that the ghost didn't know everything about the present or past. His private channel of communication with the cosmos must be faulty.

It is certain that Lord Ienobu will fall under suspicion.

If Ienobu were blamed for the stabbing, he would be put to death instead of becoming the next dictator. General Otani's goal was in jeopardy, and he needed to protect Ienobu. Hirata saw an opportunity for himself in this crisis.

"I'm not going." Hirata planted his feet firmly on the snowy ground and clamped his fingers around the iron bar of the gate.

General Otani's anger blazed up through his veins. *Don't be foolish.* Hirata's fingers tried to pry themselves off the bar. His feet involuntarily braced themselves against the gate and pushed. Hirata held on tight. Pain throbbed in his head. As he screamed, the windows of the mansion lit up.

"I'll keep us away from the palace long enough for the shogun to die and Lord Ienobu to be executed for his murder!" Hirata said, panting.

General Otani roared. Hirata felt his brain slam against the inside of his skull. Neither of them could bear it much longer, but Hirata would gladly die if he could take Otani with him. Then suddenly the pain stopped. Gasping with relief, Hirata sagged as he clung to the gate.

Sano is at the palace. The shogun has ordered him to investigate the stabbing.

Otani was dangling Sano like a carrot in front of a horse. Hirata took the bait in spite of himself. "If we go to the palace, will you let me talk to Sano-*san?*"

Yes.

Hirata didn't trust Otani to keep his word. He knew that going near Sano would put Sano in danger and protecting Lord Ienobu might interfere with Sano's ability to solve the crime, but he convinced himself that he was strong enough to prevent the ghost from hurting Sano or sabotaging the investigation.

"All right. We'll go."

His lips curved as General Otani smiled with satisfaction. He opened the gate as the guards staggered to their feet and people spilled out of the mansion. He sped through the snowy streets, trailing a fiery wake like a comet's tail, toward Edo Castle.

9

OUTSIDE THE LARGE Interior, Sano tried the door as the spectators in the corridor behind him watched. The door was locked. Captain Hosono called to the guard on the other side, "Sano-*san* is investigating the attack on the shogun. Let him in."

The guard obeyed. From the dim corridor behind him drifted women's anxious voices and sweet, tarry incense smoke overlaying the odors of aromatic unguents and women's bodies. The odors transported Sano nineteen years into the past, to the first time he'd entered the Large Interior. One of the shogun's female concubines had been murdered during his wedding. That had been the first crime he and Reiko had investigated together.

So much had happened between them since then.

The last case they'd investigated together was the murder of the shogun's daughter more than four years ago. At the end of that case Reiko had lost the baby and Sano had begun his campaign against Lord Ienobu. At first she'd been too ill and distraught to help Sano with his quest to prove that Lord Ienobu had murdered the shogun's heir, then too upset because she thought it was a mistake. Sano missed their collaboration, and he knew he'd made life hard for her, but he couldn't help feeling hurt and abandoned. Once he'd also had a corps of a hundred detectives. He was on his own now in a den of wolves.

As Sano stepped inside the Large Interior, Manabe joined him. "Lord Ienobu sent me to watch you."

"Where is he? Where's Chamberlain Yanagisawa?" Sano asked.

The expression on Manabe's hard, burnished face said it was none of Sano's business. Sano shone his lantern on the floor—polished cypress planks in which he could see his blurry reflection. There was no blood. Unable to tell where the attacker had gone, Sano headed into the labyrinth of passages and small chambers. Two male guards appeared, soldiers who preferred their own sex and wouldn't touch the women. Peering in doorways, Sano saw women huddled on beds where they slept four or five to a room amid lacquer chests and cabinets, dressing tables and mirrors, and garments hanging on stands. There were countless places where bloodstained socks or clothing could be hidden. Sano noted the many charcoal braziers. The socks could be burnt to ashes by now. There were also hundreds of potential suspects.

A commotion arose outside the Large Interior. Sano heard his son, Masahiro, and Detective Marume arguing with the guard at the door. He called, "Send them in."

"We heard what happened," Masahiro said. "We came to help you investigate."

Sano was glad to have helpers he trusted, but he felt the ever-present strain in his relationship with his son. As a child Masahiro had thought his father could do no wrong, but now he was old enough to know that his low station was Sano's fault. After each demotion it had been harder for Sano to look Masahiro in the eye. Masahiro was always loyal, and he respected Sano's dedication to honor, but he couldn't help resenting the high price that he, too, must pay for honor. He'd grown aloof toward Sano. Now Sano welcomed the chance to work with his son and restore their harmony as well as solve the crime.

"You're just in time," Sano said. "The shogun has made me chief investigator and you my assistant."

"That's great!" Masahiro visibly warmed toward Sano; his eyes shone with excitement. He was old enough to understand the danger that the attack on the shogun posed for his family, but young enough to think of the investigation as an adventure and an opportunity.

"Luck is on our side for once." Marume, scrubbed clean, looked delighted by the fact that Sano was back in favor with the shogun. "What do you want us to do?"

Their enthusiasm buoyed Sano's spirits. "You search for socks and clothes with blood on them. Masahiro and I will question everybody."

A tall, square woman, neatly dressed in a dark brown kimono, marched up to Sano. "If you are going to speak with the women or enter their rooms, you will do it under my supervision." Her deep, stern voice was crusty with age. Her white hair, pinned atop her head, gave off a strong odor of peppermint-and-jasmine-scented hair oil. The bristly mustache on her upper lip was white, too. She must be in her sixties now, but Sano recognized her from that long-ago investigation.

"Madam Chizuru," he said. "So you're still the *otoshiyori*."

The *otoshiyori* was the chief lady official of the Large Interior. Her most important duty was to keep a vigil outside the shogun's chamber when he slept with a female concubine, to ensure that the concubine behaved properly. There had been little need for that service. Her other duties included keeping order in the Large Interior.

She looked surprised to see Sano. "So you're a detective again."

Sano had reason not to let her oversee the search and interviews. He knew something about her that he didn't mention now. "Where were you when the shogun was stabbed?"

Her prim, dainty lips thinned in dislike. "I was in bed, asleep."

"Did anyone see you?"

"No, I have my own room."

"Then you're a suspect." Sano told Marume, "Put her under guard, apart from the other women. I'll talk to her later."

Cloaked in indignation, Madam Chizuru let Marume lead her away. Masahiro said, "That was fast."

Later Sano would tell Masahiro why he thought his first suspect was a likely culprit. They began questioning the women, who all had roommates to confirm their statements that they'd been asleep during the

attack on the shogun. Sano noticed things that had changed in the Large
Interior since his previous case. The concubines were all homely. Lord
Ienobu must have ensured that if the shogun should ever want a female
bedmate, none of them would tempt him into fathering a new heir. And
the shogun's mother was gone. Lady Keisho-in had died a few years ago,
at age seventy-six. Sano and Masahiro questioned female relatives of the
shogun, and the ladies-in-waiting and maids. They, too, had alibis. So did
the male guards.

"I think they're telling the truth," Masahiro said.

Sano agreed. With each moment that passed he felt increased pressure
to find witnesses and evidence. Detective Marume called, "Hey, I can't
get this door open."

Sano and Masahiro hurried around the corner. Manabe, their shadow,
followed. They found Marume rattling the locked door of a chamber.
"Break it down," Sano said.

Marume heaved his shoulder against the door. The wooden panel fell
into a room that exhaled warm, damp air. Sano saw a round, sunken bathtub filled with steaming water, surrounded by a floor made of wooden
slats. "Who's there?" he called.

No answer came. Sano, Marume, and Masahiro stepped inside the bath
chamber. In the corner crouched a young woman dressed in a white cotton
robe. She was small, slim, and beautiful, perhaps eighteen years old. Her
long black hair hung in damp straggles. Her limpid eyes were huge with
fright.

"Who are you?" Sano asked.

"Tomoe," she whispered. "A concubine."

So the shogun still had one beautiful concubine, Sano thought. "Why
would you bathe at this hour?"

Cringing, Tomoe shook her head.

"Why did you lock yourself in?" Masahiro asked.

"I heard screams." She shivered. "I was afraid."

"Did anyone see you come in here?" Sano asked.

"No." Her eyes pleaded for mercy. She looked like a fawn sighted on
by a hunter. "Everybody else was asleep."

Marume's and Masahiro's faces showed the same sympathy for the beautiful, vulnerable girl that Sano felt. Manabe waited in the doorway, his face impassive.

"If she was in the bathtub when the shogun was stabbed, she couldn't have done it," Masahiro said.

"She could have run in here after he was stabbed," Sano pointed out.

"To wash off his blood?" Caught between his inclination to believe Tomoe was innocent and the need for objectivity, Marume examined the floor. "I don't see any."

Sano glanced at the sponge, a bag of rice bran soap, and a bucket on the wet floor by the drain hole in the wooden slats. He tried to picture Tomoe scrubbing and rinsing herself and bloody water trickling down the drain and failed. He couldn't imagine her capable of stabbing anyone, but he was sworn to conduct an honest investigation; he'd dedicated his life to the pursuit of truth and justice. That was his personal code of honor, as important to him as Bushido.

"She's a suspect," Sano said. "We have to treat her like one." Masahiro and Marume reluctantly nodded. Sano called to Captain Hosono, who'd joined Manabe at the door. "Put her under guard, away from everybody else. Marume-*san*, continue searching for bloodstained socks and clothes."

Captain Hosono led the meek Tomoe away. As Sano and Masahiro headed down the corridor together, Masahiro said, "Aren't we done questioning everybody?"

"No." Sano opened a door, and they looked through it across the snowy night to a little house attached to the Large Interior by a covered corridor and surrounded by an earthen wall and a narrow garden of bamboo thickets.

Masahiro frowned. "Lady Nobuko. The shogun's wife."

There was bad blood between Sano's family and Lady Nobuko. She'd lured Sano into investigating the death of the shogun's daughter, and their troubles had begun then. Furthermore, her actions had almost gotten Masahiro killed. Masahiro clearly hadn't forgiven Lady Nobuko. Now here she was again, at the center of another crime they were investigating.

"I'll talk to Lady Nobuko by myself," Sano said.

Masahiro opened his mouth to object. Sano silenced him with a stern look and said, "Go talk to Dengoro, the boy who was sleeping with the shogun during the attack."

A hint of the usual tension between them returned. Sano knew that Masahiro's chafing at his authority went deeper than just a young man's natural desire for independence. After more than four years of watching Sano try and fail to prove that Lord Ienobu was guilty of murder and treason, Masahiro no longer trusted Sano's judgment. That hurt.

"The boy couldn't have done it, could he?" Masahiro said. "Don't the bloody footprints mean it was someone from the Large Interior?"

Sano sensed that something else was bothering Masahiro, but they didn't have time for a personal discussion. He also feared that Masahiro's lack of faith in him would prove to be justified. They were several hours into the investigation, with no results in sight. Lord Ienobu's threats loomed large.

"It's too soon to rule Dengoro out, and he's an important witness," Sano said. "Maybe he's remembered something."

10

MASAHIRO WENT TO the section of the palace where the shogun's boys lived. It consisted of small chambers built around a court-yard, and a theater where the shogun and the boys performed in Nō plays with professional actors. Masahiro walked the deserted corridor, peering into the chambers that smelled of dirty socks and contained wooden swords, balls, horses, and other toys. The beds were unoccu-pied. Masahiro heard shouts, followed them out a door, and found a furious battle waging in the dark courtyard. Some twenty boys pelted one another with snowballs, ran, and laughed. Standing on the veranda, Masahiro smiled. For the first time since he'd been caught with Taeko, the tension inside him eased.

"Dengoro?" he called.

Boys turned toward the sound of his voice. One said, "What?" An-other flung a snowball at him and hit his chest. He yelped.

Masahiro scooped up a handful of snow and hurled it at the boy who'd hit Dengoro. His snowball splattered the boy's face. Everyone started yelling and throwing snowballs at Masahiro. He dodged some, was hit by others. Laughing, he packed more snowballs and returned fire. For a moment he didn't have to worry about Taeko and her talk of eloping. He didn't have to think about what would happen if he and his father couldn't prove Lord Ienobu was responsible for the attack on the shogun. But soon his bare hands were freezing; a snowball melted down his neck. He couldn't forget that he had a job to do.

The investigation was his chance to help himself, his father, and their whole family get out of trouble for good. He mustn't flub it. When it was done, he would figure out how to fix things so that he and Taeko could be together.

"That's enough!" He help up his hands, surrendering. The boys groaned. "Dengoro, come inside with me."

Dengoro smiled, happy to be singled out by the man who was so good at snowball fights. He led Masahiro to a chamber, sat on his unmade bed, and waited, bright-eyed and expectant.

Masahiro knelt on the floor and introduced himself. He felt under pressure because although he'd helped his father with past investigations, this was the first of his adult life, and more would be expected of him. He'd also realized that his father wasn't infallible. In four years Sano hadn't managed to defeat Lord Ienobu, and Masahiro had begun to doubt that he could. Masahiro couldn't deny that his own life had been adversely affected by Sano's actions. But that didn't diminish his love or respect for his father. It only applied more pressure. Sano needed help, and Masahiro couldn't let him down.

"My father and I are investigating the attack on the shogun," Masahiro said. Dengoro's expression filled with the awe of a younger boy impressed with an older one. Pride boosted Masahiro's confidence. "We have to find out who did it. I'm hoping you can help us."

"Help you, how?" Dengoro looked eager to do whatever Masahiro wanted.

"I'm going to ask you some questions. Do you swear to answer them honestly?"

Dengoro nodded solemnly. "I swear."

He didn't look tough enough to stab the shogun or clever enough to plant bloody footprints leading to the women's quarter, but Masahiro remembered his father saying that appearances could be deceptive. "Did you like the shogun?"

The boy's forehead wrinkled. "I guess so. He gives me food to eat, and a place to live, and clothes and toys and everything. I'm an orphan. My parents died in the earthquake. If not for him, I would be dead, too."

He sounded as if he were quoting the palace official who procured the shogun's concubines. Masahiro hinted, "But you don't like him as much as you should?"

"I don't like the things he makes me do." Dengoro looked guilty.

"Well, I wouldn't, either." Although manly love was common and accepted by society, Masahiro wasn't interested in it, and he felt sorry for the boys who were forced to have sex with the shogun. He felt particularly sorry for Dengoro, a nice child, but couldn't go easy on him. "Do you ever get angry at the shogun?"

". . . Sometimes. When it hurts."

"What about tonight?"

Dengoro chewed his fingernails. "I didn't want to sleep with him. He has the measles. I'm afraid of catching it."

"My next question is the most important one." Masahiro paused to let the gravity of it sink in. Dengoro waited, smiling eagerly. "Did you stab the shogun?"

"No!" Dengoro reacted as if Masahiro had played a cruel joke on him.

Masahiro didn't like to hurt the boy, but he understood that being a detective sometimes required hurting people, and he would do it for the sake of his father. "Maybe it was an accident," he suggested. "Maybe you just wanted the shogun to leave you alone, and you didn't mean to hurt him. If it was an accident, you can tell me. I'll make sure you don't get in trouble." Being a detective sometimes also meant lying.

"I didn't." Dengoro's sweet face crumpled. "Do you think I did? Is that why you wanted to talk to me?"

Masahiro thought Dengoro was telling the truth. "No, I believe you," he said in an apologetic tone. "And I still need your help. All right?"

"All right." Dengoro's willingness to forgive made Masahiro ashamed.

"You told my father you didn't see anything when the shogun was stabbed. But maybe you did and you forgot. Think back to when you woke up. Try to remember."

Dengoro stared into space and concentrated. ". . . I think I saw somebody running away. An old lady. It might have been the shogun's wife."

If Masahiro couldn't pin the attack on Lord Ienobu, then Lady Nobuko was his second choice. She'd almost gotten him killed. "Why do you think it was Lady Nobuko?"

"It looked like her."

"How many times have you seen her?"

"Once. During a New Year ceremony."

Masahiro thought it unlikely that the boy could identify a running figure glimpsed in the dark as a person he'd seen once before. "Do you know that my father is looking for the attacker in the Large Interior?"

"Yes. I heard the guards talking."

So he knew the women were under suspicion. Masahiro asked, "Which of the other women do you know?"

Dengoro named a few servants. "And there's the *otoshiyori*." His brow wrinkled. "It could have been Madam Chizuru. After I woke up, I think I smelled her. She smells like peppermint and flowers."

Masahiro had smelled her tonight. Her scent was certainly strong enough to have lingered in the shogun's bedchamber and distinctive enough for Dengoro to remember. Heartened by this clue, yet skeptical, Masahiro decided to try a test. "Do you know any of the shogun's girl concubines?"

"No. They're kept away from us. But we sneak up on the roof and spy on them in their garden. They're all ugly except one. Her name is Tomoe. She's really pretty. And she sings really nice."

Masahiro gave him a sly man-to-man smile. "You like her?"

Dengoro blushed and shrugged.

"I know you wouldn't want to get Tomoe in trouble, but could it have been her that stabbed the shogun?"

Dengoro hesitated, eyeing Masahiro, gnawing his thumbnail. "Maybe."

Masahiro rotated his hand, prompting Dengoro.

"I think I heard the person muttering before she ran away. I couldn't hear what it was, but . . . it sounded like Tomoe's voice." Dengoro looked unhappy to incriminate Tomoe but hopeful that he'd said the right thing.

Exasperation filled Masahiro. His hunch had been correct: Dengoro was inventing evidence to please him. Dengoro probably would have said he'd seen the Buddha stab the shogun, if Masahiro had suggested it.

Although flattered because the boy wanted so much to be liked by him, Masahiro was also angry. "You didn't really see Lady Nobuko, or smell Madam Chizuru's hair oil, or hear Tomoe's voice, did you?"

Dengoro's face showed alarm and confusion that gave way to chagrin.

"Then don't say you did!" Masahiro grabbed Dengoro by the chin and glared down at him. "This isn't a game. By making things up, you could get innocent people put to death. You could be helping whoever stabbed the shogun get away with it." He was furious at the boy for misleading him, furious at Lord Ienobu and Chamberlain Yanagisawa for mistreating him and his father, furious at everything that was keeping him and Taeko apart.

"I was just trying to help." Dengoro's voice wobbled.

"You're wasting my time!" Masahiro let go of Dengoro.

"I'm sorry." Dengoro jumped to his feet. "Please don't go. Please don't be mad at me."

Ashamed of hurting the boy's feelings, Masahiro relented. "I'm not mad. But I have work to do."

"Will you come back and see me again?" Dengoro pleaded.

Maybe he actually did have information about the stabbing. Just because he'd made up stories tonight didn't mean he hadn't actually seen something he'd forgotten and would remember later. "All right," Masahiro said.

If he could help his father solve the crime, maybe it would change things enough that he and Taeko could marry. His own lack of progress increased the pressure and his determination.

Dengoro smiled, cheerful again. As Masahiro left the room, he reminded himself that Dengoro had been at the scene during the attack. Maybe he wasn't just a terrible witness. Maybe he had stabbed the shogun.

SANO WALKED THE wet, slushy gravel path to Lady Nobuko's quarters. Manabe doggedly followed. The sky was more gray than black above the glow of lights from the castle; morning was near. The bamboo thickets hid any sign of life in the little house. When Sano knocked on the door a long time passed before it was opened by a gray-haired man dressed in a dark blue coat—Lady Nobuko's personal physician.

"Lady Nobuko isn't receiving visitors," the physician said. "She's ill."

The shogun's wife suffered from headaches, a convenient excuse for avoiding unwanted conversations. Sano had no patience for his old adversary's games. "I'm investigating the attack on the shogun. She has to speak with me whether she wants to or not."

"She was very upset to learn about her husband. I gave her a sedative. She won't wake up for a few hours."

Sano wanted to barge in on Lady Nobuko and thrash her until she begged him to let her talk. Pent-up frustration, pressure to solve the crime, and his ravenous hunger for revenge on Lord Ienobu frayed his control over his temper. But there was no use trying to interrogate an unconscious woman. "Tell her I'll be back later," Sano said.

As he departed, Manabe fell into step beside him. Sano said, "How about telling me what you really did the night of Yoshisato's murder?"

Manabe just smirked. Sano determined that he would eventually get the better of both Manabe and Lady Nobuko. In the meantime, he had two other suspects to question.

HIRATA LOITERED OUTSIDE Edo Castle, apart from the crowd of beggars, priests, and nuns soliciting alms that began to gather along the avenue as the gray sky brightened. He squinted up at the guards in the watchtowers, the covered corridors on the walls, and the guardhouse built over the main gate at which a long line of officials, troops, and visitors stood. The sentries questioned people one by one before letting them enter.

"How am I supposed to get into the castle?" Hirata asked.

How many times do I have to tell you not to talk to me out loud when other people are around? said General Otani's irate voice inside his head. *You'll draw attention to yourself.*

Those sentries know me, Hirata said silently. *They know I'm wanted for treason. If I try to go in, they'll try to arrest me, and it would create a scene.*

Don't worry.

Compelled by the ghost's will, Hirata drew a deep breath. His lungs expanded and expanded. Energy currents spread through him. His aura changed, a sensation like pins pricking the surface of his skin and a sound like metallic tinkling from the part of his mind where the ghost kept its secrets. He looked down at his body—and saw only the snow on the street where his feet had stood. He let out a yell that General Otani stifled by contracting his throat muscles. He held up his hands and saw Edo Castle where they should have been. They, and the rest of him—clothes and all—had disappeared. *I'm invisible! What did you do to me?*

An ancient spell. General Otani sounded amused at his terror.

Hirata patted his hands over himself. His body, and the rough cotton of his garments, were as solid as ever. He gasped with relief. A soldier coming toward him frowned, wondering where the sound had come from. General Otani made him step aside before the soldier walked right into him.

The spell makes your aura reflect whatever is around you, General Otani said. *You're like a chameleon.*

Under other circumstances Hirata would have been delighted to have such a handy skill. But he knew the ghost was bound to put it to evil use. *Please let it not be against Sano!*

General Otani's will propelled him alongside the queue outside the castle. When the sentries let in a group of officials, Hirata slipped through the gate behind them. Otani's voice said, *You'll be undetectable as long as you don't bump into anybody and don't make any noise.*

11

THE SOUND OF voices quarreling filled the Large Interior. The attack on the shogun had upset the peace like a kick to a beehive, Sano thought as he and Manabe arrived at Madam Chizuru's room. The guard outside it let Sano in while Manabe waited in the corridor. The room smelled of peppermint and jasmine. Madam Chizuru sat on the floor, embroidering flowers on a doll-sized pink kimono. She jabbed and yanked, her delicate mouth pressed into an angry line. When she saw Sano, she threw her embroidery in a sewing box and rose.

"I can't be kept locked up. I must tend to the women."

Sano was already in bad temper from his confrontations with Manabe, Lord Ienobu, and Chamberlain Yanagisawa. "As soon as you convince me that you didn't stab the shogun, you're free to go."

The room was crammed with wooden chests and wicker baskets stacked up to the ceiling. Sano and Madam Chizuru stood on a small, bare patch of floor where she would lay her bed at night. Shelves bulged with ledgers and scrolls—records she kept and official communications she received. Cabinets too full to close contained her garments, shoes, and linens. A portable desk equipped with writing brushes, inkstone, and water jar sat atop a table alongside a mirror, comb, brush, jars of makeup, a teapot and cup, and playing cards. Sano could see the red veins in the whites of her angry eyes.

"I'm innocent," she said. "My word should be enough to convince you. I've worked for His Excellency for thirty years. My trustworthiness has never been doubted."

"His Excellency isn't the only one you work for. You're also employed by Lord Ienobu." That was the fact Sano knew about her.

Madam Chizuru reacted with dismay. "How did you know?"

For years Sano had been compiling a dossier on Lord Ienobu, and he'd cultivated a spy in the treasury. "Lord Ienobu pays you a monthly stipend."

"He pays everybody who works in the Large Interior. He likes to know what goes on here."

"But he pays you the most," Sano said. "What do you do for him?"

Chizuru hesitated, trapped between fear of lying and fear of being punished by Lord Ienobu for talking. "I keep track of his concubines' monthly courses. I'm supposed to tell him if any of them are pregnant."

Of course Ienobu would be on the lookout for a pregnancy, Sano thought. No matter if the shogun had actually fathered the child, if it was a boy, he might claim it as his own even if he knew it wasn't; he was that desperate to leave the regime to a direct descendant, and a new son would displace Lord Ienobu. But Sano suspected Madam Chizuru wasn't telling the whole story of her arrangement with Ienobu.

"What else?" Sano asked.

"I'm paid not to tell anyone except him."

"So he buys your silence," Sano said, still unconvinced. "How many pregnancies have there been in the Large Interior since he started paying you?"

"None."

"Then he hasn't gotten his money's worth, has he?"

"If there is one, I'm to make sure the baby isn't born," Chizuru admitted reluctantly.

Sano was shocked even though abortion was common and Lord Ienobu had already masterminded the murders of the shogun's daughter and Yoshisato, the former heir. To pay someone to discover and kill unborn babies, as if they were vermin . . . "That's pretty dirty work."

Chizuru looked offended rather than shamed by his repugnance. "Not all of us can afford to turn down money. I have a granddaughter to support. My stipend isn't enough." She glanced at the doll's dress in her sewing basket. "And you of all people should know what happens to somebody who won't do what Lord Ienobu wants."

Sano did, but he couldn't let sympathy get in the way of justice, and if he didn't solve the crime, the shogun would put him to death. If he couldn't pin it on Lord Ienobu, then Lord Ienobu would. "So you couldn't say no to Lord Ienobu. Did he tell you to stab the shogun?"

"No. He didn't. And I already told you: I'm innocent."

"He wants to rule Japan, and he was tired of waiting for the shogun to die, so he decided it was time for you to earn your pay. He sent you to assassinate the shogun."

Chizuru folded her arms across her stout chest. "If he sent some-body, it wasn't me."

"You're the only woman in the Large Interior who doesn't have an alibi," Sano lied. "The shogun has to blame somebody for stabbing him. It's going to be you."

The fear rekindled in her eyes; she apparently didn't know that Tomoe and Lady Nobuko were also suspects.

"Do you think Lord Ienobu will protect you? No—he'll let you take the fall."

Chizuru backed away from Sano, but a stack of trunks against the wall stopped her. She glanced at the door. Manabe and the guard blocked her escape.

"You may as well confess and make Lord Ienobu share your death sen-tence." Sano heard her breath rasp. Perspiration soured her peppermint-and-jasmine scent.

"When the shogun was stabbed, I was here, asleep. I can't prove I was, but you can't prove I wasn't." With an emphatic nod, Madam Chizuru clamped her prim mouth shut.

Sano couldn't break her without using more persuasive tactics, and he didn't believe in torture even though it was legal and commonly em-ployed. It often produced false confessions, and Madam Chizuru might be innocent. Even without a confession he could make a case for his theory that she had tried to assassinate the shogun on orders from Lord Ienobu. The shogun, who was in a drugged, vulnerable state, might believe it and put Lord Ienobu to death. Sano and his family could make a fresh start.

But no matter how much he wanted that fresh start, Sano also wanted the truth about the crime, even if the truth was that Ienobu was innocent. It was a matter of honor as well as justice. Honor was the source of strength that had sustained him through the most difficult times in his life. If he ever gave up his honor, he was finished no matter how this investigation turned out.

And there were still at least two other suspects.

A guard came to the door and said, "Excuse me, but some man is trying to take that girl Tomoe out of the castle."

YANAGISAWA STALKED THROUGH the gate of his secluded compound within Edo Castle. He ran past the barracks where his many retainers lived, then across the courtyard. A young woman skipped down the steps of the mansion to meet him. She was slender and graceful, with shiny black hair that reached her knees. It streamed out behind her like a cape. Her delicate face was stunningly beautiful. Her smile revealed perfect white teeth; her luminous black eyes sparkled. She opened her arms, and the long sleeves of her brilliant pink, flower-embroidered kimono spread like wings.

"Papa," she cried. "See my new kimono!"

His daughter Kikuko was twenty-four years old, but she spun like a little girl. Yanagisawa shuddered with revulsion. Kikuko was feeble-minded; she would never grow up. Yanagisawa was ashamed to have fathered a defective child, mortified because she looked like him. He sidestepped to get away from her as she fluttered around him and giggled.

His wife hurried out of the mansion. She was as ugly as Kikuko was beautiful. Her face was flat and dour, with slits for eyes, a broad nose and lips, and thin, greasy, graying hair. Yanagisawa had married her only because she came from a rich, powerful clan and had a large dowry. He'd only bedded her to get an heir, and after Kikuko had shown early signs of retarded development, he'd avoided touching his wife.

"Don't bother your father. He's busy." His wife's voice was soft and hoarse, like a rusty iron hinge creaking. She gently drew Kikuko away from Yanagisawa.

He disliked having her and Kikuko in his house. He'd only moved them in because their villa had been damaged by the Mount Fuji eruption two years ago. Before that he hadn't seen Kikuko in almost ten years. When he'd discovered how beautiful she'd grown up to be, he'd realized that she might not be completely useless. As he strode past her, she stared vacantly at him. Saliva pooled at the corners of her smile. His wife beheld him with naked, miserable yearning. She was in love with him, Yanagisawa knew but didn't care. His wife and daughter meant nothing to him. All his love, all his passion, were for Yoshisato, his absent son.

He hastened into the mansion, shouting, "Nakai-*san*!"

His chief retainer appeared in the corridor that led past offices where his staff worked. Yanagisawa spoke in a low, furtive voice. "Are there any new leads?"

Nakai was one of the few people Yanagisawa had told that Yoshisato was alive. The others were the troops searching for Yoshisato. "Not since that sighting in Kamakura last month that turned out to be false."

Yanagisawa fought down despair. "Beat every bush in Japan for more leads. I have to find Yoshisato before the shogun dies and Lord Ienobu—"

A woman came hobbling toward him. Her brown kimono hung on her gaunt figure. It was Lady Someko, Yoshisato's mother. She didn't know that Yoshisato, her only child, was alive. Yanagisawa didn't trust her to keep the secret. Once a beautiful woman, now devastated by Yoshisato's death, she neglected her appearance. Her gray-streaked hair straggled around a face devoid of makeup. Her skin was waxy, her eyes set in dark hollows. As she neared Yanagisawa, he smelled her rank odor of urine, sweat, and dirty hair. She sucked in her cheeks and spat. A blob of saliva splattered on the front of Yanagisawa's robe. She grinned, baring scummy teeth, then hobbled away.

Yanagisawa didn't retaliate because she stirred a quagmire of pity and guilt in him. She'd hated him since the day twenty-three years ago when he'd stolen her from the husband she loved and made her his concubine. After she'd borne his son, he'd sent her away to an isolated villa. He'd ignored her and Yoshisato for seventeen years, then reentered her life and devised his scheme to put Yoshisato at the head of the regime. He and Lady Someko had become lovers again, even though she'd still hated him and her own desire for him. Now Lady Someko blamed him for the loss of Yoshisato.

She wasn't entirely mistaken. If he hadn't passed Yoshisato off as the shogun's son—if he hadn't made Yoshisato a political pawn—then Yoshisato would be safe with her now. Lady Someko had done everything possible to punish Yanagisawa. She'd yelled curses and insults; she'd thrown things at him. While making savage love to him in a futile attempt to conceive another child, she'd clawed and hit him. Yanagisawa still had the scars. Now she was so broken that spitting at him was all she could manage. He felt as if he deserved the abuse for letting her think Yoshisato was dead, for letting her suffer. It was fair retribution for what Yoshisato must be suffering at the hands of Lord Ienobu's men.

If Yoshisato wasn't already dead.

Lady Someko only lived in Yanagisawa's house because she had nowhere else to go. But it wasn't only pity or guilt that made him keep her with him; nor was it love or desire. They'd never loved each other, and he liked his sexual partners young and beautiful. Lady Someko was a connection to his son.

"Find Yoshisato," he whispered urgently to Nakai. "Or you and I and everyone in this house are finished!"

12

SANO FOLLOWED THE guard to a room down the passage. Inside a samurai was arguing with another guard. Tomoe stood watching anxiously, her hands tucked inside the sleeves of her white robe.

"She's my cousin." His back to Sano, the samurai held a wicker hat in his gloved hand and gestured with it at Tomoe. His proud posture made him seem taller than his average height. His copper-colored, padded silk cloak was damp from the snow. He wore two swords with elaborate gold inlays at his waist. "I'm the head of our clan. She's under my protection."

"Who are you?" Sano asked.

The samurai turned. He bore a disconcerting resemblance to the shogun. If one shaved about thirty-five years off the shogun's age, and gave him a backbone, this man would be the result. Sano recognized him. "Honorable Lord Tokugawa Yoshimune."

"Greetings, Sano-*san*." Lord Yoshimune's speech was confident instead of hesitant like the shogun's, his refined features firmly set instead of slack. He wasn't handsome, but his eyes had a hard, clear look of intelligence that made him attractive.

As they exchanged bows, Sano recalled that Yoshimune was a second cousin to the shogun and Lord Ienobu. He belonged to the Tokugawa branch clan that ruled Kii Province, a rich yet troubled agricultural region. He'd become the *daimyo* of it at the young age of twenty-one, after his father and elder brothers died. His clan had been in debt to the government for many years and still owed a fortune in tributes, and two years ago a tsunami had destroyed villages and killed many people in his province. Yoshimune had taken strong measures to help the survivors, trim expenses, and reduce the debt. With a growing reputation as an expert in finance and administration, he was spoken of as a new player on the political scene.

"The guards outside told me you were investigating the attack," Yoshimune said.

"How did you get past them?" Sano asked.

"I convinced them that letting me in would cause less trouble than trying to keep me out." Yoshimune said with a brash, youthful grin, "I brought some of my army along. That usually opens doors."

"I didn't know Tomoe was your cousin," Sano said.

"Third cousin. She's been a concubine since last year."

Noble families, Tokugawa branch clans included, sent their girls to the palace on the off chance that the shogun would father a son on them. A son eligible to inherit the regime would make the sacrifice worthwhile.

"Would you have treated Tomoe more kindly if you'd known she was my cousin?" Hostility tightened Yoshimune's expression. "I came as soon as I heard the news about the shogun and you'd already broken down a door and terrified her. I'm taking her home with me." He turned to Tomoe. She smiled gratefully at him. His manner turned gentle. "Put on some warm clothes. It's cold outside."

Tomoe sidled to a cupboard and took out a cloak and sandals. Sano blocked the door. "She's not leaving."

"You can't seriously believe she stabbed the shogun?"

"She doesn't have an alibi, and she wouldn't explain why she was taking a bath in the middle of the night."

Tomoe stood on tiptoe to whisper in Yoshimune's ear. As he listened, his hand clasped her waist in a gesture more intimate than a man of his station would normally use toward a younger, distant, female relative. He conveyed her words to Sano. "She can't take baths while the other concubines are around. They hold her head under the water. Plain girls like to pick on the pretty one." He asked Tomoe, "Why didn't you tell me?"

"I didn't want to bother you," she murmured.

"Well, you should have. I'd have taken you away sooner."

Pity for Tomoe didn't change Sano's mind. "She's still a suspect. She stays here, under house arrest, until my investigation is finished."

"She can be under house arrest at my estate."

Sano began to see that this crime might not be as straightforward as he'd first thought. Nor did Yoshimune's turning up to rescue his cousin seem innocent. "Why are you so anxious to take her home with you?"

"To protect her." Impatient, Yoshimune explained, "She grew up in my house. She's like a sister to me. I don't want her tormented by you or the girls or anyone else."

Sano saw Yoshimune's hand on Tomoe's waist and suspected that the two were a little more than like brother and sister. He began to see a motive for Tomoe to kill the shogun. "What place in line are you for the succession?"

Startled by the change of topic, Yoshimune said, "Second, after Lord Ienobu. I'm a great-grandson of Tokugawa Ieyasu, who founded the regime." His eyes narrowed. "But you must have known that. Why did you ask?"

"Do you want to be shogun?"

"Who wouldn't?" Yoshimune's laugh was loud, boisterous, uninhibited. "My bad luck, I drew the short straw."

He wasn't like the current shogun, who'd always seemed to consider his rank as much a fearful burden as a blessing. Yoshimune was as ambitious as his other cousin, Lord Ienobu. "Did you decide to change your luck?" Sano asked.

Yoshimune was also as mentally adroit as Ienobu. "You're asking if I arranged the attack?" He laughed again. "If I had, you'd be investigating a murder and not a stabbing. But why would I assassinate the shogun? That would make Ienobu the new shogun, not me."

"It would make you the new shogun if Lord Ienobu were blamed for murdering the old one and put to death."

"Oh, I see." Vexation tinged Yoshimune's enlightenment. "You think I cooked up a scheme to get rid of the shogun and Ienobu with one swipe. Well, I'm afraid it never occurred to me." He grinned, pointing a gloved finger at Sano. "It's a good thing you're not in line for the succession. You would bump off everybody else who was ahead of you."

It had been a long, difficult night, and the mockery taxed Sano's patience. "I don't believe you never thought about how to put yourself at the head of the dictatorship." Throughout history samurai had assassinated their relatives in order to gain power. "And you had someone to help you." He pointed at Tomoe, whose bare toes peeked out from under the hem of her robe. "Her feet match the size of the bloody footprints leading from the shogun's chamber. Where are her socks?"

"That's ridiculous. I didn't send my poor cousin to kill the shogun. I would never." Yoshimune took the cloak from Tomoe and draped it over her shoulders. "Enough of this!" He thrust his hand against Sano's chest and shoved.

"Hey!" Taken by surprise, knocked off balance, Sano stumbled out the door. Disagreements at Edo Castle rarely turned physical. Sano had thought he could talk his way around Yoshimune, but the *daimyo* had yet to tame the short, hot temper of youth. Having gained so much power at such an early age, used to having his own way, he thought himself exempt from protocol. He pulled Tomoe out of the room and hurried her down the corridor.

"Stop!" Sano yelled, running after them.

"Try to make me." The grin Yoshimune flashed over his shoulder said they both knew that if Sano laid a finger on him, his army would rush to his defense, drag Sano out of the castle, and beat him to a pulp. Sano needed to pick his battles, and this wasn't a good one, even though he could have gladly fought Lord Yoshimune to the death.

The rude young pup was yet another obstacle between Sano and the truth about the most important crime of his career.

Following Yoshimune and Tomoe outside the palace, Sano blinked in the sudden brightness. The morning sky was white with opaque clouds. Snowflakes materialized out of it and swirled before Sano's tired eyes as he halted on the veranda. Yoshimune paused to help Tomoe put on her shoes, then led her down the steps. Troops standing around the palace let the couple pass.

"If you have any more questions for her, you can ask them at my estate," Yoshimune called before the troops closed ranks and he and Tomoe disappeared from Sano's view.

Manabe chuckled at Sano's frustration. Masahiro came out the door and said, "What was that about?"

"That was one of our suspects escaping." Sano explained about Tomoe and Yoshimune.

"I talked to Dengoro, the shogun's boy," Masahiro said. "He said he thought he heard Tomoe's voice right after the stabbing."

Sano rubbed his forehead in dismay. This was more evidence that pointed to Tomoe, she'd just absconded, and the investigation was leading away from Lord Ienobu.

"But Dengoro also said he thought he saw Lady Nobuko and smelled Madam Chizuru's hair oil. So we'd better not trust anything he says."

Detective Marume and Captain Hosono joined them. Marume said, "That's the worst kind of witness—the kind that makes things up."

Sano was disappointed because the shogun's boy couldn't identify the attacker. "Have you finished searching the Large Interior?"

"Yes," Marume said, dejected. "No bloody socks. Not a thing out of the ordinary. And the snow under the windows was undisturbed. There's no sign that anybody tossed anything out or climbed through them."

"So we're left with Tomoe, Madam Chizuru, and Lady Nobuko as suspects, and without any evidence to say which is guilty." Sano was discouraged, but at least the array of suspects was still narrow, manageable. He asked Captain Hosono, "How is the shogun?"

"He's asleep. The guards and the physician are with him."

"At least he's still alive," Marume said.

But Sano knew that didn't guarantee his recovery. Sano had to prove that Lord Ienobu was responsible for the stabbing before the shogun died. If he couldn't, then Lord Ienobu would inherit the dictatorship and there would be no way to hold him accountable even if he was guilty.

"People are starting to show up for work." Captain Hosono gestured beyond the cordon to the growing crowd of officials. "Can I let them in?"

"Yes," Sano said. The government had to continue its business despite the circumstances. "I'm finished here for the time being."

13

AFTER EXITING THE castle, Manabe rode with Sano, Marume, and Masahiro to make sure they really were going home and not just pretending in an attempt to get rid of him so they could continue their inquiries by themselves. He left them at the edge of the *banchō*.

In the blank white daylight, the small estates looked especially rundown with the leftover New Year decorations. Ash from Mount Fuji coated sacred rope hung on the gates to keep out evil spirits and the pine branches staked to bamboo poles by the doors—symbols of strength, longevity, and resilience. Dismounting outside his estate, Sano saw the shabby little house with his flying crane crest on the gate as a shameful reminder of how far he'd fallen in the world.

Marume took the horses to the stable in the backyard. Masahiro went into the house. Carrying the cloth-wrapped iron fan he'd brought from the castle, Sano followed his son and mustered the courage to face his wife.

INSIDE THE HOUSE, Reiko opened the back door to the racket of dogs barking. Akiko was standing in the yard, holding a wooden bowl and unlatching the gate. In rushed a pack of huge stray dogs. Rough-furred and lean, frantic with hunger, they jumped and pawed at Akiko. She emptied the contents of her bowl onto the ground. As the dogs pounced on the food, growled, and fought over it, Reiko called, "Akiko!"

Akiko turned, her face a picture of guilty defiance.

"I told you not to feed stray dogs," Reiko said. "We can't afford it."

"I saved them some of my food."

Reiko hated to criticize her daughter's generosity, especially since caring for dogs was a virtue. The shogun had enacted laws that protected dogs and built kennels for them. Anyone caught killing or hurting dogs received the death penalty. A priest had once told him that his mercy would please the gods, who would then grant him an heir. Under his laws the population of stray dogs roaming Edo had exploded. The fierce, wild animals scared Reiko.

"They'll bite you," she said.

"No, they won't. They're my friends."

Reiko was caught between her need to discipline and protect her child and her wish for Akiko to be happy. She knew Akiko was lonely. Chiyoko was too young to be a close friend, Tatsuo preferred to play by himself, and Akiko's bold ways didn't endear her to the neighborhood girls who shunned her because her father was in disgrace. When they teased her, she hit them. Reiko herself had been unpopular as a child, neither able nor willing to fit in with the conventional girls of her social class. She'd been fortunate that her father, Magistrate Ueda, had occupied her with education, martial arts lessons, and listening to trials in his court. But Reiko's attempts to teach Akiko ended in fights, Sano didn't have time, and there was no money for tutors. Akiko had turned to these dogs for company and diversion.

Something had to be done about her, Reiko thought. Then she heard noises from the front of the house. Sano and Masahiro had come, at last. She'd been in a fever of impatience to see them ever since she'd heard the news about the shogun. She dreaded talking to Sano because every conversation turned into an argument, but she wanted to find out what had happened. Reiko closed the back door, leaving Akiko with the dogs, and hurried to the entryway.

* * *

SANO'S HEART LIFTED, its habit whenever he saw his wife. Then it fell like a bird with a net thrown over it, dragged back to earth by their troubles. Reiko was as beautiful as when they'd married nineteen years ago, but she was thinner, and silver threads glinted in her upswept black hair. She didn't smile at Sano across the distance created between them by his campaign against Lord Ienobu. Sano felt lonely in her presence.

"Are you all right?" Reiko asked. She was cool toward Sano; her concern focused on Masahiro.

The zest Masahiro had shown during the investigation turned to sullenness. "I'm hungry."

"Your breakfast is ready," Reiko said.

"I'll eat it in the kitchen." Masahiro hung his swords on the rack, tossed his cloak on a hook, and stomped off.

It wasn't like Masahiro to be rude to his mother. Sano noticed a new tension between his wife and son. Masahiro didn't like the estrangement between his parents and avoided being with them, but this was something different. "What's wrong with him?"

"I'll explain later."

Reiko helped Sano remove his cloak, careful not to touch him. They never touched except accidentally. They hadn't had sexual relations in two years. She'd spurned his advances until he'd given up. She'd said she didn't feel well, but Sano knew the real reason: She wasn't in love with him anymore because his actions had put them in danger, reduced them to poverty, and ruined their children's prospects. He was still in love with her despite her disapproval of him, and he felt rejected, less than a man, and miserable. He also couldn't help feeling angry.

She knew these were hard times for him, too, yet she denied him the comfort of physical intimacy and sexual release. Would it kill her to accommodate him once in a while? He would never go outside their marriage for sex, although it would be his right; many husbands did.

They went into the parlor, which was chilly despite the charcoal brazier. The alcove, decorated for the New Year, contained a table set with ferns in a porcelain vase and painted wooden lobsters—symbols of good fortune—and rice cakes topped with oranges—bribes to make evil spirits go elsewhere. If only the rituals worked, Sano thought as he sat by the brazier and thawed his hands.

Reiko put his breakfast on a tray table in front of him. Sano was starving; he hadn't eaten since dinner yesterday. Devouring rice with fish, pickles, and tofu, washing it down with hot tea, he felt guilty because Reiko bore the brunt of his demotions. Raised as a privileged member of the upper class, she'd never had to do housework for most of her life. Now they had so few servants that she cooked, waited on the family, and washed clothes. She wore cotton garments because her pretty silk kimonos had worn out and Sano couldn't afford to replace them. She never complained, but he knew she minded—and it wasn't because she was spoiled and resented having to work. It was because he'd willingly, despite the consequences, kept up the campaign against Lord Ienobu, and his honor always took priority over her wishes and their family.

"What happened last night?" Reiko asked.

He'd done more things that he knew would upset her and jeopardize what was left of their marriage. Sano started his tale with the confrontation on the highway.

Reiko leaned away from him. Her eyes filled with reproach. "You didn't tell me you'd had a tip about Lord Ienobu's men."

Four years ago Sano wouldn't have kept it a secret from her. Back then, since the early days of their marriage, they'd shared everything. Reiko, a unique woman and unconventional wife, had loved helping him with his investigations. The only child of one of Edo's two magistrates, she'd grown up listening to trials, and she'd developed an interest in crime and a flair for detective work. Sano had come to rely upon her help. Although they'd often disagreed on aspects of their investigations, they'd never disagreed about whether to pursue a murderer . . . until the case of Lord Ienobu. Sano wanted to continue. Reiko didn't. They'd had many arguments about it, but neither could change the other's mind. Their discord was complicated by other problems, one of which was that Reiko's father had been forced to retire after Sano had run afoul of Lord Ienobu. Now here came another argument, the last thing Sano wanted, that he'd tried to avoid by not telling Reiko about the tip.

"I didn't know if the tip was any good," Sano said. "I had to investigate it first."

"You could have told me you were going after them last night." Reiko spoke in a controlled, civil voice.

"I didn't want to upset you," Sano said.

"So you let me think you were out on your regular patrol? Then Detective Marume comes home alone, covered in blood?" Reiko exclaimed, "Well, I'm upset now!"

"I'm sorry," Sano said, keeping his voice low, hoping Reiko would follow suit. The house was so small; words spoken in one room were audible everywhere else. "I didn't know what would happen."

"Things always turn out badly when you take action against Lord Ienobu." Reiko repeated what she'd been telling Sano for years: "It's time to give up trying to prove that Lord Ienobu was responsible for Yoshisato's murder."

At times like this Sano wished she were a conventional wife who never criticized or opposed her husband. Her strong, independent will had attracted him to Reiko when they were first married, but he didn't like having it turned against him; yet he had only himself to blame. He'd endangered what was left of their life together. What did she see when she looked at him? Surely not the dashing samurai she'd married, but a misguided fool.

"It's a matter of honor," Sano retorted.

Reiko glanced up at the ceiling, her habit when he used Bushido to justify his misdeeds. Sano knew that losing his temper was dangerous when he was exhausted and under pressure, but he felt a flare of anger at Reiko. She knew that honor was the most important value in his life, yet she wouldn't embrace it for his sake because she didn't care enough about him.

"A wise man knows when to stop beating his head against his wall," she said.

"Are you calling me stupid?" Sano demanded.

"Just stubborn."

"And you aren't?" This trait they shared made it all the harder for them to get along, and it was worsening as they grew older. "I'm stubborn for the sake of justice."

Reiko gave him a long look that penetrated too deeply. "It's not only justice you want. It's revenge on Lord Ienobu."

"Vengeance is a matter of honor, too. It's cowardly to let your enemy beat you and not fight back."

"Vengeance can hurt you more than your enemy! It almost got you killed last night!"

"I'm alive to fight another day," Sano said, folding his arms. "That's how it goes."

"According to Bushido?" Reiko said, "You're investigating Yoshisato's murder after the shogun told you to stop. That's a violation of Bushido, which says you have to obey your lord."

"I'm disobeying it for the shogun's own sake, to prevent his murdering nephew from inheriting the regime! It's my duty as a samurai to go against my lord when my lord is going the wrong way."

"Then why not break the rule about justice and vengeance, too? Why should you be able to choose which rules to follow and which to break?"

Her logic was sound, but honor didn't always obey logic. "There's no use my trying to explain," Sano said. "You refuse to understand."

"I don't understand why you had to report Hirata. He hasn't done anything wrong. You could have given him a chance to shut down his secret society instead of making him a fugitive and his family outcasts."

She never confined an argument to one subject; she dragged in all his offenses. Sano's anger flared hotter, stoked by the frustration of unsatisfied desire. "Don't bring that up again!"

"Of course, you don't have to live with Midori and the children and their misery every day," Reiko said, angry, too. "You're hardly ever home." She shook her head, realizing the argument had gotten off track. "What's the use fighting Lord Ienobu? You never win."

"There's obviously no use expecting you to give me another chance," Sano snapped.

"Why take another chance? The shogun doesn't care about justice for Yoshisato. Let the fool leave the regime to Lord Ienobu, the traitor who murdered his heir. It's what he deserves."

"Don't talk about the shogun like that!" Sano was horrified to hear someone criticize his lord even though he knew exactly what the shogun was.

"You're trying to do him a service he doesn't want, and it's only hurting us. Haven't we suffered enough?" Reiko spread her arms.

The gesture encompassed their cold, shabby house and her thin body. The memory of their dead child occupied the space between them like a cruel apparition. Sano supposed he'd never grieved the loss as keenly as Reiko. He hadn't carried the child in his body or been present when it was stillborn. It had never seemed as real to him as his other children. He felt guilty for that as well as because she'd lost the baby while trying to save his life.

"It's because we've suffered that I'm so determined to get Lord Ienobu." Sano wanted desperately to make it up to Reiko, and this was the only way he knew how. "He set the events in motion that caused . . ." Sano couldn't say "our baby's death." They didn't talk about the baby; it was too painful.

Tears glittered in Reiko's eyes. "Don't make your vendetta about that. You can't change anything that's happened. You'll only cause more trouble for us."

"It's not just about honor," Sano said. "It's about survival now."

"You knew four years ago that it could come to that. If you'd quit then, we wouldn't be in this spot. And it's not too late for you to change."

Sano felt the rift in their marriage widen. He fervently wished they could be as they'd once been—united, facing peril together. He loved Reiko so much that he wanted to blurt it out, but she must hate him so much that if he did, she would laugh. Would they ever find their way back to each other? It seemed impossible.

In the adjacent room, the children fretted; Midori's anxious voice soothed them. Reiko drew a shaky breath, made an effort to calm herself for their sake. "Detective Marume said the shogun was stabbed." She spoke as if she thought this was a safer, neutral topic. "Will you tell me what happened?"

It was as safe as an axe hanging over his head, but Sano mustn't keep any more secrets from her. He told her about the unseen attacker. "The shogun's wounds are serious. The doctor says it's too soon to know if he'll survive."

Clasping her heart, her eyes stricken, Reiko said, "Merciful gods."

"There's good news," Sano said, delaying the inevitable while he tamped down his emotions. Their argument was about to move on to even more hazardous ground, and unless he controlled himself, he would say or do something irreparably destructive. "The shogun brought me, and Masahiro, back to court. I'm chief investigator again and Masahiro is my assistant."

Reiko brightened, then frowned, suspicious. "But why . . . how . . . ?"

Bracing himself for the axe to drop, Sano said, "I'm going to investigate the attack."

REIKO INTUITED WHAT had really happened. "You mean, you volunteered?"

"Yes," Sano admitted.

She tried to see it from Sano's point of view instead of getting angry that he'd stepped right in the middle of another dangerous investigation. He was an experienced detective; it was his duty to find out who stabbed the shogun. She couldn't help thinking, *He never learns!* The discomfort in his manner told her there was even more to the story that she wasn't going to like.

"But you've been out of favor for four years. Why would the shogun change his mind about you all of a sudden?"

"I talked him into it. With help from Yanagisawa."

Reiko was surprised that their enemy would lift a finger for Sano except to cut his throat, and even more disturbed to learn that Sano had gotten mixed up with Yanagisawa again. That surely meant more trouble, and she smelled Sano's motive for volunteering to investigate the crime. "Don't tell me: Lord Ienobu is a suspect. You think he's responsible for the attack on the shogun."

"He has the best motive," Sano said, defensive. "If the shogun dies, he inherits the dictatorship."

Reiko's anger flared again. "You're using the investigation to start up a new battle with Lord Ienobu! I don't believe it!" She shook her head as she thought of the demotions, the effect on the children, and the constant fear that next time Lord Ienobu retaliated, it would be death for the whole family.

"This is my new chance to prove that Lord Ienobu is guilty of treason and take him down," Sano said. "That's the only way to protect us."

"And if you can't?"

Sano beheld her with reproach. "Why are you assuming I'll fail?"

"After four years you still can't convict Lord Ienobu of killing the shogun's daughter and son. Why do you think you'll succeed this time?"

Sano studied her as if she were a puzzling stranger. "There was a time when you would have jumped at this opportunity, no matter the risks."

Reiko turned away from his unspoken question: *Why have you changed?* The answer hurt too much. Part of her spirit had died with the baby. It was the part that contained her courage, her taste for adventure, and her belief that she could prevail over stronger adversaries. She had become a small, frightened, helpless person who saw disaster around every corner. Sano didn't like her new self, and neither did she. Reiko could hardly remember how she'd once been, how once she would have welcomed the prospect of a new investigation with her husband.

She could hardly remember how much in love they'd once been.

She was scared because they'd lost each other as well as the baby. She didn't want that, but she didn't know how to change it, and she didn't deserve to be happy again. She was to blame for the baby's death, not Sano, not Lord Ienobu. She was the one who'd overexerted, whose body had failed to carry the child to term, but she couldn't bear to think about it, let alone tell Sano. Instead she salved her pain with anger.

"How is the investigation going?" Reiko flung the question at Sano like a challenge.

"We have the weapon and a potential witness." Obviously anxious to put matters in a positive light, Sano described the iris fan and the boy who'd been sleeping with the shogun. "Also bloody footprints leading from the shogun's chamber to the Large Interior."

A spark of curiosity lit in Reiko despite herself. "The women are suspects?"

"So far." Focused on convincing her that he'd made good progress, Sano didn't notice her interest. "There are two who don't have alibis." He told her about Madam Chizuru and Tomoe.

This was where Reiko once would have jumped right in. Her strength as a detective lay in her ability to go places where a man couldn't, talk to women, and extract information that they might withhold from a male detective or that might escape his notice. Her talents perfectly suited this crime. Reiko felt a stirring inside her spirit. Her fear quelled it like a foot stamping out a fire.

"There's also the shogun's wife," Sano said. "I haven't questioned her yet. She's ill."

Here was Lady Nobuko, her old adversary, right in the middle of another crime. Sano wasn't the only one with samurai blood that craved revenge. When Reiko had lost the baby, Lady Nobuko had played no small role. The mention of Lady Nobuko brought back the pain of that awful day. Reiko recoiled from it. A new case that involved Lady Nobuko could only bring more trouble, and Reiko had the answer that Sano had been beating around the bush to avoid.

"So there's no evidence against Lord Ienobu," Reiko said flatly.

"I only started a few hours ago. You know it takes time. And there is evidence of a sort." Sano described the connection between Ienobu and Madam Chizuru. "Lord Ienobu and Lady Nobuko are close, too. I'll get him this time."

Reiko felt a twinge of familiar restlessness. Once she'd never been able to sit idle while an investigation was underway and her family in danger. She was stuck in the past, but events were dislodging her, like an ocean current moving a sunken ship. Even as she resisted, she heard herself say, "I'll help you, then. Let me question Lady Nobuko."

Sano looked surprised that she would volunteer to help with an investigation she didn't want him to conduct, then offended. "You think I can't handle it by myself?"

"That's not why I want to help," Reiko said, dismayed because he'd misunderstood her.

"Isn't it?" Sano's voice was bitter. "You wanted me to stop trying to get Lord Ienobu for Yoshisato's murder. You don't approve of my doing this investigation, either, but you think I'm so incompetent that I'll fail again, so you offer to help me even though you don't want to."

They'd fallen into a bad habit of not getting along, Reiko supposed. Not even a new case and the heightened threat to their family could break the habit. Angry at Sano for jumping to the wrong conclusion, she said, "It's my neck in danger, too. And I want to take on Lady Nobuko."

Sano nodded, admitting her point, frowning in concern. "Won't your personal bias against her get in the way?"

"Won't your personal bias against Lord Ienobu?"

Sano sighed, tired of arguing, still reluctant to give in. "Are you sure you're up to it?"

"You're calling me incompetent?" Reiko was the one on the defensive now. "After all the times I've helped you solve crimes?"

"That's not what I meant!" Sano said, frustrated. "I'm talking about your health."

Reiko knew she was so thin the wind could blow her away, and she hadn't practiced martial arts in years, but she said, "I can handle Lady Nobuko. Besides, it's dangerous enough sitting here waiting for Lord Ienobu to strike again." She wanted to be in on this investigation, more than she'd realized at first.

Sano reluctantly conceded. "All right. Talk to Lady Nobuko."

They rose, and he hesitantly put his arm around Reiko's waist. Reiko shied away, picked up his food tray, and said, "I should wash the dishes before I go to the castle."

He held his arm out, circling the empty space she'd vacated, then let it drop. Reiko was immediately sorry. He thought she didn't want him to touch her because she was disgusted by him, his actions, and his failures. But she still desired him, and she was still in love with him even though she tried to deny it to herself because he obviously didn't love her anymore. The way she'd treated Sano, she was lucky he didn't divorce her and throw her out. The real reason was that she was afraid to arouse him, afraid of sex. She longed for another baby, but she'd failed to conceive after two years of trying. She couldn't bear to get her hopes up and fail again and again. Nor could she bear the thought of miscarrying another child. But she couldn't tell this to Sano. Every time she tried, she choked on tears. It seemed that nothing could heal the pain she carried inside her like a bleeding wound.

After a moment of uncomfortable silence, Sano said, "What's wrong with Masahiro?"

That was another sore topic. "Midori caught Masahiro and Taeko . . . together, in the storeroom last night."

Sano looked surprised, then disheartened by this trouble on top of trouble. He sighed. "I'll talk to him."

Carrying the tray to the kitchen, Reiko thought of things she might have said. *You have the most dangerous case of your life to solve, and I'm only making things worse, I'm sorry.* But she still thought she was justified in criticizing Sano for starting a new campaign against Lord Ienobu, and he hadn't apologized for putting honor ahead of their family. Neither was going to back down; they were both too sure they were right, both too proud.

Maybe the investigation would bring them back together. Reiko felt hope glimmer inside her, like a lighted window glimpsed through a snowstorm. Fear tempered hope. She was about to step into the same, treacherous political quagmire that she'd begged Sano to stay out of. But she found herself looking forward to another chance at Lady Nobuko.

14

SANO FOUND MASAHIRO swinging a wooden sword, hacking savagely at the falling snowflakes, in the fenced yard behind the house. His breaths puffed out angry white vapor. His face was strained with distress. Sano remembered practicing martial arts with Masahiro when he'd been younger. Masahiro had worked hard but often clowned and laughed. Sano missed that carefree little boy, but he bore much of the blame for Masahiro's present unhappiness.

Masahiro saw Sano, froze, and lowered his sword. His expression darkened.

"Your mother told me about you and Taeko," Sano said.

"I suppose *you* don't want us to marry, either," Masahiro said.

"It's not that I don't want you to." Sano had an inkling of how Masahiro felt. Before he'd married Reiko, he'd fallen in love with another woman. He'd known from the start that their affair was doomed, but losing her had hurt so much, he hadn't been sure he could go on living. "I wish you and Taeko could marry. It's just that you can't."

"But I love her." Masahiro's hardness melted into pleading.

"You're young, and so is Taeko. Your feelings will change."

"No, they won't! We'll never love anybody but each other!"

It was no use promising Masahiro he would find a new, better love within an arranged marriage. Sano couldn't promise Masahiro any marriage at all; no suitable family wanted him. For the first time Sano thought Reiko might be right—he should have given up fighting Lord Ienobu years ago. He had ruined, perhaps permanently, Masahiro's life. If not for his stubbornness, Masahiro would have been married, with a home and children, and perhaps concubines, before he could fall in love with Taeko. But these notions only made Sano cling harder to his convictions. To abandon them would mean he'd wasted the past four years for nothing, and his honor still required him to vanquish Lord Ienobu.

"If you really love Taeko, then you'll leave her alone," Sano was forced to say.

Masahiro waved his wooden sword in a defiant, slashing motion. "I want to be with her. She wants to be with me. You can't keep us apart forever."

"If you keep making love to her, she'll get pregnant."

"She won't. We're careful."

Sano doubted that they were careful enough. "Break it off with her," he said, all too aware that he might be permanently ruining his relationship with Masahiro. "For her sake."

Masahiro flung the sword. It struck the house's roof. Tiles shattered and fell. "We're going to marry. I promised Taeko. I'm going to keep my promise." He stalked away.

INSIDE THE HOUSE, Taeko watched Masahiro and Sano through the window. After hearing their conversation, she felt more desperate than ever. Sano didn't want her and Masahiro to marry. Would Masahiro really go against his father? If she and Masahiro couldn't marry, what was she going to do?

Everybody thought that keeping her and Masahiro apart would prevent her from getting with child, but it was too late. She was already pregnant.

"Shut that window, I'm freezing!" said Ume, the maid, in the kitchen behind her. "You're supposed to help me. Get over here!"

Taeko closed the window and knelt at the table where Ume was cleaning fish. She picked up a mackerel and slit its belly with a knife. The slime and the bloody, rank-smelling fish guts nauseated her. Taeko breathed shakily. She'd begun vomiting in the mornings and at odd times. She'd thought it was just a stomach upset, until she'd missed two monthly courses. When she and Masahiro made love, he tried to protect her by withdrawing from her before he finished, but sometimes he hadn't been able to control himself, and sometimes she hadn't let him withdraw because she wanted him so much. And now she was in trouble.

She felt so alone. She couldn't tell Masahiro. He would be upset and blame her. Maybe he wouldn't love her anymore. She couldn't tell her mother, either. Her mother would force her to take medicine that would make the baby come out dead. That was what women did with unwanted babies; she'd heard people talking. The very thought made Taeko feel sicker. She closed her eyes.

"Keep working! Don't be so lazy!" Ume scolded.

Taeko forced her eyes open and threw the fish guts in the slop bucket. What would happen if she had the baby? Although Reiko and Sano had always been kind to her, they would surely throw her out of their house. That was what happened to unwed girls who had babies. Masahiro would marry somebody else, Taeko would never see him again, and she and the baby would die in the streets. It would be better for the baby not to be born. But Taeko wanted the baby. It was hers and Masahiro's. She already loved it with all her heart. What was she to do?

Scraping off fish scales, Taeko silently prayed harder than she'd ever prayed before: *Please let Masahiro marry me soon!* She clung to her hope even though it seemed impossible.

ALONE IN THE courtyard, Sano gazed at the tile fragments that lay on the icy snow with the wooden sword, which had broken apart between the hilt and the blade. He breathed air that had grown colder in the last few moments.

A servant came out of the house. "Master, there's a message for you." He gave Sano a bamboo scroll container and left.

Glad of the distraction, Sano took out a scroll made of cheap rice paper. The characters were written in a clear but plain hand, perhaps that of a scribe hired by someone who didn't know how to write. Sano read, *If you want the truth about Yoshisato's murder, come to the Shark Teahouse in Nihonbashi today. Come alone.* Directions followed. The message wasn't signed.

Sano didn't put much faith in anonymous tips; he'd had so many that had turned out to be false. But he was desperate to break through the barrier of secrecy that surrounded Lord Ienobu. He would follow up on the tip before he resumed investigating the attack on the shogun. As he headed for the stable to fetch his horse, he decided not to tell Reiko where he was going. If the tip solved Yoshisato's murder and put the blame on Lord Ienobu, she would forgive him. If it didn't, she would never have to know about it.

15

IN THE BUSTLING Nihonbashi merchant quarter, the narrow street that sloped down to the Sumida River was oddly quiet. The snow had stopped falling, and the wind carved drifts in the streets. Shop doors were closed behind indigo curtains that hung halfway down the entrances. Smoke rose from chimneys. A few men bundled in cloaks and hoods loitered outside. As Sano rode down the street, they appeared not to look in his direction, but he knew they were watching him. A window opened as he passed a shop, and he heard dice rattle. These shops were gambling dens. One of the men outside raised a tobacco pipe to his mouth. Blue tattoos decorated his bared wrist. This street was a haunt of gangsters.

Sano's instincts went on high alert. Gangs controlled the gambling dens, operated illegal brothels, ran protection rackets, and killed people who crossed them. The tsunamis and the Mount Fuji eruption had driven them from devastated areas into Edo, and the incidence of gang-related violence had soared. Sano knew his patrol guard's uniform wouldn't protect him. Gang initiation rules required the novices to kill before they became full-fledged members, and killing a Tokugawa soldier would score them extra points. Sano thought of the battle he'd lost last night. Years ago he could have beaten single-handedly a whole mob of gangsters. Now he hoped they didn't sense his fear.

Midway down the block, two young gangsters leaned against the wall of the Shark Teahouse. Daggers and clubs hung from their sashes. The law permitted only samurai to carry swords, but that was of little comfort to Sano. Above the entrance hung a shark's jawbones with rows of sharp, pointed teeth. Sano dismounted and tied his horse to a post. The gangsters eyed him as he ducked under the curtain. The door grated open. An old man peered out.

Sano introduced himself. "Did you send me a message?"

The man stood back for Sano to enter an empty room in which two cushions sat on opposite sides of a low table that held two cups. A sake decanter warmed on a charcoal brazier. Sano wondered if Lord Ienobu had set him up to be murdered in a way that would look like a random crime, and he had an urge to run, but his inner voice whispered, *Stay.*

Sano stepped into the teahouse. The gangsters outside rammed the door shut. He faced the proprietor. "You have something to tell me?"

The proprietor looked toward the back doorway. The curtains hanging over it parted. A gangster stepped through. Compact and wiry of figure, he wore a padded brown cloak. Gray leggings hugged his muscular calves. A dagger in a black lacquered sheath hung at his waist. His hair was cut short; blue and black tattoos climbed up his neck. His face had scars on his rounded chin, his cheeks, and his wide brow. His expression was so fierce that Sano instinctively drew his sword.

The gangster laughed. Its gleeful, sardonic timbre sounded so familiar that Sano's heart skipped a beat. His face was startlingly familiar, too. "If you want the truth about my murder, you'd better let me talk before you kill me."

It was Yoshisato.

Shock dropped the bottom out of Sano's stomach. He felt unbalanced, as if the world had turned upside down. Everything he thought he knew was suddenly negated. His mouth opened as he stared. This tough, tattooed gangster couldn't be the youth he'd known as the shogun's heir. He let his sword dangle while his mind argued with his eyes.

"Yes, it's me." A mischievous smile played around Yoshisato's mouth. If this weren't an illusion, he would be twenty-two now. He was astoundingly more like Yanagisawa, his true father, in manner although not physical features. "I'm really alive." He held out his hand. "Touch me, if you'd like to check."

Slowly, in a daze, Sano sheathed his sword. His hand reached out. Yoshisato grasped it. His hand was warm. The back was tattooed with a dragon whose tail curled around his fingers. Sano pulled away as if burned.

"This is a poor welcome back," Yoshisato said with mock disappointment. He also sounded just like Yanagisawa. "Aren't you glad I'm not dead?"

Sano was glad because Yoshisato hadn't burned to death in the fire, because miracles were possible. But he was also aghast. The murder he'd been investigating for more than four years had never happened. He couldn't lay the blame for it on Lord Ienobu.

"While you make up your mind, let's have a drink." Yoshisato knelt on a cushion.

Sano dropped to his knees on the other. They were alone; the proprietor had disappeared. Yoshisato filled their cups. Sano swallowed the strong, smooth liquor. He felt as if he were drinking with a ghost. So many questions tangled in his mind that he couldn't sort out which to ask first.

"Are those your men outside?" he asked. Yoshisato nodded. The shogun's heir had reincarnated himself as a gang boss. "Do they know who you are?"

"They know I'm a former samurai. They think my name is Oarashi." *Great Storm.* "I've been calling myself that for almost two years."

"You've been a gangster for almost two years? The fire was more than four years ago. What happened during the time in between?" Sano slammed his cup down on the table as he realized what a cruel hoax had been played on the shogun, on the whole country. "Why in hell did you let everybody think you're dead?"

Yoshisato responded with a thin, humorless smile. "It wasn't my idea. When you hear the whole story, you'll understand."

Once Sano had thought Yoshisato a decent, honest man despite his history. Now he was so drastically changed in more than outward appearance. Sano sensed a difference inside him, a new darkness. Unsure whether to trust him, Sano folded his arms. "I'm listening."

"The night of the fire, I was almost asleep when I heard scuffling and shouting outside. I jumped out of bed, grabbed my sword, and ran to the door. They burst through it, chased me, and cornered me in my bedchamber." Yoshisato's voice conveyed none of the terror he must have felt; he could have been reciting what had happened to somebody else. "I fought hard, but it was five against one."

"'They'?" Sano prompted.

"The one in charge was Manabe Akira. He's Lord Ienobu's chief retainer. I didn't know the others. I figured they worked for Ienobu, too."

You think you know so much, but you don't know anything, said Manabe's voice in Sano's memory. Here was the information Sano had gone to Yoshiwara to learn—the role Manabe had played in what he'd thought was Yoshisato's murder. "There were five men?" His informer had told him that only Manabe, Setsubara, Ono, and Kuzawa had gone out that night. "Not four?"

Yoshisato waved away the interruption. "They tied me up. Manabe poured medicine down my throat, then gagged me. His men carried in three dead bodies—my guards. Suddenly one of the men turned on another and cut his throat. They left him with my dead guards."

Revelation filled Sano with awe and horror. "After the fire, we found four bodies in the ruins. We thought one was yours. But it was Lord Ienobu's fifth man." Lord Ienobu was even more ruthless than Sano had thought. To serve his purpose, he'd sacrificed one of his own. But what purpose? Why had he faked Yoshisato's death?

"Then they brought in a big wooden trunk," Yoshisato said. "They put me in it. Things are a little hazy after that. There must have been opium in the medicine. I only remember smelling smoke and hearing the fire bell."

Korika had set the fire after Manabe and his gang had set their scheme in motion, Sano thought. The arson and the murders had been blamed on her, just as Lord Ienobu had planned.

"When I woke up, I was locked in a cellar," Yoshisato said. "Ienobu's men had taken me from the castle and hidden me someplace."

Sano shook his head, astonished. Lord Ienobu was guilty not of murdering but kidnapping Yoshisato. Sano began to see a solution to a puzzle that had mystified him. "Does Yanagisawa know you're alive?"

An opaque expression like a coating of ice came over Yoshisato's face. "I assume so. Lord Ienobu's men made me write a letter to Yanagisawa. They told me what to say, and I had to put it in my own words. It said I'd been kidnapped and if he ever wanted to see me again, he should cooperate with Lord Ienobu."

That was why Yanagisawa had allied with Ienobu, his onetime enemy. That was why Yanagisawa had refused to help Sano prove that Ienobu was responsible for Yoshisato's murder. Ienobu had blackmailed Yanagisawa, and Yanagisawa was trying to save Yoshisato. "But if Lord Ienobu needs you as a hostage to hold over Yanagisawa's head, then how is it that you're walking around as free as a bird?"

"Be patient; let me finish. Manabe handed me off to some of Ienobu's other men. They smuggled me out of Edo. I don't know where we went. I rode in the trunk and slept. We moved around a lot."

To hide from Yanagisawa, who must have started hunting for Yoshisato as soon as he'd received the letter, Sano deduced.

"They kept me drugged during the day. They woke me up every night, at a different house or inn or temple. They would untie me and let me eat and wash. I tried to run away a few times, but I was too weak from the opium. They caught me. So I pretended to give up. They stopped drugging me. They let me walk around outside as long as one of them was with me. When we went someplace, I let them tie me up and put me in the trunk. They thought my spirit was broken. I waited for a chance to escape. I was a prisoner for more than two years."

Sano's respect for Yoshisato increased. The youth had had the intelligence, patience, and determination to foil Lord Ienobu.

"One day we were on the highway. Ienobu's men were traveling by horseback. My trunk was carried by porters who didn't know I was in there. Suddenly I heard a loud roar. The ground started shaking. At first I thought it was an earthquake. Then something started clattering onto the lid of my trunk, as if somebody was throwing rocks at us. The horses were neighing and stomping; Ienobu's men were shouting. The porters screamed and dropped me. The lid of the trunk popped open. I wriggled out and—" For the first time during his story, recollected fear crept into Yoshisato's voice. "The sky was red. Rocks were falling from it. Ienobu's men were groping and stumbling and coughing. Their horses had bolted. The air was full of black ash and smelled like sulfur."

"The Mount Fuji eruption." Sano remembered the faint roar and minor earth tremors, a rain of pebbles, and the fumes. Although Edo was distant from Mount Fuji, the effects had been dramatic. Yoshisato must have been in the zone near the volcano.

"Yes." Yoshisato said, "I was tied up. I wriggled off the road, into the woods. The trees protected me from the rocks, but I could hardly breathe. I rolled down a hill. At the bottom there was a cave. I crawled in. The air was better there. I chewed the ropes off my wrists and untied my ankles. If I went outside, I would suffocate or get killed by the rocks, so I stayed put."

Sano imagined the unbearable suspense Yoshisato must have experienced, waiting for Ienobu's men to come after him.

"The rocks kept falling until the next morning. When I came out of the cave, the woods were covered with ash. The air was like the breath of hell. I tore off a piece of my kimono and tied it over my face. Then I started walking. I never saw Ienobu's men again. Either they were dead or they'd run away because they were afraid to tell him they'd lost me."

The eruption that had killed many and caused so much suffering and damage had been wonderful luck for Yoshisato. Sano asked, "How did you survive afterward?"

"That first day I found some people dead on the road. A merchant and some servants and a samurai bodyguard. Their noses and mouths were full of ash. I stole the merchant's money and the bodyguard's swords. I traveled from village to village, living on the money until it ran out." Yoshisato said without pride or guilt, "Then I started robbing live people."

The shogun's heir had become a bandit.

"I made my way to Osaka." That was a market city, some thirty days' journey from Edo. "It was big enough to hide in. I fell in with a gang."

Now Sano understood the new difference he'd sensed in Yoshisato.

Had Sano not been so shocked to see him, he would have identified it at once. During his time with the gang, Yoshisato had killed—he'd bloodied his hands, crossed a line. That changed a person, Sano knew. He'd crossed that line, too.

"The gang was a major one, with its fingers in every illegal business in Osaka," Yoshisato said. "I eventually became the boss." Sano intuited that Yoshisato had killed the former boss. Once he'd thought Yoshisato would make a good shogun despite his dubious origins; now Yoshisato had demonstrated his leadership ability by taking over a gang.

It sounded like exactly what Yanagisawa, his father, would have done in his position.

Sano's distrust of Yoshisato grew. "So you're a gang boss. You have a new life. Why did you come back? Are you tired of beating up people who won't pay you protection money?"

Yoshisato grinned; he answered as if flinging a challenge at Sano. "I'm here to reclaim my rightful place as the shogun's heir."

He was as ambitious as Yanagisawa. "Why did you wait so long?"

"Do you think Lord Ienobu would just let me stroll into town? He's got the army scouring the country for me. In the early days, I tried several times to come back, but there were soldiers at every checkpoint along the highway. They were detaining every man who looked the slightest bit like me. Ienobu wants to find me before I can tell the shogun I'm alive. I had to wait until my disguise was good enough." Yoshisato opened his kimono and rolled up his sleeves. His arms and chest were covered with tattoos of demons and lucky symbols.

"The soldiers never suspected that the shogun's dead heir was hiding under those," Sano said. "Am I the only person who knows you're back?"

Yoshisato nodded.

"Why did you reveal yourself to me? Why not Yanagisawa?"

"I don't want to talk about Yanagisawa." Before Sano could ask why, Yoshisato said, "I need a favor from you. Will you take me to the shogun?"

Surprised that Yoshisato would ask him of all people, Sano said, "You know I don't believe you're the shogun's son. Why do you think I would help you get yourself reinstated as the heir?"

"Because you've dedicated your life to seeking truth and justice. The truth is that I'm alive. The shogun deserves to know. The truth is that even though I wasn't murdered, Lord Ienobu had me kidnapped and held prisoner for years. He deserves to be punished. And you're the one person I can trust to deliver him to justice."

Sano smiled glumly. Yoshisato had him pegged. He could guess what Reiko would think of all this. And the fact that Yoshisato was alive had other ramifications. Sano hesitated a moment before he said, "Let's go."

Yoshisato smiled as if he'd known Sano would agree; he rose.

"Not so fast. Have you heard what's happened?"

"No . . . ?"

The news hadn't trickled into town yet. "The shogun was stabbed last night. As of a few hours ago he was still alive, but he's seriously injured." Sano added, "It's a good thing you didn't wait any longer to come back. If the shogun dies before he finds out you're alive, then Lord Ienobu wins."

And now that Lord Ienobu couldn't be convicted of Yoshisato's murder, Sano's hopes of defeating him hinged on proving he was responsible for the attack on the shogun.

16

ACCOMPANIED BY ONE of Sano's few troops, Reiko walked up through the snow-blanketed passages inside Edo Castle. The trembling began as she neared the palace. Her heart raced as her memory carried her back in time.

The day she'd lost the baby had begun with her and Sano and the children escaping from house arrest and a death sentence. Since then, her mind had gone over and over each moment of that day, like a waterwheel churning a pond. Now, more than four years later, as she walked the same path as then, she again felt the weight of her pregnant belly and the painful contractions that signaled that the baby was coming soon, too soon.

"What's the matter?"

Her escort's worried voice jolted Reiko out of memory, into reality. She was bent over, panting, and holding her stomach outside the little house where the shogun's wife lived. The soldier asked, "Are you sick?"

"No, I'm fine." But the sight of the house made Reiko feel giddy and faint. She hadn't been here since that day; the last time she'd seen Lady Nobuko was four years ago, at her own home. This was where she'd come to confront Lady Nobuko, to extract information that would save her family. She'd succeeded at the cost of her baby's life. Black spots coalesced in her vision, as if from the darkness that the house exuded.

She couldn't go in there. Sano was right: She wasn't up to it. The boldness that had sustained her through fifteen investigations was gone.

"Do you want me to take you home?" asked the soldier, a fatherly, kind man.

But she'd made Sano let her question Lady Nobuko. It was her duty to help him, no matter how bad things were between them, and she had to protect her family. The gods help them if they didn't solve this crime.

"No," Reiko said. She mustn't be a coward. "Wait here."

As she walked up to the door and knocked, she strained against panic as if against a fierce wind. A woman with a mouth like a pickled plum opened the door, looked at Reiko, and said, "You're not welcome here."

"I know," Reiko said. Lady Nobuko had declared, during their last conversation, that she was severing all ties between them. The memory of that conversation dredged up anger, which formed a screen between Reiko and her panic. "I don't care."

She pushed through the door and moved down the passage even though she was shaking. Lady Nobuko was in her chamber, kneeling at a low table, ink brush in hand. The brush's tip was poised above a sheet of paper covered with spiky black calligraphy. All manner of evil memories buzzed like wasps behind the mental screen of Reiko's anger.

Lady Nobuko glared up at Reiko. "I told you I never wanted to see you again."

Her right eye was half closed, the muscles on that side of her narrow face bunched together by the pain of her constant headache. Her figure was as bony as a skeleton in her padded lavender silk robe, and her hair had gone white since Reiko had last seen her, but she'd held up remarkably well. She looked as if she were sustained by drinking vinegar, unaffected by the events that had devastated Reiko.

"If you hadn't pretended to be too sick to speak with my husband, then I wouldn't have had to come," Reiko said.

Lady Nobuko didn't argue that she really had fallen ill upon hearing the news that the shogun had been stabbed. She regarded Reiko with a dislike colored by amusement. "So you're dabbling in another investigation. I would have thought you'd learned your lesson. After all, you gave birth to a dead baby last time."

Reiko felt as if Lady Nobuko had stabbed her in the heart. To hear the baby's death mentioned in such a callous manner was unbearable. Tears welled up from the bottomless reservoir inside Reiko.

"Besides that, you and your husband came to a mistaken conclusion about the murder of the shogun's daughter," Lady Nobuko said. "Lord Ienobu wasn't responsible."

"We weren't mistaken." Reiko's voice quavered.

"So you told me the last time we met. I must say this for you: You never give up." Lady Nobuko's tone scorned Reiko's persistence. "I hope you think it was worth it." She obviously knew all about Sano's downfall. Studying Reiko, she said, "You're losing your looks." Her facial spasm relaxed a little; Reiko's loss was balm to her headache. "You used to be beautiful."

Her cruelty worsened Reiko's anguish. Reiko had insisted to Sano that she could handle Lady Nobuko, but she'd been wrong. Struggling not to cry, Reiko lashed back at Lady Nobuko. "You should have listened to us and helped us avenge the death of the shogun's daughter. But you prefer to believe the official story because you don't like to think that Lord Ienobu got away with conspiring to kill Tsuruhime. You'd rather think that my husband and I are wrong than that you let Tsuruhime down."

Lady Nobuko winced with grief. She was Tsuruhime's stepmother, but she'd loved Tsuruhime as if she'd been her own child. In a fit of anger she threw down her writing brush. "You have the gall to say I let Tsuruhime down! You're the one who killed your baby!"

The low blow hit Reiko right in the tender, vulnerable center of her guilt. Her tears spilled even as she furiously blinked them away. To talk back would invite more personal attacks, but there was no other choice except running out of the room, and Reiko could imagine Lady Nobuko jeering at her. "You're the one who's made a mistake, by allying with Lord Ienobu after he learned that my husband was reinvestigating Yoshisato's murder."

Sano had tried to keep his investigation secret, but someone he'd questioned had informed on him. Ienobu had begun persecuting Sano with Lady Nobuko's help. Lady Nobuko was a powerful ally, but not because she was married to the shogun—theirs was a marriage of convenience; they rarely, if ever, spoke. Lady Nobuko had amassed a fortune by investing an inheritance from her father. She had Japan's biggest bankers under her thumb because she was their best client. They extended credit or called in debts on her orders. Reiko hadn't known that about Lady Nobuko until she'd become Sano's enemy. Lady Nobuko had persuaded her powerful relatives who were allies of Sano to desert him and pressure other powerful clans to do the same. Rather than let her bankrupt them, they'd obeyed.

Blotting the page she'd written, Lady Nobuko said, "I don't believe Lord Ienobu is guilty of Yoshisato's murder, either."

"It's in your interest not to." Reiko heard her voice rise too high and break as she recalled how much of her family's trouble was due to Lady Nobuko. The information that Lady Nobuko had withheld could have prevented Sano from being charged with Yoshisato's murder. It might have prevented Reiko from losing the baby during her strenuous efforts to prove Sano's innocence. She was flustered by anger as well as grief. "Lord Ienobu stands to inherit the dictatorship. You need his goodwill." She had to breathe deeply and swallow a sob before she said, "Did he tell you to kill the shogun? What did he offer you in return?"

Lady Nobuko squinted at Reiko. "Do you really think I stabbed my husband as a favor to Lord Ienobu?"

"I'm beginning to." Reiko thought the old woman was ruthless and heartless enough.

"And you came here to make me admit it?" Lady Nobuko chuckled. "Look at you! You're so weak, you're still crying over a baby that died four years ago. You couldn't make a mouse squeal!"

Humiliated, Reiko couldn't hold back the tears any longer.

"There, there, it's all right." Lady Nobuko's false sympathy was like sugar syrup mixed with lye. "I'm going to make things easy for you." She picked up her jade signature seal and pressed the carved end into a red ink stick. "I've written out my statement." She applied the seal to the paper, under her spiky writing, then handed the paper to Reiko.

Reiko read, *I did not stab the shogun. I was asleep in bed when it happened. My lady-in-waiting can vouch for me. I had no reason to want him dead. I am innocent.*

"Take it to your husband. Then you can go home and have a good cry."

Hating herself because that was what she wanted to do, insulted because Lady Nobuko thought Sano would be stupid enough to accept this statement, Reiko said, "Your lady-in-waiting would say anything you ordered."

"Nevertheless, she is my witness." Lady Nobuko radiated complacency. "*You* don't have a witness to prove I wasn't asleep when my husband was stabbed. Now get out."

She was obviously not going to give Reiko any evidence against herself or Lord Ienobu. Reiko had failed. Longing to escape before she completely broke down, Reiko said, "First I'll search your quarters."

"You will not." Bracing herself on the table, Lady Nobuko stood up. Her skeletal body leaned toward the distorted side of her angry face, as if the pain were an unbalancing weight.

"If you won't let me, it must mean you have something to hide." Reiko resorted to a threat that was stronger than her own power of persuasion. "My husband will tell the shogun."

Lady Nobuko gave an exasperated, conceding sigh.

AT EDO CASTLE, Sano on his horse, accompanied by Yoshisato and the gangsters on foot, marched up to the main gate. The sentries said to Sano, "You can come in. They can't."

"This is the shogun's son," Sano said.

The sentries laughed; they thought Sano was joking. Yoshisato said, "Bow down! Show some respect!" The sound of his voice choked off their laughter. They stared at him with shocked recognition.

"But—but you're dead," one said.

"Obviously not," Yoshisato said.

The sentries fell over themselves in their rush to open the gate and spread the news. Sano dismounted and walked Yoshisato and the gangsters up the hill, through the stone-walled passages inside Edo Castle. An uproar followed them. Patrol guards shouted, "Yoshisato is back!" Curious faces peered from watchtowers. Running footsteps echoed as people flocked to see the shogun's resurrected son. Officials poured out of their quarter, blocked the passage, and craned their necks.

Plowing through the crowd, Sano and Yoshisato hurried to deliver the news to the shogun before anyone else could. At the palace Sano rushed Yoshisato past the sentries and in through the door. "Wait outside," Yoshisato called to his gangsters.

Sano and Yoshisato raced through corridors, past gawking officials and servants. Yoshisato strode into the shogun's bedchamber, then Sano did. The shogun was asleep, his eyes closed in his pale, damp face. A soldier knelt near each side of the bed, the doctor at the end. Along the wall, Yanagisawa and Lord Ienobu sat with Captain Hosono between them. Everybody except the shogun looked up in surprise.

"Mind if I join you?" Yoshisato said.

The shogun's eyelids fluttered. Everybody else stared at Yoshisato and reared up on their knees. Yanagisawa slumped forward. His right hand braced him against the floor. His left hand clutched his heart. Lord Ienobu's eyes bulged.

"You weren't expecting me, were you?" Yoshisato directed his question at Yanagisawa and Ienobu, who'd known all along that he was alive.

Mouth open, Yanagisawa wheezed. Lord Ienobu coiled into himself like a snake trying to hide under a rock. The shogun opened bloodshot, sunken eyes. He gasped, propped himself up on his elbow, and said in a voice filled with awe, "Yoshisato? My son?"

Yoshisato moved toward the shogun. "Yes, Honorable Father, it's me."

"Am I dreaming?" The shogun blenched with sudden fear; he raised his hand to stop Yoshisato. "Are you a ghost?"

"No, Honorable Father." Yoshisato knelt and took the shogun's hand in his. Sano had told him the shogun had measles, but he appeared unconcerned about catching it. "You can feel that I'm real."

The shogun pressed his nose and mouth to Yoshisato's hand as if to inhale Yoshisato, devour him. "You are! The gods have brought you back to life!" He sobbed in ecstasy, then convulsed with pain and moaned.

Lord Ienobu and Yanagisawa watched, dumbstruck. Yoshisato smiled, gratified by the drama he'd created. A woman burst into the room. She had disheveled, graying hair and a sallow complexion; her soiled gray kimono hung on her emaciated figure; she smelled stale, fetid. She cried, "I heard the news. I had to come and find out, is it true? Is Yoshisato alive?" Her hollow eyes spied Yoshisato. She screamed, pushed the shogun away, and flung herself on the young man, then caressed his face while she keened, "Yoshisato! Yoshisato!" and wept.

Yoshisato held her. "Mother." His voice trembled; his eyes glistened.

It was a scene that Sano wouldn't have missed for the world. It was a scene that nobody here would ever forget.

"Mother, I have business to discuss with these people." Yoshisato had his emotions under control again. "Go home and wait for me."

She stumbled out, weeping with joy. The bewildered shogun studied Yoshisato. "Where have you been all this time?" Noticing Yoshisato's tattoos, he gasped. "Why are you so changed?"

"I'm glad you asked," Yoshisato said. "It's time you learned the truth about my so-called death."

As he told his story, Sano watched Yanagisawa and Lord Ienobu. Yanagisawa's face darkened with anger as he heard how Yoshisato had been drugged, kidnapped, and imprisoned. Ienobu's protuberant eyes skittered, chasing frantic thoughts.

"He let everyone think I was dead." Yoshisato pointed at Lord Ienobu. "He wanted me out of the way so that he could be the next shogun."

The shogun collapsed back on the bed. His horrified stare turned on Ienobu. "Is this true, Nephew?"

"It certainly is not." Ienobu regained his haughty poise. His eyes were steady now, brimming with scorn. "Yoshisato is lying."

"Of course you would deny it, to save your own ugly skin," Yoshisato retorted.

Waving his frail hand to interrupt the argument, the shogun said to Ienobu, "If he's lying, then how do *you* account for the extra corpse in the fire? How do *you* explain the fact that my son is alive?"

"The corpse must have been a servant who was in the heir's residence when the fire started. Yoshisato is responsible for his own absence. He didn't want to be the next dictator. He has no stomach for politics." Ienobu's contemptuous glance called Yoshisato a coward. "When the fire started, he saw his chance. He ran away."

Yoshisato uttered a shout of disdainful laughter. The shogun demanded, "If Yoshisato doesn't want to inherit the regime, then why did he come back?"

Perspiration beaded Ienobu's forehead, but he sat his ground. "Because starting a new life isn't easy. He decided that being shogun would be nicer than being a gangster."

"I have to admire you, Lord Ienobu—you think fast on your feet," Yoshisato said with a pitying smile. "But I have a witness to prove I'm telling the truth." He looked to Yanagisawa.

YANAGISAWA STILL COULDN'T believe that after he'd searched for Yoshisato for so long, Yoshisato had just strolled into the palace. He felt as if the sun had come out after an endless night. Yoshisato glowed so dazzlingly that Yanagisawa could barely see the other people in the room. Even Sano, the blight on his existence, was a mere shadow. Yanagisawa wanted to feast on the sight of Yoshisato, but if he looked directly at him, he would break down and blubber; his heart overflowed with so much love for Yoshisato, so much joy.

How he regretted that they'd parted on bad terms! He'd let Yoshisato go away thinking he was nothing to Yanagisawa except a political pawn. Now Yanagisawa could tell Yoshisato how he felt. But not yet. Later he could marvel at Yoshisato's miraculous return. Later he would find out what in the world Yoshisato and Sano were doing together. This was his long-awaited chance to send Lord Ienobu to hell.

Engorged with vengefulness, Yanagisawa rose. Ienobu looked like a snake cornered by a man with an axe. "A few days after the fire, you came to me and told me Yoshisato was alive." Yanagisawa's voice was clear, resonant, and loud with the anger that had reopened the airway constricted by shock. "You showed me the letter you made him write to me."

He felt a sensation like a tight iron band around his chest snapping loose. "My silence and cooperation were the price you put on Yoshisato's life." To speak freely again was an exhilarating relief. "You said that unless I helped you become the next shogun, you would kill Yoshisato. But now I don't have to do any more of your dirty work. I don't have to keep quiet." Yanagisawa told the shogun, "Lord Ienobu duped you. He tried to take over the regime by kidnapping your son and holding him hostage. He's a traitor! He should be put to death!"

Anger encroached on the confusion on the shogun's face. Yanagisawa had planted a seed of suspicion in him, and it had taken root.

Lord Ienobu stood up on his rickety legs. "Yanagisawa-*san* is lying! There was no letter, no such conversation. Here's what really happened, Uncle: After the fire, *he* came to *me*. He was terrified that with Yoshisato dead, he would lose his position at court. He begged me to let him work for me so that he wouldn't become a *rōnin* and starve!"

"Look at him," Yanagisawa jeered. "See him shaking. Do you want to know why he's so afraid?"

The shogun nodded, rapt with attention. Here Yanagisawa had the advantage over Lord Ienobu: Yanagisawa had controlled the shogun for almost three decades; the shogun had been under Ienobu's influence for a fraction of that time. The shogun raised a hand to prevent Ienobu from speaking. Now Yanagisawa had to make the most of his advantage. There had never been a situation like this; it was an unfamiliar battle-ground in fast-moving flux. All his instincts, honed by a lifetime in politics, told Yanagisawa that persuading the shogun that Ienobu had kidnapped Yoshisato wouldn't carry the day. The shogun had limited concern for other people. Yanagisawa had to exploit the shogun's selfishness in order to stick it to Lord Ienobu.

"Lord Ienobu is afraid because what's happened today proves he's responsible for the attack on Your Excellency," Yanagisawa said. "He knew that Yoshisato was alive and on the loose and if Yoshisato returned to court, he would take back his place as your heir. There were two ways for Lord Ienobu to prevent that. He had to find Yoshisato and kill him—or to make sure you died and he became shogun before Yoshisato showed up." Yanagisawa held up his thumb, then his forefinger. "But he couldn't find Yoshisato." Yanagisawa folded down his thumb. "So he chose option number two." He pointed his forefinger at Ienobu, who was jittering so hard that the floor shook. "He sent an assassin to murder you, Your Excellency."

The shogun sat up, panting. "Yanagisawa-*san* is right!" His red, tearful eyes blazed at Ienobu. "You tried to have me killed so that you could rule Japan!"

Yanagisawa tasted victory coming, so sweet after years of humiliation from Ienobu.

"I didn't!" Terrified, Ienobu extended his clasped hands to the shogun. "Please, Uncle, believe me!"

To cap his argument, Yanagisawa said, "If the assassin had succeeded, you would be dead now, Your Excellency. Ienobu would be shogun. And if your son ever surfaced, Ienobu would slaughter him like a lamb."

"Traitor!" the shogun screamed at Ienobu. Spasms gripped him; he moaned. "I want your head on a post by the Nihonbashi Bridge!"

"I swear on my life, I'm innocent!" Ienobu bleated.

Sano stepped forward. "Pardon me, Your Excellency, but even though Lord Ienobu's motive for the attack on you looks stronger in light of these new circumstances, there's still no evidence against him. There are other suspects."

"He's right!" Ienobu gasped with relief that someone was taking his side. "Let him finish his investigation. It will prove that someone else is guilty!"

The angry determination on the shogun's face wavered. *A curse on that bastard, Sano!* Yanagisawa thought. He wouldn't let Sano redirect the tide that was finally flowing in the direction he wanted. "Sano-*san* is right," he said. Sano frowned in surprise at his capitulation. "We don't know for sure who stabbed Your Excellency, but one thing is certain: Yoshisato is back." He felt the warmth of Yoshisato's dazzling light. "Yoshisato was your first choice for an heir. Lord Ienobu was only a poor second. You should rename Yoshisato as your heir."

"Yes, yes!" the shogun exclaimed, clutching at Yoshisato. "You are my heir."

"And Acting Shogun," Yanagisawa prompted.

"And Acting Shogun. Nephew, I don't need you anymore. Good-bye!"

17

SANO, YANAGISAWA, YOSHISATO, and Lord Ienobu exited the palace. A crowd of officials, troops, and servants outside, abuzz with gossip and speculation, halted them on the veranda. Yoshisato smiled and bowed to them. They quieted, gawking at the soul risen from the dead. Sano saw Masahiro in the back, craning his neck. Yanagisawa spoke into the pool of silence.

"The shogun has renamed Lord Yoshisato as his heir. Lord Yoshisato is now the Acting Shogun." Yanagisawa's voice rang with triumph.

Exclamations burst from the crowd. Sano recognized officials who were Ienobu's allies, saw panic on their faces. Under his stoic manner he, too, was reeling with shock. Never had he imagined that the investigation he'd started four years ago would end like this. He was delighted to have Ienobu knocked out of first place in line for the succession, but he'd delivered control of the regime into the hands of Yanagisawa and his pawn.

Yoshisato stepped forward. An anxious hush descended as his new subjects waited for the changes they knew would come. "Many thanks for coming to welcome me back." He surely knew that many of these men were loyal to Ienobu, but he spoke as if to friends. "I shall visit each of your departments soon. You shall brief me about everything that has happened while I've been away, and we shall discuss how we can work together on behalf of my father's government."

Before the fire, Yoshisato had asked Sano to be part of a coalition to improve the government, stamp out corruption, and reduce political strife. Evidently he still wanted the coalition; he was still idealistic. But his pleasant words to Ienobu's friends contained a threat: *Switch your allegiance to me, or woe betide you.* He was making good use of his experience as a gangster boss, but that didn't alleviate Sano's qualms.

The crowd quickly dispersed. Only Masahiro, the sentries, and Yoshisato's gangsters remained. Sano supposed that everyone else was eager to discuss this historic event, spread the news, and figure out how to survive the coup. "Find your mother and tell her what happened," Sano said to Masahiro. She wasn't going to be pleased. He couldn't leave yet, and if she couldn't hear it directly from him, better Masahiro than the gossips.

Masahiro ran off to obey. Yanagisawa and Yoshisato faced Lord Ienobu. Vindictive satisfaction shone in their eyes, but Sano perceived a strange, uncomfortable air between the two.

"How does it feel to have the power shifted to the other hand?" Yanagisawa gloated.

Fuming yet helpless, Ienobu started to sidle around his two enemies.

"Not so fast," Yoshisato said. "Here's my first order to you: Vacate the heir's residence by sundown."

Ienobu spoke through gritted teeth. "I'll see the two of you in hell before I let you rule Japan." He scuttled away like a fleeing cockroach.

"I've waited four years for this day," Yanagisawa said, watching Ienobu's retreat.

"So have I," Yoshisato said.

Sano had noticed that they hadn't looked at each other since he'd sprung Yoshisato on the shogun. They were a united front against Ienobu, yet somehow divided. Yoshisato said to Sano, "We'll talk soon."

Yanagisawa's eyes narrowed with disapproval at this hint of camaraderie. Sano found himself caught in a familiar spot—between his liking for Yoshisato, his bad blood with Yanagisawa, and his duty. "Talk about what?" Sano asked Yoshisato. "The fact that you're Yanagisawa-*san*'s son and not the shogun's?"

"Oh, come now, you can't really want to fight about that again!" Yanagisawa regarded Sano with exasperation.

Much as he liked Yoshisato, Sano resisted being sucked into an allegiance with him. "You shouldn't be allowed to inherit the dictatorship. You're a fraud." And Yanagisawa was his partner in his fraud and his quest to seize power.

"So why did you bring me to the palace? You knew the shogun would rename me his heir." Antagonism tinged Yoshisato's voice. Sano had the peculiar sense that he really had died in the fire and been reincarnated as this gangster who would thrash anyone who crossed him. "Why didn't you tell Lord Ienobu that I was in town and let him do away with me?"

"Because the shogun deserved to know the truth about what happened to you. Because Ienobu engineered the death of the shogun's daughter even though he didn't kill you."

"Which means you have to choose between a fraud and a murderer," Yanagisawa said.

"That's no choice!" Sano was exasperated, too. "Neither Yoshisato nor Ienobu deserves to be the next shogun! And you certainly don't deserve to control the regime."

"One or the other of us will be," Yoshisato said, "and I'm the top contender, not to mention Acting Shogun."

The threat gleamed like a knife blade through his civil manner. And Sano had once thought that Yoshisato had inherited none of Yanagisawa's ruthlessness! By bringing Yoshisato back to court had he supplanted Ienobu with a worse villain?

Yoshisato read the dismay and confusion on his face and smiled faintly. "Don't worry, I'm not going to have your head for defying me. I'm going to help you do something you've been wanting for four years—deliver Lord Ienobu to justice."

Sano chuckled at the irony of one criminal offering to help him get another. "Lord Ienobu's not the only one who should be delivered to justice." His gaze encompassed both Yoshisato and Yanagisawa.

"We've more important things to do than fight among ourselves," Yanagisawa said impatiently. "You once asked me to help you prove that

Lord Ienobu murdered Yoshisato. That's obviously impossible, but Yoshisato and I can offer you a sweeter deal: We'll help you prove that Ienobu was behind the assassination attempt on the shogun."

The offer was like a strange new breed of flower spawned from the alien soil laid down by today's events. Sano couldn't ignore its allure. With Yanagisawa's cooperation instead of his hindrance, it would be easier for Sano to solve the crime, do his duty by the shogun, and destroy Ienobu. But Sano smelled poison at the flower's heart.

"What about the other suspects?" Sano asked.

"What about them?" Yoshisato's tone was dismissive. "You think Lord Ienobu is guilty. So do we." He and Yanagisawa behaved as if each were alone with Sano yet keenly aware of the other. "The evidence will bear it out. You'll just find it faster with our help."

Sano also knew better than to trust the notoriously unscrupulous Yanagisawa, to whom the truth meant little and victory everything. And Yoshisato was a wild card, unpredictable. "Suppose we prove that Ienobu is guilty?" Sano asked. "Then what? He's put to death; you the fraud become the next shogun. That's a violation of samurai duty, loyalty, and honor!"

"Forget Bushido for a moment. Suppose you refuse us and you don't prove he's guilty?" Yanagisawa said. "You'd be giving Ienobu a chance to bite you again another day. If he manages to become the next shogun, it won't be just Yoshisato and me he'll put to death. Do you think he'll let you live?"

Here was the crux of his dilemma, the devil's bargain Sano had to make. How drastically the new circumstances had changed the political arena! With Yoshisato restored as the official heir, Lord Ienobu unwilling to give up his hope of ruling Japan someday, and the shogun in bad shape, the battle over the succession was a whole new game. The stakes in his investigation had risen drastically.

The results would determine who inherited the dictatorship and who died.

Sano looked back over his long feud with Yanagisawa. If Yanagisawa came out on top in the war with Ienobu, would *he* let Sano and his family live?

The choice came down to the fact that Sano believed Ienobu was guilty of the attack on the shogun and so did Yoshisato and Yanagisawa. That gave Sano more in common with them than with Ienobu. "All right," Sano said reluctantly. "We'll work together."

Heading back to the Large Interior to resume his investigation, he wondered what form Yanagisawa's participation would take.

WHILE SHE SEARCHED Lady Nobuko's quarters, Reiko took a spiteful pleasure in riffling through cabinets, messing the piles of neatly folded clothes and bedding. Lady Nobuko angrily watched her every move.

"Be careful, you idiot!" Lady Nobuko said.

Reiko went to Lady Nobuko's dressing table and disarranged the little celadon-glazed porcelain jars of medicines and hair oil. Lady Nobuko snatched them out of her hands and put them back in order. Reiko scattered writing supplies, ledgers, and papers in the office niche. Still tormented by Lady Nobuko's cruelty, and still close to tears, she didn't know what, except for bloodstains, she was seeking. The need to find evidence paled before her need to keep busy so she wouldn't break down. She went through all three rooms. Lady Nobuko hobbled after her with a look savage enough to disembowel.

"Help me lift the tatami," Reiko ordered the lady-in-waiting.

They pulled up the heavy straw mats. Reiko looked under each, inspected the floor for secret compartments. In the privy—a little shed connected to the building by an enclosed corridor—she peered into the malodorous basin set on the ground beneath the raised floor. She went outside and searched the bamboo thickets, then yanked off one of the lattice panels that covered the foundation of the building and crawled around under the house. An hour later, she was tired and cold, her clothes dirty. She found no bloody socks. She had a vague yet troubling sense that she'd missed something. There must be incriminating evidence here, but she'd been too upset and distracted to recognize it. She couldn't hear the voice of her intuition.

She was failing at a time when she, and Sano, couldn't afford a single misstep. Each misstep decreased their chances of victory over Lord Ienobu.

"Are you satisfied?" Lady Nobuko asked as she followed Reiko to the gate to make sure she left.

"No." Ashamed of her haphazard effort, Reiko added with false bravado, "You haven't seen the last of me."

"Leave me alone, or you'll wish you'd seen the last of me," Lady Nobuko said. "Lord Ienobu and I can make things worse for your family than we already have."

Masahiro burst through the gate, breathless and upset. Reiko asked, "What's wrong?"

Lady Nobuko grimaced in annoyance. "Is your whole family going to invade my home?" She and Masahiro glared at each other.

There was bad blood between them, too; it stemmed from the events following Yoshisato's murder. Lady Nobuko had known who had set the fire, but she'd kept quiet when she should have told the shogun and prevented Sano from being charged with arson and murder. When the truth had finally come out, it had set off a chase that had almost killed Masahiro. He blamed his brush with death on Lady Nobuko's lie by omission. So did Reiko. She hated Lady Nobuko for that as much as for her part in the loss of the baby.

"Get out," Lady Nobuko ordered Masahiro. He'd done nothing to hurt her, but her dislike of Sano and Reiko extended to their son.

"Not until I've told my mother the news," Masahiro said. "You'll want to hear it, too. Yoshisato is alive."

It sounded so incredible, Reiko felt nothing but irritation. "Where did you hear that gossip?"

"It's not gossip. It's true! Yoshisato didn't die in the fire. He's back! I just saw him. He's here in the castle."

Reiko's heart slammed in her chest like a pounded drum. The man that everyone had thought had been murdered more than four years ago hadn't been murdered at all. Sano's crusade to put the blame for Yoshisato's death on Lord Ienobu had been for naught.

"Yoshisato is the shogun's heir again," Masahiro said. "He's also Acting Shogun."

Reiko was too stunned to perceive all the ramifications. She stammered, "But how did Yoshisato get out of the fire alive? Where did he come from?"

"I don't know. You'll have to ask Father."

Confusion assailed Reiko. "How would he know?" Sano had given her no hint of this miracle or disaster or whatever it was.

"He's with Yoshisato at the palace."

A scream that deepened into a groan issued from Lady Nobuko. Her good eye rolled up in its socket. She fell in a limp faint, her head striking a stone lantern beside the path. A gash on her temple spilled red blood onto the snow.

18

INSIDE HIS ESTATE, Yanagisawa walked toward the mansion with Yoshisato, trailed by the gangsters. His body quaked with pent-up sobs. Tears watered his eyes. He wanted to embrace Yoshisato and say how much he'd missed him, how thankful he was to have him safe and sound. But Yoshisato gazed straight ahead with a face like stone. He showed no sign that this reunion with Yanagisawa meant anything to him. Four and a half years spread like a sea between them, fathomless and treacherous.

Yanagisawa blinked, cleared his throat, and spoke in a casual tone. "I'll have rooms prepared for you and your friends."

"That won't be necessary." Yoshisato sounded as cool and businesslike as if talking to an innkeeper. "We'll be leaving as soon as I've visited my mother."

"It will be a while before Lord Ienobu is moved out of the heir's residence and it's been cleaned up," Yanagisawa pointed out. Ienobu would probably leave booby traps for Yoshisato.

"I have lodgings in town," Yoshisato said. "I can stay there."

His refusal of Yanagisawa's hospitality was like a slap in the face. He was as contrary as ever! Offense subdued Yanagisawa's tender feelings toward Yoshisato. "The shogun's heir can't live in some flophouse. You'll stay with me."

They stopped at the stairs leading to the veranda. As Yoshisato faced

Yanagisawa, hostility showed through his indifference like black water seeping through cracked ice. "The shogun's heir can do as he chooses."

Yanagisawa didn't like Yoshisato pulling rank on him, but now that he had Yoshisato back, he couldn't bear to let him out of his sight. "You won't be safe in town."

Yoshisato responded with the insolent smile that had vexed Yanagisawa so often. "Remember what happened to me the last night I spent inside the castle."

After the fire, the kidnapping, and four years apart, they were even more at odds than before. "Why are you so angry at me?" Yanagisawa asked, honestly puzzled.

Yoshisato looked as if he couldn't believe Yanagisawa needed to ask. "You let Lord Ienobu hold me prisoner. Was it too much to expect you to rescue me?"

Hating himself for letting Yoshisato down, Yanagisawa hurried to defend himself. "I tried! I've spent the last four and a half years searching for you!"

"That's not what I heard." Yoshisato seemed caught between distrust and wanting to believe Yanagisawa. "Sano says you've been working the whole time for Lord Ienobu."

Sano, the constant thorn in Yanagisawa's side. "I kept my search secret so that Ienobu would think I was cooperating with him and he wouldn't kill you."

"Do you really expect me to believe that with all your resources you couldn't find me?"

"You made it hard. My spies were looking for a group of Ienobu's samurai traveling with a young man who appeared to be drugged or an invalid or restrained, not a tattooed gangster. Lord Ienobu's army couldn't find you, either. Your disguise was good."

Yoshisato nodded, conceding the point, but suspicion drew his eyebrows together. "Maybe you decided to hitch your cart to Ienobu for real instead of gambling that you would be able to find me before the shogun died. You had your own future to think about." He said with bitter rancor, "It would have been practical for you to give me up for lost and move on."

"Is that what Sano told you?" Yanagisawa demanded.

"There you go again, blaming Sano for everything. You haven't changed." Yoshisato grimaced in exasperation. "No—this has nothing to do with Sano."

"Then what were you and Sano doing together?"

When Yoshisato explained, Yanagisawa was wounded and jealous. "Why reveal yourself to Sano instead of me? Why ask him to bring you to the palace?"

Yoshisato smiled briefly, pleased that he'd gotten a rise out of Yanagisawa. "Because I trusted Sano more than I trusted you. You might have done Ienobu a favor and stabbed me in the back instead of letting me near the shogun."

"I did everything in my power to save you! I sacrificed my pride. I rubbed my nose on Lord Ienobu's bony rear end!" Yanagisawa shouted, "You ignorant, insufferable brat!" He grabbed Yoshisato's neck and throttled him. The warmth of his son's living flesh made him sob. "I should have left you to die!"

Yoshisato seized his wrists, broke his grasp. "Don't you ever touch me!" Blood engorged his face above the lurid tattoos. A terrible look came into his eyes. His fist shot out and belted Yanagisawa's mouth.

Yanagisawa tasted blood; he roared with pain and fury. "How dare you?" He swung at Yoshisato.

Yoshisato ducked. "You allied with Ienobu to fulfill your political ambitions! And now you want to switch back to my side because the wind is blowing the other way! You two-faced whore!"

They threw punches. One to the chin knocked Yanagisawa's head sideways. He struck out and his knuckles connected with Yoshisato's cheekbone. He was beating up the son he'd longed to see, but he couldn't stop. "I'm going to make you sorry you came back!"

"I'm going to destroy you and Ienobu both!" Yoshisato pummeled Yanagisawa.

Lady Someko came running out of the house, crying, "Stop it!"

Yoshisato kicked Yanagisawa in the gut. "That's for my mother. You should have told her I wasn't dead."

Yanagisawa doubled over and retched. "I couldn't! I thought she would let it out and Ienobu would kill you, you damned fool!" He rammed his head into Yoshisato's stomach.

As they wrestled, Lady Someko grabbed Yanagisawa around the waist and pulled. She shrieked at the gangsters, who'd been watching as if they thought they should stay out of this private spat, "Help me stop them before they kill each other!"

The gangsters pulled Yoshisato away from Yanagisawa. Father and son glared at each other and panted. The many sleepless nights he'd passed during Yoshisato's absence caught up with Yanagisawa. He felt a sudden, overwhelming, despairing exhaustion.

Their reunion had only set them at each other's throats.

"You're both bleeding," Lady Someko said. Yanagisawa and Yoshisato stared at her. She was dressed in clean, opulent maroon silk robes, her hair neatly coiffed and spangled with ornaments, her makeup immaculate. Yoshisato's resurrection had made her beautiful, vibrant, and imperious again. "Come inside, and I'll clean you up."

IN THE PARLOR, Lady Someko wrung out a cloth in a basin of warm water. Yoshisato let her bathe the scrape on his cheek. Her touch was tender, her eyes filled with adoration. He knew she wanted to hug him but she remembered he didn't like being babied. Today he wouldn't mind, but for Yanagisawa sitting nearby. He was suddenly exhausted after years on the lam, fighting in gang wars, keeping out of Lord Ienobu's sights, and the long journey back to Edo. He wanted to curl up in his mother's lap and let her rock him to sleep. But he wouldn't show such childish weakness in front of Yanagisawa. He sat rigid and silent.

Lady Someko ministered to Yanagisawa. Obviously furious at him for not telling her that Yoshisato was alive, she scrubbed his split lip so hard that he winced. She dabbed healing balm on it, then said, "What's wrong with you two?"

Neither answered. Yoshisato supposed that Yanagisawa didn't want to continue the argument in front of Lady Someko because he knew she would take Yoshisato's side. Yoshisato didn't want either of them to figure out why he was so upset with Yanagisawa. This quarrel was only part of a story that had begun long ago.

During his childhood, the absence of his father had been a constant, sore emptiness inside Yoshisato. He'd been four or five when he'd asked his mother, "Why don't I have a father?" She'd promised to explain when he was older, but he'd kept after her. "Who is my father? Why can't I see him? Where is he?"

Finally she'd taken him to a festival at Zōjō Temple and pointed out a samurai amid a party of officials. "He's the chamberlain—the shogun's second-in-command." That was Yoshisato's first sight of Yanagisawa. How tall, handsome, and fierce a man he was!

"He's a very important person, very busy," Lady Someko had said. "That's why he can't come to see you."

Yoshisato had interpreted that to mean he wasn't worth his busy, important father's time. He decided to make himself worthy. He studied hard; he diligently practiced martial arts. If his father ever came to see him, he wouldn't embarrass himself, and if his father didn't, then it would be his father's loss. Yoshisato later found out that Yanagisawa had four other sons—half brothers that Yoshisato had never met. One day Yoshisato learned that Yanagisawa had taken Yoritomo, the eldest, to live with him. Yoshisato was so hurt, jealous, and angry that he decided to hate Yanagisawa. Even after he learned that the unfortunate Yoritomo was the shogun's concubine, he still felt slighted.

When Yoshisato was seventeen, his father finally came calling. It wasn't because he'd heard about Yoshisato's accomplishments. It wasn't to have wonderful adventures together, as Yoshisato had fantasized. It was because Yoritomo was dead.

Thence began Yoshisato's war with Yanagisawa. Yoshisato was angry because Yanagisawa didn't care about him; Yanagisawa only needed a new political pawn. Yoshisato was thrilled to meet his father, but he had a deep well of resentment, Yanagisawa hadn't the patience to win Yoshisato over, and they both had hot tempers.

And the first thing Yanagisawa had done was to pass Yoshisato off as the shogun's son.

Yoshisato knew Yanagisawa had done it to save his life. He even wanted to be shogun; he wanted to try his hand at ruling Japan, to leave his mark on history. He wanted to outrank Yanagisawa and become so important that he needn't crave his father's approval. But Yoshisato couldn't help feeling that Yanagisawa had disowned him, had foisted him off on the shogun, because he didn't want him. The wound cut deep.

Then Yoshisato had been kidnapped. He'd found himself in a night-marish reprisal of his childhood, waiting for Yanagisawa to come for him, feeling empty and hurt because Yanagisawa didn't. And now he was plagued by the same knowledge that Yanagisawa didn't care about him except as a political pawn. If Yanagisawa had indeed tried to rescue him, it was for the selfish reason that Yanagisawa wanted him to inherit the dictatorship and rule Japan through him. The wound had festered for more than four years. Yoshisato couldn't forgive, or trust, Yanagi-sawa.

"All right, go ahead and pout," Lady Someko said. "But whatever you were fighting about, you'd better make it up."

"Why? I don't need him, now that I'm the shogun's heir again." Yosh-isato was angry at himself because it wasn't true. Being with Yanagisawa reopened his wound, but it also filled the emptiness that winning the dictatorship couldn't fill.

Yanagisawa offered a weary yet adamant protest. "Yes, you do need me. You've been away too long; you don't know what's going on here."

"I seem to remember that when we did things your way, I got kid-napped." Yoshisato wanted to prove to Yanagisawa, and himself, that he could stand on his own two feet, and he didn't like Yanagisawa's strate-gies for solving problems.

"Stop it!" Lady Someko hurled the cloth into the basin. Bloody water splashed. "Lord Ienobu would love to see you at each other's throats. He would love for you to be so busy arguing that you don't notice him yank-ing the regime out from under your feet!"

The reminder that they had a common enemy silenced Yoshisato and Yanagisawa. Yoshisato said glumly, "She's right." Yanagisawa exhaled and nodded.

"I'm glad you've gotten that through your thick heads. I'll let you figure out how to handle Lord Ienobu." Lady Someko picked up the basin and rose gracefully. "Yoshisato, I won't hear any nonsense about you leaving. You're staying here." She glided out of the room.

Yoshisato hid his massive relief. He and Yanagisawa were unwillingly stuck together, but he wouldn't have to swim alone in the treacherous waters of the court or feel that aching emptiness. He studied Yanagisawa. Was that relief in Yanagisawa's hollow, tired eyes? For a moment he dared to hope that his father wanted to be with him and help him not only for the sake of defeating Ienobu and fulfilling lifelong political ambitions, but because his father cared about him. Then he cast aside the childish hope.

"Well?" he said in a belligerent voice. "Do you have any ideas?"

Yanagisawa's smile was triumphant yet somehow sad. "Don't I always?"

LADY NOBUKO LAY unconscious in bed, her eyes closed, covered up to her chin by a gray quilt. Reiko sat watching the physician clean, stitch, and bandage the gash on Lady Nobuko's head. This was the first time Reiko had ever seen her face completely relaxed. She looked like a corpse, shocked to death by the news about Yoshisato. Reiko herself was still quaking from shock as her mind teemed with questions. How would Yoshisato's return affect the investigation into the attack on the shogun? What did it portend for her family as well as the fate of the regime?

The physician held smelling salts under Lady Nobuko's nose. She grimaced at their sharp, astringent odor; she opened bleary eyes. "What happened?" she murmured.

"You fainted and hit your head," the physician said.

She touched the bandage. Memory filled her expression with anguish. "Damn Yoshisato," she whispered. The spasm bunched up her facial muscles like a thread stitched through fabric and pulled to draw the folds together. She gasped. "Merciful gods, the pain."

"Drink this." The physician held a cup to her mouth.

Lady Nobuko glugged the opium potion. She saw Reiko, and anger cleared the bleariness from her good eye. "Why are you still here?"

"I wanted to make sure you were all right," Reiko said.

"Don't be a hypocrite. You just want to rub Yoshisato in my face."

Reiko supposed she should feel bad about bothering an old, injured woman, but she didn't. Lady Nobuko deserved no pity, and Reiko had a second chance at her. "Do you realize what Yoshisato's return means? It's no longer certain that your friend Lord Ienobu will take over Japan when the shogun dies."

"Go away," Lady Nobuko whispered.

"Now there are two contenders for the succession. Yoshisato was the shogun's first choice. He's likely to inherit the dictatorship."

"No! He mustn't!" Squirming under the quilt, Lady Nobuko moaned. "I was so happy about his death. It was the best thing that could have happened, after what Chamberlain Yanagisawa did to me."

Eight years ago Lady Nobuko had been kidnapped and raped after a series of similar crimes against other women. Sano and Reiko had solved those other crimes, and they didn't believe Lady Nobuko was part of the series. They, and Lady Nobuko, believed she'd been kidnapped and raped by Yanagisawa's henchmen, as punishment for crossing Yanagisawa. She and Yanagisawa had been enemies ever since.

"I couldn't prove it, and he got away with it! When his bastard was burned up in the fire, I thought that was his comeuppance. Why couldn't Yoshisato stay dead? It's not fair!"

"Life isn't fair. Everybody has bad luck sometimes." Reiko was as brutal to Lady Nobuko as the woman had been to her. "You're no exception."

"All right, you've rubbed it in. Do you feel better now?" Lady Nobuko started to cry.

Reiko took a cruel pleasure in retaliation. "You picked a bad time to stab the shogun. If he dies, you'll have put Yoshisato, and Yanagisawa, at the head of the regime."

Lady Nobuko pulled the quilt over her face. "Just leave me alone."

Reiko pulled the quilt down. "I'm going to do you a favor and point out a fact to you: Yoshisato is going to be the next shogun. You need to get in good standing with him and Yanagisawa. The best way to do that is to sell out Lord Ienobu."

"I didn't stab my husband! You're deluded!"

"Confess that Lord Ienobu conspired with you to kill the shogun. Yoshisato and Yanagisawa will put him to death." Gripping Lady Nobuko's arm, Reiko said, "They'll pardon you because you did them a favor by getting rid of both the shogun and Lord Ienobu."

"Take your filthy little hand off me!"

"Don't protect Lord Ienobu. He's already murdered the shogun's daughter. He wouldn't protect you. Betray him and save yourself!"

"No, no, no!" Lady Nobuko pounded her fists and heels on the bed like an elderly child having a tantrum.

"She must calm down or she'll hurt herself," the physician told Reiko. "Please go."

Frustrated because she couldn't even beat Lady Nobuko while the old woman was down, Reiko had no choice except to leave. And even if she could prove that Lord Ienobu was guilty, how much good would it do, when Yanagisawa and Yoshisato were set to seize power?

19

YANAGISAWA AND YOSHISATO stood before a huge map of Japan that hung on the wall of Yanagisawa's office. Black lines divided the country into provinces. Ocean, lakes, and rivers were colored blue, mountain ranges brown, farmlands green. Red highways connected cities labeled in purple ink.

"These are the *daimyo* that will take my side against Lord Ienobu." Yanagisawa jabbed black pins into the map, in provinces ruled by those lords.

"That's not many," Yoshisato said, "and they're not the ones with the largest armies. You've lost a lot of ground since I've been gone."

The brat had no idea how hard Yanagisawa had worked to maintain even those few allies! Yanagisawa stifled a sharp retort rather than waste time on another argument. "Here are the *daimyo* in Ienobu's camp." He stuck red pins in the richest provinces. When he was done, the map looked as if it were infested with red ants.

"What about the *daimyo* in the unmarked provinces?"

"They're neutral."

"Meaning, they don't like either you or Ienobu."

"Here's how to change that," Yanagisawa said. "We strip Ienobu's most powerful allies of their titles and confiscate their wealth and lands. We make you *daimyo* of those provinces."

Yoshisato gazed at him in disbelief. "Can we do that?"

"You're Acting Shogun. You have the Tokugawa army to back you up." Yanagisawa pulled red pins out of the map, tossed them in a lacquer box, and replaced each with a black pin. "Once these provinces are under your control, the neutral lords won't be able to hold out against you. Meanwhile, you'll have purged Ienobu's cronies from the government and replaced them with your supporters or turned them into your allies."

"This will change the political map of Japan!"

"To your advantage. Shall we proceed with it?"

The atmosphere in the room felt as hazardous as the air during the Mount Fuji eruption. Yoshisato was the one person Yanagisawa couldn't manipulate. Yanagisawa would never have the same degree of influence over Yoshisato that he had over the current shogun, but for now, putting Yoshisato in power was top priority, and there was more riding on Yoshisato's decision besides a victory over Ienobu.

This plan was Yanagisawa's gift to Yoshisato, a compensation for all the evils Yoshisato had suffered on account of being Yanagisawa's pawn. He hoped that when he'd put Yoshisato securely at the head of the regime, they would be at peace.

"It's the most audacious thing I ever heard." But Yoshisato spoke with grudging, admiring acceptance.

Yanagisawa suppressed his smile. He didn't want Yoshisato to think he was showing off his cleverness, gloating over how much Yoshisato needed his help. "Then let's go mobilize the troops. Not all of Ienobu's *daimyo* are in town, but we can start with the ones who are." The law of alternate attendance required the *daimyo* to spend half of each year in Edo and the other half in their provinces, on staggered schedules. This prevented them from forming alliances and revolting, at least in theory.

Yoshisato hesitated. Yanagisawa said, "What are you waiting for? You know how the shogun is—he could easily change his mind about you. We have to act fast."

"This won't settle the matter of who stabbed the shogun," Yoshisato said. "Unless the blame lands squarely on Ienobu, he'll keep fighting us. And Sano will fight us no matter what."

"Ienobu will go down for the attack on the shogun," Yanagisawa said confidently. "Don't worry about him, or about Sano."

"THIS IS WHERE Sano lives?" Hirata gazed with dismay at the shabby little house behind the leafless, snow-frosted bamboo hedge.

Keep quiet, General Otani warned.

Hirata was shocked at how far Sano had fallen in the world. Guilt tormented him because he hadn't been there to help Sano.

It's his own fault for going against Lord Ienobu.

The thought of his wife and children, as well as Sano's family, living in such reduced circumstances, deepened Hirata's hatred for Lord Ienobu, General Otani, and himself. His foolishness had put him on Ienobu's side against Sano. As he loitered in the cold, near Sano's house, a woman came out of the gate. She wore a padded blue cotton cloak, a gray scarf over her head, and carried a large wicker basket. Hirata was shocked to recognize Midori. Her face, once plump and rosy, was thinner, mottled, and careworn. The hair above her brow was streaked with gray. But Hirata saw in her the pretty girl he'd married fifteen years ago. He wanted to run to Midori, catch her up in his arms, and weep.

General Otani's will clamped down on him. *Not here.*

Midori walked right past Hirata without a glance. In his wicker hat and plain cotton garments, without his swords, and his hair cropped instead of shaved at the crown and tied in a topknot, he looked like a peasant. General Otani let him follow Midori to the Nihonbashi merchant district. Townspeople thronged shops where clerks ladled tofu and pickled vegetables from vats. Coins changed hands amid talk and laughter. Smoke that smelled of fish grilling and noodles boiling in miso broth wafted from outdoor food stalls. Seagulls, stray dogs, and beggar children snatched at scraps. Midori entered a grocer's shop. Hirata watched her buy daikon and turnips. At another shop she bought eggs. The proprietor made some joking remark and she smiled. When she came out, Hirata accosted her. "Midori!"

Her smile froze then vanished as she heard his voice; she clutched the handle of her basket. "You," she whispered.

Hirata pulled her into an alley where they could have some privacy. The alley extended between the back walls of shops. Laundry hung from balconies on the second stories. Hirata and Midori faced each other amid reeking garbage bins and vats of night soil.

"What are you doing here?" she asked in a tremulous voice.

Hirata felt a needle of pain inside his head, a warning from General Otani. Midori hated it when he lied to her, but he couldn't tell her the truth. "I wanted to see you."

She didn't look glad to see him. She looked horrified. "Do you know that Sano-*san* reported you for treason? Do you know that the army is after you?"

"Yes. But I had to come." Hirata saw her through a scrim of tears. "I've missed you so much!" He hadn't realized how much until this moment. He remembered when they'd fallen in love and their families hadn't wanted them to marry. He remembered waking in bed with Midori the day after their wedding. They'd laughed as they made love, happy that they could sleep together every night. He remembered when she'd put their first baby in his arms, and he'd looked into Taeko's little face and seen himself and Midori there.

Midori's disgusted expression said she remembered something very different. "You missed me so much that you abandoned me and let me live on charity from Sano and Reiko?"

"I didn't want to," Hirata protested.

"I suppose you didn't want to choose those troublemaking friends of yours over me." Midori's voice was replete with scorn. "But you did anyway."

"Things happened—" Another jab from General Otani silenced Hirata.

"Things always happen, and it's never your fault, is it? You never take any responsibility for the things you do."

"I'm here to take it now." Hirata swallowed his pride. "I'm sorry."

She stared, incredulous. "What good is apologizing? It won't change the fact that you're a wanted traitor, or that the children and I will share your punishment."

The thought of the children drove another spear through Hirata's heart. "How are Taeko and Tatsuo?" They would be almost grown up now. "And Chiyoko?" She wouldn't remember him; she'd been a baby when he'd left.

"You don't deserve to know."

"But I'm their father."

"You should have remembered that before you put their lives in jeopardy."

Hirata fought despair. "Is there anything I can do to make it up to you and the children?"

"Yes." Angry tears sparkled in Midori's eyes. "You can go kill yourself. Then maybe the government will be happy you're gone and they'll let me and the children live."

She cared so little about him that she wanted him to die! "I tried to kill myself. But I couldn't—" General Otani held his tongue before he could explain.

"Shut your mouth before any more nonsense comes out! I'm going home."

Desperate to keep her with him, Hirata grabbed her arms. "Wait."

"Let go!" As she tried to wrench away, Midori dropped her basket. Hirata held tight.

"Please! Forgive me!" His voice was hoarse with emotion and tears. He pulled Midori to him. "I love you so much."

"Leave me alone!" She struggled and thrashed.

For years Hirata had felt no lust. Mystic martial arts training, and later his problems, had diminished his sex drive. But now it was revived by the softness of Midori's body against him, the heat of her breath and anger. He was suddenly erect, wild with desire.

"Stop!" Midori cried. Terror filled her eyes as she twisted in his grasp. "Please!"

Hirata didn't want to frighten her or hurt her, but he was so excited. He nuzzled her neck, caressed her body through her clothes, and groaned. He couldn't remember how long it had been since he'd experienced sexual release. A hunger that wasn't his own fanned the fire of his need. The ghost inside him roared with excitement, urging him on. It had been even longer since General Otani had had sex. The ghost overpowered Hirata's self-control. Hirata shoved Midori against a wall and yanked up her skirts.

Midori bit Hirata on the cheek. He shouted in pain. General Otani howled with rage. Hirata let go of Midori and staggered backward. Touching his cheek, he felt warm, wet blood. Midori pulled her skirts down and began to cry. Hirata's desire vanished. He felt a shame and remorse so strong that they drowned out General Otani's angry frustration.

"I'm sorry," he said. "That wasn't me, I didn't mean to—"

Sobbing, Midori picked up her basket and flung it at Hirata. It struck his chest, then fell to the ground, spilling its contents. "I hate you!" she screamed. "I never want to see you again!"

She ran out of the alley. Hirata dropped to his knees amid the broken eggs, miserable, wishing he hadn't seen Midori. It had only made things worse.

I told you so, muttered General Otani.

INSIDE THE HEIR'S residence, servants scurried about, preparing for Lord Ienobu's departure. They bundled up clothes and bedding, tied straw mats around furniture, nestled ceramic vases in straw in wooden crates. In the garden, porters loaded the packed items onto litters and carried them out of the castle. Lord Ienobu stood with Manabe in the empty reception chamber. His face was set in resolute lines; his protuberant eyes didn't blink. Ignoring the people emptying his home, he was the still center of the storm.

Manabe watched Ienobu with concern. His master's reaction to the crisis was unnatural, unnerving. "Are you all right?"

"I'm fine," Ienobu said. "Don't fuss over me like a nursemaid."

Once Manabe had, in effect, been Ienobu's nursemaid. They'd met forty-seven years ago, when Manabe was ten and Ienobu an infant. Manabe had been a page in the household of a retainer to Ienobu's father, the now deceased Lord Tokugawa Tsunashige. Lord Tsunashige was the older brother of the current shogun. He'd fathered a baby on a chambermaid. The baby Ienobu's birth was hushed up, lest it jeopardize Lord

Tsunashige's betrothal to a noblewoman. Ienobu was sent to live with the retainer, who would raise Ienobu as his own child. Manabe remembered the day the baby arrived and everyone had discovered why its existence needed to be kept secret.

The newborn Ienobu was deformed. Should the family of Lord Tsunashige's fiancée find out, they would cancel the betrothal for fear that Lord Tsunashige had bad blood and would sire more defective children. Horrified by Ienobu's misshapen body and face, the adoptive parents confined him to a separate wing of their house with a wet nurse, a maidservant, a bodyguard, and Manabe. The nurse, bodyguard, and maidservant, repulsed by Ienobu, gave him minimal attention. Manabe felt sorry for the poor little thing. He took over Ienobu's care. It was Manabe who played with Ienobu, and held Ienobu's hands while Ienobu learned, at the late age of four, to walk. He'd grown fond of Ienobu, and he'd discovered how clever Ienobu was. Ienobu had taught himself to read by the time he was six. By that time he already spoke with big words, and when other children teased him, he responded with devastating insults that made them cry. He'd never let abuse go unpunished.

Manabe was worried to see Ienobu so passive now. His long history with Ienobu allowed him to speak bluntly. "Yanagisawa and Yoshisato are set to take over the regime. Why are you just standing there with one foot in the grave?"

"This is just a temporary setback. They won't win."

"Yoshisato is the heir and Acting Shogun. He'll be the real shogun, and probably soon."

"He won't," Ienobu declared. "*I* am destined to be the next shogun."

Manabe remembered an eight-year-old Ienobu crawling out of a mud puddle where a gang of samurai had pushed him. Manabe had drawn his sword and been ready to do battle, but Ienobu had stopped him, saying, *It doesn't matter. I'll be shogun someday.* He'd always had a peculiar way of making the most outlandish things sound perfectly reasonable. From then on Manabe felt a commitment to Ienobu that went beyond a samurai's usual duty to his master. Manabe was no longer just a caretaker of a deformed, unwanted child; he was the guardian of a future shogun. And soon there came a sign that it was true. Lord Tsunashige's noble wife died; there was no more reason to keep secret the existence of his deformed only child; and Ienobu was recognized as Lord Tsunashige's legitimate son and a true member of the Tokugawa ruling clan. He was eligible for the succession.

Thirty-nine years later, he still had that peculiar quality. But now, for the first time, Manabe wondered if Ienobu's longtime sense of destiny was self-delusion.

"We kidnapped and imprisoned Yoshisato." Manabe had denied it to Sano, but it was true. "Yoshisato knows. He has the shogun half convinced. You saw."

"Are you afraid?" Ienobu sounded disappointed by Manabe's lack of faith in him.

"Yes." Manabe wasn't afraid for himself; his fear was all for Ienobu. If the shogun came to believe that Ienobu had kidnapped and imprisoned Yoshisato and faked his death, it would be the beginning of the end of Ienobu. Manabe would gladly die alongside Ienobu if it came to that, but he desperately hoped it wouldn't. "Yoshisato isn't the only problem. Yanagisawa has the shogun half convinced that you tried to have him assassinated."

Manabe gave the words an inflection that asked, *Did you?* He'd been Ienobu's confidant for a lifetime, but he didn't know whether Ienobu had engineered the attack on the shogun. He was Ienobu's right hand, but Ienobu had many hands. Ienobu wasn't the outcast, helpless child anymore. He'd used his wits, his position in the Tokugawa clan, and his peculiar quality to gain friends and control them. Two of those friends were Madam Chizuru and Lady Nobuko, both suspects in the stabbing.

"What do you think?" Ienobu challenged. "Are *you* half convinced that I'm guilty?"

More than half, Manabe thought. He was afraid to know for sure. He would willingly carry most burdens Ienobu placed on him, but he didn't want the attempted murder of the shogun on his conscience. That was too extreme a violation of Bushido. "It doesn't matter what I think. It matters what the shogun believes. You should do something to counteract Yanagisawa and Yoshisato."

Screams interrupted the conversation. Ienobu's two-year-old son toddled into the room, stamping his little feet as he cried. Ienobu's wife hurried after the child and picked him up.

"Can't he ever be quiet?" Ienobu demanded.

"He's just a baby," his wife said apologetically.

Ienobu jabbed his crooked finger in the child's face. "You'd better learn to discipline yourself." The child shrank from him and cried harder. "You're going to be shogun after me."

His wife carried the screaming child out of the room. Ienobu smiled and said, "I have a bet with myself that Yanagisawa and Yoshisato will be taken care of for me." He tilted his gaze toward the ceiling. "The gods want me to be shogun."

Manabe experienced a familiar discomfort in his gut. "Not that again."

"Don't act like it's nonsense. What else can explain the money that regularly appears on my doorstep?"

"The gods leave you gold coins in dirty sacks?"

"You couldn't prove otherwise."

Manabe had kept watch outside the house for many nights. On some mornings he'd found a sack of gold beside him with no idea how it had gotten there. "But I still think the money was left by a human." It wasn't that he didn't believe in mysterious cosmic forces; he just didn't like the idea of them meddling with Ienobu. Cosmic forces were dangerous.

"What about the other things that have happened?" Ienobu demanded.

The thought of those other things worsened the discomfort in Manabe's gut. They were much more serious than gold magically appearing. "Coincidences."

"They're too good to be coincidences. They're signs that the gods are on my side and my plans will be successful."

Manabe's gut churned. Acid burned up to his heart. He was as leery of those plans as he was of cosmic forces, but there was no winning this argument with Ienobu. He tried a different tactic. "You wouldn't want the gods to think you've grown lazy and dependent on them. They may decide to fulfill someone else's destiny instead. Do something about Yanagisawa and Yoshisato. And Sano. He's probably halfway toward proving you tried to assassinate the shogun." Manabe stated his firm belief: "The cosmic forces help those who help themselves."

Ienobu said with a sly smile, "Would you like to make a bet with me?"

"What kind of bet?" Manabe didn't like gambling.

"By tomorrow the tide will turn in my favor without my having to do anything."

Manabe could only nod. He realized that he'd made the riskiest bet of all forty-seven years ago, when he'd cast his lot with Ienobu.

20

AT THE PALACE, the search for evidence and witnesses in the Large Interior continued. Masahiro ransacked chambers while Sano and Detective Marume questioned the women. So far none had seen or heard, or admitted to seeing or hearing, anything unusual during or immediately before or after the attack on the shogun. Sano had just finished another fruitless interview when a squadron of soldiers marched into the Large Interior.

"Chamberlain Yanagisawa sent us to help you with your investigation," said the leader, a stiff-necked lieutenant named Haneda.

Sano saw that Yanagisawa's help was a mixed blessing. "Come with me." He herded the soldiers out of the Large Interior, to the wide corridor in the public part of the palace. "Now undress."

"What?"

"You heard me."

The men reluctantly stripped while clerks, officials, and servants passing along the corridor gawked. All except one man unwound their loincloths. Sano gave him a stern look. As he peeled away the long white strip of fabric, out fell a small ceramic jar.

Sano picked up the jar and uncorked it. Inside was fresh red blood, probably from a horse. He asked the naked soldiers, "Where were you planning to sprinkle this?" They were silent, nervous. Sano didn't waste his anger on them; they were only following orders from Yanagisawa.

After they'd dressed, he took them back to the Large Interior and told Marume and Masahiro, "These are Yanagisawa's men. They'll help you move things around. Keep an eye on them, and search them before they leave. I'm going to talk to Lord Ienobu's people."

Leaving the Large Interior, he passed Madam Chizuru's chamber. The old woman peeked out past the guard stationed by her door and beckoned Sano. When he entered the cramped, cluttered room, she stood with her hands clasped inside the sleeves of her gray kimono and said in a low, unsteady voice, "I want to confess."

It was so unexpected that Sano tilted his head and frowned.

"Lord Ienobu told me to stab the shogun," Madam Chizuru said.

Sano's heart gave a huge, thumping leap. This was the answer to his prayers—a confession that not only solved the crime but incriminated Lord Ienobu.

It seemed too good to be true.

His instincts sent out a warning that sliced through his elation like a knife through a sail. He looked closely at Madam Chizuru. "Why are you confessing?"

Head bowed, she gazed at the floor. She gulped several breaths, then spoke in a rush. "Because I'm guilty."

Suspicion bred in Sano. "That's not what you said yesterday."

"Yesterday . . . I lied."

Sano thought she'd sounded more convincing then than she did now. "What changed your mind?"

Madam Chizuru lifted her head. Her eyes were rimmed with red. "I—I don't want it on my conscience any longer." Oddly, she also seemed more afraid that he wouldn't believe her.

"Very well," Sano said, still dubious. "Tell me what happened that night."

"I waited in my room until everybody was asleep." Now Madam Chizuru spoke too fast, too fluently, as if her speech were rehearsed. "Then I tucked the iron fan under my sash." She pantomimed. "Then I—"

"Wait," Sano said. "Where was the fan?" She responded with a worried, uncomprehending frown. "I mean, where did you keep it?"

Madam Chizuru glanced uncertainly around the room. "There." She pointed at a shelf. "Behind those ledgers."

"So you took the fan from behind the ledgers. What next?"

"I tiptoed through the palace."

"Did you see anyone?" Sano wanted to know whether a witness he hadn't located yet had seen Madam Chizuru and could corroborate her story.

"No."

"It must have been dark. How did you find your way?"

Her breath made a little hitching sound. "I took a lamp with me. I forgot to say." She hurried on. "I went in the shogun's chamber." Her jowls trembled, the loose flesh like empty, shaken sacks. "I—I shone the lamp on the bed. The shogun was asleep. I—I drew back the quilt. And then I took the fan and I stabbed him." She sounded relieved to finish rather than upset because she was guilty of attempted murder.

"How many times?" Sano asked.

Panic glazed Madam Chizuru's eyes. "Why, I—I don't remember. I just did it. Then he started screaming, and I ran away."

Sano wondered whether the number of stab wounds was a detail missing from the news that had spread through the castle. He urgently wanted a reason to believe her confession. "Let's back up for a moment. When did Lord Ienobu ask you to stab the shogun?"

"A few days ago?" She spoke as if she hoped it was a good answer.

"How did he ask you?"

"What do you mean?"

"Did he come here to speak with you? Did you go to see him?" Those were events that might have been witnessed by someone.

The fear in Madam Chizuru's expression deepened. "Lord Ienobu sent me a letter?"

"How was the letter delivered? By messenger?"

"I—I don't know. I found it in my room. He—he must have had someone put it there."

"Where is this letter?" Sano asked skeptically.

"It said to burn it after I read it. So I did."

Disappointed, and more skeptical than ever, Sano asked, "Where did you get the fan?"

"In a shop in Nihonbashi." She sounded as if she were on firmer ground.

Sano had seen similar fans for sale in the merchant district. She probably had, too, even if she'd never bought this one. "Which shop?"

"I don't remember."

"What is the design on the fan?"

Her hands twisted together like a small, frightened animal under her sleeves. Sano thought she didn't know because she'd never seen the fan and hadn't heard about the painted irises. She blurted, "Why must you ask me all these questions?"

"I'm trying to make sure you're telling the truth." And the truth was in the details.

"I am!"

Never had Sano met a criminal so determined to convince him of her guilt or so inept at it. "Did somebody put you up to confessing?"

"No." Madam Chizuru met Sano's gaze for a moment before averting her eyes. "It was my own idea."

Sano leaned out the door to ask the guard if anybody had visited Madam Chizuru since yesterday. He saw the crowd of people eavesdropping in the passage—Masahiro, Detective Marume, and Yanagisawa's troops.

"I'm not answering any more questions!" Madam Chizuru cried. "I stabbed the shogun. I confessed. That should be enough."

"It's enough for me," Lieutenant Haneda told Sano. "Arrest her. Tell the shogun."

"Not until I've checked out her story," Sano said. "It's as full of holes as your head."

Glowering at the insult, Haneda advanced. "If you won't, I will."

Madam Chizuru moaned and covered her mouth with her hands. She seemed to realize for the first time what trouble she was in. Sano blocked the door and said, "You're not in charge of the investigation. Get out."

"Sano-*san*, listen." Marume inserted himself between Sano and Haneda. "She confessed. The shogun deserves to be told."

"This is our chance to get Lord Ienobu!" Masahiro called over Marume's shoulder.

Now Sano found himself set against his son and his retainer. "I won't let her or Lord Ienobu be condemned until I'm sure they're guilty." According to his code of honor, even Ienobu, damn him, deserved fair play.

"It's not up to you," Haneda said.

Yanagisawa's other men invaded the room and dragged Madam Chizuru out. She began howling. Her legs collapsed. The troops carried her down the corridor. Women emerged from their chambers, gasping and murmuring as they watched.

"Lock her in the tower," Haneda told the troops. "Tell Yanagisawa-*san* what happened. I'm going to the shogun." He said to Sano, "You and your people can come if you like."

THE PHYSICIAN MET Sano, Marume, Masahiro, and Lieutenant Haneda at the door of the shogun's bedchamber. "His Excellency is asleep. He shouldn't be disturbed."

"He'll want to wake up for this." It was Yanagisawa, arriving with Yoshisato, both short of breath from running and jubilation.

"Did you force Madam Chizuru to confess?" Sano asked. When he saw Yoshisato, he did a double take. Yoshisato was groomed as a samurai—shaved crown, oiled topknot, and silk robes. Except for the tattoos, it was as if he'd never left the court.

"You give me too much credit," Yanagisawa said. "Not even I could make that tough old bag put her neck on the chopping block."

He swept past the physician into the chamber where two bodyguards sat by the shogun's bed. Yoshisato followed; he seemed occupied with his own thoughts. Sano eyed him curiously as he entered with Marume and Masahiro.

Yanagisawa knelt beside the shogun. "Your Excellency?"

The shogun opened sunken, crusted eyes in a gray face. He'd declined since morning. A different smell tainted the air—the smell of decay.

"Good news," Yanagisawa said. "The person who stabbed you has been arrested."

Interest animated the shogun's groggy expression. "Who is it?" His voice was a croak.

"It's Madam Chizuru, the *otoshiyori*. She confessed."

Sano stepped forward. "It's not certain she's guilty. Her confession—"

The shogun spoke over him. "Why did she do it?"

"Excuse me, Your Excellency," Sano said, "but her confession is extremely dubious."

"Because Lord Ienobu told her to," Yanagisawa said. "He wanted you dead so that he could be shogun. He sent Madam Chizuru to assassinate you."

"Merciful gods, it's true." The shogun's face turned grayer. "My nephew is responsible."

"She couldn't tell me how many times you were stabbed," Sano said. "She couldn't describe the fan."

Detective Marume whispered, "Sano-*san*, for the love of all of us, be quiet." Masahiro whispered, "Father, please." Yoshisato observed the spectacle with dawning distrust.

Sano was well aware that he was arguing against his own interests, but his hunger for justice had become so entrenched. He was too stubborn to change, or too old. "I think it's because she doesn't know. She may be innocent, and so may Lord Ienobu."

"Yesterday you were ready enough to believe that Ienobu was responsible for the attack." Yanagisawa gave Sano a look that reminded him of their pact, threatening him with mayhem if he didn't cooperate.

The opium spread blankness across the shogun's expression. Yanagisawa hurried to press his case. "It's for Your Excellency to decide. Madam Chizuru confessed. Either she's guilty and she'll be punished, or she's not and you may never get revenge on the person who stabbed you."

"Those aren't the only outcomes," Sano said, sick and tired of Yanagisawa's fast talk. "If Your Excellency accepts her confession without letting me verify it, you could be condemning innocent people while letting the real assassin go free."

The shogun's gaze moved back and forth between Sano and Yanagisawa, his eyes skittering like pebbles in their hollow sockets. "Nobody in her right mind would confess if she were innocent. She must be guilty." He moaned at a spasm of pain.

He was impatient to know his attacker's identity; delay was a luxury that a man gravely injured couldn't afford. It was Sano's duty now, more than ever, to give the shogun what he wanted. Vengeance might be the shogun's last wish—a solemn demand that Sano couldn't refuse to fulfill. It came down to a choice between his lord versus Madam Chizuru and Lord Ienobu.

That was no choice.

But although Sano still disbelieved the confession, he must give it the benefit of the doubt. "Let's hear what Lord Ienobu has to say for himself."

"Find him. Bring him here," Yanagisawa told Lieutenant Haneda. "Don't tell him why."

Soon Haneda and his troops brought in Lord Ienobu, accompanied by Manabe. Excitement flushed Ienobu's usually sallow complexion. His lips stretched over his big teeth in a grin. "You sent for me just in time, Uncle." He obviously thought the shogun meant to take him back into his favor. "I was ready to vacate the heir's residence. Now I won't have to——"

He noticed Yanagisawa and Yoshisato. Yanagisawa smiled a wolfish smile at him. Yoshisato's straight face was equally malevolent. Ienobu looked around the room and saw Sano, Marume, and Masahiro. Alarm inverted his grin. "What's going on here?"

Sano almost felt sorry for Ienobu. "I've found evidence that you conspired to assassinate the shogun."

"You're under arrest," Yanagisawa said in a tone vibrant with glee.

"What are you talking about?" Lord Ienobu demanded.

Yoshisato spoke in a cold voice as sharp as the needles that had etched the tattoos on his skin. "Your accomplice betrayed you."

"What accomplice?"

"Oh, spare me the innocent act," Yanagisawa said. "You know it's Madam Chizuru."

Sano wasn't so sure Ienobu was acting. He seemed genuinely flabbergasted. Then again, Ienobu's talents had surprised Sano in the past.

"Madam Chizuru?" Ienobu's eyes bulged as he realized that the connection between him and his spy in the Large Interior was an open secret.

"She confessed that she stabbed the shogun and you told her to do it," Yoshisato said.

Ienobu sputtered. "She's lying! I never told her any such thing!"

"I believe her," the shogun said weakly through a fog of opium, fever, and pain. "You tried to have me assassinated! You, my own nephew!"

"Uncle, I swear on my honor I didn't!" Ienobu said.

With a strength born of anger, the shogun lifted his head from his pillow. "You have no honor! You flattered me and pretended to love me so that I trusted you. And then you betrayed my trust." The pain constricted his voice. "You ought to be ashamed of yourself!"

Ienobu turned on Sano. "You made Madam Chizuru incriminate me!"

Stung by the accusation and the insult to his honor, Sano was forced to defend the confession. "I didn't make her. She confessed voluntarily."

"That's right," Yanagisawa said. "There are plenty of witnesses."

"Uncle, this is a trick! They're all in league against me! They've set me up to take the fall so that he can inherit the dictatorship!" Ienobu pointed his bony finger at Yoshisato.

"*You're* trying to trick *me!*" The shogun's voice was shrill with fury. "Haven't you hurt me enough already?" He sobbed and moaned. "Can't you at least be honest?"

"I didn't tell Madam Chizuru to kill you. She's lying!" Ienobu was too distraught to think up a better defense than denying his guilt. "I'm being framed!"

Doubts about Madam Chizuru's confession, suspicion about Yanagisawa's possible role in it, and the passion in Ienobu's manner nudged Sano toward deciding, against his wishes, that Ienobu really was innocent.

"Lord Ienobu would say the sky was green if he thought it would save his ugly skin," Yanagisawa said.

"Lord Ienobu had your daughter killed. He had me kidnapped," Yoshisato reminded the shogun. "You were the last remaining obstacle between him and the dictatorship."

Easily persuaded while in his miserable state, anxious to believe the person responsible for it had been unmasked, the shogun said, "He's right! You never cared about me. All you wanted was my position. Well, I won't let you have it. Take him away! Put him to death!"

"Wait!" Ienobu turned to Sano, the man he'd tormented for more than four years, now his only ally among the company. "Tell my uncle he's wrong! Make him understand!"

Sano was sorely tempted to let matters take their course. Masahiro put his finger to his lips, and Marume waved his hands, urging Sano to give Ienobu up, but Sano couldn't stand by while a possibly innocent man was framed. "Your Excellency, suppose you put Lord Ienobu to death. If something happens to Yoshisato, who will inherit the regime?"

The shogun was dumbstruck by this new concern. He'd apparently forgotten that Lord Yoshimune was third in a long line of relatives eligible for the succession.

"Nothing's going to happen to me," Yoshisato said quickly; he'd perceived Sano's intention.

"Surely my son won't die before I do," the shogun protested feebly. "Look at me."

"He's already been kidnapped," Sano reminded them.

Yanagisawa had caught on, too; he hurried to head Sano off. "That was Lord Ienobu's doing, Your Excellency. All the more reason to get rid of him—so that Yoshisato will be safe."

"Safe from man-made danger, perhaps," Sano said, "but he could be killed by a disease or an earthquake, and then who will be your heir, with your nephew gone?"

The shogun paled with consternation. "Why, I, ahh, haven't had time to think about it."

"You should think about it." Sano spoke bluntly; he had no time for tact. "You need Lord Ienobu."

Ienobu scowled, insulted because Sano had styled him as nothing but a backup for the shogun's preferred choice of an heir, but he knew better than to deride the hole-ridden logic that Sano was weaving like a net to catch him as he fell.

"Your Excellency doesn't need the man who tried to have you

assassinated." Yanagisawa brought the subject back to Ienobu's alleged guilt. Furious and exasperated, he said, "This discussion is so far off the point!"

Sano was only borrowing a page from Yanagisawa's book: Yanagisawa would steer a discussion to the far ends of the earth to achieve a desired aim. "The point is, Your Excellency has a choice." He talked fast and loud before Yanagisawa or Yoshisato could get a word in. "Decide who should be your alternate heir or have the decision made for you later."

The shogun groaned as if his wounded gut were a rope in a tug-of-war. "Merciful gods, I'm too ill to think about it."

"But you could delay Lord Ienobu's death until I find out whether Madam Chizuru's confession is true," Sano said, "and if it's not, then you'll be glad you waited."

"Those aren't the only choices!" Yanagisawa protested.

"I only ask Your Excellency to delay it for one day." Sano knew this was an impossibly short time. He hoped it was enough for him to verify or disprove the confession.

"Very well," the shogun said. "One day. I may not have much longer."

Yanagisawa said, "But Your Excellency," and Yoshisato began, "Honorable Father," as the shogun convulsed in dry heaves. "I can't bear any more talk!" He begged the doctor, "Merciful gods, give me some more opium, I'm in agony!"

Lord Ienobu scrambled for the door, followed by Manabe, before the shogun could change his mind. He gave Sano a grudging look that said, *I owe you.*

Outside the chamber, Yanagisawa said to Sano, "Knock down that confession and we'll see each other in hell." As he and Yoshisato walked away together, Yoshisato flung Sano a backward, enigmatic glance.

Masahiro stalked off, his expression stormy, without a word. Marume opened his mouth. Sano said ruefully, "Don't say it. I know."

21

"I STILL THINK you should have let it go," Masahiro said.

"I still stand by my decision," Sano said.

"It was wrong! You threw away our chance to get rid of him for good!"

Reiko heard them arguing as they came in the door. Masahiro sounded defiant, so unlike when he'd been a little boy, when he'd worshiped the father he'd thought could do no wrong. She hurried to meet them in the passage. Masahiro looked furious, Sano exhausted. She said, "Are you arguing about Yoshisato?"

"So you know he's alive," Sano said.

"You said to tell her. I told her," Masahiro said.

"How can it be? Don't keep me wondering," Reiko begged. When Sano explained about the anonymous letter, she was stunned and furious. "Why didn't you tell me this morning?"

"You wanted me to quit investigating Yoshisato's murder. I knew you'd be upset."

"Didn't you think I would be upset when I found out you kept another secret from me?"

Sano rubbed his tired face. "I'm sorry. I thought the letter was another false tip. Seeing Yoshisato was the biggest shock of my life."

"So you brought him to the castle," Masahiro said with disgust. "You gave the shogun back his 'son' and Yanagisawa back his chance to rule Japan. Whose side are you on, anyway?"

"Don't speak to your father in that tone of voice!" But Reiko herself didn't like what Sano had done. "Why did you bring Yoshisato to the shogun?"

Vexed at both his wife and son, Sano flung up his hands. "What was I supposed to do? Tell Yoshisato, 'Go back to being dead,' and walk away?"

"You should have killed him," Masahiro said. "He's a fraud. He deserves to die."

"Masahiro!" He was right, but Reiko was disturbed by Masahiro's readiness to shed blood.

"I don't murder people for my own convenience," Sano said in a low, tight voice.

"Then you should have let me," Masahiro said.

Although glad that she and Masahiro were in agreement that Yoshisato's return was a bad thing, Reiko didn't like her son taking sides against his father. It was sad as well as a violation of filial piety, and another rift within their family.

"I've finally found out the truth about Yoshisato's 'murder.'" Sano explained that Lord Ienobu had had Yoshisato kidnapped and held hostage and Yoshisato had escaped and had become a gangster boss. Reiko listened in amazement. "So it wasn't what I expected—still, I had to tell the shogun. He thinks Yoshisato is his child. If your child that you thought was dead was really alive, wouldn't you deserve to be told?"

Reiko felt as if he'd slapped her. Her eyes filled with tears, and she turned away to hide them. If only her baby could be resurrected; if only someone would come and tell her he was alive! That Sano would make his point with such an insensitive remark! It showed that he didn't care about the baby or her feelings and he didn't love her anymore.

He started to say something, but she wouldn't let him rub in the fact that he'd won this round of the argument. She spoke lightly, so as not to give him the satisfaction of knowing how much his insensitivity hurt. "There is a bright side to Yoshisato coming back. He's trouble for Lord Ienobu."

"Not enough trouble," Masahiro said. "He's knocked Lord Ienobu out of line for the succession—again. The shogun has renamed Yoshisato as his heir." He shot a bitter glance at Sano. "But Father has kindly given Lord Ienobu a helping hand."

Reiko was disturbed to realize that Yoshisato wasn't the only bone of contention. "What else happened?"

"Madam Chizuru told Father that she stabbed the shogun," Masahiro said. "She said Lord Ienobu told her to kill him. She voluntarily confessed."

Stunned again, Reiko sank to her knees on the cold floor. "So the crime is solved, just like that? Lord Ienobu is guilty and he'll be put to death?" She couldn't believe the investigation was finished so soon and Sano's risks had finally paid off.

"Not just like that." Sarcasm permeated Masahiro's voice. "Father convinced the shogun to give Lord Ienobu a stay of execution."

"*Why?*" Reiko spread her hands as she stared up at Sano. "Have you lost your mind?"

A breath gusted from Sano as he crouched opposite her. "Madam Chizuru's confession stank like rotten fish. She doesn't know that the shogun was stabbed four times or that the fan has irises painted on it. Those are details the attacker would know."

"It doesn't matter!" Masahiro shouted. "She said she stabbed him! She fingered Lord Ienobu. That's exactly what we wanted!" He said to Reiko, "We'd have had him, except Father wouldn't let it go!"

Now Reiko understood the full meaning of the argument she'd overheard: Sano had disputed the confession rather than allow Madam Chizuru—and Lord Ienobu—take the consequences. That was just like Sano, but Reiko was shocked nonetheless. "You've been trying to defeat Lord Ienobu for four years, and now—" She remembered what she'd heard Masahiro say. "You had a chance to get rid of him forever, and you threw it away!"

Sano hastened to defend himself. "It was only fair. Someone put Madam Chizuru up to incriminating Lord Ienobu. I'm certain."

"*He* hasn't been fair to *us!*" Masahiro said. "Why should you be fair to him?"

"It comes down to honor," Sano said. "I couldn't live with myself if I didn't give Ienobu the same chance I would give anybody that I thought had been framed."

It always came down to honor with Sano. The argument Reiko could never win reared its armor-plated head again. She rose to it anyway. "Lord Ienobu is guilty of conspiring to murder the shogun's daughter. What difference does it make if he's been framed this time? Why defend him when he's already a criminal and a traitor?"

Masahiro eagerly followed her line of reasoning. "Lord Ienobu deserves to die." He crouched beside Sano and hollered into his ear as if he were deaf. "By defending him, you're standing in the way of justice!"

"Justice for whom?" Sano demanded, wincing at the noise. "So I wasn't able to deliver Ienobu to justice for murdering Tsuruhime or Yoshisato. I tried, I failed, I'm sorry. But the issue now is justice for the shogun. If Ienobu and Madam Chizuru are put to death, and they aren't really guilty, then the real culprit will go free. Is that what you want?"

Reiko and Masahiro fell silent. Sano said to Reiko, "You learned justice in your father's court. You've been helping me fight for it since the day we married. Are you turning your back on all that now?" He addressed Masahiro. "When you were little, you wanted to help me defeat bad people and protect innocent ones. And now you don't?" He knelt, his knees hitting the floor with a thump. "Maybe I've lost my mind, but the two of you seem to have lost your principles!"

Reiko glanced at Masahiro. He looked as defeated as she felt. They both knew Sano's accusation was valid, but it didn't make her any less angry about what Sano had done. It also did nothing to restore their family harmony. Sano looked more regretful than glad about his victory over them, but he said, "I think Yanagisawa is responsible for Madam Chizuru's confession."

"You haven't proven it," Masahiro said.

Frustrated yet unwilling to concede, Sano said, "Yanagisawa and Yoshisato stand to gain the most from Lord Ienobu's downfall." As if a sudden thought had occurred to him, he asked Reiko, "What did Lady Nobuko have to say?"

"That she's innocent. Her lady-in-waiting is her alibi." Reiko couldn't bear to admit that Lady Nobuko had upset her so much that she'd been unable to get anything else out of the old woman and she still had the gnawing sense that she'd missed something during her search.

"Well," Sano said, "that doesn't exactly help decide the issue of Lord Ienobu's guilt." Reiko felt even worse, because she'd contributed so little to this most crucial investigation. "But one thing is certain: Whether Lord Ienobu comes out on top or Yanagisawa does, it's bad for us. Neither one will let us live long."

"What do we do?" Masahiro suddenly sounded more like the boy he'd been, looking to his father for guidance, but there was a dubious note in his voice: He no longer believed Sano had all the answers.

"We do what we've always done," Sano said with too much confidence. "We find the truth."

And hope it somehow straightens everything out, Reiko thought. The plan sounded like one whose time had come and gone years ago.

IN THE PARLOR, Taeko sat eating dinner with her chaperone, her mother, and the children. She heard Sano, Reiko, and Masahiro arguing, and although she couldn't discern what they were saying because of the children's noisy chatter, their angry voices upset her. Nausea struck. She dropped her chopsticks on her tray table of food, covered her mouth with her napkin, and spat out partially chewed noodles. Midori and Umeko glanced at her as they ate. Did they suspect?

Masahiro stepped into the room. Hope and anxiety replaced nausea. She needed to tell him why they had to elope, but she was terrified that he would say no. He looked tired, troubled by his argument with his parents.

Midori clambered to her feet like a mother bear ready to protect her young. "Don't come near Taeko."

Masahiro held up his hands. "I'm not going to touch her."

"If I were to leave you alone with her, those hands would be all over her," Midori retorted. Umeko and the children watched with interest, like an audience at a Kabuki play.

"I just want to talk to her."

Midori folded her arms. "There's nothing you should be saying to her that you can't say in front of me."

"We'll stand over there." Masahiro pointed to the corner. "We won't leave your sight."

Midori shook her head.

"Please, Mother!" Taeko cried in desperation.

"Get out! And if I ever catch you with her again, I'll kill you!" Midori ran to Masahiro and beat him with her fists.

Umeko clapped her hands in delight. "Get him!"

"Hey, stop!" Masahiro tried to fend off Midori without hitting her back.

She tore at his hair, clawed his arms, and screamed. Taeko was alarmed because something was different about her mother. She was even angrier and less able to control her temper than yesterday. Taeko jumped up and tried to pull her mother away from Masahiro. Akiko came to her aid, saying, "Stop beating up my brother!" Umeko laughed gleefully. Tatsuo and Chiyoko started to cry.

"Go!" Midori shoved Masahiro toward the door.

He gave Taeko a defeated, helpless look, then slunk out.

"You showed him," Umeko said to Midori.

Midori flounced back to her tray table, plopped down on the cushion, and glared at everyone. The children shrank from her, frightened. Taeko said, "Mother, what's wrong with you?"

"Nothing." Midori's chin trembled; her eyes were shiny with tears. "Just shut up and eat."

AFTER A TENSE, silent dinner with Reiko and Masahiro, Sano thought of going out to investigate Madam Chizuru's confession, but he was so tired that as he walked down the passage he felt as if he were wading through mud. He hadn't slept in two days. Drowsiness engulfed his brain in a numbing fog. He desperately needed a few hours' rest.

In the bath chamber he stripped, scrubbed, then soaked in the hot water and almost fell asleep before he hauled himself out. Clean and dry, swathed in a towel, he went to the bedchamber and found Reiko undressing. She quickly turned away as she put on her night robe. She never wanted him to see her naked. Sano smiled without humor. If she knew how tired he was, she wouldn't worry about him making advances. He turned his back on her while he stripped off the towel and donned his own night robe, sparing her the sight of his body. She didn't speak. Neither did Sano.

It was safer not to say anything. What a terrible blunder he'd made when he'd asked her whether she would want to be told that her child she thought was dead was really alive! Fatigue and temper had made him careless. He hadn't realized how bad it sounded until too late. He'd hurt Reiko, so much that she hadn't let him apologize when he'd tried.

Reiko tucked herself in bed. Sano blew out the flame in the lantern and crawled under the quilt. They lay side by side in the chilly darkness, facing away from each other. As tired as Sano was, he couldn't fall asleep. His muscles stiffened; his old battle wounds ached. He turned, trying to find a comfortable position. Reiko was restless, too. The atmosphere buzzed with echoes of their argument. His defenses weakened by exhaustion, Sano felt Reiko's doubts about his judgment seep into him like an infection penetrating broken skin. Had he gone too far for honor? Would it be so bad to quit his crusade for truth and justice? If it brought his family peace, why not? Nobody but himself would fault him. Weren't his twenty years of fighting enough? These blasphemous ideas were palatable when combined with fatigue.

"What should Masahiro and I do tomorrow?" Reiko asked.

Sano was glad she'd spoken, encouraged because she was still apparently willing to work with him. Troubled by his new doubts, he had to cudgel his tired brain to come up with an answer to her question. "Masahiro should talk to the shogun's boy again. Maybe he's remembered something else. You talk to Madam Chizuru. After a night in jail, maybe she'll be ready to tell the truth."

"All right," Reiko said.

Sano realized, too late, that it wasn't the best idea to employ his wife and son on his quest for the truth about the confession; they were hardly objective. But Sano couldn't tell Reiko he'd changed his mind and put him at further odds with her and Masahiro, and he had to admit that he was just as biased.

"What are you going to do?" Reiko asked.

Sano heard the accusation in her words: *What other trouble are you going to get us into?* She probably wanted to work with him only to counteract what she saw as his wrong thinking and actions. His hope for a reconciliation waned. "I'll go back to the Large Interior and try to figure out who, if anybody, got to Madam Chizuru."

"Yanagisawa?"

"Him in particular. I forgot to tell you, I caught one of his men trying to smuggle blood into the Large Interior. But not just him."

Reiko was silent a moment, thinking. "Yanagisawa isn't the only person who would like Madam Chizuru to take the blame for the stabbing. There are the other suspects—Lady Nobuko, and Tomoe and her cousin Lord Yoshimune."

The quickness of her mind, and the interest in her voice, lifted Sano's low spirits. Maybe she hadn't entirely changed. Hope was a stubborn creature that refused to die. Glad that for once they were talking without arguing, Sano said, "Yes. Madam Chizuru's confession lets them off the hook."

"How could they have forced her to confess if she's innocent?" Reiko sounded reluctant to believe it possible.

"By the same means as Yanagisawa. Money, power, and cunning. Lady Nobuko and Lord Yoshimune have all those things." The fog of drowsiness thickened. Sano yawned; he roused himself to say, "Maybe Lord Ienobu wasn't meant to figure into the confession. If someone did force Madam Chizuru to confess, maybe whoever it was didn't care whether Lord Ienobu was incriminated. Maybe all that he—or she—wanted was a good scapegoat."

He heard Reiko's hair rustle against her pillow as she nodded. "Madam Chizuru is the only commoner among the suspects. She has no powerful connections to protect her. But why would she say Ienobu told her to kill the shogun if it's not true? How could anybody make her say it?"

Sleep was irresistible. Sano mumbled, "Those are good questions. Maybe we'll find out the answers tomorrow."

He turned his head toward Reiko. Before his eyes closed, he saw her lying wide awake, facing him. Did he sense a fragile truce spreading across the cold space between them, like thin ice? Maybe it was just wishful thinking. Sano teetered on the brink of sleep, then fell into its dark embrace.

22

THE NEXT MORNING Sano, Marume, and Masahiro rode to Edo Castle. The sun shone in a brilliant blue sky, and the snow on the street and rooftops sparkled, but the air was colder than yesterday, with an edge that bit Sano's face. At the main gate, troops from the night watch streamed out while troops arriving for day duty streamed in. Masahiro headed to the palace to see the shogun's boy while Sano and Marume went to army headquarters, located in a watchtower high on the hill. From among the troops reporting for duty Sano chose ten soldiers he'd known when he was chamberlain, who'd had good reputations then. They accompanied Sano and Marume to the palace. The physician came out, medicine chest in hand.

"How is the shogun?" Sano asked.

"Worse, I'm sorry to say. He can't keep down any food or water or medicine, and he passed bloody stools last night. There's internal hemorrhaging. I'm going to mix up some medicine for it. I pray it works."

So did Sano. He took little comfort from the fact that Lord Ienobu was no longer the shogun's heir. If the shogun died, Yoshisato and Yanagisawa's grip on the regime would become permanent. He took Marume and the soldiers to the Large Interior. The women were dressing and breakfasting; maids lugged bedding outside to air. The chatter was subdued by the news of the shogun's condition. Guards loitered in the passages. Sano accosted Lieutenant Arai, the man who'd been watching Madam Chizuru yesterday.

"Who else is assigned to guard Madam Chizuru?" Sano asked.

"Lieutenant Fujisawa. He just went off night duty."

"Go bring him back. And bring everybody else who had any contact with Madam Chizuru while she was locked in her room. I want to talk to all of you outside."

Soon the two guards and two maids were gathered on the veranda. The soldiers stood aside while Sano and Marume eyed the lineup. Arai and the other guard were strong men in their forties. One of the maids was a girl with a round, bland face, the other an older, surly-looking woman. They shivered in the cold and clasped their hands under the sleeves of their blue cotton kimonos. They looked puzzled and nervous, the guards stoic.

Marume conducted the questioning. "Did any of you bring Madam Chizuru a message?"

Sano watched for reactions. When Marume turned his gaze on each in turn, they all said, "No," but Sano could smell that someone was lying.

"What about a letter?" Marume asked. Heads shook. "Did you tell Madam Chizuru to say that she stabbed the shogun and Lord Ienobu told her to kill him? Did you threaten to do something bad to her if she didn't?"

Astonishment showed on all four faces. Guards and maids shook their heads again. Sano had to consider the possibility that they were all innocent and Madam Chizuru had confessed voluntarily, but he still believed she'd been pressured by Yanagisawa.

Marume directed his next question to the guards. "Did you let anyone else in her room?"

They chorused, "No."

Sano and Marume exchanged a conspiratorial glance. Sano announced, "Somebody's lying. I'm going to count to ten. If that person doesn't speak up, I'm going to kill one of you."

The maids gasped, clutching their throats. The guards looked at each other, then turned angry, fearful gazes on Sano. Lieutenant Arai said, "You can't do that!"

"This is about the attempted murder of the shogun," Marume said. "Anything goes."

Sano began counting: "One, two . . ."

The ten soldiers stared at him in surprise. They knew his reputation for eschewing violence during interrogations.

"Somebody's going to die," Marume taunted.

The guards protested loudly. The maids fell to their knees, wept, and begged, "Please, have mercy!"

Sano finished counting. Nobody confessed. Sano's instincts pointed him to the likely culprit: Lieutenant Arai, muscular with coarsely handsome features, had an arrogance that even fear for his life didn't quell. Sano pointed at him.

"Hey!" Arai protested. Marume seized him by the arm. He jerked, yelling, "Let me go!"

"Don't just stand there," Marume said to the shocked, bewildered soldiers as he wrestled with Arai and tore off his swords. "Let's get him out of here."

They reluctantly stepped forward. Sano ordered five of them to help Marume. "The rest of you, take these folks inside and guard them." He gestured at the kneeling, weeping maids and the other guard, whose face had turned white with terror. He had serious qualms about threatening innocent people, and breaking Madam Chizuru's confession went against his own interests, but honor was at stake. "I'll be back after I cut off Lieutenant Arai's head. If nobody confesses, I'll keep killing people until you're all dead."

MASAHIRO WENT TO the section of the palace where the shogun's male concubines lived. There he met a boy he remembered from the snowball fight. "Where's Dengoro?"

"In the sickroom." The boy pointed to the end of the corridor, which was hazy with incense smoke. "Nobody's supposed to go in there. He has the measles."

Dengoro must have caught it from the shogun, Masahiro thought, feeling sorry for him. Although he was afraid of catching it himself, that wasn't the main reason for his reluctance to go near the boy. If he discovered that Madam Chizuru's confession was true, it would put his father in the wrong. Masahiro was torn between his father and his mother. He loved them both, even though he was furious at them about Taeko. He hated being caught in the middle of their fights, and it seemed that whoever won, things wouldn't work out so that they would let him and Taeko marry. Mixed up and distraught, he didn't know what else to do except what they'd asked—question Dengoro again.

As he headed down the corridor, the incense smoke used to banish the evil spirits of disease was so pungent that he coughed. It emanated from brass burners hung by the door to the sickroom. Masahiro slid open the door, waved away smoke, and saw Dengoro sit up in the bed. A red, mottled rash covered his face, but Dengoro smiled at Masahiro.

"You came back. I was wishing you would."

"How are you feeling?" Masahiro asked.

"Not too good." Dengoro's smile dimmed. "I get to drink as much tea with ice and honey as I want, but I don't want much. And I have to take nasty medicine."

"You'll be all better soon." Masahiro hoped so. He liked the boy despite his stories. "And then we'll play together."

Dengoro cheered up. "That would be fun."

"In the meantime, I wanted to ask if you remembered anything else from the night the shogun was stabbed," Masahiro said.

"I wanted to talk to you about that." Dengoro admitted with chagrin, "I make things up sometimes. It's funny, as soon as I say them, they seem so real, I start thinking they really happened." Worry knitted his rash-covered brow. "If I tell you the truth, do you promise not to get mad at me again?"

If Dengoro lied again, Masahiro would be even madder, because the situation was even more serious than before. But he wanted to give Dengoro a chance to redeem himself, and he needed whatever real, honest evidence Dengoro might have. "I promise."

Dengoro sighed with relief, then said sheepishly, "I didn't really see Lady Nobuko. And I didn't really hear Tomoe's voice."

There went the evidence against those two suspects. So far so good.

"What about Madam Chizuru?" Masahiro was afraid Dengoro would recant his story about her, too.

"I really did smell her," Dengoro said. "She was in the shogun's chamber."

Masahiro was caught between jubilation and distrust. He welcomed this evidence that supported Madam Chizuru's confession and incriminated Lord Ienobu, but a man once bitten by a puppy should be careful about putting out his hand again. "Are you sure?"

"Yes." Dengoro sounded confident. "I thought it over, and I'm sure I didn't make it up."

A liar who fooled himself into believing his own lies wasn't a good witness. "Did you hear that Madam Chizuru confessed to stabbing the shogun?"

"Yes. That's why I'm sure. She said she stabbed him. That proves I really smelled her. And my smelling her proves she really did it." Seeing the skepticism on Masahiro's face, Dengoro said anxiously, "Don't you think so?"

Masahiro exhaled as he saw yet another reason to doubt Dengoro, aside from the fact that the boy's story hinged on the confession itself. Now that Dengoro had admitted lying about Tomoe and Lady Nobuko, his story about Madam Chizuru was all he had left to offer Masahiro in exchange for friendship. Still, Masahiro knew his mother would be pleased by it, and maybe he could convince his father that Lord Ienobu had in fact ordered Madam Chizuru to kill the shogun. Maybe he would soon have good news for Taeko.

THE WATCHTOWER ROSE from the retaining wall on a tier of Edo Castle halfway up the hill. Built on a wide base faced with flat stones, three square stories with white plaster walls decreased in size up to the smallest at the top. The eaves of tile roofs curled like wings over the barred windows of each story. Reiko approached the tower through the covered corridor atop the wall. She carried a wicker basket in one hand and a cloth bundle in the other. Patrolling guards eyed her. Cold drafts blew in through the windows. She looked out with yearning at the bright blue sky. If only she could fly away to someplace where there was light, freedom, and peace! But her troubles bound her to the dark earth as if by iron chains.

"I want to talk to Madam Chizuru," she told the sentries at the tower door. "Sano-*san* sent me. I'm his wife."

One sentry escorted her up the narrow wooden stairs that zigzagged through the tower, past troops stationed in the two lower levels. At the top story he unlocked the door, let Reiko in, and locked the door behind her. The room was dim, as cold as outside, and smelled of peppermint and jasmine hair oil, urine, and excrement. Gaps in the shutters admitted faint light. As her eyes adjusted, Reiko saw what looked to be a blanket covering a pile of straw by the wall. The pile shivered; the straw rustled.

"Madam Chizuru?" Reiko said.

A head of disheveled white hair emerged from under the blanket. Daylight striped Madam Chizuru's face. Her lips were blue with cold. Her teeth chattered as she shivered on the bed of straw. Her red, sunken eyes brimmed with misery. A bucket in the corner contained her waste, frozen solid. Reiko wanted to believe that Madam Chizuru was guilty and deserved no better, but she hated seeing an old woman treated like an animal. And Lord Ienobu, the alleged instigator of the attack on the shogun, was probably warm and comfortable under house arrest. Reiko set down her basket and untied her bundle, a silk quilt stuffed with goose down. She spread the quilt over Madam Chizuru, then called to the guard, "Bring a brazier with hot coals."

"She's a traitor," he said. "Let her suffer."

"If you don't warm up her room, she'll freeze to death before she can be executed, and the shogun will have your head instead."

The guard brought the brazier. Soon the room was warm enough that Madam Chizuru, wrapped in Reiko's quilt, stopped shivering. "Thank you," she said, wincing as she sat up and her stiff joints creaked. "You are too kind."

It wasn't only kindness that had motivated Reiko to provide comforts for Madam Chizuru; they might induce her to talk. "Have you been given anything to eat?" Madam Chizuru shook her head. Reiko said,

"I've brought food," and removed lacquer lunch boxes and a jug of hot tea from her basket.

Madam Chizuru drank thirstily and devoured the rice balls, steamed fish with fermented black beans, sesame noodles with prawns, and pickled lotus root, carrots, and radish. Reiko knelt beside her and waited. Her hunger satisfied, she beheld Reiko with startled recognition. "You're Sano-*san*'s wife." Suspicion hooded her eyes. "What do you want?"

Reiko wanted her to prove that she and Lord Ienobu were guilty. But Reiko felt sorry for Madam Chizuru, and she had to consider that there was at least a chance that the woman was innocent and think twice about forcing her to incriminate herself again. Reiko had her own conscience, even if it wasn't as exacting as Sano's code of honor. But she also had a fierce loyalty to her family, whom she must protect above all.

"I want to talk to you about your confession," Reiko said.

Madam Chizuru pulled the quilt tighter around her, as if Reiko might snatch it away.

"My husband says you were uncertain about some points, such as the number of times you stabbed the shogun."

"It was four times." Madam Chizuru seemed suddenly eager to talk.

Reiko was startled by the correct number. "How are you so sure now?"

"I remembered."

"Do you remember the design on the iron fan?"

"Irises," Madam Chizuru said promptly. "Blue irises on a gold background."

"Did someone tell you?"

"No." Madam Chizuru repeated, "I remembered."

Reiko thought of Yanagisawa's men. They'd heard her confession; they knew where its holes were; they would have told Yanagisawa, who had all the information about the stabbing. He could have told them the details and sent one of them to help Madam Chizuru fill in the holes. But Lady Nobuko and Lord Yoshimune were also possibilities. They, too, had spies in the palace; they, too, could have smuggled the information to Madam Chizuru. Reiko began to suspect, against her will, that Sano was right and Madam Chizuru's confession was false.

She asked the question that loomed large in her mind. "Why are you trying so hard to make everybody believe you're guilty?"

Madam Chizuru tightened her jowls. "I already told your husband."

"You're about to be executed. Why are you so eager to die?"

"I don't want to talk anymore." Madam Chizuru began shivering again, even though the room was warm.

"Have you a grudge against Lord Ienobu? Did you confess to get him in trouble?"

Obstinacy stiffened Madam Chizuru's spine. "He's guilty. So am I."

Reiko felt pulled in opposite directions. This talk was going exactly as she'd hoped—Madam Chizuru had filled in the holes in her confession, which indicated that she and Ienobu were in fact guilty—but Reiko intuited that something was terribly wrong. On a hunch, she said, "Do you have any family?" She recalled hearing that Madam Chizuru had been widowed long ago, before she'd become a concubine to the previous shogun.

Madam Chizuru maintained her stiff posture, but her lips quivered. "Only my granddaughter," she whispered. "She is eleven years old."

"Have you thought about what will happen to her if you're executed for treason?" Reiko asked. "She'll be executed, too. It's the law." She pictured a little girl who looked like Akiko kneeling on the dirt while the executioner raised his sword over her. The awfulness of the image touched on Reiko's grief for her baby. She blinked away the tears that were always ready to fall. "If your confession is a lie, it's not too late to take it back." Aware that every word she said went against her own family's interests, Reiko said, "Why don't you try to save yourself, for your granddaughter's sake?"

"I'm doing it for her!" Madam Chizuru burst out. Her self-control shattered with an abruptness that stunned Reiko. She rocked back and forth. "Chamberlain Yanagisawa kidnapped her! He said that if I confessed that I stabbed the shogun because Lord Ienobu told me to, he would let her go. I would be put to death, but she would be safe. If I didn't, or if I told anybody what he told me, then he would kill her!" She leaned over, beat her forehead on the plank floor, and sobbed violently. "I should have kept my mouth shut! Now we'll both die!"

Reiko experienced an overwhelming astonishment and distress. She'd broken Madam Chizuru's confession so easily, so exactly against her wishes. For a moment she considered not telling Sano. What if she convinced Madam Chizuru that the best way to protect her granddaughter was to keep Yanagisawa's threat a secret and let herself and Lord Ienobu be executed for a crime they hadn't committed? That would be the end of the danger Ienobu posed to Reiko's family. But Reiko felt responsible for this poor woman desperate to save her granddaughter who was only a little older than Akiko. She couldn't not tell.

MARUME AND THE soldiers dragged the shouting, cursing Lieutenant Arai out of the palace. Sano led the way down the hill to a watchtower. He ordered the guards inside to leave. Marume and the soldiers dumped Arai on the floor of the cold, square bottom level.

"I'll give you another chance to tell me the truth before I take you out of the castle and kill you." Sano drew his sword. "Are you working for Chamberlain Yanagisawa? Did he tell you to make Madam Chizuru confess?"

Arai leapt to his feet. "No." Insolence shone through the fear in his glare. "You can't make me say I did."

Sano wondered what he would do if Arai wasn't Yanagisawa's messenger or wouldn't admit it. He wasn't really going to kill anybody . . . or was he? To kill under circumstances like these was a line he'd always refused to cross. Sano felt a terrifying, disorienting uncertainty. How far would he go to learn the truth about a confession that he would do better to let stand?

How far to uphold honor?

Last night's doubts, temporarily quelled by a restorative sleep, reawakened in Sano.

There was a scuffle outside. A guard said, "You can't go in there." A woman shouted, "I have to speak with Sano-*san*! I have something important to tell him!" It was Reiko.

23

"ARE YOU SURE this is where she's being kept?" Marume asked Sano as they rode across the bridge that spanned the Nihonbashi River. Below them, boats converged on the fish market on the north bank. The sounds of merchants haggling over the catch, seagulls screeching, and the stench of rotten fish drifted up.

"No. He owns several properties that I know of," Sano said.

They spoke in low voices that wouldn't carry to the army troops riding behind them through the district known as the Large Post-House Quarter. Stables and lodging houses clustered near the starting point of the four major highways that led out of Edo. The streets were crowded with travelers who had come to rent or return horses and government officials come to hire the fleet-footed messengers who ran messages all over Japan. Sano hadn't told the troops they were here to rescue Madam Chizuru's granddaughter. He hadn't let them hear Reiko whisper to him that Madam Chizuru had admitted that Lieutenant Arai had told her that Yanagisawa had kidnapped her granddaughter and forced Madam Chizuru to incriminate herself and Lord Ienobu.

He was amazed that Reiko had managed to break the confession she wanted to be true. He wished she hadn't. He, too, had hoped the confession was good.

He'd sent her home with instructions not to tell anyone outside their family. He didn't want Yanagisawa to find out what she'd discovered.

He hoped he could count on help from these troops when the time came.

"I think this is the likeliest place." Sano confessed, "I used to wait outside the castle for Yanagisawa. Then I would follow him." He'd been trying to find out what Yanagisawa was up to and why he'd allied with Lord Ienobu. He hadn't told anyone then; it seemed shameful, his futile dogging of his old enemy.

They stopped in a street, between the neighborhood gates at each end that closed at night to keep the residents contained and troublemakers out. Sano pointed to a low house flanked by two stables and enclosed by a fence that concealed it up to the bottom of its tiled roof. Across the street, trees rose from within the earthen walls surrounding large inns. Sano had seen Yanagisawa use the house for meetings with men who appeared to be spies newly arrived in town, but he'd been unable to get close enough to eavesdrop. Now, as he and Marume and the troops dismounted, servants carried bales of hay into the stables. Sano led the way to the house. It was run-down, with cracked and missing roof tiles. He and Marume peered between the moss-stained planks of the fence. In the side yard, two horses were visible through the barred windows of a small stable. Sano's heart sank even as it beat faster. Two horses there meant two samurai in the house. This had to be the place where Yanagisawa was keeping his hostage. Otherwise, it would have been vacant.

Marume heaved his shoulder against the locked gate. It broke off its hinges. He and Sano stepped over it and ran up the path, drawing their swords. The half-timbered house with peeling plaster walls squatted in a garden of snow and dead weeds. Sano beckoned the troops to follow. As they neared the door, it opened. They burst in on two samurai in the entryway. Sano recognized them as Yanagisawa's enforcers—hardmuscled, strong-jawed. When they recognized Sano, Marume, and the Tokugawa crests on the troops' helmets, they faltered for an instant before they drew their swords and lunged.

"Don't kill them!" Sano shouted as he parried their strikes. "Capture them!"

Three of the soldiers had already ganged up on one of Yanagisawa's men. He fell, blood pouring from a fatal gash across his belly. The other turned and ran into the house. Sano and Marume pounded after him, through an entryway that contained empty racks for shoes, down a corridor with rooms on either side. Marume tackled Yanagisawa's man, then sat on him while Sano wrested his long sword from his fist and his short sword from the scabbard at his waist.

"Chamberlain Yanagisawa will kill you for trespassing on his property!" the man said as he kicked and bucked.

The soldiers, who'd followed Sano and Marume inside, watched with astonishment. One said, "This place is Yanagisawa's? What the hell are we doing?"

"I'll explain in a moment," Sano said. "Tie him up."

"You should have told us. Now we're in trouble!"

"Not as much trouble as Yanagisawa," Marume said.

The troops bound the captive's wrists and ankles with his sash. Sano asked him, "Where's Madam Chizuru's granddaughter?"

"Who?"

Marume kicked the man. "The girl you kidnapped for Yanagisawa."

"I don't know what you're talking about."

Sano and Marume searched the building. In one room, Yanagisawa's men had set up camp with bedrolls, charcoal braziers, and food. The other rooms were vacant. The soldiers talked among themselves, fretting about how to excuse their actions to Yanagisawa.

"See?" the captive called. "I told you so."

Sano hoped Yanagisawa hadn't really kidnapped the girl, Madam Chizuru had lied, and her confession was good. Then he heard a faint sound like a cat mewing. "Everybody shut up!"

He and Marume listened. The sound repeated. Sano followed it to the kitchen. Nobody was there, nothing except a hearth black with cold ashes. Sano looked down at the floor. He pointed at a large, square wooden board set between narrower planks. Marume crouched, inserted his fingers into a hole cut in one edge, lifted the board, and flung it aside. The mewing sound and a pungent smell of urine-soaked earth wafted up from a cellar. There lay a girl, immobilized by ropes tied around her body. A cloth gag muffled her screams. Her eyes were huge with fright.

Marume groaned. "Please tell me I'm not seeing this!"

Despair coursed through Sano. Madam Chizuru hadn't lied. Sano had been right in thinking her confession was false, but he wished with all his heart that he'd been wrong.

OUTSIDE THE PALACE, officials turned to watch a procession march up the path. Sano led with Madam Chizuru and her granddaughter. The girl and the old woman clung to each other, weeping. Next came Detective Marume escorting Lieutenant Arai, the guard from the Large Interior. The army soldiers followed with Yanagisawa's man from the house in the Post-Horse Quarter. Masahiro came running across the grounds, calling, "Father! What happened?"

"Your mother found out that Yanagisawa forced Madam Chizuru to confess," Sano said. "He took her granddaughter hostage. We just rescued her granddaughter." His heart was heavy; he'd traded saving Madam Chizuru and the girl for his chance to convict Lord Ienobu.

Masahiro reacted with dismayed astonishment. "But Dengoro said he really did smell Madam Chizuru in the bedchamber after the shogun was stabbed."

"He lied again. I've got all these witnesses to prove it." Sano glanced at Madam Chizuru and her granddaughter, Lieutenant Arai, and Yanagisawa's man. "I have to tell the shogun."

"Can I come?" Masahiro asked.

"No," Sano said. Things were going to get ugly. "Go home. Take care of your mother and sister and the others."

He led the procession to the shogun's chamber. There, Yanagisawa and Yoshisato knelt on either side of the bed. When they saw Sano at the door and the angry expression on his face, they quickly stood. So did the shogun's two guards stationed by the wall.

"Many thanks for your help with my investigation," Sano said to Yanagisawa.

"What——?" Yanagisawa's nostrils flared as he scented danger. He moved between Sano and the shogun. "Get out. The shogun is asleep."

174

Marume called from the corridor, "He'll want to wake up for this."

Sano stepped aside to reveal Madam Chizuru and her granddaughter. He'd made his trade-off; it was too late to back out. Yanagisawa's face blanched.

"What a clever plan to frame Lord Ienobu," Sano said. "It almost worked."

"There you go again, giving me credit I don't deserve," Yanagisawa said. "I didn't frame anybody."

Yoshisato came to Yanagisawa's side. "Who are these people?" he said with confusion that seemed genuine.

"That's Madam Chizuru," Sano said. "The woman who said that she and Lord Ienobu conspired to assassinate the shogun. The girl is her granddaughter." Madam Chizuru cringed from Yanagisawa and hugged her granddaughter as Sano pulled them into the room. "Yanagisawa-*san* forced her to confess by holding her granddaughter hostage. I found the girl trapped in a cellar with two of his retainers guarding her." He said to Yanagisawa, "One of them is dead, I'm sorry to say."

Yoshisato stared in horror at Yanagisawa. "You did what?"

Yanagisawa saw his retainer and Lieutenant Arai. Rage darkened his face. Lieutenant Arai fell on his knees and whimpered, "I didn't tell!"

"Neither did I!" Yanagisawa's retainer said.

"Shut up!" Yanagisawa ordered.

A thin, wavering, furious voice said, "No, *you* shut up!"

Yanagisawa and Yoshisato whirled. The shogun glared at them from the bed. His face was even more ravaged than yesterday, his body like a bundle of sticks under the quilt. His eyes were feverish but lucid.

"I heard everything! Sano-*san* said you made that woman confess. You framed my nephew. You tricked me!" The shogun's voice rose to a shrill, harsh pitch. The last offense he'd named was obviously the one that angered him most.

Yanagisawa hid his horror behind the smooth, reassuring manner he always used to coax the shogun. "Your Excellency, Sano-*san* is mistaken. I didn't—"

"Yes, you did! There are all these people to prove it. You wanted to make sure that Yoshisato will succeed me, so you cooked up a plot to get rid of Ienobu." The shogun pointed his withered finger at the door. "Get out!"

"Your Excellency, I can explain——"

"I said, shut up!" The shogun turned his feverish, angry gaze on Yoshisato. "You should be ashamed of yourself, conspiring with Yanagisawa-*san* to make me put my innocent nephew to death. Thank the gods that Sano-*san* found you out in time! You get out, too!"

Alarmed and indignant, Yoshisato said, "Honorable Father, I had nothing to do with it! I didn't even know about it until now!"

"Don't call me 'Father,'" the shogun said. "Sano-*san* was right all along: You're not really my son. No son of mine would be party to such an evil scheme!"

Sano's breath caught. He heard gasps from the other men. The shogun was finally wise to the fraud. Yanagisawa's hold on him was slipping like a rope through a greasy fist.

"I'm disinheriting you!" the shogun told Yoshisato.

This was what Sano had been wanting for years—the imposter knocked out of line for the succession—but at what cost?

Yoshisato turned a face livid with fury on Yanagisawa. "See what you've done?"

Yanagisawa spoke between clenched teeth to Sano. "You're going to be sorry for this."

"You're no longer chamberlain," the shogun informed Yanagisawa. "I'm demoting you to patrol guard. Move out of the castle, to someplace far away from me!"

Sano saw Yanagisawa realize that he was not only losing his chance to rule Japan, he'd fallen to the bottom of the hierarchy, the same rank to which Lord Ienobu had consigned Sano. He couldn't hide his panic as he said, "But you and I have been friends for more than thirty years! Surely we can——"

"It's only because we're old friends that I'm letting you stay in my regime at all! If we weren't, I would put you and Yoshisato to death! Now go, before I change my mind!"

Yanagisawa and Yoshisato walked out with identical proud, straight-backed postures, their fierce gazes trained straight ahead. Sano's minimal doubt that they were father and son was gone now. He couldn't rejoice in Yanagisawa's fall from favor. His own fall was coming, and he'd as good as asked for it.

Breathless, weakened by exertion, the shogun said to Sano, "Fetch Lord Ienobu. Tell him I want to reinstate him as my heir. And hurry. I may not have much time left."

24

A COLD, UNCOMFORTABLE ferryboat ride took Sano and Marume across the Sumida River. Beyond the entertainment district in Honjo on the other side, past the vegetable markets along the canals, rich government officials lived in villas where they could take refuge from the summer squalor of the city. At Lord Ienobu's villa, porters carried in hampers and trunks brought from the castle as Sano and Marume arrived.

"I'd rather shovel dung than give Lord Ienobu this message," Marume said.

"An order is an order." Never had Sano been charged with such a distasteful errand. It was small comfort that he'd thwarted Yanagisawa's scheme to seize power. He already regretted his decision, but what else could he have done? Let Madam Chizuru die for a crime she hadn't committed? And Yanagisawa probably would have killed her granddaughter to erase the evidence of his role in her confession.

The granddaughter had reminded Sano of Akiko.

The sentry at the guardhouse told Sano, "You can come in. Your man stays outside. Give me your swords first." Sano handed them over. The guard frisked him, checking for hidden weapons, then led him into the reception chamber. Lord Ienobu knelt on the dais, Manabe beside him. Manabe puffed on a tobacco pipe.

"Have you come to rub salt in my wounds?" Ienobu asked. Yesterday he'd been within arm's reach of ruling Japan. Today he looked like a crippled beggar plucked off the street and dressed up in opulent silk robes. His face was as gray as old meat.

"No," Sano said. "The shogun has disowned Yoshisato and demoted Yanagisawa. He ordered me to bring you back to the castle so he can reinstate you as his heir."

The tobacco pipe fell from Manabe's open mouth. An odd, serene smile crept across Lord Ienobu's face. He said to Manabe, "Didn't I tell you?" He laughed a wheezy chuckle. "Better put out that fire." Smoke rose from embers on the floor mat in front of Manabe; the smell of burning straw filled the room. Manabe picked up his pipe and tamped out the fire with his calloused hand. Lord Ienobu asked Sano, "What occasioned my uncle's change of heart?"

Sano was not only puzzled by Lord Ienobu's reaction but offended. The shogun's change of heart was a huge blow to honor and decency as well as to Sano, and Lord Ienobu seemed to take it for granted as his due! "His Excellency learned that Madam Chizuru's confession was false and Yanagisawa blackmailed her into incriminating you."

Lord Ienobu laughed in exultation, slapping his bony knee. Color returned to his face, as if from an infusion of fresh blood. "How did he find out?"

"Madam Chizuru told my wife. I told the shogun."

"You did?" Lord Ienobu's eyebrows lifted; he seemed more surprised by this second piece of news than the first. "Why, when you could have kept quiet and let me die?"

"You were wrongfully incriminated." Never had Sano hated conceding any point as much as this one. The truth was a double-edged sword, and this time it had cut him instead of his enemy. "It was the right thing for me to do."

"I'm moved, Sano-*san*." Genuine sincerity inflected Ienobu's raspy voice. "You did me a good turn even though you don't like me."

"I hope it's the last thing I ever do for you," Sano said, tasting his own bitterness.

"I suppose I owe you something in return. What would you like?"

"I'd like you to refuse the dictatorship and crawl back under your rock."

Angered by the insult to his lord, Manabe made a move toward Sano, but Ienobu waved him down and said, "Come now, Sano-*san*, don't take that attitude. Suppose we let bygones be bygones, and when I'm shogun, I'll make you my chamberlain. You can help me rule Japan."

That Ienobu would keep him alive, let alone want him in his regime! Then Sano recalled that Ienobu's battle for power wasn't over yet. Powerful men—*daimyo* and Tokugawa branch clan heads—didn't want him to be shogun, and Yanagisawa and Yoshisato were still lurking in the wings. Ienobu needed all the help he could get. Sano knew he should consider Ienobu's proposition, for his family's sake if not his own, but he was appalled by the conditions attached.

"Which bygones do you mean?" Sano asked. "The fact that you're responsible for the murder of the shogun's daughter? That you had the shogun's heir kidnapped?" Lord Ienobu shrugged; his smile said he was proud of these maneuvers he'd never admitted to. Sano laughed in disdain. "Those are pretty big bygones to let slide."

Lord Ienobu's smile turned cunning, malicious. "Face it, Sano-*san*: I'm set to rule Japan. If you want to live, you make peace with me."

"There are other contenders for the succession. Lord Yoshimune, for example." But Sano recalled that with Madam Chizuru's confession discredited, Yoshimune and his cousin Tomoe were once again suspects in the attack on the shogun. Yoshimune could take the fall for it. He wasn't a safe harbor for Sano.

"There are no other contenders as closely related to the shogun as I am."

"The others aren't suspects in the attempted murder of the shogun," Sano went on even though he knew he was digging his own grave.

"Madam Chizuru's confession was false," Ienobu pointed out. "You said so yourself."

"So you didn't order her to stab the shogun. You could have sent a different assassin. Your friend Lady Nobuko, perhaps."

Frowning in displeasure but not surprised, Ienobu said, "Are you refusing my offer?"

Honor decreed that Sano should, but this was surely his last chance for security for his family under Lord Ienobu's seemingly inevitable rule. The doubts that infected Sano swelled like a boil filling with pus. But Sano would rather live with the boil than stomach serving a man he believed was responsible for the murderous attack on their lord. And he didn't trust Ienobu. A man capable of assassinating the shogun wouldn't hesitate to do the same to Sano rather than keep his part of a bargain.

"I am," Sano said with regret as well as conviction.

"Then we have nothing more to discuss."

Ienobu and Manabe rose. Ienobu seemed more limber than yesterday, his back less stooped, like an insect hatching from its cocoon with fresh, damp wings. Transformed by the knowledge that the dictatorship was once again within his grasp, he said with a sly smile, "I'm afraid you'll have to do me one more service: Escort me to the palace."

OFFICIALS AND TROOPS were massed outside the palace when Sano and Marume returned with Lord Ienobu and his retinue. News of Ienobu's impending reinstatement had spread. People lined up alongside the path to witness his triumphant return or curry his favor. They bowed as he shuffled past them. Ienobu acknowledged them with formal nods. His lips strained to repress a grin that peeled them back from his teeth. Sano was disgusted with himself as well as Ienobu. After more than four years of fighting to keep Ienobu from inheriting the dictatorship, he was practically joining Ienobu's and the shogun's hands as if he were the priest at a wedding.

At the palace entrance, Ienobu said, "Have you had second thoughts about my offer?"

"No." Sano imagined the sound of an iron door clanging shut.

"You'll wish you'd accepted," Ienobu called over his shoulder as he hobbled up the steps to the palace.

"No, you won't," Marume said. "The man's a monster."

But Sano knew the consequences of his decision would be bad. He hadn't jumped into the grave he was digging; honor had pushed him in, and he would pull Reiko and the children in with him. But he clung to the stubborn hope that serving honor would get him out of trouble. It always had. Let it not fail him now!

A soldier came up to him and said, "Yanagisawa wants to see you at his compound."

"Who cares what he wants?" Marume scoffed.

Yanagisawa didn't have the authority to command him anymore, but Sano said, "I'd better go." A new phase of the battle for the succession was beginning, and his refusal of Lord Ienobu's offer had driven Sano straight into Yanagisawa's camp.

YANAGISAWA'S COMPOUND WAS secured with extra troops stationed outside the walls. Sano handed over his swords to the guard who frisked him. Inside the mansion, Sano found Yanagisawa huddled in his office with his top retainers, conversing in low, agitated tones. When Yanagisawa saw Sano at the door, he dismissed his retainers. They departed; he stood. The look he gave Sano could have sliced through stone.

"We had a deal," he said, "and you stabbed me in the back."

"Our deal was to work together to prove that Lord Ienobu is responsible for the attack on the shogun," Sano said. "I'm not the one who broke it."

"I held up my end of the bargain," Yanagisawa said. "I gave you the proof."

"Madam Chizuru's confession wasn't proof. It was fraud!" Sano was exasperated because Yanagisawa didn't seem to know, or care about, the difference.

Yanagisawa's hostile eyes accused Sano of stupidity. "Well, you should have gone along with it. Now look what you've done! You've handed the dictatorship to Lord Ienobu!"

Sano badly regretted it, but he said, "It's not my fault he's the shogun's heir again and Yoshisato is disowned." How infuriating that Yanagisawa should put the blame on him! "If you hadn't played your trick, and wasted my time on a false confession, maybe I would have found real proof that Ienobu is guilty. Maybe he would be put to death instead of getting ready to inherit the regime."

" 'Maybe, maybe,' " Yanagisawa mocked. "What's certain is that Lord Ienobu is on top again, and see where your lofty principles have gotten you? You're stuck with me, down here in the mud."

As much as these facts distressed Sano, he couldn't deny them. "Our deal is still on, if you're willing."

"Let bygones be bygones?" Quizzical humor edged into Yanagisawa's cruel smile. "Why didn't you make a deal with Lord Ienobu? He must be grateful to you for saving him. Grateful enough to keep you alive in exchange for helping him get rid of his enemies."

Sano knew how astute Yanagisawa was, but he was nonetheless surprised that Yanagisawa had read the situation so well. Yanagisawa saw his surprise and said, "So Lord Ienobu did offer you a deal. You turned it down. Why not go with him instead of me?"

He sounded honestly puzzled. He had no idea that one reason was Yoshisato. Sano saw Yoshisato as a counterweight to Yanagisawa's villainy. Lord Ienobu had no such redeeming factor. Sano said, "Just be satisfied that I won't be joining Lord Ienobu's attack on you." Yanagisawa didn't need to know that Sano hoped to drive a wedge between him and his son.

"How can I be sure you won't stab me in the back again?"

The price of a rift in their alliance was much higher now, with the shogun weakening by the moment and Lord Ienobu set to claim the dictatorship. Sano said, "You have my word."

"You've shown me that your word is worthless. I want collateral."

"Squeeze blood out of a turnip. I've nothing to my name but a little house and a few coins. Take it all if you want."

A sly smile leavened Yanagisawa's expression. "Oh, you have something much more valuable. Your son Masahiro."

Sano frowned, disturbed and wary. "What do you want with Masahiro?"

"He's of marriageable age. So is my daughter Kikuko. We'll wed them to each other."

Intermarriage was the traditional method by which samurai clans cemented their alliances. Intermarriage between hostile clans made the bride and groom, and any children they had, hostages to each clan's good behavior. Intermarriage was a completely unreasonable, shocking, and outrageous demand for Yanagisawa to make on Sano.

"No!" Sano was horrified, and not just by the idea of a legal, familial, entrapping bond with Yanagisawa, his ally not by choice and his enemy these twenty years. Nor was it because Reiko would hate the idea or because Masahiro wanted to marry Taeko. "Your daughter tried to drown Masahiro when he was a child! Your wife told her to do it."

"That was a long time ago." Yanagisawa sounded annoyed that Sano would bring up such a trivial matter.

Sano wasn't finished relating his grievances against Yanagisawa's wife and daughter. "Your wife tried to kill mine! I don't believe she's changed. I'm not letting her or Kikuko near my family!" Infuriated and adamantly opposed, Sano headed for the door. "I'm going to tell Lord Ienobu I accept his offer. *He* didn't try to marry his child to mine." Sano knew the offer had expired, but Yanagisawa didn't. He had to make Yanagisawa retract his demand.

Yanagisawa moved swiftly to block Sano's exit. "I'm going to change your mind. Three words should do it." His eyes glinted with determination and malice. "Dr. Ito Genboku."

Sano's heart flipped like a speared fish. "Who?"

"You know—your friend at Edo Morgue. The old man who was caught practicing foreign science."

Foreign science, along with books and religion acquired from Western barbarians, was banned by Tokugawa law, due to a policy of isolation established some seventy years ago. The shogun at that time had feared that foreign weapons and military aid were a threat to Japan's stability. People caught doing anything that smacked of foreign science were usually exiled, but the government had made an exception for Dr. Ito.

"He was sentenced to a lifetime as the custodian of the morgue." Yanagisawa's taunting smile said he saw and relished Sano's discomfiture. "He's been helping you with your investigations. He dissects the corpses of murder victims and finds clues for you. Which means you've been a party to foreign science." Triumph broadened Yanagisawa's smile. "Don't bother denying it. I've had you followed to the morgue; I have spies there. I know."

Sano experienced a falling, perilous sensation. His collusion with Dr. Ito, begun twenty years ago, had set him up for this moment of reckoning. He'd been young and impulsive then, a single man with little to lose, and he'd unwittingly put himself under Yanagisawa's power. "How long have you known?"

"Oh, seven or eight years."

All those years of wearing disguises to the morgue, delivering the corpses there by circuitous routes—all for nothing. Sano didn't need to ask why Yanagisawa had kept his secret, had let him think he was safe. "You've been hoarding the information in case you ever needed it to use against me."

The corner of Yanagisawa's smile twisted upward. "How well we know each other."

"And now, if I don't agree to marry my son to your daughter, you'll report me for practicing foreign science."

"The shogun is too sick to care about it, but Lord Ienobu will like the excuse to banish you to the silver mines on Sado Island. He won't have to worry that any friends of yours will rally to your defense. They won't want to be associated with you and share your exile. Which your family will."

Banishment to Sado Island was tantamount to a death sentence. Nobody lasted long in the mines. Sano hurried to find the advantage in the catastrophe. "So you have my secret to hold over my head. You don't need Masahiro to marry Kikuko."

Yanagisawa's expression told Sano not to take him for a fool. "When I tie up a man, I don't give him room to wriggle free."

The falling sensation stopped as Sano hit bottom in a pit of despair. Events had flung him back and forth like a ball between Yanagisawa and Lord Ienobu, and although Yanagisawa was losing the game, he'd claimed Sano's soul as a prize.

But it wasn't Sano who would ultimately pay for his sins. It was his beloved son.

"The wedding needs to happen soon," Yanagisawa said. "Tomorrow, I think. Afterward, Masahiro and his bride will live with me, to guarantee your cooperation."

Sano felt sick at heart as he nodded. His actions had already caused Reiko and Masahiro enough pain. They would never forgive him for this. He would never forgive himself. And he could see no way out of it . . . except to kill Yanagisawa.

The solution was so simple, would be so satisfying.

But he didn't have his swords, and he was trapped in Yanagisawa's domain, surrounded by Yanagisawa's men.

He didn't have any other friends able to help him. Unless Masahiro married Kikuko, the whole family was at Lord Ienobu's nonexistent mercy.

Yoshisato poked his head in the door and said to Yanagisawa, "Sorry to interrupt, but the word from the palace is, Lord Ienobu has been officially reinstated as the heir and Acting Shogun, and he's issued orders for our arrest." He looked at Sano. "Yours, too."

25

IN THEIR HOUSE in the *banchō*, Reiko waited anxiously in the parlor with Masahiro, Midori, Taeko, and the other children. Masahiro had told them that Lord Ienobu was back in power. When Sano burst through the door, distraught and breathless, everyone jumped up in alarm. Reiko asked, "What is it?"

"Lord Ienobu is coming after us. There's no time to explain. Pack your things!"

"Where are we going?" Akiko asked.

"You'll see," Sano said, heading out of the room.

Midori put her arms around her children. "Us, too?" She and Taeko looked frightened, the younger children puzzled.

"Yes. And the servants. Hurry!"

Reiko followed Sano, blinded by heart-hammering panic. She didn't know what to do first; she didn't have time to be angry at Sano. Lists of which items to bring, and things to do before she went, unspooled in her mind. "My father—we can't leave him!"

Reiko's father was the only family that Reiko and Sano had in Edo. Since his forced retirement he'd lived in a little house in town. Reiko and the children visited him often. Magistrate Ueda never reproached Sano, but Reiko felt guilty, and although Magistrate Ueda was always glad to see them, he was sad about losing the work he loved. He had a new hobby—growing bonsai. Now Magistrate Ueda, too, was in danger from Lord Ienobu.

"Marume's getting him." In the bedchamber, Sano bundled up spare clothes, swords, and the small iron box of money he kept for emergencies. He packed the cloth-wrapped iron fan he'd brought from the castle. Reiko hurriedly packed her belongings.

Soon the household was on the road. Sano and Marume led on horses laden with baggage. Reiko, Midori, Taeko, the children, and the servants went on foot, bundles on their backs. Masahiro and two retainers, also mounted on laden horses, brought up the rear.

"Mama, I didn't say good-bye to my dogs," Akiko cried.

"You'll see them later." Reiko didn't know if they would ever return to their house. Once again Akiko and her needs had been shuffled aside; the family had no attention to spare for her. It was unfair to the little girl, Reiko knew, but it was unlikely to change any time soon.

In the *daimyo* district, sunlight sparkled on the black-and-white geometric tile patterns that decorated the long barracks surrounding the estates. Thousands of troops milled in avenues wide enough to parade an army. The news had spread: Lord Ienobu was in charge, and the *daimyo* clans expected trouble. Sano stopped outside a gate with a double roof and brass-trimmed double portals. Reiko felt her heart thump and a flood of horrific memories assail her. Staggering under her bundle, she panted up to Sano.

"This is Lord Mori's estate," she said. "This is where we're staying?"

Eleven years ago she'd been framed for a murder in this very place. She saw in her mind a naked man lying dead, a red wound where his genitals had been, and a white chrysanthemum in a puddle of blood.

"Yes, we're staying here." Sano identified himself to the sentries in the guardhouse.

"Do you know Lord Mori?" Masahiro asked.

"Slightly," Sano said.

Lord Mori had been a suspect in that long-ago murder that Sano had investigated. Everybody was acting as if everything were normal. All the while, Reiko was caught in a nightmare deeper and more real than when she'd gone to the castle to see Lady Nobuko.

"Yanagisawa's messenger said you would be coming." The sentry opened the gate and said with cool courtesy, "Welcome to you and your people."

Surprise joined the horror, nausea, and panic that gripped Reiko. "Yanagisawa got us invited here? He's friends with Lord Mori?"

"That's right." Sano dismounted and told his household, "Get inside."

"But why would Yanagisawa protect us?" Masahiro asked.

"He and I are allies now," Sano said.

It was an alliance made in hell. But Reiko had more immediate cause for objection. "I can't go in there!" she cried.

Sano grabbed her shoulders, brought his face close to hers, and said urgently, "I know why you don't want to, but this is the only place that would take us in. The people who hurt you aren't there. Go in or you'll be arrested!" He pushed Reiko.

As she stumbled with Midori and the children into a courtyard, she retched. Only water mixed with bile came up; she'd been too anxious to eat today. Mori troops loitered outside the barracks and around the inner gate to the mansion. She wiped her mouth on her sleeve and kept her head down, afraid someone would recognize her. More memories fed the panic that squeezed her chest; she couldn't breathe. She'd been pregnant with Akiko when she'd been framed for murder here. Had she not been exonerated, they both would have died.

Sano and his few retainers and Masahiro led in their horses. He asked a guard, "Has Yanagisawa arrived?"

"Not yet."

"He's staying here, too?" Reiko couldn't believe this horror on top of everything else. "With his family?"

"Yes." Sano seemed even more uncomfortable than the occasion warranted. He glanced around, as if seeking something to distract her. "Look—here's your father."

Magistrate Ueda rode through the gate with Detective Marume. His stout figure bounced on a horse laden with bulging saddlebags. He cradled a little potted bonsai pine tree in one arm. Akiko ran to him, calling, "Grandpa!"

He handed her the pine tree and grunted as he climbed off the horse.

"This is my favorite. I didn't want to leave it behind." Tatsuo and Chiyoko danced around him. Shunned by their own relatives, they'd adopted him as their substitute grandfather. He patted their heads, hugged Akiko, then greeted Sano and Reiko.

Reiko clung to her father, a source of comfort. He put his arm around her, but he didn't seem to notice that she was upset or recall what had happened to her inside this estate. "Well." He looked around with lively interest. His topknot was white, he was short of breath, and his mind wasn't as sharp as it had been before his retirement. "This is a nice change." He was happy to be in the thick of the action.

"We all got away just in time," Marume said. "On our way here I ran into a friend of mine from the army. He warned me that Lord Ienobu's sent troops after us."

From the street came the sound of hooves and footsteps pounding, men yelling. In the distance a war trumpet made from a giant seashell blared like the voice of a sea monster. Reiko heard Yanagisawa shout, "Open up! Let us in, damn it!"

Into the courtyard galloped Yanagisawa and Yoshisato on horseback, then their mounted troops and two gangsters on foot. An oxcart carried in three women wearing hooded cloaks. One was Yoshisato's mother. The others clung to each other, a homely older woman pressing a younger one's face against her bosom. She gazed at Reiko with flat, expressionless eyes.

"Lady Yanagisawa. Kikuko." The last people in the world Reiko wanted to see. The gate slammed shut. She was trapped in here with these two who'd tried to kill her and Masahiro. They'd all died and reunited in hell.

The war trumpet blared louder. The children covered their ears. Distant hoofbeats escalated to a rolling thunder. Their rhythm broke into splatters and stomps as the legion halted on the slushy road outside the estate. "It's the Tokugawa army!" called a soldier in one of the fire-watch towers that rose from within the estate on wooden stilts. "They're surrounding us!"

Reiko's horror worsened as she realized that she had more to fear than Lady Yanagisawa, Kikuko, and the memories that the Mori estate harbored.

The soldier in the fire-watch tower yelled, "They're surrounding other estates, too!"

Voices clamored outside as Lord Mori's troops faced the army. A sentry at the gate shouted, "What do you want?"

"Yanagisawa, Yoshisato, and Sano," replied the army's spokesman. "We have orders to arrest them and their people."

Reiko, Midori, and the children gathered fearfully around Sano, Masahiro, Marume, and Magistrate Ueda. Yanagisawa called, "We're not coming out!"

A pause, then, "We have a message for Lord Mori."

In the courtyard, the *daimyo*'s troops muttered and agitated. Reiko supposed they didn't know what to do; there had never been a situation like this in their lifetime.

Yanagisawa took charge. "Go get Lord Mori."

Troops scrambled to obey. Reiko heard garbled commands from nearby estates—the same thing was happening there. The gate that led to the mansion opened. Into the courtyard marched guards with huge, fierce dogs on chains. The dogs bared sharp teeth as they barked. Akiko smiled at them. Chiyoko squealed in fright; Midori drew her and Tatsuo close. The guards accompanied Lord Mori Enju, *daimyo* of Suwo and Nagato provinces. He was much the same as when Reiko had last seen him eleven years ago. In his midthirties now, he still had a tall, lithe build and fine features. Cool and self-possessed, he seemed untroubled by the uproar. His gaze alit on Reiko. She wished the ground would open up and swallow her. She felt as naked and exposed as on that day eleven years ago. But Lord Mori looked right through her. If he remembered that he'd once accused her of murder, she couldn't tell.

He acknowledged Sano and Yanagisawa with a curt nod, then called through the gate, "What is Lord Ienobu's message?"

A dark, cylindrical object flew in over the wall and landed on the ground near Lord Mori. It was a black lacquer scroll container. He picked it up, opened it, read the scroll, and frowned. "Lord Ienobu is stripping me of my title. He's taking over my province." His cold anger reminded Reiko of a burn from touching ice. "The army is here to confiscate my property. He's sent the same message to the other *daimyo* who don't want him to become shogun."

His men exclaimed in outrage. Lord Ienobu's action would make them *rōnin*. Their protests were echoed by those from other estates where the message had been delivered.

Yoshisato said to Yanagisawa, "That was a great idea you had, seizing control of the provinces. Too bad it's Lord Ienobu carrying it out."

"Don't surrender," Yanagisawa said fiercely to Lord Mori.

"I have no intention of surrendering." Lord Mori called out, "Here's my reply to Lord Ienobu." He hurled the scroll over the wall, then addressed his men in a loud voice that would carry to the soldiers in the fire-watch towers. "We'll resist. So must everyone else. If we all do, Lord Ienobu can't take us. Spread the word!"

"Resist! Resist!" The cry rang through the air, taken up by other soldiers in towers at other estates. Outside, yells arose as the army tried to force its way to gates and *daimyo* troops rallied to protect their masters. Lady Yanagisawa enfolded Kikuko in her arms. Magistrate Ueda clutched his bonsai. Taeko clung to Masahiro, whose eyes shone with excitement. Reiko, with Midori and the children, couldn't believe this was happening. She wanted to shut her eyes, scream, dig her fingernails into her arms, and wake herself up from this insane nightmare.

"Fire!" Lord Mori shouted to the archers on his roofs.

They and the archers at other estates let loose a barrage of arrows. The army yelled, then the commotion outside quieted. Lord Mori said, "They'll be sending messengers to tell Lord Ienobu what's happening. They'll wait for his orders."

Yanagisawa smiled with satisfaction. "If he thought we would go down without a fight, he's in for a surprise."

Lord Mori nodded and turned to Sano. "Forgive my bad manners. I welcome you and your family to my humble home." He didn't mention the murder investigation during which he and Sano and Reiko had clashed.

Sano bowed. "Many thanks."

Lord Mori's cool gaze included Yanagisawa. "This may be a long standoff. You might as well get your people settled. I'm giving you guest quarters in the same wing of my house. It seems appropriate."

This was no nightmare. It really was hell. Reiko looked at Sano, aghast that they would be living in close proximity to Yanagisawa and his family. And there was apparently even more to the situation than she'd thought. "What does he mean?"

Yanagisawa smiled with sardonic amusement at Sano. "I gather you haven't told her yet. Now would be the time."

"TOLD ME WHAT?" Reiko asked.

She and Sano were in the guest quarters, a series of rooms built around a garden and connected by covered corridors to the *daimyo*'s mansion, a large, half-timbered structure with multiple wings and peaked tile roofs, mounted on a granite foundation. The space was as large as their whole house, furnished with clean, fresh-smelling tatami, elegant landscape murals, and well heated by charcoal braziers under the floor. Akiko, Tatsuo, and Chiyoko happily explored. Sano busied himself with stowing his clothes and swords in the cabinet.

His gut clenched.

The moment he'd been dreading was here. Just when he'd hoped things between him and Reiko were improving, now this.

He knew he'd done a terrible thing by bringing her here. The sick pallor of her face told him how terrible. This was exactly the wrong place and time to tell her about his deal with Yanagisawa.

Masahiro dumped his own baggage on the floor. "What did Yanagisawa mean?"

Sano faced his wife and son. His stomach felt sick, his heart heavy as lead. "Sit down."

Reiko ran to him. "You're scaring me. Out with it!"

This was the hardest thing Sano had ever had to do. He would rather disembowel himself. "Yanagisawa wanted assurance that I wouldn't betray him. He demanded that we cement our alliance with—" Sano swallowed. He forced himself to go on. "A marriage between his daughter and Masahiro."

Reiko and Masahiro smiled and frowned as if he'd made a bad joke. Their smiles vanished; their frowns deepened. "You didn't agree?"

Reiko asked. Sano swallowed again. Her eyes and Masahiro's widened in alarm. "Did you?"

Sano wished that one of the many people who'd tried to kill him during the past twenty years had succeeded. "I agreed." He watched his wife's and son's stricken faces. He forced himself not to run away like a coward. "After the wedding, Masahiro and Kikuko will live with Yanagisawa."

Masahiro shouted, "No!"

"How could you?" Reiko turned from side to side, caught between puzzlement and horror. "You and Yanagisawa are enemies, and you know Kikuko tried to kill Masahiro when he was little."

"I won't do it!" Masahiro cried.

Reiko pointed to the door. "Go tell Yanagisawa that Masahiro isn't going to marry Kikuko. Offer him anything else but that!"

"That's what he wants." More wretched than ever, Sano said, "It's settled."

Masahiro shouted, "I'm not marrying anyone but Taeko!"

"Why are you giving in so easily?" Reiko demanded.

"What did Yanagisawa say he'll do unless I marry Kikuko?" Masahiro asked.

They were too perceptive and too strong-willed. Sano couldn't put anything over on them or make them accept his decision without argument. "He knows about Dr. Ito."

Reiko and Masahiro stared at him with appalled enlightenment. Sano didn't need to say more. They were among the few people who knew about his illegal business at Edo Morgue. They also knew what would happen to them should Yanagisawa make the secret public.

Reiko snatched up her baggage. "Masahiro, we're leaving."

"Where are we going?"

"Someplace else." Reiko glared at Sano. "You let Yanagisawa find out about Dr. Ito, and I'm not letting our son pay the price!"

Sano knew she was angry at him for more than this fiasco, which was only the latest in the series of troubles he'd brought upon his family. "You can't go. We're surrounded by the army. If you leave the estate, they'll arrest you and deliver you straight to Lord Ienobu."

Reiko groaned in agony and frustration. "This is all because of your bullheaded honor! You've sold our son to it!" She flung her bundles at Sano. He didn't try to dodge. They hit his chest; he welcomed the punishment he deserved.

"You betrayed us! I'll never forgive you!" Reiko screamed. "If we get out of this alive, I'm leaving you. I don't want to be your wife anymore!"

She knelt and moaned into her hands. Masahiro's face was a tragic mask. Nobody needed to tell him it was his duty to honor his father's agreement, marry Kikuko, and protect his family. Masahiro knew that Bushido demanded filial piety. Sano had often struggled with Bushido's harsh dictates, and now he'd used them to bind his son.

"All right," Masahiro said in a hard voice fissured with pain. "I'll marry her. When is the wedding?"

"Tomorrow." Sano stood in the ruins of his marriage and his relationship with his son. Knowing he'd destroyed all chance of reconciliation was a desolate, lonely feeling.

He heard a sob and looked toward the open door. There stood Taeko, biting the back of her hand, her eyes filled with tears. She'd overheard the conversation. She turned and fled.

TAEKO RAN DOWN the corridor, crying so hard she couldn't see where she was going. Her worst fear had come true: Masahiro was going to marry someone else.

He called her name. She ran faster, blindly, outside to a cold garden of boulders, snow, and twisted, leafless shrubs. She fell to her knees by a boulder, leaned against it, and wept. Masahiro knelt beside her and awkwardly patted her shoulder.

"Go away!" Taeko could barely speak through the sobs that erupted deep within her and tore at her stomach, lungs, and throat on their way up. It seemed that her body, in its agony, was trying to expel her broken heart through her mouth.

"I'm sorry you had to find out this way." Masahiro's voice shook. "I wish I could have told you myself."

As if that were the only thing wrong! She turned to him and cried, "You broke your promise!"

"Let me explain." Masahiro's face was blurred by her tears, filled with his own sorrow.

"There's nothing to explain! You're dumping me to marry Yanagisawa's daughter!"

"I'm not. I love you. I want to marry you, but I have to marry Kikuko or my family will die. So will yours."

Taeko understood that. She knew he was trapped and he was unhappy about it, but she said, "I don't care! You said we would marry, and now we aren't going to." And the baby was due in a few months. She sobbed harder. "What am I supposed to do?"

Masahiro grabbed her hand. "Listen." Taeko tried to pull away, but he held tight. "After I'm married, you can be my concubine."

Married men often had concubines; it was the custom. If she were Masahiro's concubine, she could live with him and the baby would be recognized as his and supported by him, and his wife would have no right to object. But the very idea revolted Taeko.

"No!" she cried.

"It will be all right," Masahiro tried to soothe her. "Our parents will be upset, but they can't stop us."

"I don't care about them," Taeko said, angry because he'd misunderstood her objection. "I won't share you with your wife!" His wife would have all the privileges of marriage. Her children would be legitimate, his official heirs. Taeko and her child would be second-class members of his household. And her heart sickened at the thought of Masahiro making love to another girl.

"Yanagisawa's daughter will be my wife in name only," Masahiro said. "I won't touch her. I won't even look at her."

Taeko's resistance started to crumble. She wanted so much to be with Masahiro, and this awful compromise was better than nothing. "Do you promise?"

"I promise." Masahiro's eyes overflowed with sincerity. "It's you I love. My being married to somebody else won't change anything between us."

He clasped her hands to his chest. "I'll never love anyone but you as long as I live."

She had to trust him. She had no choice. She nodded and whispered, "All right."

Masahiro dropped her hands. "Here comes your mother. I'd better get lost."

He ran off. Confused and forlorn, Taeko leaned against the boulder, shivering in the cold. Footsteps crunched the snow. Warm, soft fabric draped her. Her mother was wrapping her in a padded cloak.

Midori put her arms around Taeko and said, "I'm so sorry." Her voice was gentler than Taeko had heard in a long time. "I know you thought I was being mean when I separated you from Masahiro, but I was just trying to protect you from something like this." She'd apparently heard about his engagement to Yanagisawa's daughter. "I didn't want you to be hurt."

Her unexpected sympathy made Taeko cry again. Midori rocked her like a baby. "I know what it's like being in love with the wrong man," Midori said. "It happened to me when I was about your age."

Taeko was surprised. Her mother never talked about her youth.

"My father didn't want me to marry your father," Midori went on. "My father is a *daimyo*. Yours was only a police patrol officer. But your father and I fell in love, and I was desperate for us to marry." She sighed. "I was pregnant, with you."

Shocked, Taeko pulled back and stared up at her mother.

"Yes." Midori smiled sadly, shamefaced. "We were so much in love that we couldn't help ourselves."

Not only was it hard for Taeko to imagine her parents having sex, but they'd been so at odds for so many years that Taeko couldn't believe they'd ever loved each other.

"I don't want the same thing to happen to you," Midori said.

Now would be the time to confess that it already had. Taeko longed to unburden herself, but her mother's moods changed so fast. She kept quiet rather than set off a fit of temper.

"Things worked out," Midori said, "or so I thought at the time. Now I'm not so sure."

Taeko felt a pang of hurt. "Are you sorry you had me?"

"No, no." Midori tightened her arms around Taeko. "You and your brother and sister are the best things that ever happened to me." She sighed again. "But your father has been so much trouble." Her manner turned hard and brisk. "Masahiro is trouble for you. Try to forget him. Be glad that after the wedding tomorrow he'll be his wife's problem."

Now wasn't the time for Taeko to tell her mother that she was going to be Masahiro's concubine. "Yes, Mother," she said unhappily. "I'll try."

IN THE SECTION of the guest quarters on the other side of the garden, Lady Yanagisawa unpacked her baggage. Kikuko said, "Mama, where are my dolls?"

"Here, darling." Lady Yanagisawa found the dolls in a trunk. Her daughter's childishness always provoked mixed feelings in her. She was distressed because Kikuko would always remain a five-year-old girl in a woman's body but glad that Kikuko would always need her, unlike other children who eventually left their mothers.

Kikuko chattered to the dolls as she changed their kimonos. Lady Yanagisawa smiled fondly at her, thankful that she'd inherited her father's looks. Putting away clothes, Lady Yanagisawa listened for her husband. She always thrilled to the sight and sound and smell of him, his slightest attention. She loved him with a passion that persisted regardless of his indifference toward her and his revulsion toward their daughter. She often wished she didn't love him, but nothing could change her feelings— not even the fact that he'd just moved her and her daughter into the same house as her worst enemy.

She'd admired, envied, and hated Reiko since the day they'd met fifteen years ago. Reiko had everything she didn't. Reiko was beautiful; Reiko had a loving husband; Reiko had two normal children whom their father loved. Lady Yanagisawa wished with all her heart that she'd managed to kill Reiko when she'd had the chance. She wished Kikuko had managed to drown Masahiro. That would have taught Reiko that she couldn't be lucky all the time! When Lady Yanagisawa had seen Reiko today, it had been like acid thrown in her face.

Reiko was as beautiful as ever. Her daughter looked just like her. Masahiro was a man, as tall and handsome as his father. Reiko's children had grown up, but Kikuko never would. Lady Yanagisawa's envy was as corrosive as poison.

A familiar step at the door set her pulse racing. She looked up to see Yanagisawa. A shiver of joy rippled through her. Her body ached with desire. He'd made love to her only a few times, and she couldn't honestly call it making love; he'd taken his pleasure so fast, with no care for hers. She breathed a sigh that expressed all her hopeless love and yearning. She lived for two things—her beautiful, childlike daughter and her beautiful, cruel husband.

He spoke to the air above her head. "I've arranged for Kikuko to marry Sano's son, Masahiro, tomorrow. Get her ready." Then he left.

A loud, wild howling racketed in Lady Yanagisawa's ears. She covered them to block out the noise. She didn't realize it was coming from her until Kikuko ran to her and cried, "Mama, what's wrong!"

My daughter is to marry Reiko's son!

Lady Yanagisawa clapped her hand over her mouth to suppress the howling. She wheezed, coughed, and retched so hard that the pressure behind her eyes caused a dark tangle, like a scrawl of red-tinged ink, to swim across her vision—blood from ruptured veins. Dizzy and breathless, she collapsed to the floor.

Kikuko knelt beside her, patting her back. Lady Yanagisawa moaned and writhed, caught in the throes of a savage anguish. *Reiko already has everything, and now her son is going to take my only child, the only person in the world who loves me!*

"What did Papa mean?" Kikuko asked in her babyish voice. "Who's Masahiro?"

26

LEGIONS OF ARMY foot soldiers and mounted troops occupied the streets of the *daimyo* district all night. Concentrated outside the estates of the clans that opposed Lord Ienobu, they prevented anyone from leaving and deliveries of food, coal, and other necessities from entering. They burned bonfires to keep warm. In the guest quarters of the Mori estate, Reiko lay rigid and sleepless in bed. She smelled the smoke from the bonfires, watched the orange light from the flames flicker through the window shutters, and listened to the *daimyos'* watchdogs barking. Once during this long night she'd fallen asleep and dreamed that her naked body was drenched in the blood of the man she'd been accused of murdering eleven years ago. She'd not dared to close her eyes again. And the evils weren't only in her dreams or memory.

Yanagisawa and his wife and daughter were under the same roof, separated from her only by corridors and paper walls. Reiko felt Lady Yanagisawa's animosity like a deer scents a wolf's meaty breath. In the adjacent chamber Masahiro stirred and muttered in his sleep. Reiko heard muffled sobs from Taeko. Her heart ached for the poor girl who was suffering the pain of lost love.

Reiko looked at Sano, asleep beside her. He thrashed his arms, kicked, then lay still, as if disturbed by intermittent bad dreams. They hadn't spoken since he'd told her and Masahiro about his deal with Yanagisawa. Whenever she tried to see it through his eyes, she understood that he'd done the best he could in an impossible situation, but understanding didn't negate the fact that he'd not only pitted himself against Lord Ienobu, he'd inadequately hidden his collaboration with Dr. Ito, and that secret had put him under Yanagisawa's power. His actions had been based on honor, and their son was paying the price. What Reiko could understand, but not forgive, was that their family would always lose out to Sano's honor.

She turned her face away from him; she lay as far from him as possible, so he wouldn't accidentally touch her. She hated him so much! The fact that she'd once loved him passionately made her hatred all the more strong. She had to get away from him. She didn't know where she would go or what she would live on, but leave him she must.

Temple bells rang; it was dawn. The guard that Lord Mori had assigned to the guest quarters spoke at the door, "Excuse me, Sano-*san*?"

Sano bolted upright beside Reiko. "What is it?"

"There's a message from Lord Ienobu. He wants a meeting with you and Yanagisawa and Yoshisato."

THE MORNING WAS warmer, cloudy, with a deceptive, springlike mildness. Fog shrouded the hills outside Edo and hung in the air. In the *daimyo* district, troops formed cordons along the avenue that separated the Mori estate from another, which belonged to an ally of Lord Ienobu. Archers crouched on roofs on both sides. At one end of the avenue, Sano stood with Yanagisawa and Yoshisato. Behind them were fifty of Lord Mori's mounted soldiers. At the far end, Lord Ienobu and Manabe stood, backed by their own fifty troops from the Tokugawa army. The conditions of the meeting had been specified in the message Lord Ienobu had sent to Sano, Yanagisawa, and Yoshisato. They'd included the stipulation that although their troops could wear armor and weaponry, the four men would not. Clothed in ordinary robes and wicker hat, minus his swords, Sano felt naked and vulnerable. Cold mist filmed his skin as he gazed down the long avenue.

In the middle, set off to his right, between the two rival camps, stood a tent such as generals used as battlefield headquarters. The tent was made of white fabric, mounted on four poles. Flaps open on all four sides showed a tatami mat, charcoal brazier, and five cushions in the tent. Sano's mind reeled with disbelief. Never had he imagined attending a war council between rival contenders for the dictatorship, right in the middle of Edo, to discuss the fate of the Tokugawa regime.

Temple bells rang the hour of the dragon. Lord Ienobu and Manabe stepped forward. Yoshisato, Yanagisawa, and Sano followed suit. Matching pace by pace, trailed by their armies, they advanced through an unnatural quiet disturbed only by a stray cough, a horse's stomp, and dogs barking in the distance. Sano kept his eyes trained on Lord Ienobu and Manabe. Lord Ienobu shuffled in thick, padded winter robes that disguised his deformities. A broad-brimmed hat enlarged his small head, shadowed his ugly face. Sano was keenly aware of the troops outside the estates, the archers on the roofs. His instincts rang out danger signals.

This could be a trick. Maybe Lord Ienobu meant to kill him and Yanagisawa and Yoshisato and gamble that he could escape before Lord Mori's troops killed him. Or Yanagisawa might have secretly ordered the assassination of Lord Ienobu. If either side attacked, Sano would be caught, unarmed, in the crossfire of the first battle in a war.

Both parties halted at the tent. Lord Ienobu's, Yanagisawa's, and Yoshisato's faces were rigid with their effort to conceal anxiety. Sano felt the same rigidity on his own features. The damp atmosphere was hard to breathe, as if the tension had wrung all the air out of it. Lord Ienobu said, "One of my men will search you." A soldier from among the troops behind him stepped forward. "One of yours can search Manabe-*san* and myself."

Sano, Yanagisawa, and Yoshisato stood with their arms spread and feet apart as a soldier examined them for hidden weapons. Sano imagined dirty handprints left on him from so many recent friskings. Lord Ienobu flinched as he and Manabe endured the same indignity. Then he gestured for Sano, Yoshisato, and Yanagisawa to enter the tent. He and Manabe followed them in. Manabe closed the tent flaps. The two sides knelt on the cushions, facing each other, the charcoal brazier between them. Gray daylight penetrated the white tent. The space was too close, too full of animosity. Sano, seated between Yanagisawa and Yoshisato, knew he was at a worse disadvantage than the other men: Each of them had an ally present; he was the only one to whom everyone else was an adversary.

Each side bowed with cold politeness to the other. Lord Ienobu said, "The shogun is weaker this morning. He's passed more blood, he's on such a heavy dose of opium for the pain, he's rarely conscious."

Sano hadn't expected better news, but he hoped Ienobu was exaggerating the graveness of the shogun's condition.

"If you're saying there's not much time left before he dies, then get to the point," Yanagisawa said, his belligerence coated with suavity.

Lord Ienobu ignored Yanagisawa and said to Yoshisato, "You and I are the rivals for the succession. This is between us."

"So talk to me." Yoshisato was calm; maybe he'd attended similar councils with rival gang bosses. He exuded menace toward the man who'd had him kidnapped and imprisoned.

"I called you here to discuss a peace treaty," Lord Ienobu said.

It was as Sano had suspected: Lord Ienobu didn't really want a war. Cautious hope vied with disappointment in Sano. War was a samurai's proper element, and Sano instinctively hungered for it, but he had personal reasons for wanting to forestall this one. After destroying his marriage and his son's happiness, the least he could do was make peace so that his family wouldn't be killed in a war. Maybe then Reiko would forgive him; maybe she wouldn't leave him. And if there was peace between Yanagisawa and Lord Ienobu, his alliance with Yanagisawa wouldn't be necessary and they could call off Masahiro's wedding.

Maybe, maybe, said Yanagisawa's mocking voice in his memory.

"Why a peace treaty?" Yoshisato said with a tight half smile. "Are you afraid of losing a war?"

"Indeed not. I have the Tokugawa army, and the most powerful *daimyo* clans, backing me." Bravado puffed up Lord Ienobu. "*You're* the one who should be afraid."

"That's your idea of making peace?" Yanagisawa said indignantly. "You bluff us into surrendering?"

Sano surmised that both sides had come to the meeting because both wanted a way out of a war. But he knew they would fight if they had to;

their pride was at stake. The peace negotiations would fail if left up to them. Sano said, "Stop." The other men turned to him, surprised he'd interrupted. He appealed to Yoshisato. "At least listen to Lord Ienobu's terms."

Yoshisato's and Yanagisawa's expressions hardened. Sano sensed Yanagisawa remembering that he'd already lost one war. He surely must know he couldn't afford to lose this one. Second chances were rare.

Yoshisato flicked a warning glance at Yanagisawa, then asked coolly, "What are your terms?"

"Smart boy." Lord Ienobu grinned. "Here's what I want: You admit you're not the shogun's son. You give up your claim on the succession."

"Forget it!" Yanagisawa said with a scornful laugh, ignoring Sano's frown.

Lord Ienobu and Yoshisato had eyes only for each other. Yoshisato said, "What's in it for me?"

"I won't have you put to death when I'm shogun," Lord Ienobu said.

Yanagisawa said, "Hah!" Yoshisato glowered and said, "You insult me."

"That's not good enough, and you know it," Sano told Lord Ienobu. "Sweeten the deal."

"All right, all right." Lord Ienobu patted the air. "I'll make you both *daimyo*. You can each have your own province to rule."

"You can't buy us off!" Yanagisawa exclaimed.

"At least consider it," Sano urged. The carnage that would result from a war was dreadful to contemplate, and so was the outcome—Ienobu or Yanagisawa in power. Whoever won, Sano and his family would lose their lives. Sano had to keep both sides in play, to check each other. And this was a better deal than he'd thought Ienobu would offer.

"What, and be Lord Ienobu's subject?" Yoshisato's voice filled with disdain. "And pay him tributes every year? While he keeps my family in Edo as hostages to my good behavior? Never!"

Lord Ienobu shrugged with a false nonchalance that didn't hide his consternation. "Well, it was worth a try."

"Here's my counterproposal." Yoshisato leaned toward Ienobu. "You step down as Acting Shogun. *You* give up *your* claim on the dictatorship.

You crawl back in your hole, and when I'm shogun, I won't dig you out and step on you."

Ienobu reared up on his rickety knees. "You insolent young bastard!"

Yoshisato laughed, a breathy sound like tinder bursting into flame. "*I'm* a bastard? That's the skunk calling the tiger striped."

Morbidly sensitive about his illegitimacy, Ienobu wheezed and turned purple. Yanagisawa smiled, proud of Yoshisato for giving as good as he got. Frustrated because the men were foiling his attempts to save them and their country from themselves, Sano said, "Quit the personal remarks! The fate of Japan is the issue!"

"You're not just insolent, you're naïve," Lord Ienobu told Yoshisato. "You're so eager to go to war, but you don't know what war is like!"

"How would you know? How many battles have you fought?" Yoshisato's superior manner said he'd fought in plenty. His gaze raked Ienobu's scrawny physique, noted the shame on Ienobu's face. "Just as I thought. Not a single one."

"I've studied history," Ienobu huffed. "War destroys cities and crops and leaves thousands dead, both samurai and commoners. And you would risk that, on the small chance that you could beat me?" Scorn twisted his features. "You're a fool."

Manabe began to look anxious, for the first time Sano had ever seen. Yanagisawa lost his smile. Sano said, "That's enough!"

"You're a hypocrite," Yoshisato retorted. "Do you really expect me to believe you care about the crops or the commoners or anybody but yourself? But supposing you do, here's how to settle this: We fight a duel, one-on-one. Just you and me." He stood and flung his open palm at Ienobu. "Right here, right now."

"It's not a fair match," Manabe protested.

Even as he uttered a disdainful laugh, Ienobu recoiled from Yoshisato's hand. His involuntary reaction betrayed how much the challenge terrified him. "Don't be silly."

Yoshisato's lip curled with contempt. "Coward! You're not fit to be shogun."

Infuriated by the worst insult that anyone could level at a samurai, Lord Ienobu scrambled to his feet. His eyes bulged so large that they strained at the mesh of red veins across their whites. Manabe jumped up and reached for his sword; he'd forgotten he wasn't wearing it.

"And you think you are fit to be shogun? I at least have Tokugawa blood." Ienobu thumped his chest, then pointed a shaky finger at Yoshisato. "You're just Yanagisawa's dirty, stinking spawn."

Yanagisawa lunged at Ienobu. Sano stood and caught Yanagisawa. "How about a compromise? You both rule Japan—as co-shoguns."

Everyone stared at him in disbelief. "Are you insane?" Yanagisawa asked.

"In all of history there have never been two shoguns at the same time," Lord Ienobu said.

"There's not enough room at the top of the regime for both of us," Yoshisato said.

"A truce, then," Sano said in desperation. "To think this over. While I find out who stabbed the shogun."

Yanagisawa narrowed his eyes. "And give the shogun time to die, and Lord Ienobu time to steal the regime for good? Whose side are you on?"

"That would only postpone the inevitable." Yoshisato stood shoulder to shoulder with Yanagisawa. He said to Ienobu, "You won't be a battle virgin much longer."

White with rage now, Lord Ienobu spoke in a low voice that hissed through his bared, protruding teeth. "You won't have your head much longer."

27

AN EERIE HUSH lay over the guest quarters of the Mori
estate. It seemed to Reiko as if the world were holding its breath in suspense while she waited on the veranda for Sano to come back from his
meeting with Lord Ienobu. She didn't want to see him or speak to him,
but she was anxious to know what was happening.

In the empty garden below her, snow melted, exposing muddy brown
grass. Water dripped from the eaves. She pulled her cloak tighter around
her and paced to keep warm. She could have waited indoors with Midori
and the children, but the house was polluted by the evil spirits of the
people who'd once framed her for murder. She wondered how many
women throughout the ages had waited like this for their men to come
back. Had they been as restless and hungry for action as she?

She felt a prickling sensation of someone watching her. Across the
garden, on the opposite veranda, stood Lady Yanagisawa. Her flat face
was as expressionless as ever, but her anger blasted at Reiko like a
flame from a torch.

Tonight the two of them would be kinfolk, locked together by their
children's marriage.

Reiko's heart beat like wings that were trying to fly her body out of
a trap. She ran down the stairs without knowing where to go. She ran
through a gate, out of the guest quarters, and around the silent hulk of
the mansion. She ran away from the husband who'd betrayed her and

her son; she ran as if running could save her from the wedding, Yanagi-sawa, Lord Ienobu, and a war. She stopped when she lost her breath. Panting against the wall of the servants' barracks, she sank into despair. She couldn't leave her family, and she couldn't outrun her problems.

As she trudged back toward the guest quarters, a huge black dog with a blunt face, thick, sinewy muscles, and a sleek pelt bounded up to her. A leather collar studded with iron spikes circled its neck. Vapor puffed like smoke from its nostrils as it growled. It was one of Lord Mori's watch-dogs. Frightened, Reiko backed away into a narrow, vacant passage be-tween two outbuildings. The dog came closer and growled louder. She froze, afraid to move.

"Help!" she called.

The dog barked and bared its sharp teeth. Reiko slowly reached for the dagger strapped to her arm under her sleeve. She meant to use the weapon to scare the dog, not hurt it, but it interpreted her movement as aggression. It lunged. She screamed and flung up her arms to protect her face. The dog's massive weight knocked her down. Pinned under its huge paws, she beat at it while it slavered at her throat.

A high voice yelled, "Stop!"

The dog climbed off Reiko and sat beside her. She gasped with relief. Someone came running down the passage. Reiko sat up and stared in surprise at her daughter.

"Here, boy!" Akiko called. The dog trotted to her, wagging his stumpy tail. She knelt and scratched him behind his ears. His long red tongue licked her face.

"Be careful, he'll bite you!" Reiko cried.

"No, he won't, will you?" Akiko addressed the dog in a friendly but firm voice. He let her pet him, as though he recognized her as his mas-ter. She seemed suddenly much older than her nine years, her fierce spirit connecting her to her samurai ancestors. Then her face regained her usual childishly defiant expression. "I followed you. Are you mad at me?"

"No, no," Reiko said, ashamed of ever scolding Akiko for befriend-ing dogs. "You saved my life."

A long gaze bridged the distance between them. Much was spoken in silence that words couldn't convey. Reiko told Akiko how thankful she was. Akiko's face bloomed into a radiant smile: She was glad that for once she'd earned Reiko's approval. Reiko felt that even though she'd lost the baby and was about to lose her son, she'd found her daughter.

The moment was as fragile, perfect, and short-lived as a spring snowflake.

"Where were you going?" Akiko asked.

Reiko started to say she didn't know. Despair returned. Sano's meeting with Lord Ienobu could have no good outcome. Time was speeding toward Masahiro's wedding. Then she looked into Akiko's bright, lively eyes. Reiko felt a tingle, as if she'd tapped into Akiko's energy. She suddenly saw her young self in Akiko—the girl who'd once dressed as a boy, stolen a horse from her father's stable, and ridden around town. She hadn't been any more afraid of mean, unruly horses than Akiko was afraid of fierce dogs.

That girl wouldn't have let herself be trapped like a mouse in a box. She would have found a way out. Reiko felt boldness and adventurousness flowing back into her. She focused her attention on the dog, now tame and friendly. Her heart beat faster with sudden inspiration.

"Come with me," she told Akiko. "Bring the dog."

They hurried to the guest quarters. The dog trotted after Akiko. He waited on the veranda while Reiko found the iris fan, swathed in white cloth, which Sano had brought from the castle. She unwrapped the fan. The iron ribs and the cloth were stained with the shogun's blood. Reiko set the fan on a lacquer chest. It was the cloth she wanted.

"What are you going to do?" Akiko asked.

"I'm going to the castle to find the bloodstained socks," Reiko said.

Sano or Masahiro would have asked her why the missing socks mattered now, when the investigation had ceased. Reiko would have had to explain that she wanted to prove that Lord Ienobu really was responsible for the stabbing even though Madam Chizuru's confession was false. If Ienobu was condemned to death as punishment, Sano's alliance with Yanagisawa wouldn't be necessary and neither would Masahiro's marriage to Kikuko. Yoshisato would have a new chance to become shogun, but Reiko would worry about that later. Sano or Masahiro would have forbidden Reiko to leave the estate because it was too dangerous and her plan was foolish, but Akiko said, "Oh, I see! The dog can track the socks! Good!"

Akiko was smarter than Reiko had thought, another surprise. They hurried outside. Akiko held the cloth under the dog's nose. He sniffed the shogun's blood, sniffed the air, then barked and ran down the stairs. At the bottom he turned and barked.

"He wants you to follow him," Akiko said. "Can I go, too?" She looked suddenly peeved, expecting Reiko to say no.

Reiko hesitated. A mother shouldn't take her child into a city on the brink of war. But Reiko's notion of her maternal responsibility underwent a sudden change. Akiko was a member of the family; she shared its fate. Better for her to help her mother find the truth about the crime that had put them in peril than to sit at home waiting for their enemy to attack.

"Yes," Reiko said. If a war started, Akiko would be safer in the city streets than in this estate with Lord Ienobu's enemies, and Reiko needed her to handle the dog.

Delighted, Akiko smiled. The dog led them to a small gate near the kitchens. Reiko and Akiko struggled to lift the heavy bar. Opening the gate, Reiko saw the backs of four sentries who were stationed outside. The dog barked at the men. Startled, they turned. The dog bounded down the street.

"Come on, Mother!" Akiko cried.

Holding hands, they ran after the dog. Reiko felt connected to her daughter in a way she'd never thought possible. For once they were moving together instead of Reiko leaving, Akiko clinging, and Reiko pushing her away. The emptiness left by the baby Reiko had lost didn't feel so big or hurt quite so much.

"Hey!" the sentries yelled, but they couldn't desert their post to pursue two female guests who were running away with the master's dog.

Reiko and Akiko laughed at the sentries. Reiko knew they were foolhardy; Lord Ienobu's troops might recognize them as Sano's kinfolk, capture them, and use them to force him to surrender. But it felt so good to laugh again.

Nose snuffling, the dog loped through the *daimyo* district along narrow side streets, avoiding the army troops massed outside estates that belonged to Yanagisawa's allies. "How will we get in the castle?" Akiko asked.

Reiko envisioned the three of them marching up to the gate with no passes and no one to tell the sentries they were allowed to enter. But the missing socks must be inside the castle. The dog was leading her and Akiko in that direction. "I'll think of something."

Whereas Sano or Masahiro would have challenged her plan, Akiko blithely accepted it. The dog veered to the right, down a street that led away from the castle. "He's lost the scent," Reiko said, disappointed even though she'd known that this search was a long shot and the socks had probably been destroyed by the shogun's attacker. "He's going the wrong way."

"No, he's not." Akiko spoke with confidence in her new friend.

They followed the dog. He trotted faster to a canal that separated the *daimyo* district from the Nihonbashi merchant quarter. Reiko and Akiko and the dog crossed an arched wooden bridge. Behind them the walls of the *daimyo* estates rose straight up from the retaining wall that lined the canal; below them the gray water was frozen into muddy ice along the banks. The dog raced into a street of houses with balconies concealed by bamboo blinds above shuttered fronts on the ground floors. Nihonbashi was strangely deserted and quiet. The townspeople must have seen the troops massing in the *daimyo* district, realized a war was coming, and either hidden themselves indoors or fled. The dog rounded a corner and loped down the alley behind the houses. The stench of rotten food and human waste came from wooden bins and ceramic vats outside back doors. The garbage and night soil collectors must have stayed home or fled, too. Rats scampered as the dog sniffed around the bins on his way down the alley. A gray heap partially blocked the far end. The dog sat by it and barked.

"He's found them!" Akiko ran to the dog and petted him. "Good boy!"

The heap was ashes emptied from hearths and braziers. The dog began digging. He unearthed a tiny bundle just beneath the surface. He nosed it and looked up at Akiko. She picked it up and gave it to Reiko.

Reiko examined the wad of cloth, brushed off the soot, and separated it into two crumpled pieces stuck together by a reddish brown substance. Her breath quickened with excitement as she held up the bloodstained socks.

HIRATA STOOD IN a fire-watch tower high above Nihon-bashi, gazing down at the city. Commoners in palanquins and on foot streamed along the roads, heading out of town. The estates in the *daimyo* district were laid out like territorial divisions on a giant game board. Miniature troops lined the street outside Lord Mori's estate. Hirata trained his eyes on the white tent. His supernatural vision and hearing couldn't penetrate it, but he sensed Sano inside. Sano's aura resembled a jagged steel mesh around his core of courage. Auras from Yanagisawa, Yoshisato, and Lord Ienobu impinged on Sano like cannons firing red-hot missiles. The tent was the center of a cosmic storm, the focus of the fear, excitement, and anticipation crackling from the spectators' auras.

"Sano is in trouble," he said, appalled by the situation that he had helped create.

Before he could climb down the ladder and rush to Sano's aid, General Otani locked his hands onto the railing. *Stay away from Sano.*

The tower swayed on its stilts as Hirata, enraged, struggled to break his own grip. The fire bell suspended by a rope from the little roof above him swung and jangled. "I've done everything you asked. The least you could do is let me help Sano!"

Sano must be allowed to play his role.

"What role?"

You'll see.

"I'm sick of this!" Hirata demanded, "Why don't I just kill the shogun and Lord Ienobu can take over the regime?" He didn't balk at the trai-torous idea. The shogun was close to death; at worst Hirata would shorten his time on earth by only a few days.

Things must continue along their present course.

"Why? If you want Ienobu to be shogun, let's take the quickest route.

Then you won't need me anymore, or Sano. You can get the hell out of my body."

Laughter resounded through Hirata. *What makes you think that after Ienobu is shogun I'll let you go?*

Taken aback, Hirata said, "Won't our work be finished then?"

I want to destroy the Tokugawa regime. Helping Ienobu take it over is just the first step.

"The first step?" Dismay opened a cold chasm in Hirata's heart. "I thought that when he became shogun, he would destroy the regime for you. What more would there be for me to do?"

Lord Ienobu has enemies, as you well know. They'll interfere with his plans and try to oust him. We have to make sure he stays in power.

In that terrible moment Hirata understood that his enslavement to the ghost wasn't nearing its end. It had only begun.

28

WHEN SANO RETURNED to the guest quarters, he found Magistrate Ueda sitting alone by a brazier with a sake decanter warming on it and two cups on a tray table.

"I thought you might need a drink," Magistrate Ueda said.

Sano realized how much he did. "A thousand thanks." He knelt while Magistrate Ueda poured two cups. He emptied his cup, and the liquor spread a fire through him that simultaneously calmed and invigorated. "Where's Masahiro?"

"I thought he was at the gate, waiting for you."

"I didn't see him there."

Magistrate Ueda looked grave. "Maybe he needed some time alone. He's very unhappy about the wedding."

"I know." Sano's spirit sagged under the weight of his betrayal of Masahiro, no matter that he was within his rights to force his son to do whatever he asked. "Where is Reiko?"

The concern in Magistrate Ueda's expression deepened. "She went out with Akiko. They didn't say where they were going."

Sano felt a stab of fear. Reiko was as unhappy about the wedding as Masahiro. She'd been unhappy with Sano for a long time. She'd said she would leave him. Had she really gone and taken their children with her? Had his actions finally driven his family away?

214

One of Lord Mori's guards brought in Reiko and Akiko. Their faces were rosy from the cold. "Your wife and daughter took Lord Mori's dog for a walk." Annoyed by the whims of females, he said, "You'd better keep them in from now on," and left.

Sano's fear turned to anger at Reiko, then surprise as he noticed how animated, young, and bright-eyed she looked. He hadn't seen her look like that in years. Her beauty was stunning. "You went outside and you took Akiko? Don't you know it's dangerous out there?"

Akiko ran off to avoid an argument between her parents. The flush on Reiko's face darkened: She was still furious at Sano, and the nature of her fury had changed. No longer frantic, helpless, and wild, it was like fire blasting in a kiln. She said to her father, "Tell my husband that it's not any safer in here than it is outside."

Unhappily caught in the middle of the war between his daughter and son-in-law, Magistrate Ueda repeated Reiko's words. Sano, upset because Reiko wouldn't speak directly to him, afraid that the next time she left it would be permanent, said, "Never mind. She's right."

"Ask him what happened with Lord Ienobu," Reiko said, unappeased.

Magistrate Ueda asked. "He tried to bribe Yanagisawa and Yoshisato into backing down," Sano said. "It didn't work. They exchanged threats and insults. I tried to negotiate a truce, but I was unsuccessful."

Reiko and Magistrate Ueda looked disappointed but resigned. "So there will be a war?" Reiko said, not looking at Sano.

"Yes."

"Starting when?" Magistrate Ueda asked. "Who's going to make the first move?"

"It's anybody's guess." Sano went along with the pretense of communicating through Magistrate Ueda. "My wife didn't really go out to walk a dog. Ask her what she was doing."

Reiko described how the dog had attacked her and Akiko had saved her. "It gave me an idea." She explained that the dog had tracked the scent of the shogun's blood to an ash heap in Nihonbashi. "He found the bloodstained socks."

Sano didn't know whether to be more impressed with Akiko's talents or Reiko's ingenuity. He was surprised that the socks had somehow made their way out of the castle. "Ueda-*san*, ask your daughter to let me see them. And ask her why she looks so upset."

"Because my honorable husband isn't going to like this part." Reiko took the wadded, dirty socks from under her sash and handed them to Magistrate Ueda; he handed them to Sano. "Look inside the ankles."

Sano saw tiny characters embroidered in pale gray thread: *Tomoe*. He crumpled the socks in his fist.

"I take it that they incriminate someone other than Lord Ienobu?" Magistrate Ueda said.

"Yes. Lord Yoshimune's cousin, the concubine."

They all sat in glum silence, wishing the evidence proved that Lord Ienobu had conspired to assassinate the shogun, for then the shogun would disown him and put him to death and the war would be nipped in the bud.

"But the socks are still an important clue," Reiko announced to the air. "It could solve the crime."

"And the shogun wants the crime solved." Duty was duty for Sano, even though the expected outcome—Tomoe and Lord Yoshimune put to death for the crime; Lord Ienobu off the hook—wasn't to his liking. "I'll have to pursue it."

"Pursue what?" Yoshisato said from the doorway.

Sano, Reiko, and Magistrate Ueda tensed. A chill penetrated the warm room. Even though Yoshisato was ostensibly their ally, it was as if the enemy had just breached their sanctuary. "What are you doing here?" Sano said, angry at Yoshisato for throwing away the chance of peace with Lord Ienobu.

"Yanagisawa-*san* asked me to deliver a message. The wedding is still on. It will take place tonight, at the hour of the dog."

Reiko's breath made a soft, angry hissing sound. Sano said, "Yanagisawa-*san* virtually has my whole family hostage." And he was sitting on Sano's secret about Dr. Ito. "Isn't that a good enough guarantee of my loyalty?"

Yoshisato shrugged, as if to say, *you know Yanagisawa*. He backtracked to the question he'd asked. "What are you going to pursue?"

When Sano hesitated, Yoshisato said, "You leave the estate, you walk straight into the army's hands. I'll give you an escort, but only if you tell me what you're up to."

Sano realized that he couldn't expect to get anywhere safely by himself. He told Yoshisato about Reiko and Akiko and the dog, then showed him Tomoe's bloodstained socks.

Yoshisato thoughtfully stroked his chin. "I see." Sano had an odd feeling that Yoshisato saw more than just the fact that the socks were evidence against the wrong person. "You should have a talk with Tomoe and Lord Yoshimune." As he departed, he said, "I owe you something for putting up with Yanagisawa-*san*. Some of our troops will be waiting for you at the gate."

Sano had an even odder feeling that Yoshisato's motive was different from what he'd said, but Sano was in no position to quibble.

"Well!" Reiko said. "He's much better than I expected. I do believe he really wants to find out who stabbed the shogun even if it's not Lord Ienobu."

She felt Yoshisato's power of attraction, Sano thought. He found himself jealous because Reiko admired another man and she hadn't admired Sano for a long time. "Don't be too sure about that." He rose as he cautioned himself as well as Reiko, "He's still Yanagisawa's son."

ACCOMPANIED BY TWO hundred soldiers borrowed from Lord Mori, Sano rode to Lord Yoshimune's estate. The army troops didn't try to arrest him. Sano figured that Lord Ienobu didn't want them starting a fight that would begin the war before he was ready.

There were no army troops outside Lord Yoshimune's estate. Yoshimune numbered among the *daimyo* who hadn't taken sides in the power struggle. The gate sentries quickly obtained permission for Sano to enter. They made him go in alone, but they didn't confiscate his swords or frisk him. That constituted a friendly reception these days.

Inside the mansion, Sano found Lord Yoshimune and Tomoe seated in the reception chamber. Musicians played flute, samisen, and drum while the young *daimyo* and his beautiful cousin sang a romantic song to each other. The duo exchanged fond smiles and soulful looks as they finished their song. Whatever doubt Sano had had that they were lovers was gone now. The *daimyo* saw Sano standing in the doorway, smiled, and said, "Greetings. Please come in."

He didn't seem embarrassed to be caught in an intimate moment. Nor did he seem to think he had anything to fear, Sano thought as he knelt near the group. Either Lord Yoshimune had no idea why Sano was here or he was supremely self-confident. But fear widened Tomoe's limpid eyes.

"Have you eaten? May I offer you refreshments?" Lord Yoshimune gestured toward a spread of sliced raw fish and pickled vegetables.

"No, thank you," Sano said politely.

Cunning sharpened Lord Yoshimune's good humor. "Of course this isn't a social call. It wouldn't be, while we're on the brink of a war." He'd evidently heard what had happened at the council. "If you're here to ask me to join Yanagisawa's faction, my answer is no. I shall remain neutral."

"I understand." Sano understood that Lord Yoshimune was content to let Yanagisawa and Lord Ienobu fight it out by themselves. Then, whoever won wouldn't punish him; he would keep his fief, his wealth, and his life. "That's not why I'm here."

Disconcerted, Lord Yoshimune said, "Well," then dismissed the musicians. Tomoe rose to follow them out of the room.

"Stay here," Sano said. "This concerns you, too."

She threw a pleading glance at Lord Yoshimune. He nodded at her, and she reluctantly sank to her knees beside him. He narrowed his eyes at Sano. "What do you want with us?"

Sano was uncomfortably aware of being alone in the territory of a powerful man he was about to accuse of murder. "There's been a new development in my investigation."

Lord Yoshimune's eyebrows lifted. "You're still investigating the attack on the shogun? At a time like this?"

"The shogun's order is still my duty to obey."

"What has this new development to do with us?"

"We found the socks that the attacker wore." Sano took a pouch from under his sash, loosened the drawstring, and removed the bloodstained socks. Holding one between the thumb and forefinger of each hand, he dangled them in front of Tomoe. "They're yours."

Tomoe shrank from him, her mouth opening wider than her eyes. Inarticulate with panic, she turned to Lord Yoshimune.

Lord Yoshimune patted her hand. "Don't worry." He told Sano, "Those look like any pair of women's socks."

"Observe the labels." Sano pointed out the embroidered characters.

Lord Yoshimune snatched the socks, brushed off soot, frowned at the characters and the stains. Was he genuinely surprised to see his cousin's socks with the shogun's blood on them? Or was he only surprised because he'd thought they would never show up? Unable to tell, Sano turned to Tomoe. "Are these yours?"

The horrified recognition on her face was her answer.

"Did you stab the shogun?" Sano asked.

She shook her head. Her eyes pleaded with Lord Yoshimune to rescue her. Lord Yoshimune demanded, "How do you know that's the shogun's blood?"

"Lord Mori's watchdog smelled the blood from the iron fan and tracked down the socks. It's the same blood."

Lord Yoshimune studied Sano closely and seemed to decide that he was telling the truth. "My cousin didn't do it." He sounded certain of that but distressed by the evidence to the contrary. "There must be some other explanation."

Tomoe tugged his sleeve, reached up to whisper in his ear.

He listened; his face relaxed. "She says a pair of her socks was missing from her room in the Large Interior. She noticed right before she came home with me. The shogun's attacker must have stolen them because they were marked with her name, and worn them in order to make her look guilty."

It wasn't impossible, and Sano wondered if Tomoe had the presence of mind to invent this quick excuse, but he said, "If the attacker wanted to frame Tomoe, then the socks would have been left in the open, someplace where they'd be easily found. But they weren't."

Lord Yoshimune's features tensed again. "Where were they?"

"In an ash heap just outside the *daimyo* district." Sano watched realization darken Lord Yoshimune's eyes. "You see the problem: There are two other suspects—Lady Nobuko and Madam Chizuru. Neither left the castle after the stabbing. But Tomoe did. With you."

"Are you accusing me of hiding these?" Indignant, Lord Yoshimune shook the socks at Sano.

"She could have concealed them under her clothes and given them to you outside the castle. It would have been easy for you to bury the socks on your way home."

Lord Yoshimune uttered an irate laugh. "If she had stabbed the shogun—which she didn't—and if I had wanted to hide the evidence— which *I* didn't—then I would have been smart enough to destroy them, not dump them a short distance from my estate."

Although Sano had to admit it was a good point, he said, "You might have thought they were hidden well enough because nobody would look outside the castle."

Lord Yoshimune stood with an impatient, angry motion. Tomoe scrambled to her feet and cowered behind him as he said, "Don't you see what's going on? Someone is trying to frame Tomoe, just like Yanagisawa tried to frame Lord Ienobu. Only this person has learned that you won't accept a fake confession."

"If you really think the socks were planted and Tomoe is innocent, then you won't mind if I search your estate."

Lord Yoshimune chuckled. "Go right ahead." Either he was sure he'd gotten rid of any other evidence against Tomoe or he was sure no one could have planted any inside his own domain. "It's a big place for you to search by yourself, and I'm not letting you bring in helpers. I heard that Yanagisawa's men tried to smuggle blood into the Large Interior."

A search was a long shot as well as a huge undertaking. Sano didn't want to believe that Tomoe and Lord Yoshimune were guilty, but he had to follow up on his clue. "I'll start with Tomoe's room."

Displeased, yet confident that he would be vindicated, Lord Yoshi-mune led Sano to the women's quarters. Tomoe anxiously trailed them to a chamber lively with color. A painted mural depicted butterflies in a garden; brightly patterned kimonos hung on stands; on the dressing table, hair ornaments made of beads and silk flowers adorned a carved jade tree. Shelves held a collection of dolls. It was the room of a child, but Sano smelled a man's wintergreen hair oil and a faint animal odor of sex. Lord Yoshimune had recently visited Tomoe here, and not to play dolls. Lord Yoshimune watched with alert, unfriendly eyes as Sano looked inside a cabinet full of clothes. Tomoe clung to Lord Yoshimune; he absently stroked her hair. Sano's attention moved to a red lacquer writing desk. He crouched, lifted the lid, and revealed a jumble of writing brushes and inkstones amid papers covered with childish, blotched calligraphy. The top sheet was a love poem, probably a lyric from a popular song. Sano riffled the others and stopped at a page written in a different hand.

"What's that?" Lord Yoshimune left Tomoe and swiftly crossed the room.

Sano rose, held up the page, and pointed at the character stamped in red ink at the bottom. "It's a letter signed with your seal." He read aloud, " 'Tonight, while the shogun is asleep, sneak into his chamber and stab him to death with this iron fan. Then go back to the Large Interior and wait for me. Don't be afraid. I'll take care of everything. I love you.' "

"*What?*" Lord Yoshimune said with bewildered indignation, "Let me see that." He snatched the letter from Sano. "I didn't write this! It's not even my handwriting! I never told Tomoe to stab the shogun!"

"Then who did write it?" Sano asked even as he realized that the letter could be a forgery, another attempt to steer him in the wrong direction. "Who put it there?"

Lord Yoshimune looked at his cousin, who hovered near the door. "Tomoe-*san*?" For the first time his confidence seemed shaken, his fondness for her shaded by suspicion. "Have you seen this before?"

She wordlessly shook her head. A tear welled in each of her eyes and rolled down each cheek. Lord Yoshimune gave her a brief, intense scrutiny, then turned back to Sano. His eyes flashed with anger. "I think *you* stole Tomoe's socks, and stained them with the shogun's blood, after I took her away from the castle."

Sano had expected Lord Yoshimune to invent an explanation, but this one offended him. "I didn't!"

Lord Yoshimune jabbed his finger at Sano. "And *you* forged the letter. Who planted it in my house? Which of my people is your flunky?"

"No one," Sano said, angered by the suggestion that he was so corrupt. "I haven't anybody in your house working for me. Why would I want to frame Tomoe?"

"For Yanagisawa. Is this his ploy to force me to ally with him against Lord Ienobu? Did he send you to 'find' this letter? Were you going to threaten to expose me as a traitor?"

"No!" But Sano supposed that was the real reason Yoshisato had sent him here—to blackmail Lord Yoshimune into an alliance.

Lord Yoshimune shoved Sano. "Get out of my house before I kill you!" Again he'd lost his veneer of civility along with his temper and resorted to physical force. "Tell Yanagisawa he'll rot in hell before I cave in to him!"

29

WHEN SANO RETURNED to Lord Mori's estate, the Tokugawa troops were camped in the street, fanning their bonfires, and eating rations of dried fish, pickled vegetables, and rice balls. Sano felt their restlessness, their impatience for battle, as they raked him with their hostile gazes. Inside the estate, troops dragged guns, cannons, kegs of gunpowder, and crates of bullets from the arsenal. Lord Mori strode about with his watchdogs, inspecting the munitions. Archers on the roofs attached written messages to arrows and fired them into the estates of Lord Mori's nearest allies. That was the securest form of communication; a message carried by hand or shouted could be intercepted by Lord Ienobu's men. Sano found Yoshisato and Yanagisawa in the main reception chamber with Lord Mori's officers. The chamber was now a command station. The men crouched on the floor over a huge map of Edo Castle, conversing in urgent tones as they pointed to locations on the map.

"What's going on here?" Sano asked.

Yanagisawa and Yoshisato looked up; their faces were aglow with excitement, resolute with purpose. "We're planning to invade Edo Castle," Yanagisawa said.

Astonishment silenced Sano. This was wrong for so many reasons! Yanagisawa smiled thinly at his expression. "Did you swallow your tongue?"

"We're going to capture the castle, kill Lord Ienobu, and seize the dictatorship," Yoshisato said. "His allies will fall into line with us. Or would you rather we wait like ducks on a pond for his army to blast us out of the water?"

Sano forbore to point out the dishonor of attacking the seat of the regime they were duty-bound to serve. Yanagisawa didn't care about that. Nor did he or Yoshisato apparently care that they were taking a huge risk. "In case you've forgotten, the shogun is inside Edo Castle." Sano reminded Yoshisato, "You're supposed to be his son, in case you've forgotten that, too. Attack the castle, and he could be killed."

"My father has disowned me. We're nothing to each other." Yoshisato spoke in a strange tone of voice, with a sidelong glance at Yanagisawa. "If he dies during the invasion, he'll be just another casualty of war."

It was no more use appealing to Yanagisawa's feelings, but Sano tried. "The shogun has been your friend for more than twenty years." *And your lover for some of them.* "Would you really fight a war around him while he's helpless in bed? Have you no loyalty at all?"

"Loyalty is beside the point," Yanagisawa said, more impatient with than offended by Sano's criticism. "The shogun is done for. He may be dead even as we speak. I haven't been able to get any more news about his condition. But you can bet that if he's still alive, Lord Ienobu will hurry him into the grave. He's already tried to assassinate him once."

"It looks as if Lord Ienobu isn't responsible for the stabbing," Sano said.

"Oh?" Yoshisato said. "What did you learn from Tomoe and Lord Yoshimune?"

Startled, Yanagisawa said, "You went to see them?"

"Yes," Sano said.

"When was this?"

"Just now." Sano explained about the bloodstained socks. "Tomoe admitted they're hers, but she and Lord Yoshimune still claim she's innocent and they were framed. Then I found this in her room." Sano produced the letter, handed it to Yoshisato.

After Yoshisato read it aloud, Yanagisawa exclaimed in fury, "You sneaked behind my back to follow a clue that pointed to someone other than Lord Ienobu? And you criticize *my* loyalty?"

"I didn't sneak," Sano said. "Yoshisato gave me permission."

Yanagisawa turned to glare at Yoshisato, who nodded coolly and asked Sano, "What happened with Lord Yoshimune?"

Sano explained. "He accused me of fabricating the evidence and trying to blackmail him into joining our faction. He threw me out."

"You should have tried." Yoshisato's lack of surprise told Sano that really was why Yoshisato had let him pursue a line of inquiry that seemed counter to his and Yanagisawa's interests—to force Lord Yoshimune's allegiance.

"Did you plant the letter in his estate?" Sano asked.

"No. It wouldn't have been a bad idea, but I couldn't have gotten in there." Yoshisato sounded truthful; Sano believed him.

Yanagisawa's anger encompassed both Sano and Yoshisato. "Never go behind my back again." He jabbed his finger at Sano. "Keep quiet about this."

"The shogun deserves to know what's happening with the investigation," Sano said.

"How are you going to tell him? Lord Ienobu won't let you in the palace." Yanagisawa said impatiently, "Enough of this. We have an invasion to plan." He turned to the generals, who'd been eavesdropping while they pretended to study the map.

"I'm opposed to the invasion," Sano said.

"It's not up to you," Yanagisawa said.

"We're allies. I should have a say."

Yanagisawa laughed scornfully. "You should have remembered that we were allies when you discredited Madam Chizuru's confession. If you'd left well enough alone, Lord Ienobu wouldn't be a problem now."

"Don't go through with it," Sano said with increasing desperation.

"Skip the speech about honor. If you want to demonstrate honor, save it for the battle. In the meantime, if you're not going to help with the plans, go prepare for your son's wedding."

* * *

TEMPLE BELLS RANG the hour of the dog. Their discordant peals echoed across the dark, misty city and sank into the anxious hush that engulfed the wedding party assembled in a small reception chamber at the Mori estate. Sano, Reiko, and Magistrate Ueda, Akiko, Midori, Taeko, and Detective Marume knelt in a row on the right side of the alcove decorated with a scroll that bore the names of Shinto deities and an altar that held rice cakes and a jar of sake. A Shinto priest in a white robe and tall white cap, and the estate's female housekeeper, knelt in front of the alcove, near a dais on which stood a miniature pine and plum tree and bamboo grove in a flat porcelain dish, and the statues of a hare and a crane—symbols of longevity, pliancy, and fidelity. On the alcove's left side, Yanagisawa knelt by his wife. Lord Mori sat behind Kikuko, the bride, in the center of the room. Kikuko wore a white silk kimono; a long white drape covered her face and hair. The place beside her, reserved for the groom, was vacant.

Yanagisawa leveled a warning gaze at Sano. "Your son had better show up."

"He will," Sano said curtly.

Reiko twisted her cold, damp hands under her sleeves. She was horrified by Masahiro's deliberate flouting of authority, furious at him because unless he honored the bargain Sano had made, his family would lose their alliance with Yanagisawa and be thrown to Lord Ienobu like meat to a wolf. But she was even more furious at Sano. She couldn't help hoping Masahiro would stay away. She wanted to shake Sano and curse him for getting them into this.

Sano sat there, impervious to her thoughts. Reiko remembered their own wedding, and her heart ached. She'd been so young and innocent, so fearful of marriage yet so hopeful for happiness. Now, after almost nineteen years together, the bridegroom she'd fallen in love with had sold their son into this travesty of a marriage. Everything about it was wrong. A proper wedding required two priests instead of just the one who resided at the Mori estate, and two Shinto shrine attendants instead of the housekeeper. But the troops outside wouldn't let anybody enter the estate. The incorrect procedure seemed to put the final seal of doom on Masahiro. Reiko had wanted so much better for him! Her anger at Sano flared so hotly, she thought that if she looked directly at him she would catch on fire.

Magistrate Ueda regarded her with the helpless sorrow of a parent who cannot ease his child's pain. Midori wore the same expression as she watched Taeko. Taeko had begged to attend the wedding, but her eyes were red and puffy from crying. Lady Yanagisawa sat so stiffly that the body inside her drab maroon silk kimono could have been made of stone. Her flat, homely face was still, except for her eyes; they darted as if chasing unruly thoughts between her husband, Kikuko, and Reiko. Her rouged lips were parted, and a flush reddened the skin at the opening of her robe, where the white powder applied to her face and neck stopped. A chill tingled through Reiko.

This was how Lady Yanagisawa had looked just before she'd tried to kill Reiko.

If the wedding proceeded, this woman would be Masahiro's mother-in-law. Heaven only knew what she would do then.

AS LADY YANAGISAWA beheld her daughter, her outrage escaped her body like hot, poisonous wisps of smoke from a volcano. Poor, innocent Kikuko, blinded by the drape over her head, was like a white calf ready for slaughter. She didn't know what was happening. Lady Yanagisawa had tried to explain, but the best she could do was playact a wedding using Kikuko's dolls, to teach Kikuko how to behave at the ceremony. Kikuko thought marriage was a game. She didn't understand that she was chattel in a pact her father had made with the husband of her mother's enemy. Lady Yanagisawa desperately wished Masahiro wouldn't show up. The boy would defile Kikuko for his own pleasure while scorning her because she was feebleminded. Murderous thoughts and impulses swirled through Lady Yanagisawa. She viewed Reiko through the black scribble of blood in her ruptured eye.

If only Kikuko had drowned Reiko's son when he was a baby! This horrible day would never have come.

Lady Yanagisawa wanted to grab Kikuko and run, but the presence of her husband, seated beside her, held her down like an iron anchor. A small, craven part of her hoped that if she did what he wanted . . . love was too much to expect; she would settle for an occasional friendly word and visit to her bed. She couldn't give up her hope that he would change. She would do anything to keep that hope alive. She would even offer up Kikuko as a sacrifice, no matter her awful guilt. Her husband and her daughter were her two loves; they had equal claims on her heart.

A stir rustled through the room. Lady Yanagisawa heard breaths released by the other people. An awful, sick sensation caved in her stomach as she looked in the direction of their gazes. There in the doorway stood Masahiro.

NO, NO, NO!

Taeko pressed her hand to her mouth, stifling the cries that rose in her. She'd been praying that Masahiro wouldn't come for the wedding. All day she'd hoped he was making arrangements to run away with her and they would elope and then she could tell him about the baby. But now, as he stalked into the room, Taeko understood that his tardiness was the only protest he would make against this marriage. His loyalty to his parents was too strong to break.

Masahiro didn't look at her, or anyone else, as he dropped to his knees beside Kikuko. He wore his ordinary clothes instead of the black ceremonial garments appropriate for a wedding. Taeko smelled liquor on him: He must have sneaked out to a teahouse. But his eyes were clear; he looked completely sober and utterly defeated.

Lord Mori, the master of ceremonies, said, "We are gathered here to unite Sano Masahiro and Yanagisawa Kikuko in marriage."

Taeko flung a pleading glance around the room. Her mother looked distraught, Sano grim, Reiko desolate. No one objected. The priest rose, bowed to the altar, swished a long wand tasseled with white paper strips, and intoned, "Evil out, fortune in!" He chanted an invocation to the gods and beat a wooden drum. The familiar ritual brought tears to Taeko's eyes. She'd so hoped to wed Masahiro, and there he sat like a chained prisoner beside another girl.

The housekeeper brought Masahiro and Kikuko a tray containing three flat wooden cups, graduated in size, nested together. She poured sake out of the jar from the altar into the smallest cup, then bowed to Kikuko and offered her the cup. Jealousy assailed Taeko like a wolf tearing at her heart as Kikuko accepted the cup, raised it to her mouth under her white head drape, and took three sips with her face still concealed. Taeko wanted to snatch the cup, fling it against the wall, and halt the *san-san-ku-do*—the "three-times-three sips" pledge that would seal the marriage bond between Kikuko and Masahiro. But if she interfered, it wouldn't stop the wedding; it would only get her thrown out of the room, and she wanted to be with Masahiro for as long as she could.

Kikuko handed the empty cup back to the housekeeper, who refilled the cup and offered it to Masahiro. His expression was surly as he took it. Knowing that he didn't want this marriage gave Taeko some comfort. He turned the cup in his hands so that he wouldn't have to put his mouth to the rouge-stained place on the rim where Kikuko's lips had touched. He drank his three sips quickly, as if downing poison. Sourness lapped Taeko's throat. Fighting the urge to vomit, she blinked back tears while the pair drank from their second cup. As Masahiro sipped from the third, final cup, she felt her bond with him dissolve, like a spiderweb immersed in acid.

He and Kikuko were now married. No matter how much he loved Taeko, he wasn't hers anymore. Under her sleeves Taeko clasped her hands tight over her belly, shielding the child within, containing her grief.

The housekeeper served sake to Sano, Reiko, Yanagisawa, and Lady Yanagisawa, honoring the new alliance between the two families. Taeko's lips formed the words that everyone else spoke: "*Omedetō gozaimasu—* congratulations!" The housekeeper handed Masahiro and Kikuko branches with white paper strips attached and led them to the altar to make their offering to the gods. They bowed and laid the branches on the altar.

"The ceremony is completed," the priest announced. "The bride and groom can begin their married life."

Despair crushed Taeko. Tears fell, burning on her cheeks. The housekeeper began to lift the drape off the bride's head. Taeko thought, *Please let her be ugly!*

The drape slipped from Kikuko. She was the most beautiful girl Taeko had ever seen. A cold, sickening hollow opened up inside Taeko. It filled with awe, envy, and so much pain that she couldn't breathe.

Kikuko turned to Masahiro. Her long-lashed black eyes sparkled at him. Her delicate lips curved in a shy smile. Masahiro gazed at Kikuko with eyes and mouth wide open, as dazzled as if struck by lightning. Taeko's heart gave an agonized thump. Masahiro had never looked at her that way.

Masahiro bowed to Yanagisawa and, in a dazed voice, thanked him for the honor of joining his clan. He never took his eyes off Kikuko as she bowed and murmured her thanks to Sano and Reiko. He seemed to have forgotten that anyone besides his new wife existed.

No, no, no!

THE WEDDING BANQUET was the most miserable affair Sano had ever attended. He and Reiko, Akiko, Magistrate Ueda, and Detective Marume sat in the dim, drafty hall, opposite Yanagisawa and his wife. Masahiro and Kikuko sat together at the head of the room. Maids put food on tray tables set before the members of the party. Taeko had run out of the house sobbing; Midori had gone after her. Lord Mori had excused himself, saying he had to prepare for the war. The bridal couple and their families were left to go through the motions of celebration.

No one spoke. Sano glanced at the dishes of miso soup, dried fish, pickled vegetables, and rice cakes on his tray. It was poor fare for a wedding banquet, which normally featured many courses of delicacies. Food stores in the estate were already running low due to the blockade by the army. Sano couldn't eat. The sight of his son wedded to Yanagisawa's daughter filled him with so much anger that his body had no room for nourishment. Reiko and Magistrate Ueda didn't eat, either. Sano knew they were sick at heart behind their stoic expressions. Marume and Akiko didn't touch their food, although they were probably starving. Yanagisawa shoveled in his meal, fortifying himself for the battle. His wife toyed with her chopsticks, her face blank as she watched Masahiro and Kikuko.

Kikuko ate hungrily, dropping morsels on her white kimono, smiling at Masahiro. Masahiro chewed and swallowed as if unaware of what he was eating. He hadn't taken his eyes off Kikuko since he'd first seen her face. Although Sano had hoped Masahiro could accept his marriage, his obvious infatuation with Kikuko made Sano feel more uneasy than relieved. Sano glanced at Reiko. She wouldn't look at him. He knew with a desolate heart that this wedding marked the end of his own marriage.

Yanagisawa raised his eyebrow at Masahiro and Kikuko and said with a sardonic smile, "It's time the newlyweds retired for the night."

A maid helped Kikuko rise. Masahiro jumped to his feet so fast that he upset his tray table. He flushed with embarrassment. Yanagisawa chuckled. Sano felt Reiko seething with helpless anger beside him. Masahiro shambled out of the room beside Kikuko. Sano was so furious, he would have done something catastrophic had Lord Mori not returned at that moment.

"There's news from the castle," Lord Mori said to Yanagisawa. "One of your spies managed to smuggle out a message."

Apprehension clutched Sano's heart. He heard Reiko gasp. Yanagisawa demanded, "Is it about the shogun?" His features were taut with his fear that the shogun had died, Lord Ienobu was the new dictator, and his own chances of ruling Japan were drastically diminished.

"The shogun is worse than yesterday but still alive," Lord Mori said. "Lord Ienobu has requisitioned troops from the Tokugawa branch clans, and he expects them to arrive by tomorrow afternoon. He plans to attack us then. By the way, someone did die at the palace today. It was the boy who was sleeping with the shogun during the stabbing."

30

"WHAT MAKES YOU think the boy was murdered?" Detective Marume asked. "Didn't he have the measles?"

"Young, healthy people often recover from the measles," Sano said. "The circumstances of his death are suspicious."

"The only witness to the stabbing dies suddenly while Lord Ienobu, our favorite suspect, is in charge at the castle? You're right," Marume said.

Their voices echoed in dank, earth-scented air. They were walking single file, Marume leading, through Lord Mori's secret emergency exit. All *daimyo* estates had at least one. This was a narrow, low-ceilinged tunnel that started beneath the mansion and ran under the streets. The lantern Marume carried illuminated earthen walls shored up with planks and posts driven into a rocky clay floor. Sano felt as if he were marching to hell, but they couldn't risk another trip through Lord Ienobu's troops.

The tunnel angled sharply to the left. Water that smelled of sewage dripped down Sano's neck. His feet sloshed in puddles from cesspools aboveground. Marume suddenly stopped. "Here we are, not a moment too soon."

Breathing welcome fresh air, they pushed on the iron grille at the end of the tunnel. The grille swung outward. They emerged from a hole in a stone wall and skidded down the steep, slippery bank of a canal. They hurried along the footpath, then through a city lit by a moon that shone through the fog. Smoke from chimneys was the only sign of the citizens who hadn't fled town. Sano and Marume took a circuitous route through alleys foul with accumulated garbage and night soil, avoiding the army troops who patrolled the main streets. They reached the slum district of Kodemma-chō. Its shacks, piles of debris left over from the earthquake, and roving stray dogs glowed eerily in the light from a fire burning within the high walls that surrounded Edo Jail. The smoke stank of charred human flesh.

"At least we don't have to worry about Yanagisawa finding out where we're going," Marume said.

Sano had had to tell Yanagisawa. He wouldn't have been able to leave the estate without cooperation from Yanagisawa and Lord Mori. At first Yanagisawa had objected because he'd thought Sano meant to betray him again. Sano hadn't wanted to leave his family alone with Yanagisawa, but his instincts told him that investigating Dengoro's death could change the course of events. He'd explained that he had to examine the body; he'd promised Yanagisawa evidence that would prove Lord Ienobu was responsible for the attack on the shogun and the elimination of the witness, and the evidence of his guilt should turn his allies among the *daimyo* and Tokugawa branch clans against Ienobu. After a heated argument, after warning Sano that his family would suffer if he didn't behave himself, Yanagisawa had capitulated. Lord Mori had shown Sano the secret exit. Sano only hoped he could deliver on his promise.

"I never thought I'd be glad that Yanagisawa knows about my business here," Sano said as he and Marume crossed the rickety bridge over the canal that served as a moat for the jail.

The sentries at the ironclad gates recognized Sano even though he hadn't been there in more than four years. He paid them to keep quiet about his visits. They let him and Marume in. The smoke grew thicker, acrid, and nauseating as Sano and Marume walked through the prison compound, past the guards' barracks and the dungeon, to a yard enclosed by a bamboo fence. Flames roared from a pit dug near the morgue, a low building with a thatched roof. Human shapes swathed in white cloth lay in a row on the ground—people who'd died of the measles and had to be cremated right away, lest they spread the disease. A man dressed in a leather cape, hood, boots, and gloves dragged a corpse over to the pit and pushed it in. The thud puffed cinders and ash up through the smoke and flames. Sano hoped Dengoro's body wasn't already burned up. Another man, stoop-shouldered in his fire gear, leaning on a wooden cane, watched from a safe distance.

"Dr. Ito?" Sano said.

Both men turned. The watcher said, "Who's there?" and pulled off his hood. His shaggy white hair blew in the smoky wind. His face was deeply lined, his skin blotched with brown spots. Missing teeth slackened his mouth. Although Sano had known Dr. Ito must be at least ninety, he was shocked by the changes that time had wrought upon his old friend.

"It's Sano-*san*," the other man said, bowing to Sano and Marume.

Sano recognized Mura, Dr. Ito's longtime assistant. His hair was white, too, his square face craggier. Mura took Dr. Ito's arm. Ordinarily a man of Mura's status would never touch a man of Dr. Ito's. Mura belonged to the class of outcasts, who were considered spiritually unclean because of their hereditary link with dirty, death-related occupations such as butchering and leather tanning. They also collected garbage and night soil and worked as corpse handlers, torturers, and executioners. Dr. Ito was a renowned physician, but after he'd been caught practicing foreign science and sentenced to a lifelong custodianship at Edo Morgue, he'd been cut off from polite society. Mura had become his friend. Now Dr. Ito extended a groping hand into the air and Mura guided him to Sano, who experienced a stab of concern.

"Can't you see me?" Sano asked.

Dr. Ito's once-keen eyes were filmy with cataracts. "I've gone blind," he said in the matter-of-fact tone of a man who has accepted his disability.

"I'm sorry." Sano was grieved by his friend's loss, the end of Dr. Ito's life as a scientist. He felt selfish, having two more or less good eyes, his relative youth, and his health. No matter that he'd alienated his wife and son for the sake of an alliance with his worst enemy—he'd had a choice.

Dr. Ito smiled with the sardonic humor he hadn't lost. "I hope you're not here because you want me to conduct an examination of a murder victim. My days of practicing illegal science are over. I just pretend to supervise the morgue while Mura does all the work."

"That is why I came," Sano said, "but never mind. It probably wasn't a murder. The boy had measles. Chances are, examining his body wouldn't have revealed anything else." He didn't want Dr. Ito to think he'd let Sano down. "I'm glad just to see you again."

"I am glad, too, but I have heard that things have not gone well for you." Dr. Ito's expression mixed concern with pleasure. "Associating with me is an additional hazard."

"Not as much of a hazard as before. Yanagisawa knows." Sano gave a brief summary of recent events.

Dr. Ito chuckled. "No matter how old one gets, surprises never cease." He grew somber again. "Even if Yanagisawa isn't a problem, you are running the risk of capture by Lord Ienobu's troops. I would hate for you to have taken the risk for nothing. Let us examine this boy who died. What was his name?" Sano hesitated, wondering how much good an examination by a blind scientist would do. Dr. Ito said, "Mura can show you the body. Perhaps there is evidence to be found without doing an autopsy."

"Dengoro. He was one of the shogun's male concubines," Sano said.

Mura walked to the row of swathed corpses and lifted the smallest one; it lay closest to the fire pit. Marume whistled. "We got here just in time. I'll wait out here."

Sano followed Mura into the morgue. Dr. Ito trailed them. He knew his way so well that he didn't bump into the waist-high tables, the stone troughs for washing the dead, or the cabinets filled with equipment. Mura laid the corpse on a table, lit lanterns on stands around it, then asked Sano, "Can you cover your nose and mouth? That's what we do when we work with the bodies of people that had measles."

"To keep out the evil spirits of disease," Dr. Ito explained. "I have a theory that diseases are caused by something other than evil spirits, but I have not yet devised a means of proof." He added wistfully, "I probably never will."

Sano had already been exposed to the shogun, but he tied his kerchief around the lower half of his face. Mura, after covering his own face and exchanging his heavy leather gloves for thinner ones, unwrapped Dengoro. The boy's body, dressed in a green night robe, was stiff and shrunken, the gray skin blotched with darkened red measles rash. Eyes closed, mouth slightly open, his delicate face wore a peaceful expression. Sano felt sorry for this child whose innocence had been destroyed before the end of his short life. At least Dengoro didn't look as if he'd died violently.

That was good for Dengoro, bad for Sano's hope of proving that Lord Ienobu was responsible for the attack on the shogun and the witness's death.

Mura took up a knife and cut the robe off the body. Dengoro's skin was smooth, unmarked except for the measles and a scab on a skinned knee. Mura turned the body over, with the same disappointing results.

"Any wounds or blood on him?" Dr. Ito asked.

"None," Sano said.

"He could have been poisoned," Dr. Ito said. "That's a common way of making a murder look like a natural death. Examine his mouth."

Mura laid the body on its back and used a bamboo stick to push back the flaccid lips. Sano peered at grayish-pink gums, tongue, and throat. "No burns or swelling." Had his instincts steered him wrong? Were they, like his physical strength, compromised by age? Suspicious timing didn't mean Dengoro's death was in fact murder.

"An autopsy might or might not reveal signs of poison," Dr. Ito said. "Some poisons are undetectable."

Loath to subject Dengoro to an autopsy on the off chance that evidence would turn up, Sano said, "Let me take a closer look at him before Mura does any cutting." He held a lantern near the body while he examined Dengoro, starting at his head and moving downward. Something on Dengoro's thigh caught his attention—what looked to be a smudge of dirt in an odd place. His instincts quickened in spite of his cautioning himself not to imagine clues. He asked Mura for a magnifying glass and held it over the smudge. Enlarged, it took on a blue color and revealed a distinctive pattern of curved lines and whorls. Sano's heart thumped.

"What is it?" Dr. Ito sounded impatient because he sensed that Sano had found something he couldn't see.

"A bruise shaped like a fingerprint."

Recollection shone in Dr. Ito's blind eyes. "I've seen that before. Once."

"Fourteen years ago," Sano agreed. "During my investigation into the series of deaths of high-ranking officials. They were murdered by *dim-mak*."

Dim-mak, the touch of death. It was the ancient martial arts technique of delivering a light tap that the victim might not even feel but was nonetheless fatal—sometimes immediately, sometimes days afterward. The speed of death was directly proportional to the force the killer used. The energy from the tap traveled through the victim's body to the brain and caused a hemorrhage that oozed blood until the victim dropped dead.

"Very few people have ever mastered the technique," Dr. Ito reminded Sano. "Could this be the same killer as in your previous case?"

"No. He's dead. I'm sure because I killed him." This investigation seemed like a tangle of sharp-edged vines from which he'd been trying to fight his way out. Now a tendril he hadn't noticed glowed with the red-hot light of revelation and slipped free of the tangle.

"Do you know of anyone else who is capable of *dim-mak*?" Dr. Ito asked.

"Yes." The clue that Sano had never expected seemed to pulse like a cut vein, pumping out poisoned sap that burned his flesh. It wasn't going to prove Lord Ienobu was responsible for the attack on the shogun, turn his allies against him, or stop the war. It explained so much, and in hindsight made perfect sense; yet it pointed Sano in a direction he was so loath to go.

"Hirata."

31

IN A SECLUDED garden inside Lord Mori's estate, moon-light shone through the mist around a picturesque wooden cottage. Light from the windows gilded the snowy grass. Inside the cottage, Masahiro and his new bride stood on opposite sides of a bed laid on the floor. Kikuko smiled. Her eyes, her long black hair, her pale skin, and the white silk of her wedding kimono gleamed. Masahiro stared at her and gulped.

He'd been ready to hate Kikuko because she wasn't the girl he'd wanted to marry. But he felt a heart-pounding attraction to her. His promise to Taeko had been easy to make before he'd seen Kikuko, whom he'd barely remembered from when they'd been children, but he couldn't tear his gaze off her. He grew erect at the very thought that she was his wife, that he could bed her tonight.

He had to keep his promise. He was in love with Taeko, and he wanted to be true to her, but his guilt didn't lessen his desire for Kikuko.

Kikuko skipped around the bed. He couldn't help turning toward her. She tilted her head, batted her eyes, and said, "I like you."

Masahiro knew she was feebleminded, but his body didn't care. He wanted her with an urgency he'd never felt before. He backed away from Kikuko. It reminded him of the time he'd grabbed a metal spear during

238

martial arts practice on a freezing day. His fingers had stuck to it, and when he'd pulled them free, pieces of his skin had ripped off.

A frown wrinkled Kikuko's smooth brow. "Don't you like me?"

This wasn't her fault, and Masahiro didn't want to hurt her feelings. She'd had no more choice in the matter than he. It was a good thing that she probably didn't know what a bride and groom were supposed to do on their wedding night.

"I'm just tired," Masahiro said. "I'm going to sleep."

With an expression that was strangely adult yet disconcertingly childish, she placed her hand against his bare chest above the neckline of his kimono. Her fingers were soft and warm. Gasping, Masahiro flung her hand off him. "Don't touch me!"

"Why not?" Kikuko asked in a pouty, wheedling voice. "I can make you feel good. Don't you want to feel good?"

Masahiro was astonished. She sounded like the bathhouse girls he'd sometimes visited before he and Taeko had fallen in love. She squeezed his erection. The pleasure made him groan. She giggled. "You like that, don't you?"

"No! Leave me alone!"

"Would you like to see me?" Kikuko untied her sash, let her white silk kimono and red under-kimono drop to the floor, and stood naked, preening like a little girl. Her body was slim, her skin sleek, her breasts bigger than they'd looked under her clothes. Her long hair fell over her narrow waist and curved hips, tickled her crotch. Masahiro was so hard that the pressure from his loincloth hurt. He breathed as if he were running too fast. He tried to avert his eyes from Kikuko, but they wouldn't move.

She cupped her breasts in her hands, teasing her nipples into pink buds. She dimpled with mischievous pleasure. "Wouldn't you like to make me feel good, too?"

Masahiro trembled with his desire and his effort to stanch it. His lips moved in a silent curse or plea. Kikuko inserted her finger between her legs, then held it up. It glistened wetly. As Masahiro watched, thrilled and horrified, she put her finger to her mouth, licked it, and purred. She seemed to know everything he liked, everything he would never ask of Taeko because Taeko was too good. As Kikuko tore off his clothes, he let her. He let her push him onto the bed. Crouching over him, she nuzzled, cooed, and murmured down his chest and belly. She took his erection in her mouth and sucked. The sensation was so arousing that Masahiro nearly climaxed right then. Shocked by her behavior, desperate not to betray Taeko, he pushed Kikuko away.

"Where did you learn this?" he demanded.

Saliva drooled down her chin as she smiled. "From Daiemon and Genzo."

"Who are they?"

"They work for my papa. He doesn't know they're my friends. Neither does Mama. It's a secret." Kikuko positioned herself on her hands and knees on the bed, her bottom pointed toward Masahiro. Looking over her shoulder, she said, "Do you want to play dogs?"

It was irresistible. Masahiro tried to think of Taeko, but her face was a blur in his mind. All he could see was Kikuko's bare buttocks, the cleft between them, and her saucy smile. He tried to remember how much he loved Taeko, but only Kikuko was here now and real. Hating his weakness and faithlessness, Masahiro knelt behind Kikuko. As he plunged into her, his last coherent thought was that Taeko would never have to know.

TAEKO STOOD IN the snow outside the cottage, sobbing as she spied on Masahiro and Kikuko through a hole she'd torn in the paper windowpane. They didn't hear her. They were moaning too loudly while Masahiro held Kikuko by her hips and rammed himself against her. Taeko watched in misery and disbelief.

Masahiro couldn't even keep his promise for one day! He'd said he loved her, but look at him! His eyes were closed, his mouth open. Sweat glistened on his skin. Taeko had never seen him so excited. Not that she'd ever really seen him while they'd made love; they'd always done it in the dark. He plunged so wildly that his penis slipped out of Kikuko for a moment. Taeko wailed. This was her first clear sight of Masahiro naked, and he was with someone else!

Her anger at his faithlessness turned on herself. She wasn't beautiful or exciting enough for him. She hadn't even known that people did the things she was seeing! Kikuko was beautiful, and she was giving Masahiro what he liked, so why shouldn't he want to be with her? Taeko cried so hard that she choked. Self-hatred consumed her as she beheld her rival.

Kikuko panted. Her breasts jiggled while Masahiro coupled with her. She rocked forward and backward, her buttocks meeting his thrusts, crying, "It feels so good!"

Taeko moaned, tore at her hair, and clawed her face. Kikuko was married to Masahiro. She didn't have to sneak around to make love to him, and she could be as noisy as she wanted. Taeko couldn't console herself with the thought that she was the one Masahiro loved. Masahiro threw back his head, arched his back, rammed Kikuko hard, and shouted as he climaxed and shuddered. Kikuko squealed, "Yes, yes, yes!" Taeko's tears blurred their images. They were so passionate, they would surely fall in love, and Taeko would be where she was now—alone in the cold. She felt an ache in the pit of her belly, as if the baby was also suffering.

Masahiro and Kikuko collapsed onto the bed together. Kikuko stroked Masahiro's heaving chest and cooed. Taeko wanted to rush into the cottage, tear them apart, and yell, "You can't have him! He's mine!" But he wasn't. He never would be. Taeko couldn't bear to watch any longer. She turned and ran.

WHEN SANO AND Marume returned from the morgue, Yanagisawa was waiting for them, tapping his foot as they crawled up through the trapdoor. They joined him in the chamber in which a lacquer chest, now pushed aside, had concealed the secret exit. His nose wrinkled at their odor of cesspools.

"What did you learn?" He sounded skeptical yet hopeful.

"Nothing," Sano said. He and Marume had agreed not to tell

Yanagisawa about the fingerprint. Yanagisawa wouldn't care; the fact of the boy's murder, wasn't ammunition against Lord Ienobu. And Sano still felt compelled to protect Hirata, bound by a loyalty that persisted in spite of everything. Although Marume disliked Hirata and wouldn't have minded holding him accountable for the murder, he disliked Yanagisawa more. He saw no good in giving Yanagisawa ammunition against someone Sano cared about. And both Sano and Marume realized that Hirata's role in the boy's murder put the attack on the shogun in an entirely different light.

"The boy died of the measles," Sano said.

Yanagisawa looked as if he'd expected as much but was disappointed anyway. "No more wild-goose chases. I'm going to bed. I suggest you do the same." Striding out the door, he called, "It might be our last chance of sleep for a long time. Tomorrow we attack Lord Ienobu."

Sano had failed again—failed to protect his family and the shogun, failed to solve the crime. He and Marume exchanged troubled yet elated glances. The war they'd never thought to see in their lifetime was nigh. They hurried to their quarters. Marume went to tell Sano's other men. A lamp glowed in the chamber where Sano found Reiko. She sat up in bed, put her finger to her lips, and pointed at Akiko, asleep beside her; she started to turn away from Sano.

"I have to talk to you," Sano said in a quiet, pleading voice.

Reiko's expression warned him not to try to placate her with futile apologies. They both felt the absence of Masahiro, who was with his new bride. Sano said, "We're attacking Lord Ienobu at the castle tomorrow."

She merely nodded, unsurprised.

"Hirata murdered the boy."

"What?" Reiko exclaimed, startled out of her aloofness. Akiko stirred. Reiko lowered her voice. "How do you know?"

At least she was finally willing to talk to him. Sano explained about the bruise. Reiko put her hands to her cheeks, dropped them, and said, "But why do you think it was Hirata? Why not one of his friends from the secret society?"

"It's as if they've disappeared from the face of the earth. But there have been sightings of Hirata. It has to be him."

"Not some other martial artist?" Reiko sounded anxious to exonerate Hirata.

"Maybe some other martial artist is able to kill with a touch, but Hirata is the one who's in league with a ghost that wants to make Lord Ienobu the next shogun."

"How would killing the boy accomplish that?"

"I think Dengoro really did see or hear something when the shogun was stabbed. Something that implicates Lord Ienobu and that he would have remembered eventually."

Reiko followed Sano's logic. "If he'd talked about it, the shogun might have heard and believed it and put Lord Ienobu to death."

"Hirata killed the boy to protect Lord Ienobu." Sano knelt, sharing a rare moment of rapport with Reiko as they saw the cold-blooded murder of an innocent child added to their friend's list of misdeeds.

Reiko cautiously broached the subject they both would rather avoid. "What else might Hirata have done?" She was finally willing to admit that Hirata had turned bad.

His discovery that Hirata was involved in the case forced Sano to view it in a new light. "I think he planted the evidence against Tomoe and Lord Yoshimune. Putting the blame for the stabbing on them would get Lord Ienobu off the hook."

"It would get Lady Nobuko off, too." Reiko frowned at the thought of her enemy benefiting from Hirata's crime. "Do you think . . . ?" She hesitated, reluctant to voice the next logical question. "Could it be Hirata who tried to kill the shogun?"

The awful possibility had occurred to Sano. Perhaps everything he'd thought he'd learned during his investigation was wrong; perhaps Hirata—not Lord Ienobu—was responsible for the stabbing. "I don't know."

"Do you think Hirata would draw the line at murdering his lord?"

"I think that if Hirata had wanted to kill the shogun, he wouldn't have failed. Then again, he wouldn't have wanted anyone to know it was him. Maybe he tried to make it look as if the shogun was stabbed by someone who didn't know how." Sano was still reluctant to believe Hirata had stooped so low and Lord Ienobu was innocent.

"We thought Lady Nobuko, Madam Chizuru, and Tomoe were the

only suspects. Hirata is a new one we almost missed. What else might we not be seeing?"

"I have to find out, even if it means starting the investigation over." Sano looked ahead to a formidable challenge at the worst conceivable time. "I'll start with Hirata."

Hostility crept back into Reiko's expression. "This is bad for Midori and the children."

Her sympathies clearly still lay with them. Sano felt the fragile rapport between him and Reiko disintegrate as he said, "If Hirata is guilty of the assassination attempt on the shogun as well as Dengoro's murder, then I have to bring him to justice. I've already let him slide for too long." Whatever Hirata had done since Sano had learned about his treasonous activities was, in effect, Sano's fault. "But if he's innocent, I must clear his name."

"How can you investigate anything? Didn't you say the war is starting tomorrow?"

"I don't have much time, but I have to try. The shogun ordered me to find out who's responsible for stabbing him." Sano believed that investigating Hirata would lead him to the truth, whatever it was. "It could be his last order to me."

The demands of Bushido had never seemed so urgent—or so onerous. Thus far the truth Sano had thought would save the day had only made things worse for his family and Hirata's. But Sano could no more ignore his duty than live without air to breathe.

"What are you going to do?" Reiko lay down in bed and turned away from Sano.

Sano imagined how angry she would be if she knew he'd turned down the final deal with Lord Ienobu, the one offered when he'd gone to fetch Ienobu back to Edo Castle. "Yanagisawa won't like it, but I feel another wild-goose chase coming on."

32

THE MORNING MIST in the air condensed into drizzle as Taeko stood alone on the veranda of the guest quarters. Her eyes were red and swollen, her cheeks puffy under the white makeup she'd put on to hide the scratches she'd gouged on them last night. She shivered despite her heavy cloak, but she couldn't go back inside the house, where she would have to face her family. If they showed her any sympathy, she would start crying again, and she didn't want to cry. She knew Masahiro would come to her, and she had to be strong enough to do what must be done.

The door behind her opened, and she heard his steps. Her body tensed. She glanced sideways at him, and his smile stabbed her heart.

"No chaperone today," Masahiro said. "We're in luck." He put his arm around her. She flung it off. "Hey, what's the matter?" He sounded puzzled, hurt.

She drew a deep, shaky breath. "I've been thinking." Her voice came out barely audible. She cleared her throat. "I've been thinking . . . it's best if we don't see each other anymore."

"What?" Fear tinged the shock in Masahiro's voice. "Why?"

Risking another glance, Taeko saw guilt on his face: He knew he'd broken his promise and didn't want her to guess. Anger steadied Taeko. "You're married," she said coldly.

"But we already decided you're going to be my concubine."

He thought she would live with him and he could go back and forth between her and Kikuko! She would have to listen to them making love all the time, and she would know he wanted Kikuko more than her. "I've changed my mind." Her voice wobbled.

"Why?" Masahiro grabbed her arm and turned her to face him. She twisted, avoiding his gaze, afraid she would cry. "All of a sudden, you don't love me anymore?"

Taeko wanted to say yes, she'd come to her senses, it was no good prolonging a relationship that their families disapproved of. Instead she blurted the truth. "If I can't have you to myself, I don't want you at all."

"But you do have me. Kikuko is my wife in name only."

Tears burned Taeko's sore, swollen eyes. "How can you say that?" She hadn't meant for Masahiro to know she'd watched him and Kikuko— she was ashamed of it—but she couldn't help herself. "After last night?"

He stiffened. "Nothing happened last night." His voice was brusque. "I promised I wouldn't touch her, and I didn't."

He thought he could lie to her and get away with it! Taeko smelled soap and fresh wintergreen hair oil on him; he'd been careful to bathe away the smell of sex. Furious, she exploded at him. "You broke your promise! You made love to Kikuko!"

"That's not true! Why don't you believe me?"

"I was watching you through the window. You were playing dogs!"

Masahiro blenched with shock and horror, then flushed with anger. "You spied on me? How could you do such a sneaky thing?"

That he would try to put her in the wrong! "It's a good thing I did! Because now I know what you are." Taeko sobbed. "You're a liar and a cheater!"

He exhaled, rubbed his mouth, and groaned. Now he looked wounded, appalled by his own actions, sick with shame and regret. "I'm sorry." His voice cracked. "Please forgive me." He reached for Taeko.

She remembered his hands holding Kikuko while he plunged in and out of her. She slapped them away. "Don't touch me!"

"It was only sex," Masahiro hurried to say. "It doesn't mean anything. I don't care about her. It's you I love."

Taeko was crying so hard, she could barely speak. "You forgot about me last night!"

"I made a mistake. I won't do it again."

"The next time she wiggles her bottom at you, you'll say no?"

". . . I will!"

His lack of conviction stabbed such pain through her heart that Taeko moaned. "Do you think I'm stupid enough to believe you? Well, I'm not!"

She could never trust him again; things would never be the same. Taeko fled down the stairs, into the wet garden.

Masahiro ran after her, calling, "I'm sorry! Let me make it up to you!"

He caught her arm. She shrieked, "Leave me alone!" and flailed her fists at him. He tried to hold her. As they struggled, she lost her balance and fell. She lay on the ground and screamed, "Knock me down! Hit me if you want!" Masahiro stood over her, looking miserable. "Kill me! Kill the baby, too! Then you won't have to bother with us!"

His face went blank. "What baby?"

This wasn't how Taeko had meant to tell him, but it was too late to take it back. She sobbed out the words. "I'm with child."

Masahiro staggered as if she'd hit him across his stomach. He inhaled, was dumbfounded, and puffed out his cheeks. "How long have you known?"

"A while."

"Why didn't you tell me?" He sounded as grieved as angry.

Her own anger helped Taeko regain her self-control. "When would have been a good time? While we were sneaking into the storeroom? After you were engaged to marry Yanagisawa's daughter?"

"You should have told me. I had a right to know. It's my baby, too." Masahiro seemed amazed by the idea that he was going to be a father, then stupidly proud, then relieved and smug. "This means you can't break up with me."

"You think my baby and I will live with you and Kikuko? So that she can be mean to it and you can ignore it while you make babies with her?" Being Masahiro's concubine had seemed possible before Taeko had seen Kikuko at the wedding. It was unthinkable after last night. Taeko sat up and glared. "Never!"

"Be reasonable," Masahiro said, impatient with her defiance, hurt because she was rejecting him. "What are you going to do if you don't become my concubine?"

Terrified of the future, enraged by her helplessness, Taeko said, "I don't know, and I don't care! I'd rather die than be your concubine! I hate you!"

His gaze softened with painful tenderness. "You don't mean that." His tone reminded her of the times they'd lain in each other's arms, whispering passionate vows of eternal love.

"Yes, I do!" Taeko had no way to salvage her pride except to lash out at Masahiro and hurt him as much as he'd hurt her. "You're selfish, and dishonest, and stupid, and cruel." He flinched at the insults; his expression grew more downcast with each. She tasted bitter satisfaction. "You're dishonorable!"

It was the worst thing she could say to a samurai. The hurt in Masahiro's eyes blazed into sudden fury. He raised his hand as if to strike her, then dropped it. They stared at each other, aghast.

"You want it to be over between us, all right, it's over," Masahiro said in a hard voice. "Do whatever you want. I'm going back to my wife." He turned on his heel and stalked into the house without looking back.

Taeko collapsed on the ground and wept.

THE COURTYARD OF Lord Mori's estate bustled with preparations for war. Troops swaggered out of the barracks, dressed in full battle regalia—iron helmets, chain-mail arm and leg guards, and armor tunics made of hundreds of leather-covered metal plates. They hoisted cannons and balls onto wagons. Grooms brought horses, also clad in armor, from the stables. Gunners rammed gunpowder down the barrels of arquebuses.

Yanagisawa stalked through the crowd, calling, "Where is Sano?"

He needed Sano to accompany the squadron that would seek out and kill Lord Ienobu. Sano was one of the few men in his faction who'd ever fought a real battle; most had only fought practice matches.

Nobody he asked had seen Sano since last night. Sudden suspicion propelled Yanagisawa inside the mansion, to the chamber that contained the secret exit. On the floor lay the two men he'd ordered to guard the exit in case Sano tried to use it again. The trapdoor was open. The men's wrists and ankles were bound, their mouths gagged.

Ripping off the gags, Yanagisawa demanded, "What happened?"

"Someone hit me on the head," mumbled one guard. The other said, "Me, too."

Yanagisawa pictured Sano and Detective Marume sneaking up behind the guards, knocking them out, and tying them up. He knelt by the trapdoor and peered into the dark, silent tunnel. Where had they gone? For what purpose? Yanagisawa only knew that Sano had deserted him at this crucial moment.

"Sano!" he roared down the tunnel, and heard only the echo of his own furious voice.

AS SANO AND Marume raced through Nihonbashi, citizens hiding in their homes peeked fearfully through windows. People scurried in and out of the few shops open for business. Moorings along the canals were unoccupied, the boats and barges gone. Sano and Marume arrived at the Nihonbashi Bridge, the starting point of the Tōkaidō, the main highway that ran from Edo to points west. All the traffic was heading out of town, the commoners who hadn't left yesterday fleeing before the war started. Porters carried baggage for rich merchant families in palanquins; poor folk with their worldly goods on their backs jostled priests, monks, and nuns.

"If I were a rat, I'd leave this ship, too," Marume said.

Sano was sad to realize that even if he could leave—even if he didn't have a mission to finish and a battle to fight—Reiko and Masahiro might not want to go with him. Things were that bad. Sano glanced at Marume. Even his old friend must have lost faith in him. But Marume willingly stuck with Sano while they went down in the sinking ship.

"Thank you," Sano said. A master didn't owe his retainer any thanks, but he wanted to tell Marume his loyal service was appreciated and he wasn't taken for granted.

Marume shrugged and said, "Don't mention it."

They stopped outside a barbershop set amid inns, teahouses, and restaurants that catered to travelers. The door behind the blue curtain that hung halfway down the entrance was open. He and Marume entered the shop. Three men knelt on the floor by the hearth. An elderly, one-armed barber shaved the scruffy beard off a samurai who looked as if he'd been living rough. Two other samurai with the same unshaven, ragged appearance ceased their conversation. All the men trained unfriendly gazes on Sano and Marume.

"If you're here to ask about Hirata-*san*, my answer is the same as last time," the barber said. "I haven't seen or heard from him."

Sano had expected as much, but the barbershop was a haunt of itinerant martial artists, the only place he might hope to get news of Hirata. "And if you had, you wouldn't tell me."

The barber oiled his customer's hair, twisted it into a topknot, tied it with twine, and trimmed the end with one deft hand. "You have your code of honor. We have ours."

"If you do see Hirata, tell him I said he's gone too far, and it's time for him to turn himself in before he hurts any more innocent people."

Concern showed on the barber's lined face. "What's he done?"

"He murdered a little boy," Sano said.

The barber squinted at Sano and seemed to decide he was telling the truth. "I never thought he was capable of that." His loyalty to Hirata visibly waned.

"That and probably worse. So if you've any news about him, you should tell me."

"I've heard news," the barber said reluctantly. "But not about Hirata. It's his three friends."

"You mean Deguchi, Kitano, and Tahara?" Marume asked.

The barber nodded. "Deguchi's body was found on a hill outside town, four or five years ago. It looked like he'd lost a terrible fight. The last I heard of Kitano and Tahara was a while later. A friend of mine who was visiting Sky Mountain Temple saw them there. They disappeared. One night he woke up to hear the monks chanting prayers, and he smelled burning flesh. I think Kitano and Tahara are dead, too."

Sano looked at Marume. They shared their relief that the secret society members were gone, the suspicion that Hirata had killed them, and the disturbing certainty that he, the only one left, was responsible for the boy's murder. What else had the ghost compelled Hirata to do?

Back on the street, Marume said, "That was hardly worth knocking out Yanagisawa's men. How are we supposed to investigate Hirata when we can't even find him?"

Sano was discouraged, too, but he said, "Hirata left a track when he murdered Dengoro—the fingerprint. He may have left other tracks. I know of a place to start looking."

STANDING UNDER THE eaves of a teahouse, Hirata watched Sano and Marume emerge from the barbershop across the street and walk away. *Sano is looking for me! I have to go to him!*

You wanted to see Sano. You've seen him. General Otani clamped his will down on Hirata. *That's enough.*

Hirata exerted his own will against the paralysis that kept him rooted to the spot. Sweat popped out on his forehead. His body wouldn't move. *Let me talk to him!*

So that you can confess everything you've done? And tell him about me? General Otani's contemptuous chuckle vibrated through Hirata. *What good would that do?*

Hirata tried to scream in frustration. General Otani silenced him as if with an iron hand that squeezed his throat. People passing by, hurrying to leave town, paid him no attention. *I want to make a clean breast,* Hirata pleaded. It was the least he owed Sano after years of deceit.

That might make you feel better, General Otani said, *but suppose you did. Sano would try to interfere with my plans. I would have to make you kill him.*

Despair fell upon Hirata like a landslide of boulders. This was the ultimate threat that the ghost held over him—that it would force him to hurt Sano or his family. He could live with anyone's blood on his hands except theirs. The fight drained from Hirata. He would have fallen to the ground had not General Otani's will kept his body standing up-right.

Ah, you've come to your senses, General Otani said with satisfaction. Hirata's paralysis dissipated. General Otani prodded him down the street with jabs of pain between his shoulder blades. *No more wasting our energy on stupid resistance. Major events will soon transpire at the castle. We have to be there in case they need a nudge in the right direction.*

33

"ISN'T THIS WHERE you grew up?" Marume asked as he and Sano hurried through a neighborhood at the edge of Nihonbashi.

"Yes," Sano said.

His background wasn't a secret, but he rarely talked about it. His father had been a *rōnin* who'd lost his samurai status when a previous shogun had confiscated his lord's lands and turned the lord's retainers out to fend for themselves. Sano's family had settled in this district amid the commoners. So had other former samurai. Sano wasn't ashamed that some people looked down on him because of his lowly origin, but his father had never gotten over the disgrace. Sano kept quiet about it out of respect for his father, dead twenty years. He sadly remembered his father being so proud of him when he earned a position in the Tokugawa regime and restored their family's honor.

"It's been rebuilt since the earthquake." Sano looked through the drizzle at the rows of humble but new houses. Streets had been rerouted; the bridge over the willow-edged canal was new. His childhood home, vacated after his widowed mother remarried and moved out of town, was gone, replaced by a building that housed several families. Sano had the disturbing sense that his past had been erased and so had all the gains he'd achieved since he'd left his old home. He'd lost his high position in the regime, ruined his marriage, and handed over his son to his enemy. Self-pity, fatigue, and strain suddenly overcame him. His eyes stung. With his future in jeopardy, he had no-where to go.

"Looks like everybody's left town," Marume said. Shops were closed, the houses deserted, the neighborhood gates unguarded.

Not everybody had, and a part of Sano's past remained. A samurai dressed in full armor stood with his horse outside the martial arts school that Sano's father had once operated, where Sano had learned and taught sword-fighting. The low building with a brown tile roof and barred win-dows resembled the original so closely that it seemed a figment of his memory.

"Aoki-*san*," Sano called.

The samurai smiled, greeted Sano, and bowed. He was Sano's father's former apprentice, now master of the school. "What brings you here?"

Sano was so glad to see a friendly face, someone he hadn't hurt. "I'm looking up a former colleague. His name is Toda Ikkyu. Do you know him?"

Aoki nodded and gave directions to Toda's house. "He's probably left already. I was just locking up before I go." He patted the wall, a gesture of love for the school that he might never see again.

"Aren't you leaving town?" Sano asked. Aoki's horse wasn't carrying any baggage.

"No. Neither are the other men from the neighborhood, except those who are old or sick. We're staying to fight in the war." Excitement bright-ened Aoki's eyes.

Sano realized this was a big opportunity for the men. "On whose side? Yanagisawa's or Lord Ienobu's?"

"Whichever one will take us."

It didn't matter to them which side they fought on; joining either would regain them their samurai status. But for a quirk of fate Sano might be in Aoki's shoes. "Good luck."

"You, too. May we meet again." Aoki bowed. "I hope we end up on the same side."

"If we don't, no hard feelings," Sano said.

Aoki rode away. Sano and Marume followed his directions to a row of houses. One entrance had the same clutter of buckets, brooms, and miscellany as the others, but the items seemed too deliberately arranged in order to make this home resemble the others so that it wouldn't stand out. Sano knocked on the door. "Toda-*san?* Are you there?"

The man who answered looked as if the right half of his face had melted and solidified into a reddish purple mask of puckered scars. A black patch covered the eye. His scalp was bald on that side; the other was shaved. Sano's heart lurched even though he'd seen Toda before and had known what to expect.

Marume, who hadn't, said, "Whoa!"

"Meet Toda Ikkyu, retired spy," Sano said.

"Is this the man you said you could never recognize?" Marume said in astonishment. "One look at that face, and I'd know it anywhere."

Toda had once been completely nondescript and forgettable, an asset in his former profession as an agent for the *metsuke,* the Tokugawa intelligence service. "Detective Marume. I've heard about you." He smiled with the undamaged half of his mouth. "This face is a reminder of my good luck."

Marume stared with open revulsion. "Give me bad luck any time."

"Some people lost their lives during the earthquake. I only lost half my face and a couple of fingers in the fire that burned down my house afterward." Toda held up his hands. They were red and scarred, both missing the little fingers. He poked his head out the door. "You'd better come in out of the rain."

His home consisted of one austere room. Sano, Marume, and Toda knelt on the frayed tatami. Shelves that held a few dishes, pots, and utensils surrounded a hearth at one end of the room. The bed was rolled neatly in a corner by a portable writing desk. A few trunks concealed everything else Toda owned.

"I haven't any liquor, but I can offer you some tea," Toda said.

"That's not necessary," Sano said, knowing how poor Toda was. He hid his pity, sparing Toda's pride. "We won't impose on you for long. You must be anxious to leave."

"Leave? And miss the war?" Toda laughed. "It will be the greatest spectacle of my lifetime."

He either had no place to go or no means for getting there, Sano thought. "Be careful."

"If a stray bullet gets me, fine. There are worse ways to die." Toda asked Sano, "Who let you out? I thought Yanagisawa had you sewed up tight. Congratulations on your son's marriage."

"I see that you're still well informed."

"Even though Lord Ienobu kicked me out of the *metsuke* after thirty years of loyal service, I still have friends who bring me news."

"Not so loyal service," Sano reminded Toda. "You were never completely in his camp or anyone else's. You played for all sides."

Toda smiled wryly. "Help all of the people some of the time, and I'll be fine whoever ends up on top. That was my survival strategy, but it didn't work with Lord Ienobu—he's an all-or-nothing sort of man."

"So why are you still alive?" Marume asked.

"He likes knowing there's someone uglier than he is."

Sano and Marume laughed. Toda said, "No, it's because he thinks he may need me someday. I have a lot of information stored up here." He tapped his scarred head.

"That's why I'm here," Sano said. "To mine your memory."

Toda turned serious now that they were getting down to business. "Lord Ienobu took away my stipend. I can't afford to give anything away for free."

"I'll give you back your stipend after we defeat Lord Ienobu," Sano said.

"Hah! Fat chance. Is that the best you can offer?"

"Yes."

Conceding with a shrug, Toda said, "Ask away."

"Have there recently been any sudden, unexpected deaths in the regime?"

Toda's eye gleamed with interest. "Yes, as a matter of fact. Nobody's looked too closely at them, for fear of running afoul of Lord Ienobu."

Sano felt the sinking sensation that presaged bad news. "Who died?"

"The assistant to the treasury minister."

"He used to divert money from taxes and tributes into Yanagisawa's pocket." Sano saw that putting him out of action would have benefited Lord Ienobu. "How did he die, and when?"

"About two years ago. He had severe indigestion after a banquet. He was a glutton and a big drinker. He died after being violently ill all night."

"Who else?"

"A captain of the palace guard. He was Yanagisawa's man, too. He got bronchitis during the Mount Fuji eruption, and he'd had trouble breathing ever since. One night he couldn't get enough air and suffocated."

The guard captain would have been able to arrange a lapse in palace security so that Yanagisawa could assassinate Lord Ienobu. Sano and Marume exchanged grave looks as they saw the pattern. Dengoro was the most recent case in which someone who'd posed a threat to Lord Ienobu had had a health problem that could account for his sudden death.

"Do you think the deaths were murders?" Toda asked. "Is that why you're interested in them? Because you think Lord Ienobu is responsible and you can use it against him? If so, then I'm sorry to disappoint you. There were no wounds or evidence of poison on the bodies."

No one would have thought to look for a fingerprint-shaped bruise, Sano realized. No one would have suspected that Hirata was involved. If not for his hunch that had sent him to Edo Morgue, Sano wouldn't have seen the telltale sign on Dengoro.

"I knew it was a long shot digging for dirt on Lord Ienobu. I just asked on the off chance that you had some." Sano couldn't tell Toda that it was Hirata whose crimes he was trying to uncover. His own former chief retainer and friend! "I figured you wouldn't mind helping me take Lord Ienobu down."

"Believe me, I would be glad to. But his hands are clean as far as I know."

But Hirata's weren't, Sano was now certain. Sano wondered if Lord Ienobu had any idea that someone was secretly killing his enemies on his behalf.

"The third sudden death doesn't seem to have benefited Lord Ienobu," Toda said.

Two out of three was bad enough. "Who was it?"

"A samurai named Ishikawa Kakubei."

"Never heard of him," Marume said.

"He didn't live in Edo, although he died here," Toda said.

"What was he doing here?" Sano asked.

"He was from Nagasaki. He accompanied an envoy of Dutch traders when they came to Edo to visit the shogun."

Nagasaki was the only place in Japan where foreigners were allowed. A previous shogun had decided that foreigners—and their strange religions and advanced weaponry—posed a danger to the regime and had closed Japan's other ports. The Western barbarians were the most feared foreigners of all. Only the Dutch, who'd signed an agreement not to meddle in local affairs or spread Christianity, were permitted to trade with Japan. They lived in a prisonlike compound in Deshima, an island off the coast of Nagasaki.

"I remember that visit," Sano said. "It was a few months after the earthquake." He also remembered his own visit to Nagasaki nineteen years ago, in another lifetime.

"It was a bad time for them to come," Marume said. "The roads were barely passable, and the city was still in ruins."

"The shogun was afraid he would lose face if the Dutch saw his castle in such bad shape," Toda said, "but they'd been granted official permission for their annual journey to pay their respects to him, and protocol is protocol."

Sano had been busy organizing relief for the people left homeless and destitute by the earthquake and tsunami. He'd briefly met the Dutch, and he didn't recall their Japanese escorts.

"Ishikawa was a translator," Toda said. "He was one of three who interpreted for the Dutch during their visit."

There were only a few translators in Japan. It was against the law for anyone except those trusted, officially appointed men to learn foreign languages. People who spoke foreign languages might conspire with foreigners against their own government.

"How did he die?" Sano asked.

"He caught a bad cold during the journey. By the time he reached Edo, it had settled in his lungs. He had a high fever, which is what killed him, according to the doctors. He died the day before the Dutch went back to Nagasaki."

Sano unwillingly spotted another example in the pattern. But why would Hirata have killed a translator? That couldn't have done Lord Ienobu any good.

"The poor sap," Marume said. "He made the trip and died for nothing. He must not have interpreted while the Dutch met with the shogun. The shogun never lets anybody who's sick get near him."

"That's right," Toda said, "but Lord Ienobu had a private meeting with the Dutch envoys. Ishikawa translated during that."

Here was the connection between Lord Ienobu and Ishikawa. An unpleasant, ominous feeling told Sano that the meeting was an important clue and Hirata was involved in the translator's death. "What happened at that meeting?"

"I don't know. I didn't find out about it until after Ishikawa was dead and the Dutch had gone back to their country. I could hardly ask Lord Ienobu."

"Was anybody else present?" Sano asked.

"Just Lord Ienobu's chief retainer. Manabe."

Sano experienced a sense of inevitability. He'd circled back to the unfinished business that had put him on the cold, dark road from Yoshiwara on a winter night. His quest for the truth about Yoshisato's death had led him to Manabe. His quest for the truth about Hirata and the attack on the shogun had led him to the same person, again.

34

THE IRON GRILLE that covered the hole in the stone wall swung open. Reiko and Akiko cautiously poked their heads out of the tunnel and looked both ways along the footpath and canal below them. "I don't see Papa and Detective Marume," Akiko said.

"We can go, then," Reiko said.

They'd followed the men down the tunnel. "Papa would be so angry if he knew." Akiko sounded delighted to be misbehaving with Reiko.

Reiko knew Sano would be furious at her for risking her own and their daughter's safety, but she didn't care. Masahiro was married to Kikuko, their family's fate was tied to Yanagisawa's, and there was going to be a war. Anything Reiko did couldn't hurt, and if she discovered who'd stabbed the shogun, it might help. She was glad to take her fate into her own hands, and although she had qualms about taking Akiko's, they belonged together. She was also glad she wouldn't be at the Mori estate when Sano found the note she'd left.

She and Akiko scooted out of the hole and slid down the bank of the canal. Holding hands, they hurried through a city that Reiko had never seen so empty. Even the neighborhood gate sentries were missing. The castle's guard towers and walls loomed on the hill. Reiko and Akiko stopped in an alley that gave onto the avenue that circled the castle. It was crowded with thousands of mounted troops and foot soldiers. Gun and cannon barrels poked through the barred windows of the towers, the covered corridors, and the guardhouse above the main gate. The gate was protected by a whole squadron of sentries.

"Is the war going to start today?" Akiko asked.

"Yes," Reiko said. The castle was prepared. Her husband and son would be among the forces attacking.

"How are we going to get inside the castle?"

The thought of entering Lord Ienobu's stronghold, and the prospect of war, excited as well as terrified Reiko. She saw the same emotions in her daughter. Samurai blood ran in their veins. They could have waited at the Mori estate for Lord Ienobu's army to come; they could have prepared to commit suicide to avoid being captured and savaged by their enemies. That was what samurai wives and daughters did during wars. But they had stepped outside the bounds of womanhood. They would not retreat to the false security behind the front lines.

"Come with me." Reiko took Akiko's hand.

Keeping to the streets of Nihonbashi, they circled the castle to a small gate used by servants. This gate was open to admit porters lugging in rice bales; people inside the castle still needed to eat. Pages carrying message pouches hurried out; the court still needed to communicate with the outside world. Before she could lose her nerve, Reiko walked Akiko up to the gate. Fortunately they weren't the only women in line. The others were maids. Reiko and Akiko, dressed in cotton kimonos and head kerchiefs, fit right in. The maids carried baskets or bundles. Reiko hoped their empty hands wouldn't mark her and Akiko as imposters.

"Don't speak unless you're spoken to," Reiko whispered to Akiko as the line advanced.

Heads bowed, they shuffled up to the sentries. Reiko was glad Akiko stayed so calm. Her own heart pumped currents of fear through her. This wasn't the first time she'd impersonated a servant in order to gain entry to a forbidden, dangerous place, but it was the first time she'd brought her daughter. They were officially kin to Yanagisawa. If caught sneaking into the castle, they could be deemed enemy agents and killed. At the front of the line, they removed folded papers from beneath their sashes. Reiko handed the papers to a sentry and waited in a fever of anxiety as he examined the passes she'd forged. She'd given herself and Akiko the names of two maids who worked in the Large Interior. She hoped he didn't know the real maids and wouldn't look too closely at the blurry red signature seals on the forged passes.

He handed the passes back to her and Akiko and waved them through the gate. Reiko almost fainted from relief. Akiko stifled a giggle as they hurried up the wet passage. She turned serious as they were scrutinized by troops stationed at the checkpoints. Reiko died a small death of fright each time. She recognized some of the men, whom she'd seen often when she'd lived in the castle. If they recognized her and Akiko, how many could she kill with the dagger she wore hidden under her sleeve? Could she buy Akiko enough time to escape?

They reached the top tier of the castle. Akiko flashed Reiko a triumphant smile. Reiko forced herself to smile back as she noticed how strangely quiet the palace grounds were—so quiet that the plop of icicles falling from the eaves of the building onto the damp snow seemed loud. The guards usually stationed at the entrance were nowhere in sight.

"Mama, do you hear that sound?" Akiko whispered.

A soft hum rose and fell within the palace, from hundreds of voices. Reiko hazarded a guess. "They must be chanting prayers for the shogun. He must be dying."

His death would make Lord Ienobu dictator and undermine Yanagisawa's chance of victory. It was one thing to attack the shogun's heir apparent, another to revolt against a sitting shogun. Some of Yanagisawa's allies would desert him on the grounds that they couldn't violate the samurai code of loyalty to their lord. Bushido was also a good excuse for those who would rather accept Lord Ienobu's rule than fight a war. A takeover by Lord Ienobu would mean death for his enemies and all their close associates—including Sano and his family. Never had their plight seemed so gravely real to Reiko. She hadn't much time to prove Lord Ienobu was responsible for the attack on the shogun, guilty of treason, and unfit to inherit the regime.

She hurried Akiko around the palace to the separate wing of the Large Interior where Lady Nobuko lived, retracing a path she'd followed four years ago under circumstances equally dire. Memories impinged, as harmlessly as the raindrops, on Reiko. Her newfound confidence, and Akiko's company, kept her fixed in the present moment. The palace grounds were deserted. Everybody must have gone to the vigil for the shogun. Reiko cautiously opened the door of the little house attached to the main building and listened to the silence. She and Akiko stole through the entryway and down the corridor to Lady Nobuko's inner chamber. The house exuded a fusty, medicinal, old-woman smell. The chamber was empty, but two cups of cold tea and two bowls of half-eaten gruel on tray tables suggested that Lady Nobuko and her lady-in-waiting had left in a hurry to go to the shogun. There was no telling when they would return.

Reiko stood in the room she'd searched three days ago. She eyed the table where Lady Nobuko had sat writing, the cabinets, and the dressing table. All seemed the same.

"Mama, what are we looking for?"

"I'll know when we find it." Reiko knelt and opened scroll cases on the writing table. Akiko rummaged through Lady Nobuko's toiletries. The first scroll was a letter from a *daimyo*'s wife, inviting Lady Nobuko to a tea ceremony. Suddenly Reiko smelled a sharp, strong fragrance of peppermint and jasmine. She felt a startling sense of vindication that she didn't immediately comprehend. She exclaimed, "What is that?"

Akiko held a little, celadon-glazed porcelain jar in one hand and the stopper in the other. Her face showed the guilty defiance that it always did when Reiko caught her disobeying. "I just wanted to see what was in it." She set the jar and lid on the dressing table. "I'm sorry. I won't touch anything else."

"No, it's all right, you haven't done anything wrong, I'm not angry." Reiko snatched up the jar, sniffed the thick, cloudy oil in it, and exclaimed, "You found what I was missing!"

Akiko sighed with relief, frowned in confusion. "I did?"

"Yes." Reiko cupped the jar of hair oil in her hands as if it were a sacred treasure. "Now I know what happened the night the shogun was stabbed. Lady Nobuko did it."

The transparent specter of Lady Nobuko materialized. She tucked the iron fan under her sash, then dipped her fingers in the jar Reiko held. She smeared the oil on her hair. "She used the same hair oil as Madam Chizuru," Reiko said. Lady Nobuko's specter lifted a lantern from the stand and tiptoed from the room. Her sock-clad feet padded down the corridor toward the shogun's private chambers. "It was dark. If she met anyone, they would think she was Madam Chizuru, because they would smell the peppermint and jasmine." Reiko envisioned the shogun's bedchamber. The light from Lady Nobuko's lantern illuminated the sleeping figures of the shogun and his boy. Lady Nobuko bent over the shogun, the iron fan clutched in her fist. The shogun slept; the boy stirred, his nostrils twitching. "Dengoro really did smell Madam Chizuru's hair oil. He lied about everything else, but not that."

And Lady Nobuko had lied about why she'd refused to let Sano question her immediately after the stabbing. She hadn't been too upset or just wanting to avoid him. "She needed time to wash her hair, so he wouldn't smell peppermint and jasmine on her and realize there were two women who'd been wearing the oil when the shogun was stabbed and guess that she was the one Dengoro smelled." Reiko thought of Tomoe's bloodstained socks. Her intuition said the hair oil was the genuine evidence, hidden in plain sight by Lady Nobuko, not planted. But Reiko needed more evidence, solid proof.

"Let's keep searching." She yanked open more scroll cases and scanned the letters inside. "Look for anything that doesn't belong."

They ransacked the chamber. Akiko inspected the other toiletries then flung them aside like garbage. Reiko did the same with the items in Lady Nobuko's desk. They moved on to the cabinets, pulled out garments, shook them, and dropped them on the floor. They didn't find the bloodstained socks Lady Nobuko had worn; she must have burned them before Reiko's first search. While Akiko examined shoes, Reiko tore into a stack of kimonos packaged in white silk bags. These were Lady Nobuko's best clothes—opulent satin robes reserved for special occasions and brightly patterned ones saved from her youth. Expensive kimonos were a significant portion of a rich woman's wealth. Reiko shook out a gorgeous kimono with red peonies splashed on a black, white, and yellow geometric background. As she ran her hands over the smooth, heavy fabric, she felt a crackly thickness in the hem of one sleeve.

Her heart jumped.

Turning the hem inside out, she saw a loose yellow thread where the stitching had been cut. The hem had been sewn up with lighter-colored thread. Reiko tore open the hem. Tucked inside was a folded sheet of paper. She pulled it out and unfolded a letter scribbled hastily, dated two months ago.

> *Honorable Lady Nobuko,*
> *Yesterday, while traveling along the Tōkaidō, I thought I saw the shogun's son. I knew it couldn't be Yoshisato—he was burned to death in that fire. This fellow has gangster tattoos, but he looked so much like Yoshisato, it was as if I'd seen a ghost. I asked around the town where I saw him. His name is Oarashi and he's from Osaka. He was heading to Edo. Maybe my eyes deceived me, or maybe he's a relative of Yoshisato, but you asked me to report any news that had the slightest connection to Yanagisawa, and I am*
>   *Your obedient servant,*
>   *Shiga Mondo, Courier*

"Mama, what's that?" Akiko asked, dropping a quilt she'd just shaken.

"It's proof that Lady Nobuko stabbed the shogun." Reiko could hardly believe what she'd found. Her voice shook with excitement as she said, "She knew Yoshisato was alive before everyone else did." Or at least she wasn't taking any chances. "She knew he was coming back, and she wanted to prevent him from becoming the next shogun!"

Reiko basked in triumph because she'd solved the crime, against all odds. Exhilaration lifted the cloud of despair that had weighed upon her since she'd lost the baby. It didn't matter that the hair oil and the letter incriminated only Lady Nobuko. Lady Nobuko and Lord Ienobu were allies; her killing the shogun would have helped Lord Ienobu take over the regime before Yoshisato showed up. They must have been in on the crime together.

Akiko frowned as she tried to make sense of what Reiko had said. "What are we going to do now, Mama?"

Reiko folded the letter, grabbed the jar of hair oil, and tucked them under her sash. "We're going to tell the shogun that Lady Nobuko and Lord Ienobu conspired to assassinate him and Lady Nobuko stabbed him. He'll disinherit Lord Ienobu and put both of them to death." It was fitting punishment for Lady Nobuko's evils. "Let's hurry. We have to get to the shogun before he dies."

35

WHEN SANO AND Marume returned to the Mori estate, Yanagisawa's men hauled them through the trapdoor and took them straight to Yanagisawa, who was in conference with Yoshisato and Lord Mori.

"Our spies report that Lord Ienobu has troops marching toward town from the provinces controlled by the Tokugawa branch clans," Yanagisawa said. "They'll be here before sundown. Then our forces will be outnumbered ten to one. You'd better have good news."

When Sano told Yanagisawa what he'd learned, Yanagisawa threw up his hands in exasperation. "What do I care about a meeting that happened four years ago, or the death of a piddling translator? Why go after Manabe at a time like this?"

This was Sano's last chance to find out the truth about the attack on the shogun. He still craved the truth, like a man clinging to an unfaithful mistress because she'd already cost him so much and he couldn't bear to think it was all for naught. He appealed to Yoshisato. "Something secret happened between Lord Ienobu and the Dutch. Manabe was in on it. He's like a crutch that Lord Ienobu leans on. Knock him over, and Lord Ienobu will go down, too."

"You're making it up as you go along," Yanagisawa accused.

Sano was, but he said, "Get some extra ammunition against Lord Ienobu, and you won't have to fight a war you can't win." He sweetened the deal for Yoshisato. "Go after Manabe, and you'll get revenge on him for what he and Lord Ienobu did to you."

Yoshisato frowned and considered. Lord Mori said, "Extra ammunition can't hurt."

"Chasing after it will cost us time," Yanagisawa said. "We need to kill Lord Ienobu before his extra troops get here. And there's no guarantee that it will be any more use than investigating the death of the shogun's boy."

Sano knew in his heart that the boy's death was connected to the translator's; both were part of Hirata's campaign to put Ienobu on top. But he didn't say so, even though his loyalty to Hirata had been destroyed when he'd learned about the other murders. The story about the secret society and the ghost was too fantastic for Yanagisawa to believe.

"I say let's try Manabe," Yoshisato said.

"So do I," Lord Mori said.

"I'm in charge!" Yanagisawa protested. "You can't overrule me!"

"I'm the one with the claim on the dictatorship," Yoshisato said.

"And I'm the one with the largest army in your camp," Lord Mori said. "My troops don't attack Lord Ienobu unless I say so. First we tackle Manabe."

Yanagisawa was practically breathing fire from his nostrils, but he saw that arguing was no use. "You have two hours. That's all we can afford to wait." Curious in spite of his anger, he said, "How are you going to get at Manabe? He and Lord Ienobu's other top retainers are shut up inside the castle."

"I'll need your help again," Sano said.

Yanagisawa groaned. "Why am I not surprised?"

THE STREETS OF the Post-Horse Quarter were empty, and so were the stables. The proprietors had rented out all the horses to people fleeing town and closed up shop. Sano and Detective Marume lurked inside the cold, damp yard of Yanagisawa's house.

"Do you think Manabe will show up?" Marume asked.

An hour had passed since Yanagisawa had sent the anonymous note to Manabe, via his spy among the Tokugawa troops stationed outside the Mori estate.

"He'll have to," Sano said. "The note says there's a traitor inside the palace, who's going to assassinate Lord Ienobu, and if Manabe wants to know who it is, he has to come. He can't ignore that kind of threat."

But if the message hadn't gotten through, if Manabe didn't come, there went Sano's chance to get to the bottom of the attack on the shogun, Lord Ienobu's secrets, and Hirata's business, and prevent the war. Moments passed slowly. Sano and Marume tensed at the sound of trotting hooves. They stepped out of the gate to see Manabe, clad in full armor, ride up the street. Manabe reined in his horse and leaned back in the saddle.

"It was you who sent that note." Manabe seemed less surprised to learn it was a trick than angered and puzzled by the fact that Sano was behind it. "What the hell do you want?"

"Just a chat about Lord Ienobu's meeting with the Dutch four years ago."

Manabe kept his face expressionless, but his horse skittered, sensing its rider's unease. Now Sano knew he was right—something illicit, and serious, had happened at that meeting. Manabe chuckled. "Don't you remember what happened the last time you two came after me?" He put his fingers to his lips and whistled, a loud, shrill sound. Nothing happened. The smugness on his face turned to consternation.

Sano pointed behind Manabe. Manabe turned to see Yoshisato walk up the street with his two gangsters. Each man dragged an inert human body. "Look who we found sneaking around," Yoshisato called. He and the gangsters dumped the bodies in front of Manabe.

The bodies were Setsubara, Ono, and Kuzawa. Manabe jumped off his mount, crouched by his friends, shook them, and shouted their names. They lay motionless. Blood from fatal wounds on their heads oozed onto the muddy snow.

"They helped you kidnap me," Yoshisato said. "I had fun getting reacquainted."

"The note said to come alone," Sano said. "You should have."

Manabe stood up, his eyes hot with fury, and reached for his sword.

Sano, Marume, and Yoshisato drew theirs, and the gangsters their daggers and spiked clubs. Marume said, "Five against one. Are you that stupid?"

"Drop your weapon," Sano said.

Manabe realized he was beaten, yanked both swords from his waist, and threw them on the ground. "I should have known." He shook his head, disgusted with himself. "There's no traitor in Lord Ienobu's camp. This is just you and Yoshisato getting revenge."

"You're wrong," Sano said. "There is a traitor. It's you."

"WHAT HAPPENED BETWEEN Lord Ienobu and the Dutch?" Sano asked.

He and Marume, Yoshisato, and the gangsters surrounded Manabe in the cellar where Yanagisawa had hidden Madam Chizuru's granddaughter. Manabe knelt, naked except for his loincloth, in front of a wooden post that supported the low ceiling, his wrists and ankles tied behind him around the post. The air was cold and dank, fetid from the wet filth in the corner where the girl had relieved herself. Sano had never wanted to set foot again in this place of suffering. He wouldn't have brought Manabe here if he'd had an alternative.

"I won't tell you anything," Manabe said.

"Yes, you will. It's only a matter of time." Not much time, Sano hoped. When the two hours were up, Yanagisawa would attack Edo Castle. If Sano wasn't back yet, he would be left behind, unable to go after Lord Ienobu or return to the Mori estate to protect Reiko and Akiko. "You might as well talk now and spare yourself some pain."

Manabe glared. "I thought you didn't approve of torture."

Sano glanced at Yoshisato and the gangsters; their robes were stained with blood. "I'm outnumbered."

"Do your worst. I'll never betray Lord Ienobu." Tethered and shivering, Manabe said, "You might as well kill me now."

Sano mentally crossed the line he'd never thought he would cross. His heart shrank to a chip of ice. He nodded to the gangsters. One struck Manabe on the ribs with his spiked club. Manabe jerked and swallowed a yell as bone cracked.

"What happened at the meeting?" Sano said.

"Rot in hell," Manabe whispered between clenched teeth; his eyes leaked tears.

The other gangster thumped his club against Manabe's crotch. Sano's own genitals contracted. A squeal like a pig burst from Manabe. His body strained forward to curl over his injured testicles. The ropes binding him held up upright. He vomited violently.

"Had enough?" Marume asked.

His big face was pale in the light from the lantern hung on the wall. Sano felt ready to be sick himself. Yoshisato and the gangsters acted as if this were all in a dull day's work for them. Retching and wheezing, Manabe shook his bowed head. One of the gangsters brandished a rusty cleaver while his comrade untied Manabe's wrists and held his right hand against a chopping block. Manabe gasped at the sight of his hand laid out like meat to be butchered. Terror shone in his eyes. For a samurai proud of his swordsmanship, an injury to his primary hand was disastrous.

Yoshisato held up the little finger of his own right hand. Sano balled his hands into fists and swallowed a protest. The gangster brought down the cleaver. Manabe roared as the blade whacked and blood poured from severed flesh and bone. The finger sat on the block, a dead relic. Sano's gorge rose. He'd inflicted worse injuries before, but always in defense of himself or someone else, not in a deliberate effort to cause pain.

"Give up," Marume said, "or they'll keep cutting off your fingers until you won't be able to wipe your behind, let alone pick up a sword again." But he, too, looked repulsed.

"All right, I'll talk!" Manabe wept with pain, shame, and relief. "Just stop!"

The victory didn't taste as rotten as Sano had expected. He had the strange sense that Manabe had intended to confess all along. That was why he'd surrendered after his friends were killed—not because he was outnumbered, but because he wanted to talk. He'd held out longer than most men could, in order that no one could fault him for caving in. Sano wondered why, but he needed other questions answered first.

"Tell me what happened at the meeting," he said as the gangsters bandaged Manabe's hand.

"Lord Ienobu made a secret deal with the Dutch," Manabe said between gasps.

"What was the deal?" Sano asked.

"Lord Ienobu agreed that when he became shogun, he would let the Dutch trade all over Japan and sell whatever they wanted and move about as they pleased instead of being confined to Deshima. They would even be able to settle here if they chose."

Sano was shocked. "Lord Ienobu means to overturn the isolation policy?"

The isolation policy had been instituted about seventy years ago, after the most serious bloodshed in the history of the Tokugawa regime. On the Shimabara Peninsula near Nagasaki, thirty-seven thousand Christian peasants, joined by many *rōnin*, had rebelled against corrupt local government and bad economic conditions. It had taken three months and a hundred thousand troops to put down the rebellion. Almost all the rebels, and thousands of troops, had been killed. The regime had purged the country of the evils they blamed for the rebellion—Christianity and the barbarians who'd brought it to Japan. Japanese were forbidden to go abroad, on penalty of death. These measures prevented the current shogun's worst nightmare—that the powerful *daimyo* clans would collude with the barbarians to overthrow the Tokugawa regime. And now Lord Ienobu meant to reopen the door to the outside world.

"What was Lord Ienobu getting in exchange?" Sano asked.

"A fleet of battleships with modern weapons, and experts to teach our navy how to operate them."

"What for? Did Lord Ienobu want them to keep his enemies under control?" The Tokugawa army and navy, with their ships and weapons, seemed adequate to Sano.

"No." A spark of amused condescension lit Manabe's teary eyes. "Lord Ienobu is planning to conquer the world."

Sano was angry because he thought Manabe was joking. "Do you really expect me to believe that?"

Marume laughed in disgust. "Not even Lord Ienobu is that grandiose."

"Cut off another finger," Yoshisato said. "That will make him tell the truth."

"It is the truth!" Manabe cradled his maimed hand and talked fast. "Lord Ienobu is going to start by invading Korea, taking it over, then moving on to China. He's ordered a hundred thousand guns from the gun makers. He's stockpiled lumber and stone in Kyushu, to build a new naval base for the troops and ships that will cross the Tsushima Strait to Korea. The ground's already been surveyed and the plans drawn up. The morning after the shogun was stabbed, he ordered me to send two messages—one to Kyushu, telling the engineers to start building the base, the other to Nagasaki to alert the Dutch that he'll be shogun soon and they should send him the battleships."

This plethora of details took the wind out of all protest. Convinced, stunned, and dumbfounded, Sano, Marume, and Yoshisato stared at one another. Then Sano said, "Doesn't Lord Ienobu know that's been tried before?"

"Oh, yes." Manabe grinned with morose pleasure at their reaction. "General Toyotomi Hideyoshi, about a hundred years ago."

Hideyoshi was a famous warrior of the civil war era. Born a peasant, he'd started as a foot soldier in the army of Oda Nobunaga, a powerful warlord, and risen to the top rank. When Oda died, Hideyoshi succeeded him and eventually controlled most of Japan. He in turn was succeeded by Tokugawa Ieyasu, who'd defeated his rival warlords at the Battle of Sekigahara and united the entire country under his new regime.

"Hideyoshi sent a quarter of a million troops to Korea," Manabe said. "They took the Koreans by surprise. Within months they'd taken the capital and spread through most of the country. Lord Ienobu has studied the campaign thoroughly."

"Then he knows what happened," Sano said. "The Koreans started fighting back. Hideyoshi's troops suffered from diseases and the severe winter. By the next year, a third of them were dead. The Chinese Emperor sent his army to help Korea. Six years after the invasion, Hideyoshi died, and what was left of his army came limping home. And Lord Ienobu wants to try it anyway?" Incredulous, Sano spread his hands. "*Why?*"

Manabe bristled at the implication that his master was foolish. "He's not small-minded like everybody else. He's not content just to rule Japan. He has a bigger vision."

"A vision?" Marume guffawed. "Is that what he sees with those bug-eyes of his—Lord Ienobu, emperor of the world?"

"If he were, you wouldn't dare mock him."

At last Sano understood the reason for Lord Ienobu's ambition. Lord Ienobu wanted to compensate himself for being deformed and ugly. Ruling the world would show everyone who'd mocked him behind his back and to his face all his life. Sano could pity Lord Ienobu but not condone the means by which he meant to prove his worth.

"He's blind to the lessons of Hideyoshi's campaign against Korea," Yoshisato said with contempt. "It's hard to win a war so far from home. How do you feed and shelter your troops in enemy territory? And the Chinese and the Europeans have better weapons than we do." He'd obviously learned his history. "And as far as timing goes, we're at as much of a disadvantage as Hideyoshi was. He invaded Korea after years of civil war. We're still recovering from the earthquakes, the tsunami, and the Mount Fuji eruption."

"Even with a fleet of Dutch ships, Lord Ienobu is sure to lose. Why does he think he can succeed where Hideyoshi failed?" Sano studied Manabe. "I think you know better. It's your duty to set him straight. Why didn't you?"

Indignant that Sano would accuse him of shirking his duty, Manabe said, "I've tried! Lord Ienobu won't listen." He added forlornly, "He thinks he has the gods on his side."

"Ha!" Marume said. "Now I've heard everything!"

Sano wanted to laugh and cry because he'd discovered the last piece of a baffling puzzle, the connection between Lord Ienobu becoming shogun and the destruction of the Tokugawa regime.

Manabe rushed to explain. "Lord Ienobu has had some lucky breaks. Two of his enemies conveniently dropped dead." Sano remembered the men Toda had told him about. "And there's been money left on his doorstep, as if by a ghost."

If he only knew, Sano thought. Hirata had puffed Lord Ienobu up with superstition and hubris and surely brought him the money. Sano deplored Hirata's actions all the more. Hirata had manipulated Lord Ienobu to do bigger, worse evils. The ghost's purpose became clear.

"Lord Ienobu probably has no idea how big the world is," Yoshisato said. "He's never been outside of Edo. But I can thank him for giving me a broader perspective. While I was on the run from him, I traveled all over Japan. One of the places I went was Kyushu. The Tsushima Strait is so wide you can't see Korea on the opposite shore. I've also been to Nagasaki and seen the barbarian ships."

"So have I." Sano recalled how shocked he'd been by that hint of the magnitude and complexity of the world outside Japan. "I've seen the foreign maps. Japan is tiny on them compared to China and Europe. I expect they're more accurate than ours. The barbarians sail all over the world. Nobody in Japan ever leaves. Lord Ienobu's not to blame for his ignorance."

The memory of his years as a prisoner and fugitive darkened Yoshisato's eyes. "He's to blame for plenty of other things."

Sano realized that Lord Ienobu was to blame for less than he'd originally thought. Lord Ienobu had contrived the murder of the shogun's daughter, but he hadn't murdered Yoshisato. He'd humiliated Sano but not done him or his family any physical harm. And if Lord Ienobu attempted to conquer the world, the consequences—Japan defeated, occupied, and plundered by foreigners—wouldn't be entirely his fault. The real villain in that picture was Hirata. If not for Hirata's meddling, Lord Ienobu might never have lifted a finger to make his dream of ruling the world come true. But there was one crime that Sano couldn't yet lay on Hirata. Lord Ienobu was still Sano's favorite suspect in the attack on the shogun.

"What should we do with him?" Marume pointed to Manabe.

"Kill me or let me commit *seppuku*," Manabe said with a dignity admirable in a naked, shivering, battered man. "It's the only way I can restore my honor after betraying my master."

At last Sano understood why Manabe had confessed: He wanted someone to stop Lord Ienobu from making a terrible mistake. Sometimes betrayal was a duty as well as a disgrace. And Sano needed one more betrayal from Manabe.

"You're not finished," Sano said. "Did Lord Ienobu send the assassin to stab the shogun?"

Manabe rallied to resist implicating Lord Ienobu in the worst crime of all. "No."

"Oh, give me that cleaver!" Marume said.

Attempting to sit up straight, Manabe winced in pain. "You can torture me into saying Lord Ienobu was behind the stabbing, but it won't be true."

His conviction persuaded Sano. Yoshisato said, "We'll take him back with us in case we need him for something else." He told the gangsters to untie Manabe, then told Sano, "His story won't stop Yanagisawa and me from going ahead with the war."

"If we tell all the *daimyo* what Lord Ienobu is up to, they might switch sides. He'll have to surrender." But Sano knew that was too big a gamble. Manabe's confession had changed nothing for the better. It had only exposed the worst about Hirata.

"It's more important than ever to block Lord Ienobu from inheriting the dictatorship." Yoshisato said with a sarcastic smile, "Call me a fraud, but when I become shogun, I won't take Japan to hell in a Dutch battleship."

36

MEN, CLAD IN full armor and organized into regiments of mounted troops and foot soldiers, crowded the courtyard of the Mori estate. Cannons on horse-drawn wagons stood ready to roll when Sano, Marume, Yoshisato, and the gangsters brought in Manabe. Sano had known it in his mind but now he felt it as if a drum had begun to beat inside his gut: The war was really going to happen. He felt it rushing upon him, mowing down all other concerns like some gigantic, many-wheeled machine.

Yanagisawa was having a last council with Lord Mori and his officers, all of them splendidly dressed in armor and equipped with the wooden drums, the war fans bearing their insignias, and the conch trumpets they would use to direct the battle from behind the front lines.

"It's about time," Yanagisawa said.

Yoshisato pointed at Manabe, said, "Here's our first prisoner of war," and told Yanagisawa about Lord Ienobu's pact with the Dutch.

Yanagisawa seemed crestfallen because he'd underestimated Lord Ienobu as well as astonished by the idea of conquering the world. "All the more reason to slaughter the bastard. Put on your armor. We're ready to go."

* * *

IN THE CORRIDOR inside the guest quarters, Masahiro said to Midori, "Please let me see Taeko!" He was dressed in his armor, swords at his waist, bow and quiver over his shoulders, iron helmet in his hands.

"No." Midori crossed her arms, blocking the door to Taeko's room. "She told me what happened. You broke her heart."

"I have to tell her I'm sorry." Masahiro felt so guilty and awful.

"Apologies won't change anything. You're married to Yanagisawa's daughter. Any other promises you make to Taeko, you'll break."

Masahiro knew he shouldn't have bedded Kikuko, but he hadn't been able to help himself. Even now, when he was about to fight in his first war, the thought of Kikuko was arousing. She was so beautiful, so irresistible, that he'd had her three times during their wedding night. When Taeko had confronted him, he should have apologized right away and begged her to forgive him instead of lying and then blowing up.

"I'm going off to war," Masahiro said. "At least let me say good-bye."

"It's no use. She was crying so hard, it made her sick. I gave her a potion to calm her down. She's asleep."

"Then wake her up!" Desperate, Masahiro said, "I might not come back." He knew the odds were against his side; he could be killed in battle. Sudden awareness of his own mortality knocked his breath out of him. The thought of never seeing Taeko again broke his own heart.

Midori was unmoved. "It would be better for Taeko if you didn't come back."

SANO HURRIED WITH Marume to his chamber in the guest quarters. Marume opened the trunks that contained their armor and laid out tunics, undergarments, chain mail, arm and leg guards, gloves, and helmets that looked like relics excavated from the past. Sano hadn't seen them in years. He'd fought many battles, but rarely in full armor; there usually wasn't time to put it on. As Marume donned his padded undercoat and laced his armor tunic over it, Sano called, "Reiko! Akiko!"

The boundaries of his spirit were dissolving. He wasn't just himself, an individual anymore. He was melding with the vast pool of other samurai throughout history who'd ridden into battle with the anguish of knowing they might never see their families again.

Magistrate Ueda shuffled into the room. Sano said, "The war's about to start. I have to say good-bye to Reiko and Akiko. Where are they?"

His father-in-law looked a decade older than yesterday, stricken by woe. He held a paper in his hand. "Reiko left this note. I just found it. They went to Edo Castle, to find out if Lady Nobuko stabbed the shogun."

Sano snatched the paper. The words wavered before his eyes in a haze of fury at Reiko. Time after time, since they'd first married, Reiko had gone off on her own, against his wishes, orders, and pleas. Every time she'd returned triumphant and unrepentant—except last time. Last time, she'd lost the baby.

His fury extended to himself. This time it wasn't only her streak of independence or her desire to solve the crime and save their family that had motivated her to go. She must be so angry at him, and so upset by his failures, that she'd decided to take matters into her own hands. His actions had driven her into peril. But he couldn't forgive her reckless-ness. She'd sneaked out the secret exit and gone to the castle—the target of Yanagisawa's attack—and she'd taken their daughter along.

Masahiro came in, dressed for combat. "What's the matter?"

Sano was so distraught, he could hardly speak. "Your mother and sister are at Edo Castle." If Reiko was so determined to get in, she some-how would.

Magistrate Ueda extended his hands to Sano. He was crying. Sano had never seen this strong, dignified man cry, never seen him look so helpless.

"Save my daughter and my granddaughter," he said. "Please don't let them die."

FOOT SOLDIERS AND mounted samurai waited inside the front gate of the Mori estate. Behind them, Yanagisawa, Lord Mori, and their commanders sat astride their horses. Yoshisato came riding through the inner gate, clad in black armor with a red-lacquered metal breast-plate, accompanied by his gangsters, who were armed with spears as well as their daggers and clubs.

"Where do you think you're going?" Yanagisawa asked.

"To fight a war." Yoshisato's grin flashed beneath his red helmet. "Where else?"

"No, you're not. You'll stay here until it's over."

Determination hardened Yoshisato's jawline. "I have a score to settle with Lord Ienobu."

Yanagisawa didn't let on how afraid he was that Yoshisato would be hurt or killed. "Set foot outside these walls, and you could be dead before you ever get near Lord Ienobu."

"You think I can't take care of myself? I've been winning fights while you've been licking Lord Ienobu's rear end."

Yanagisawa heard a snicker among the troops. He silenced it with a glare. "Your fights were just gang brawls. This is bigger than you can imagine."

"I'll take my chances."

"I'll take care of Lord Ienobu for you. Don't worry."

"You're not the one he kidnapped. I want his head."

Such vengeful bloodlust infused Yoshisato's voice that Yanagisawa felt a thrill of awe. His son had grown into someone that the gods themselves would be afraid to cross. But Yanagisawa couldn't risk Yoshisato on the battlefield. If Yoshisato were to die—this time for real—he would die, too, of grief. "If you're killed in battle, you'll never be shogun."

"Oh, so that's what your concern for me is all about." Yoshisato's eyes glittered with resentment. "You want to safeguard your chance to rule Japan through me."

He was so blind to the real reason. Yanagisawa was sorry yet glad. "Yes, if you want to put it that way." If Yoshisato knew how Yanagisawa felt about him, Yoshisato would throw it in his face. Time was running out; so was Yanagisawa's patience. "Get inside!"

Yoshisato sat firm in the saddle, his mouth compressed.

Yanagisawa called to his personal bodyguards, "Take him."

The bodyguards advanced on their horses toward Yoshisato. Yoshisato drew his sword, his movement swift and expert. "I'll fight them. They'll have to kill me to keep me here."

"All right, never mind!" Yanagisawa said. "You can go. Just stay by me." He would put himself between Yoshisato and danger.

"No." Yoshisato sheathed his sword. "I'm not hanging back with you and the other old men. I'm going with the squadron that invades the castle. I want a crack at Lord Ienobu."

ACCOMPANIED BY MASAHIRO and Marume, Sano burst into the courtyard where the troops were gathered. Yanagisawa, on horseback amid the commanders, raked a disapproving gaze over him. "Why aren't you ready?"

"Call off the attack!" Sano shouted. "My wife and daughter are inside the castle!"

"So what?" Exasperated, Yanagisawa said, "You should have kept them on a tighter leash."

"We can't invade the castle. They could be killed!"

"They should have thought of that before they went there." Yanagisawa spoke with the indifference of a man who cared nothing for his own wife and daughter except as political pawns. "I'm not delaying the invasion for their sake."

"You heartless bastard!" Marume said. Masahiro began shouting at Yanagisawa.

Much as Sano hated to beg Yanagisawa, he fell on his knees. "Just give me a little time to rescue them!" He knew he couldn't expect Yanagisawa to wait on account of Reiko and Akiko, but he was desperate.

Yanagisawa looked sorry he hadn't the time to enjoy Sano groveling to him. "How would you manage to get inside the castle by yourself, let alone get them out?"

Sano didn't know. He would think of something. "Please!"

"Forget it," Yanagisawa said. "We march at noon."

For twenty years Yanagisawa had delivered him blow after blow. Yanagisawa had forced Masahiro to marry Kikuko. And now Yanagisawa would sacrifice Reiko and Akiko to his own impatient lust for power. Never had Sano hated Yanagisawa so much. He grabbed Yanagisawa and dragged him off his horse. "I'll kill you first!"

Yanagisawa's bodyguards hauled Sano away from Yanagisawa. Yanagisawa got to his feet, awkward in his heavy armor. "It's almost noon. The temple bells will ring soon. You have until they stop ringing to get ready. And then we're storming the castle whether you come or not."

Sano was gasping, near tears. As he made a futile lunge at Yanagisawa, Marume restrained him, saying, "We have to go with them. It's our only hope of getting inside the castle and saving Reiko and Akiko."

37

THE TEMPLE BELLS rang noon in a cacophony of peals and bongs that called across river and hills, echoed through empty neighborhoods, and faded. A vacuum stilled the atmosphere, as if the city had drawn a huge breath. A moment later the breath was released in the loud, sonorous bellow of a conch trumpet blown inside the Mori estate.

The Tokugawa army troops outside the estate lifted their heads, startled. More trumpets blared from estates owned by Yanagisawa's allies. Archers on the roofs fired down at the street. The Tokugawa troops yelled and scattered. Arrows pierced chinks in armor and faces under helmet visors. Men dropped in their tracks or fell off horses. Commanders shouted orders. Their archers shot back. Arrows struck buildings, trees. Gunners on the roofs began firing arquebuses. Shots boomed; gunpowder smoke hazed the air; more soldiers in the streets fell dead. Out from the gates stampeded legions of mounted samurai wearing the crests of their *daimyo* lords on banners on poles attached to their backs, brandishing swords and spears.

Inside the Mori estate, behind squadrons of frontline troops waiting their turn to exit, Sano, Marume, and Masahiro sat astride their horses. Sano leaned forward in the saddle, willing the army to move forward so he could go to Reiko and Akiko in the castle. He was so worried about them, and so angry at Reiko, that he couldn't think about the battle ahead. He had to rescue his wife and daughter. They mattered more to him than the code of honor that required him to fight this war and not care about anything else.

Was it too late to atone for all the times he'd put them second to honor?

Marume tapped his shoulder guard. "Stop it! Pull yourself together!"

The ranks ahead of them moved. Urging his horse forward, Sano relegated Reiko and Akiko to the periphery of his mind. If he was distracted during battle, he would be killed before he could reach them. Conditioned by years of martial arts practice, his nerves calmed; his heartbeats became even, steady, and strong. He was a samurai riding into battle, a part of a force greater than himself. The past was erased, like a story written in sand and blown by the wind. His sole purpose in the present was victory. His future depended on his fighting skills, on the whim of fate.

Gunfire boomed, echoing off buildings. Swords clanged and men yelled in the streets as fighting broke out. As Sano, Marume, and Masahiro advanced, they exchanged glances, silently wishing one another good luck. Sano noticed Yoshisato and Yanagisawa nearby.

"What are you doing here?" He'd thought Yoshisato was supposed to stay at the estate and Yanagisawa in the rear.

"Change of plans," Yanagisawa said.

Sano had only a moment to be amazed by how wrong everything was. He was going to war to put Yoshisato—the fraud—at the head of the regime. He was about to risk his life to help Yanagisawa—his enemy—gain control over Japan. Then he was through the gate.

In the street, Yanagisawa's troops fought the Tokugawa army. Horsemen against horsemen, foot soldiers against foot soldiers, one on one or in gangs, they plied swords and spears amid yells and collisions. This wasn't like the Battle of Sekigahara, when rival warlords had met on an empty field and their armies had advanced in orderly ranks while the generals directed them from opposite ends. This was like every samurai street brawl, but on a grander scale. Bodies already littered the ground. Most wore the Tokugawa crest. The attacks on Lord Ienobu's army had thinned its ranks.

Sano forged up the street with his squadron, following the advance troops that plowed through the forces ranged between him and Lord Ienobu. Other troops guarded Sano's rear and flanked his squadron. Outside this cordon, men fought at half the speed as during an ordinary brawl. Stiff, heavy armor hampered their movements, weighed down their horses. Sano, too, was as much handicapped as protected by his armor. Arrows glanced off it, but his helmet obstructed his peripheral vision and distorted sounds. His tunic dug into his waist and armpits; he or it had changed shape since he'd last worn it. His horse, encased in its own armor, labored under him. The charge toward the castle was as slow as if through sludge instead of air. More soldiers disgorged from other *daimyo* estates joined the charge. A huge, growing military procession filled the wide avenues. But the Tokugawa army rallied, its soldiers cut down *daimyo* troops, and Sano saw that casualties on his side were heavy, too heavy. The mist turned to rain. In the distance, cannons boomed.

The storming of Edo Castle had begun.

At last Sano and his regiment reached the avenue outside the castle. It was a churning mass of fighters. Ranks had disintegrated as the Tokugawa forces outnumbered and overwhelmed Yanagisawa's. The brawl had turned into a riot. Fighters ignored the trumpets, yells, and waving fans of the officers. Many had lost track of their mission—they'd reverted to young men caught up in an exciting free-for-all. Sano realized that he himself had lost track of something more vital—his duty. He was about to invade the castle where his lord lived. It was another line crossed. If the shogun were killed during the invasion, that would be blood which Sano could never cleanse off his honor.

But life-or-death combat made such concerns seem abstract and trivial, especially when one's side was losing. Sano's regiment barreled through the mass, toward the castle gate reserved for the shogun on his rare trips outside. Along the avenue, soldiers loaded cannons with gunpowder and iron balls, lit fuses, and fought off Tokugawa troops who tried to interfere. Deafened by explosions, Sano saw cannonballs fly like black comets and bombard the castle walls. Gunners fired at the towers and the guardhouse over the gate. Sparks flared in the windows of the corridors on the walls; gunshots rang out as the defenders fired down at the attackers. Men in the street, hit by bullets, went down under the fighters and horses as if sucked into a whirlpool. As Sano neared the gate, mounted Tokugawa soldiers assailed his regiment. Some of Sano's troops took mortal strikes and died in the saddle. The Tokugawa soldiers broke through the cordon around Sano, Yanagisawa, Yoshisato, and Masahiro.

Sano lashed out his blade with all his might. To penetrate armor, one had to swing hard and hope to hit lacings instead of metal plates. His own armor slowed his movement. His steel struck steel as soldiers parried. He lashed again and his blade went through a soldier's tunic. The soldier screamed, fell, and was gone. Yanagisawa and Yoshisato forged ahead of Sano toward the gate, where their troops were battering the ironclad planks with a ram. Masahiro and Marume were fighting other soldiers. They reached the bridge that spanned the moat. On the opposite side, the gate was open.

The invaders had breached the castle.

Arrows rained onto Sano and his comrades. Bullets pinged off them. Each one that hit Sano felt like a punch. For hundreds of years, samurai fathers and sons had fought together in battles, but no other father could have feared for his son more than Sano did for Masahiro as they rode into a seething crush of foot soldiers at the gate. Beyond it, battling troops crowded the passage.

"Dismount!" Sano yelled as he jumped off his horse.

Masahiro, Marume, Yanagisawa, Yoshisato, and the troops from what was left of their regiment—some twenty men—followed suit. Without horses, they could maneuver more easily and quickly. Their troops cleared a narrow path through the crush. Sano and Masahiro were through the gate. Ahead, within the uphill passage, Yanagisawa's advance troops fought the Tokugawa army. Archers and gunners in the corridor and towers above fired down. It was like shooting fish in a trough. Arrows and bullets hit defenders as well as invaders. Yanagisawa's gunners and archers fired back, but the rain-soaked passage filled with dead bodies; the gray, noxious haze of gunpowder smoke; and the storm of missiles.

The only way to Lord Ienobu—and Reiko and Akiko—was through it.

REIKO AND AKIKO ran through the Large Interior. The passages were deserted, the rooms empty. The chanting grew louder as they approached the main palace. Reiko heard booms in the distance— gunfire. The war had started. Yanagisawa's forces would soon invade the castle. She thought of Sano and Masahiro, and she felt a sudden longing for her husband.

They'd parted on bad terms. She hadn't even said good-bye to him. What if he should die before she saw him again?

This was no time for such thoughts. Reiko clung to her hope that exposing Lady Nobuko would somehow save the day. She kept moving. The building resonated with chants, a giant beehive with an ailing monarch at its heart. Drums kept rhythm. Incense smoke breathed through the passages. Reiko cautiously opened the heavy door decorated with carved flowers and found herself face-to-face with a guard who stood on the other side.

He was an older man she knew from when she'd lived in the castle. He frowned as he recognized her. "You're Sano-*san*'s wife. You're not supposed to be here."

In an instinctive, single motion, Reiko drew the dagger from under her sleeve and lashed out with the blade as she said to Akiko, "Don't scream!"

The guard staggered, clutching his gashed throat. Blood spurted between his fingers. Reiko pulled Akiko backward, away from the spraying blood as he fell dead across the threshold. Eyes wide with horror, Akiko clapped her hands over her mouth. Reiko felt a terrible, sickening guilt. A child should never have to see her mother kill. But a cold, matter-of-fact voice spoke from within Reiko's warrior spirit: *Akiko was born into this family. For us it's too often a choice between killing or being killed. She'd better get used to it.*

"We have to go," Reiko said.

They stepped over the dead guard, holding their skirts up out of his blood, and rushed through the palace. The chanting, drumming, and booms covered the sound of their footsteps. The last corridor was jammed with people. Gripping Akiko's hand, Reiko plunged into the crowd. Servants fingered wooden rosary beads while they prayed. Reiko and Akiko pushed past them, jostled them, stepped on their feet. Murmurs arose: "Isn't that Reiko and her daughter? How did they get in here?"

Wishing she weren't so notorious, Reiko kept going; she dragged Akiko behind her. She was drenched with sweat from the heat of the packed bodies and her own anxiety. They turned a corner. The crowd here was all officials down the middle of the passage and guards along the walls. Reiko's heart sank. The men heard the stir and turned.

Reiko and Akiko found themselves standing alone, conspicuous. The crowd had drawn back from the trespassers. Hostile faces stared at them. Akiko's fingernails dug into Reiko's hand. Reiko glanced over her shoulder. People craning their necks to see what was happening blocked her way out of the palace. Her fate and her daughter's hinged precariously on this moment.

"I have to speak to the shogun." Her voice was small, frightened. The chanting in the corridor stopped; people quieted down to listen. Fainter chanting and drumming came from the shogun's chamber. The officials glared, confused and indignant. Guards advanced on her and Akiko. She'd gambled their lives for this instant. Quaking inside, she gulped. "It was Lady Nobuko who—"

Loud booms interrupted. From the outer section of the palace men's voices yelled, "The castle is under attack!"

Terror sucked the breath out of Reiko. Yanagisawa's army was here; her husband and son were with it. She and Akiko were caught in the middle of the attack. Thuds rocked the palace. The corridor became a turmoil of screams and pushing as guards charged through the crowd, toward the battle, past Reiko and Akiko. Two trespassers were a minor nuisance compared to an invasion. Reiko and Akiko fought their way against the tide. A chain-mailed elbow struck Reiko on the cheek. Feet stomped hers. Akiko's hand was yanked from her grasp.

"Mama!" Akiko shrilled above the screams.

Reiko turned and saw Akiko fall beneath the mob. Akiko screamed as guards trampled her. Reiko threw herself at them, kicked, pummeled, and shoved. She pulled Akiko up, but men knocked them over. They crawled through a thrashing forest of armored legs and black silk robes. Someone kicked Reiko's chin. Her ears rang. She and Akiko crawled free of the mob to the shogun's bedchamber. Guards stood against the lattice-and-paper walls, flanking the door, ready to defend the shogun from the enemy. They didn't notice Reiko and Akiko, crawling below their line of sight, until Reiko lunged at the door and yanked it open.

"Hey! You can't go in there!"

She couldn't think about what might happen to her and Akiko. She didn't know what to do but finish what she'd started. They stumbled on their knees across the threshold. The chamber was hazy with incense smoke billowing from burners in the alcove. In a flash of mental clarity heightened by terror, Reiko absorbed the scene during the moment be-fore the guards caught up with her and anyone else noticed her and Akiko. Lord Ienobu and a physician knelt on one side of the shogun's bed, three priests beating drums on the other. At its end, Lady No-buko, her head bandaged, knelt beside the lady-in-waiting whose mouth resembled a pickled plum. Many guards stood against the walls. The shogun looked like a corpse, with his eyes closed, his face waxen. Except for the priests, whose lips moved and hands drummed as they chanted prayers, everyone was as still as the shogun. Chins raised, their expressions taut with fear, they listened to the sounds of war coming.

The guards seized Reiko. Akiko cried, "Let go of my mother!" and pounded them with her fists. Lord Ienobu, Lady Nobuko, the physi-cian, the priests, and the shogun's guards swiveled toward the commo-tion. Surprise turned their expressions blank. The priests stopped drumming; prayers died on their lips. Lord Ienobu's eyes bulged with anger. Reiko pointed at Lady Nobuko and cried, "She did it! She stabbed the shogun!"

Lady Nobuko jerked, alarmed by the accusation. Her right eye squinted with the pain from the headache that contracted her face. Her left eye glared at Reiko.

"Get them out of here and kill them!" Lord Ienobu ordered.

The guards dragged Reiko and Akiko toward the door. As they fought, Lady Nobuko twisted her gaunt body around, the better to see. The movement pulled up the gray silk sleeve that covered her right hand. Reiko saw the glint of a steel blade protruding from her fist.

"She has a knife!" Reiko cried. "Look out, she's going to kill the shogun!"

The shogun cracked his eyes open. Everyone else turned in surprise to Lady Nobuko. She froze. Both her eyes opened wider with dismay. She must have wanted to make sure the shogun died before he could change his mind about leaving the dictatorship to Lord Ienobu. Her hand quickly withdrew into her sleeve. The shogun's guards had seen the knife, and so had Lord Ienobu and the physician, but they were too stunned to react. Lady Nobuko hurled herself at the bed. She landed on her elbows and knees on the shogun. The impact jolted a grunt from him. The knife was now clearly visible in her hand. Her eyes were wild, her crooked yellow teeth bared. The bodyguards shouted, lunged at her, and grabbed her. As she scrambled toward the shogun's head, her silk skirts slipped from their grasp. The men holding Reiko let her go and rushed to catch Lady Nobuko. The frightened priests ran out of the room. The bodyguards fell across the shogun as Lady Nobuko threw herself on Lord Ienobu.

Lord Ienobu exclaimed, "What are you doing?" There was a quick, furious tussle of flailing limbs and tangled robes. It ended with Lady Nobuko seated on the floor with Lord Ienobu's head cradled in her lap. She held the knife to his throat.

"Let go of me!" Terror shrank Lord Ienobu's voice into a croaky wheeze. His eyes rolled up toward Lady Nobuko. His fingers clawed feebly at her wrist, but she held him tight. With his hunched shoulders, and his feet waggling in the air, he looked like a beetle turned over on its back.

Reiko was astonished because Lady Nobuko had gone after Lord Ienobu instead of the shogun. The physician stared, dumbfounded. The bodyguards clambered to their feet and moved toward Lady Nobuko.

"Don't come any closer!" The harsh, guttural voice sounded completely different from her ordinary one. It belonged to the animal inside the civilized woman.

The guards stopped, as much frightened by the change in her as by the possibility that she would hurt Lord Ienobu. Reiko realized what Lady Nobuko was doing. The same knowledge flashed in Lord Ienobu's eyes. He said, "You don't need me as a hostage. It doesn't matter that you tried to kill my uncle. Before the day is over, I'll be shogun. I'll pardon you." He laughed, his raspy cackle. "After all, I owe you a favor."

Lady Nobuko laughed. "Do you think I stabbed the shogun for you?"

"Of course. Because we're friends." Stammering, Lord Ienobu pleaded, "Let me go!"

"That's not why." Lady Nobuko pressed the blade against his throat. "I did it because I found out Yoshisato was alive. I couldn't let him come back and be the shogun's heir again."

Startled out of his fear, Lord Ienobu said, "You knew? Why didn't you tell me?"

Lady Nobuko leaned over and snarled in his face. "Why didn't you tell me you were responsible for Tsuruhime dying of smallpox?"

Lord Ienobu recoiled. "I'm not! You've never believed it."

"You are! I've believed it ever since Reiko told me."

Astonishment struck Reiko. "But you said you didn't."

Lady Nobuko said with sly triumph, "I fooled you, didn't I?" To Lord Ienobu she said, "I fooled you, too. All these years I've rubbed my nose on your behind, you thought I was your friend. But I was just pretending. And now I have you right where I want you."

"Have you lost your mind?" Lord Ienobu asked.

"My mind is set on the fact that you killed Tsuruhime." Grief coarsened Lady Nobuko's voice. "One reason I stabbed the shogun is that Yoshisato was coming back. The other is revenge on you."

Lord Ienobu bleated, "You're insane."

"I could have killed the shogun when I stabbed him, but I didn't. Do you want to know why?" Lady Nobuko shook Lord Ienobu. He whimpered. "I only hurt him enough to injure him seriously. I wanted him to linger while you gloated because soon you would be shogun. So that when you thought your dream was within your grasp, I could kill you. Just like this." She pricked Ienobu's throat with the blade. He recoiled violently. "As you die you'll see your dream slip away. That is your punishment for murdering Tsuruhime."

$*$ $*$ $*$

"GET DOWN!" MARUME flung his arms across Sano's and Masahiro's backs as they entered the castle, shielding them with his armored shoulder flaps and chain-mail sleeves. They crouched, heads ducked, as they climbed uphill through the battle. In front of them, troops shielded Yoshisato and Yanagisawa. This was the purest expression of Bushido—samurai putting their own bodies between their masters and danger. Sano remembered Hirata stepping forward to take a blade for him. Stray bullets struck walls. Fragments spattered Sano. He felt Marume take the punch of a bullet. Marume staggered but kept moving. The combat around them was mostly hand-to-hand, a riot of bashing and grappling. There was little room to swing a sword. Masahiro shoved aside a bleeding, unconscious soldier whose body was held upright by the packed crowd. Sano raised his head long enough to see the open gate of the first checkpoint. Through the rain and the gunpowder haze he smelled scorched oil.

"Look out!" he called.

A flood of thick, crackling, smoking liquid poured from the window of the guardhouse above the checkpoint. Fighters packed into the small, high-walled enclosure screamed as the boiling oil seeped into their armor, burnt their flesh. Trying to escape the checkpoint, they slipped on the oil and fell. Writhing bodies slid downhill toward Sano. He and his comrades hurried through the checkpoint before the guards could dump more oil. The passage beyond contained another battle. Sano now knew what the journey to hell was like—an endless slog through a narrow channel that smelled of blood and gunpowder, crowded with men trying to kill one another, where arrows and bullets barraged him, paved with corpses.

Marume was breathing hard; he leaned on Sano. Alarmed, Sano said, "Are you injured?"

"I'm all right. Don't stop!"

Higher up the hill, the shooting continued; more hot oil deluged the checkpoints. The army ranks thickened as Sano neared the uppermost tier of the castle. The passage leading to the gate to the palace was deep

292

in the corpses, awash in blood. Less than half of Yanagisawa's advance troops were still fighting. Some shot at the guards who fired down at them. Others charged through the gate, ahead of Yoshisato and his gangsters, Yanagisawa, and his bodyguards. As Sano followed with Marume and Masahiro, he glanced backward. Only a few men from his squadron hurried after him. The others had been killed.

The battle raging in the palace grounds engulfed Sano. Lord Ienobu's forces vastly outnumbered the invaders. A line of them ringed the palace, swords drawn. Gangs of soldiers attacked each of Yanagisawa's. Gunners in the nearest tower fired into the melee.

"The Large Interior!" Sano shouted, beckoning Marume and Masahiro.

Yanagisawa caught his arm. "Where do you think you're going?"

"To rescue my wife and daughter."

"Oh, no, you're not. You're coming with us!" Yanagisawa and his bodyguards surrounded Sano and Masahiro.

"I'll get them," Marume said, panting and sweating. "You go kill Lord Ienobu."

As he and his son were rushed toward the palace, Sano looked backward and saw Marume fall. The big detective struggled to get up, then lay still while men fought around him. Sano cried, "Marume!"

His good, loyal old friend was dead in the line of duty. Reiko and Akiko were alone at the mercy of fate. The soldiers guarding the palace attacked his regiment. They peeled troops away from Sano, Masahiro, Yanagisawa, and Yoshisato, like a tornado stripping leaves off a tree. The four of them, the gangsters, Yanagisawa's bodyguards, and a handful of troops made it through the palace door. Soldiers chased them down the wide corridor, along the polished cypress floor, past the mural of pine trees painted on the walls. Their troops stopped to fight the defenders. Sano, Yanagisawa, Masahiro, and Yoshisato charged ahead.

The inner passages and rooms were empty. In the sudden quiet, Sano and his comrades trod softly, swords still drawn. They met no one, but Sano's skin prickled underneath layers of armor, clothes, and sweat. He sensed Lord Ienobu at the heart of the palace, like a monstrous spider in a web. Surely Lord Ienobu must feel the web shaking as his enemies drew near. The door to the shogun's chambers was open, unguarded. Sano smelled incense and the fetid sickroom odor. He heard unintelligible voices raised in anger and fear. As he stealthily advanced, the garble resolved into words.

"Just let me go!" said Lord Ienobu, tearful, pleading. "I'll give you whatever you want!"

"There's nothing you can give me." The voice was familiar yet so distorted by rage, scorn, and gloating that Sano couldn't place it. "All I want is this."

Sano exchanged baffled glances with Masahiro. Yanagisawa and his bodyguards stormed the chamber, Yoshisato and the gangsters close on their heels. They all stopped so suddenly that Sano and Masahiro bumped into them. Sano saw what had halted them in their tracks.

38

LORD IENOBU LAY on the floor with his head in Lady Nobuko's lap. She held a knife to his throat. The shogun was a withered effigy of himself, unconscious. Sano barely noticed the physician or the guards, he was so happy to see Reiko and Akiko. His eyes filled with tears that dissolved his anger at his wife. She and Akiko were alive. It was all that mattered.

"Papa!" Akiko cried. "Masahiro!"

Reiko's expression wavered between relief and uncertainty. Sano saw that she didn't trust him to do right by her and Akiko. She looked to Masahiro, as if he were her best hope of rescue. It was like a knife puncturing Sano's happiness.

Lady Nobuko's face fell. Lord Ienobu rolled his eyes toward the door, saw Yanagisawa, and screamed to the guards, "They're here to murder the shogun! Stop them!"

The guards jumped to their feet, drawing their swords. They wore armor but had removed their helmets because the room was so warm. Masahiro drew his bow, stepped forward, and let fly. The arrow pierced one guard through the eye. He fell dead. The other guard swung at Sano. Despite his heavy armor, Sano moved with a swiftness born of his need to protect his wife and daughter and his wish to prove to Reiko that he could. He furiously hacked at the guard. The guard went down, bleeding from so many wounds that Sano couldn't say which had killed him.

Yoshisato's gangsters deployed their spears against the other guards, who looked like they were trying to fend off bolts of lightning. In an instant they, too, were dead.

Sano, breathing hard from exertion, didn't have time to ask why Lady Nobuko was holding a knife to Lord Ienobu. Akiko ran to him. He didn't have time to ask what she and Reiko were doing in the shogun's bedchamber. Akiko said, "Papa, we found out she stabbed the shogun!" and pointed at Lady Nobuko. "She wore the other lady's peppermint hair oil!"

Yanagisawa pointed at Lord Ienobu and shouted to Lady Nobuko, "Kill him!"

Lady Nobuko stared at the man who was ordering her to do his dirty work. Anger flashed in her good eye. "You." She said the word like a curse.

"If you kill me, Yoshisato will become shogun," Lord Ienobu hurried to say. "He and Yanagisawa will rule over everybody including you. So you'd better let me live."

Lady Nobuko slackened her grip on the knife. Yanagisawa said quickly, "He killed your stepdaughter. He deserves to die."

Lord Ienobu pointed at Yanagisawa and said, "He had you kidnapped and raped!"

"You got over it," Yanagisawa told Lady Nobuko. "Tsuruhime won't get over dying of smallpox. His sin against you is worse than mine."

Lady Nobuko's distorted face took on a hunted expression as she looked from Yanagisawa to Ienobu, torn between two equally strong hatreds. Lord Ienobu pleaded, "Let me go, and I'll make it up to you."

"How's he going to do that—bring Tsuruhime back from the dead?" Yanagisawa scoffed.

Reiko, Akiko, and Masahiro looked to Sano: They expected him to resolve the standoff, but he didn't know what to say. To side with Yanagisawa or Lord Ienobu—a choice from hell.

"Be quiet!" Lady Nobuko cried. "You're confusing me!"

Sano deduced that she'd stabbed the shogun in an effort to block Yanagisawa's path to power. To block it again she must spare Lord Ienobu. Her dilemma was the same as Sano's—she didn't want either Ienobu or

Yanagisawa to win. She must have known that by taking action against one she benefited the other; she wasn't stupid. But her thirst for vengeance, and perhaps her old age, had demented her. She was making decisions as she went along, and she hadn't come up hard against her dilemma until now.

"I'll set you straight," Yanagisawa said. "This is your last chance to get revenge on Lord Ienobu. If you don't kill him, we will."

He and Yoshisato raised their swords. They and the gangsters surrounded Lady Nobuko. The gangsters pointed their spears down at Lord Ienobu. Sano and Masahiro joined the circle. Masahiro drew his bow, aiming at Lord Ienobu's face. Sano motioned Reiko to take Akiko outside—the killing that his daughter had already seen was bad enough—but they stayed. Beautiful and fierce, they'd never looked so much alike.

Lord Ienobu's eyes glittered with fear and the reflections of steel blades. Lady Nobuko said, "Not yet! Let me think!"

Again that sense of wrongness troubled Sano. Wars were supposed to be won on the battlefield, with each leader having a chance of taking the head of his rival while he risked losing his own. Slaughtering one helpless cripple seemed a travesty of Bushido. But Sano had pledged himself to this assassination, and he would shed his share of his enemy's blood.

"Get out of the way," Yanagisawa ordered Lady Nobuko.

The door to the outer corridor flew open with such a force that the paper panes and wooden lattice crumpled. A violent wind swept in from the garden, knocking Sano and the other men away from Lady Nobuko and Lord Ienobu. Sano heard Akiko scream, saw her and Reiko flung backward. A dark blur, like a mass of soot carried in by the wind, zoomed over the unconscious shogun. It engulfed Lady Nobuko and Lord Ienobu. Her hand popped open and the knife fell out. Terror wrenched her mouth and both her eyes wide open. She rose up from the floor, her feet kicking and arms flailing, and flew across the room. Her back struck the solid wooden partition. She slid down it and landed sitting on the floor, stunned. The blur lifted Lord Ienobu, who moaned in terror. Set on his feet, he wobbled. The wind abruptly died. The blur turned solid, gained human shape.

A shocked exclamation burst from Sano, Reiko, and their children: "Hirata!"

Hirata stood with one arm supporting Lord Ienobu. He looked leaner, stronger, but aged far beyond the years since Sano had last seen him. Rigid with an unnatural tension that clenched his jaw and tightened the muscles around his dark-shadowed eyes, he said, "Don't come near him." His speech sounded strained, forced.

Yoshisato said to Sano, "It's your chief retainer?"

Yanagisawa said, "The traitor and fugitive?"

They were so astounded that they forgot to be angry that Hirata had disrupted their mission to kill Lord Ienobu. The gangsters made confused motions with their spears. Lord Ienobu shrank in fear from his savior. The shogun remained unconscious. Lady Nobuko sat like a broken doll; she'd fainted. His own knowledge about Hirata hadn't prepared Sano for what he'd seen; Hirata's powers were magnitudes greater than he'd thought. The confrontation that had been in the making for so long was now upon Sano, although this wasn't a time, place, or audience he could have imagined. He and Hirata gazed at each other across the space of more than four years, a valley of bitter estrangement.

"That's enough meddling." Sano wouldn't bother to rehash the past or hear excuses. He was so angry at Hirata for his latest crime—killing the shogun's boy—that he just wanted Hirata gone and all ties between them severed. "Get out."

Hirata's expression filled with misery—he knew, and cared, how Sano felt—but he said, "I can't. We have to protect Lord Ienobu. We have to make him the next shogun."

"Who is 'we'?" Yanagisawa demanded.

Lord Ienobu's little jaw sagged with dismay. "It's you that's been helping me? Not the gods?"

"Yes," Hirata said. "Me, and the ghost."

"What ghost?" Yoshisato asked.

Fear of the supernatural trickled through Sano as he looked around for the spirit that had been manipulating Hirata from beyond the grave.

"Have you been leaving money on my doorstep?" Lord Ienobu asked, incredulous. "Did you kill my enemies?"

"The ghost of General Otani. He died during the Battle of Sekigahara. He made me kill them. He made me steal money and give it to you." Hirata spoke fast, then was silenced as if by a hand squeezing his throat.

"Why?" Lord Ienobu seemed abashed because he'd thought the gods were on his side but it was really a fugitive who claimed to be in league with a ghost.

"Shut up and get out, Hirata," Sano said. "That's an order."

"Because General Otani wants to avenge his death by destroying the Tokugawa regime." Hirata forced the words out, choked on them. The authority he answered to apparently didn't want the story told, either. He flung Sano an anguished, apologetic glance.

Puzzlement joined the chagrin on Ienobu's face. "How is making me shogun supposed to accomplish that?"

"You're planning to conquer the world," Hirata said, his strangled voice barely intelligible. "You're doomed to fail. The foreign barbarians are too powerful. You'll take the regime down with you."

Dismayed to have his secret out in the open, furious because Hirata had punctured his conceit, Lord Ienobu insisted, "I will win! You don't know what you're talking about!"

"You've said your piece," Sano told Hirata. "Go. Don't add to the trouble you've caused."

Hirata shook his head. "I can't."

"Just blow out of this room the same way you blew in," Yanagisawa said.

"If you have any sense of honor left, you will go," Sano said. "You'll let us take care of Lord Ienobu, and he won't destroy the regime."

"My honor is gone. And I can't stop what's going to happen. All I can do is apologize. I'm sorry I was disloyal." Hirata's desolate gaze encompassed Masahiro, Reiko, and Akiko. "I never meant to hurt you. I was stupid and greedy and I didn't know what I was getting into, and if I could go back in time and kill myself before General Otani got hold of me, I would. Please forgive me."

Sano couldn't help feeling moved by Hirata's plight, but there could be no forgiveness while the transgressor was still transgressing.

"Quit whining!" Yanagisawa said. "Get lost!"

"I owe you an apology, too," Hirata said, "for Yoritomo's death."

"What?" Startled and distracted, Yanagisawa asked, "Why?"

"It's a long story, but I was responsible."

Yanagisawa opened and closed his mouth, dumbstruck, unsure whether to believe Sano wasn't the one at fault. Hirata turned to Reiko. "Tell Midori—" He gulped; his throat jerked. "Tell her and the children I'm sorry." His eyes glistened.

"Tell them yourself." Reiko's manner was gentle, sympathetic, entreating. She extended her hand to Hirata. "Come home with me. Midori and Taeko and Tatsuo and Chiyoko miss you so much. They would be so happy to have you back."

"No, they wouldn't." Hirata sounded certain, forlorn. "Not if they knew what I've become." His voice broke. "I'm sorry I killed the boy Dengoro, and the Dutch translator, and those officials. I'm sorry I framed Lord Yoshimune and his cousin. After the shogun was stabbed, I stole Tomoe's socks, dipped them in blood in the shogun's slop basin, and buried them outside the *daimyo* district. General Otani made me."

"Stand away from Lord Ienobu, or I'll make you sorrier." Yanagisawa waved his sword at Hirata, but the gesture was tentative; Hirata had put the fear of the supernatural into him.

"General Otani's not here," Sano said. "What you do next is up to you."

"He is here." Hirata's face bunched up; he looked like a child about to cry. "He's inside me. I'm possessed by his spirit. Watch!"

He lowered the arm he held around Lord Ienobu. Stiff and trembling, it moved down slightly, then snapped back up. His hand locked like a steel clamp on Ienobu's shoulder. His face reddened, strained, and perspired with effort while his body jerked as if punched from within. Lord Ienobu shrieked, "Help!" Hirata screamed in pain. As Sano and the others watched, amazed, Hirata stopped jerking and screaming and went limp. He and Lord Ienobu hovered above the floor, then descended to settle gently on their feet.

"See?" Hirata's voice was an agonized croak.

Sano was horrified by the grotesqueness, the indignity of having an alien presence in control of one's body. His anger at Hirata faded into sorrow. All the ardor, the talent, and good intentions in Hirata, wasted because he'd been reduced to a puppet of a demon!

The flabbergasted silence was broken by a soft, sighing groan. All attention turned to the shogun. His chest no longer rose and fell. The physician felt his neck for a pulse, then raised his own stricken face. "His Excellency is dead."

39

THE NEWS THUNDERSTRUCK Sano.

The lord he'd served for twenty years was dead.

He was catapulted out of the reality in which he and Yanagisawa and Lord Ienobu were fighting for control of the regime into another dimension of darkness and agonized howls. There he joined multitudes of samurai who, throughout history, had lost their lords. A grief as much theirs as his own stabbed Sano to the heart.

The shogun was gone! Even though Sano had often hated him for his capriciousness, stupidity, cruelty, and cowardice, none of his faults mattered now. In death the shogun claimed the full magnitude and dignity of his office. The gray, wasted effigy in the bed was to Sano what every lord had been to every samurai for time immemorial—the purpose of his existence.

Sano felt as bereft as if someone he'd dearly loved had died. His body reacted even as his mind struggled to absorb his loss. His eyes gushed tears. He sank to his knees, removed his helmet, and bowed his head. Masahiro did the same; Reiko and Akiko knelt, too; they were following Sano's example; they didn't know what else to do in this unprecedented situation. Hirata's arm dropped. His expression shifted between triumph and defeat.

Exultation dawned on Lord Ienobu. He said in a hushed voice, "I'm shogun."

The ramifications of the shogun's death snapped Sano out of his grief. The shock on Yanagisawa's and Yoshisato's faces turned to horror. They were losing the war, Yoshisato couldn't inherit the regime, and Hirata stood between Yanagisawa and his dream of ruling Japan.

Lady Nobuko wailed, "No, no, no!" She crawled to the shogun and pounded on his chest. "You can't die yet!"

"Revive him!" Yanagisawa shouted at the physician.

Yanagisawa had been so fixated on gaining power by making his son shogun that he couldn't adapt fast enough to the new circumstances, Sano realized. He couldn't think past the fact that now Yoshisato could never inherit the regime. No matter that his army was in the castle and he might still have a chance of victory over Lord Ienobu—all he could see at the moment was the shogun dead and his dream lost.

The physician dipped a cotton puff in a bowl of water and wet the shogun's lips, administering the *matsugo-no-mizu*—water of the last moment, the final attempt to revive a dead person. The shogun remained inert. Droplets scattered as Lady Nobuko pounded on him and shouted, "Come back!" The physician shook his head.

Yanagisawa turned on Hirata. "This is your fault!" He told his bodyguards, "Kill him!" Now realizing how to remedy the situation, he shouted, "Kill Lord Ienobu!"

The bodyguards hesitated, afraid of Hirata. Lord Ienobu, chortling with glee, said to Hirata, "Here's my first order as shogun: Kill them all!"

Distraught but resigned, Hirata drew his sword with a motion so fast that the outline of his arm blurred and the weapon seemed to leap into his hand. Sano hauled himself to his feet, drawing his own sword. It was his duty to rid the world of the evil thing Hirata had become.

"Don't just stand there, kill him!" Yanagisawa shoved his bodyguards forward. "Do it or I'll have your heads!"

AS THE GUARDS came at him, Hirata felt General Otani's will take control of his body, a sensation like liquid steel solidifying in his nerves, muscles, and joints. He slid into a state of amplified perception.

The auras of the people in the room crackled and sparked hot, colored light. Energy flooded through Hirata, launching him into a dimension between the present and the near future. Time stretched. The bodyguards lunged in slow motion. He saw a spectral image of each man, like a faint, greenish, twin shadow, blazing a trail in front of its owner. The images revealed where the men would be and what they would do in the next instant. Hirata slashed.

The speed of his blade caused a bang like a gunshot. An instant later the men filled the space where their images had been. He cut through armor, flesh, and bone. The friction made sparks and smoke. The men's severed upper and lower halves landed on the floor in a welter of blood. Horror gradually appeared on the faces of Yanagisawa, Yoshisato, Sano, and Masahiro. Akiko screamed. She and Reiko covered their mouths with their hands. Lady Nobuko shrieked as gore splashed her. The physician vomited. Lord Ienobu tittered with delight. The sounds distorted into groans that rose in pitch as time contracted, Hirata's perception slowed, and the world sped up to its normal pace. The smells of blood, viscera, and burnt flesh, leather, and metal suffused the air.

Sano stepped in front of Masahiro, Reiko, and Akiko. Raising his sword in his right hand, he flung out his left arm to shield his family. Yanagisawa did the same for Yoshisato. Hirata moved toward Yanagisawa. If he killed Yanagisawa, it would be something good to come of the mess he'd made of his life, a gift of atonement to Sano.

Terror froze Yanagisawa's expression. Then Hirata heard General Otani's voice: *Kill Sano first.* Hirata faltered; his body pivoted. He knew why General Otani wanted him to kill Sano: It would break his spirit; he would be softer clay in the ghost's hands. Hirata resisted. It was like pulling against chains wrapped around him. His steps changed course, toward Sano.

"So it's come to this." Sano hadn't put his helmet back on, and Hirata saw reproach in his eyes. "You've broken every other rule of Bushido, why not murder me."

"No, Hirata-*san*," Reiko and Masahiro pleaded. Akiko was crying.

Kill them all, General Otani said. *Then they won't look at you like that.*

"Run," Sano told his family, as if he could hear the voice in Hirata's head.

They didn't move. Hirata strained as General Otani moved one of his feet in front of the other. The tug-of-war pulled a muscle in his groin. Hirata gasped at the pain, step by arduous step. Lord Ienobu trailed close behind him as if he were a shield. Hirata's heart pumped madly. The war of wills between him and the ghost caused a racketing ache in his skull. General Otani roared with anger, pain, and bloodlust. Hirata tried to tell Sano he was buying him time to escape and couldn't hold off much longer, but his voice shriveled in his throat. Sano held Hirata's gaze, daring him to attack, entreating him to desist. General Otani raised Hirata's arm. It trembled, the sword waving in the air, as Hirata fought to hold it back and the ghost tried to swing at Sano. A tendon snapped. Hirata and General Otani cried out. As they struggled for dominance over the body they shared, Sano swung at Hirata.

Hirata dodged. Sano missed, but for an instant Hirata's attention to General Otani lapsed. The ghost seized control, and Hirata hacked repeatedly at Sano. As Sano ducked, his heavy armor threw him off balance. Masahiro lashed his sword and Reiko her dagger at Hirata, but Hirata easily deflected them while battering Sano. Sano spun like a suit of armor hung on a stand for combat practice. He staggered and tripped over his feet. All that held him upright was Hirata's blows whacking him from side to side. Armor plates and chain-mail links flew off him. His sword broke in two and fell from his hand. Hirata strained against General Otani. The pain in his head was so bad, he felt nauseated. Every sore muscle throbbed as he relentlessly attacked the master he loved. He wept as he delivered a mighty blow.

Sano sprawled on his back. His hand scrabbled in a futile attempt to pick up his broken sword. His armor in tatters, his breastplate scored by cuts, he was too exhausted to stand.

With a loud scream and all his strength, Hirata wrenched his hips. He kicked out with his feet. Stumbling backward, he collided with Lord Ienobu. General Otani halted his retreat and bent his body at the waist with a force that sent a painful spasm twanging through his back. As

General Otani propelled him at Sano, Hirata threw his weight forward and landed on his stomach. Yanagisawa and Yoshisato circled him, trying to reach Lord Ienobu, but Hirata lashed his sword at them, and they jumped back. Hirata crawled toward Sano. More muscles seized, tendons pulled. His heart was beating so hard it would burst from his chest.

Kill Sano!

Hirata slowly rotated, as if against a tornado buffeting him. He crawled away from Sano. Elbow and shoulder joints dislocated; bones in his arms and legs cracked. Pain exploded from the injuries. The pressure of the blood in his veins rose so high that a whooshing sound filled his ears and his head spun. He saw, through black dots that swam in his vision, Lord Ienobu cowering in a corner. Perspiration gushed from his pores. General Otani tried to rein him in. He groped on his knees and left hand, dragging his sword with his right, toward Lord Ienobu.

If he could kill Lord Ienobu, the ghost's aim of destroying the Tokugawa regime would be done for.

His spine snapped like a wire drawn too tight. His arms and legs collapsed under him. He landed with his cheek to the floor. Numbness pervaded his body. His neck and facial muscles were the only ones he could move. He could still breathe and feel the wild beating of his heart, but he was paralyzed.

General Otani bellowed with fury. His attempts to raise Hirata were like punches to the inside of a pillow. They jolted Hirata, but he couldn't feel them. He moaned because Lord Ienobu was still shogun and General Otani was still inside him. Yanagisawa and Yoshisato moved to his side, keeping their distance, as if from a poisonous snake that they didn't know for certain was incapacitated.

Get up! General Otani roared. *Kill them, damn you!*

Lifting his head, Hirata saw a blurry image of Lord Ienobu. Mental energy was all he had left. Aligning it was like trying to gather marbles while his panic scattered them and General Otani stormed in his head. Hirata trained his thoughts as best he could on Lord Ienobu. An energy burst flowed out from him like the faint light of a comet in the sky at dusk. Spent, Hirata dropped his head while General Otani raged.

* * *

LORD IENOBU UTTERED a shrill, ululating scream.

Sano, lying exhausted on the floor, panted as he raised himself on his elbow. He looked from Hirata's prone figure to Lord Ienobu. Lord Ienobu's body stiffened; his back arched. His face locked in a pop-eyed grimace. The scream choked off in his throat. His eyes rolled up, and he crumpled. The room was silent except for Hirata's labored breathing and the sounds of combat outside coming closer. Yanagisawa cautiously nudged Lord Ienobu with his foot. Lord Ienobu lay motionless. His mouth was slack, drooling.

Yoshisato crouched and felt Lord Ienobu's wrist. "No pulse."

"He's dead," Yanagisawa said in a tone of wonder.

"So much for conquering the world," Yoshisato said.

Lady Nobuko burst into sobs. "Thank the gods! Tsuruhime's death is avenged!"

The physician timidly offered his professional opinion. "He must have had a stroke. The shock to his system . . ."

Sano knew better than to think Lord Ienobu had conveniently dropped dead. As he clambered to his feet, his breastplate, armor tunic, and shoulder guards fell off, the lacings cut by Hirata's blade. He went to Hirata, knelt, and shook Hirata's shoulder. "Hirata!"

"Sano-*san*." Hirata's voice was a rasp squeezed out of his inert body. His eyes cracked open, wet with tears. ". . . I'm sorry."

"You don't have to apologize," Sano said. "You've made everything right." Hirata had not only slain Sano's enemy, he'd saved Japan from Lord Ienobu's foolhardy ambitions. Hirata, the onetime traitor, was a hero.

A sigh of relief issued from Hirata. "Do you forgive me?"

"I forgive you." Sano truly did. "Where's General Otani?"

". . . Don't worry . . . he can't make any more trouble."

Hirata could make a fresh start, Sano thought. "Let me help you up."

"I can't move." Anguish squeezed Hirata's voice tighter. "I'm paralyzed."

Reiko gasped in dismay. Akiko said, "Can't the doctor fix you?"

". . . No."

Sano was horrified by the cost of Hirata's atonement. In his struggle to overcome the ghost, Hirata had sacrificed his own body. He was still alive, but in a state worse than death. Sano was filled with grief and pity for his old friend.

"You can be shogun now," Yanagisawa said to Yoshisato. They laughed with exultation.

And here was the cost of Lord Ienobu's death. Sano rose in protest as power changed hands for the last time.

Lady Nobuko revived, beheld Yanagisawa and Yoshisato with disgust and hatred, and stumbled to Lord Ienobu. She pounded his scrawny chest, shouting "Come back! Don't let them take over!"

Lord Ienobu grunted, sat up, stretched his arms, and yawned.

40

LADY NOBUKO SHRIEKED, recoiling in fright. Sano, Reiko, Masahiro, and Akiko exclaimed. Yanagisawa and Yoshisato stared, shocked and aghast. Sano stated the obvious fact: "You're not dead."

Lord Ienobu wrinkled his brow. He suddenly resembled his uncle. He hesitantly raised his finger, as the shogun had often done when he wanted to ask a question he thought might be considered stupid.

"Speak," Sano said, startled by the change in Lord Ienobu.

"Who are you?" Lord Ienobu glanced at the other people. "Who are they?"

"Don't you know?" When Lord Ienobu didn't answer, Sano realized he was waiting for permission. "You can talk to me."

"No. I don't know." Lord Ienobu noticed the corpses of the shogun and the slain guards; he pursed his mouth. "What happened?"

"Don't you remember?"

"No." Lord Ienobu seemed only mildly worried. Hirata had tried to kill him, been too weak, and only damaged his brain, Sano thought. "Who am I?"

With the vexed air of a man saddled with unfinished business, Yanagisawa drew his sword and said, "You're dead now."

Running footsteps and excited shouts resounded. The partition between the shogun's bedchamber and the corridor opened to reveal a squadron of Tokugawa troops. "Lord Ienobu, we've beat back the invasion," the leader said. "The castle is secure." His voice trailed off as he and his men took in the scene—the dead shogun, the strewn corpses, and Yanagisawa ready to slay Lord Ienobu. "Get away from him! Drop your weapon!"

Yanagisawa froze, let his sword fall, and stepped backward. His face was a picture of outrage because his fortunes had reversed yet again.

"You're safe, Honorable Lord Ienobu," the leader said. "We'll get rid of this filth for you." He and his troops advanced into the bedchamber.

Reiko and Akiko moved nearer to Sano. Glad that they cleaved to him no matter how Reiko felt about him, Sano couldn't believe they'd come so far and gone through so much, and yet now all was lost.

Lord Ienobu looked to Sano. Sano spoke instinctively: "Tell them to back off."

"Back off," Lord Ienobu said.

The troops hesitated, confused. The leader said, "What?"

"Tell them that's an order," Sano said, "and they should leave us alone."

"That's an order," Lord Ienobu repeated. "Leave them alone."

His men gaped at one another, then backed away. Sano was stunned to discover that Lord Ienobu would do whatever he said. Everyone else looked just as stunned. Yanagisawa said, "Order them to tell their generals to surrender to my army."

Lord Ienobu looked to Sano again. He was like a baby chick just hatched from the egg, thinking that the first live creature it noticed was its mother, instinctively accepting Sano's direction. Thinking fast, Sano said, "Not surrender. Call a truce."

"Call a truce," Lord Ienobu said.

"You cast some kind of spell over him," the leader accused Sano.

"Not I," Sano said with a glance at Hirata.

"Do as I say, or I'll have your heads," Lord Ienobu said. He was apparently capable of phrasing his own sentences as well as parroting Sano's.

Vacillating between fear of him and suspicion toward Sano, the men glanced at one another. Then they departed.

"Call them back!" Yanagisawa ordered Lord Ienobu.

"Touch your nose," Sano said.

Lord Ienobu raised his finger and tapped his nose.

Yanagisawa went livid with anger as he comprehended that Sano had sole control over Lord Ienobu and therefore over the regime. "You've ruined everything. You always do." His tone was as deadly as the sword he picked up from the floor as he advanced on Sano. "But this is the last time."

Sano heard Reiko, Masahiro, and Akiko exclaim in alarm as he reached for his sword—which Hirata had shattered to pieces. "Wait." He was acutely conscious that Yanagisawa wore full battle gear while his own head was bare and his body minus its armor. "We can work something out."

Yanagisawa fumed through clenched teeth; he would have spit fire if he could. "Oh, no." His eyes blazed under his helmet. "I won't give you another chance to spoil things for me. I'm going to do what I should have done a long time ago."

The weight of his armor slowed his rush at Sano long enough for Sano to snatch up Hirata's sword. Then Yanagisawa was upon Sano, lashing and shouting, "For twenty years—whatever I tried to do, you were always there to trip me up! Well, no more!"

Sano was too busy parrying to strike back. Although he was the better fighter, he was worn out from his fight with Hirata, and Yanagisawa had the lethal energy of the insane. "This is for all the times you turned the shogun against me!" Yanagisawa hacked at Sano's head. As he recited old grievances, his blade whistled, carving wild patterns that Sano frantically dodged. "This is for Yoritomo!"

Akiko ran at Yanagisawa, grabbed his leg, and shouted, "Leave my father alone!"

"Akiko, get away!" Sano yelled.

YANAGISAWA KICKED AT Akiko while hacking at Sano, but she hung on. Reiko was horrified to see her daughter caught in the battle between Sano and Yanagisawa. She screamed and rushed to rescue Akiko. Yanagisawa swung at them. Sano whacked Yanagisawa across the chest. His blade didn't penetrate the armor, but Yanagisawa faltered; he missed Reiko and Akiko. Reiko pulled Akiko off Yanagisawa, and he resumed attacking Sano.

"I'll kill you if it's the last thing I do!"

Sano struck his knee guard. Yanagisawa yelped in pain and staggered. Yoshisato ran to help him. Masahiro chased Yoshisato, tackled him, and brought him down. Holding Akiko so that she wouldn't run back into the battle, Reiko realized that Sano was bound to lose. Without his armor, already exhausted from his fight with Hirata, he panted as he dodged Yanagisawa's frenzied slicing.

Seeing her husband attacked by Yanagisawa was different from seeing him attacked by Hirata. Somehow Reiko hadn't really thought Hirata would kill Sano, and she'd been correct. Something in her had known that Hirata's loyalty to his master would ultimately win out. Instinct had moved her to defend Sano, not the belief that he was in real danger and needed her help. But now the danger to Sano was real, mortal.

Akiko knew; that was why she'd tried to protect him. Reiko knew, too.

Yanagisawa had often tried to kill Sano. Nothing stood in his way this time.

Reiko felt a sensation like cold water dashed on her, rinsing from her eyes the haze created by her anger at Sano and from her mind the list of his misdeeds. During the past four years, she'd thought of Sano as a source of nothing but trouble. Seeing him up against Yanagisawa in their long-overdue fight to the death put him in a new perspective.

Yanagisawa embodied all that was evil and Sano all that was good.

The harsh light of comparison exposed the unshaded, black-and-white fact that Sano had taken honor too far, but Yanagisawa personified what happens when a man goes too far in the opposite direction. Sano and Yanagisawa had lived their lives in the same political arena; they'd experienced the same pressures and temptations; and Yanagisawa was what Sano would have become if not for Sano's refusal to deviate from Bushido. Reiko had deplored his honor as a blight on her and her children's existence, but now she realized that it was the talisman that had kept Sano from turning into Yanagisawa. It was the cornerstone of his relentless pursuit of justice during this investigation and all those they'd worked on together. It was an integral part of the man she'd fallen in love with nineteen years ago.

The husband she still loved in spite of, and because of, everything.

In the cold, lucid air of revelation, Reiko saw a new battle line drawn. It put her on Sano's side, where she belonged, which she'd never really left. On the other side was Yanagisawa, the real enemy. All the fury and hatred she'd once directed at Sano now blazed at Yanagisawa.

How dare he attack her husband?

If Yanagisawa killed Sano, then Sano would die thinking she wanted to leave him because she didn't want to be his wife. He would never know that it wasn't true.

Reiko shoved Akiko into a corner, shouted, "Stay there!" and snatched a sword from a dead guard.

"No!" Sano shouted at her.

He'd said she would never learn to stay out of danger; Reiko would make him thankful for it. Savage with determination, she swung at Yanagisawa's back while he fought Sano. Her blade grazed one shoulder then the other, cutting the lacing on the armor panels. They hung like broken wings. She sliced the cord around his waist and the shoulder straps of his tunic. As his tunic fell off, Yanagisawa realized what was happening. He rounded on her and lashed.

Reiko jumped back, her right arm spilling blood from a cut so deep and painful that her breath hissed out of her. She dropped to her knees, clutching the wound that immobilized her arm. Her own physical agony didn't matter. She moaned because she was of no use to Sano now, when she wanted to be, when it counted the most.

YANAGISAWA WHIRLED TO face Sano again. Sano lashed and knocked his helmet off. Except for their gloves and chain-mail sleeves, they were both vulnerable from the waist up. As they lunged and circled, retreated and trampled the dead, their whirring swords met flesh. Blood spattered. Gashes on Sano's arms and shoulders burned. Masahiro and Yoshisato wrestled, their feet kicking, metal-plated knees banging, while they clawed at each other's necks. Akiko was chattering anxiously as she tied her sash around Reiko's arm. Sano feared that his wife was mortally wounded, his son outmatched by Yanagisawa's. Lady

Nobuko hugged herself, both eyes closed tight, terrified. Lord Ienobu watched with more curiosity than apprehension. Sano raised his sword, backhanding a slice at Yanagisawa's head. His blade locked in a cross against Yanagisawa's. His arm was already strained from his battle with Hirata. A muscle inside it twisted. The pain snapped open his fingers. His sword dropped.

Unholy glee shone in Yanagisawa's eyes. As he swung at Sano, he slipped on the bloody floor. Sano hurled himself on Yanagisawa and grabbed the hilt of Yanagisawa's sword. His weakened right hand slipped off. His left clung. They fell together and landed on the bed. Fighting for control of the weapon, they rolled over the dead shogun. A furious anger boiled up in Sano. Yanagisawa wasn't the only one with twenty years' worth of grievances to redress. Something in Sano had known it would come to this—him and Yanagisawa fighting to the death, over the body of their dead lord, to settle their personal scores. It was fate.

Sano pried back Yanagisawa's fingers until bones cracked and Yanagisawa screamed. He got a clumsy hold on the sword. Yanagisawa swatted it out of his hand and punched his face. Momentarily blinded, ears ringing, nose bleeding, Sano reared back. Yanagisawa sprang and grabbed Sano around the throat. With his left hand Sano scrabbled at the thick, gloved fingers squeezing his windpipe. With his right he clawed at the floor in desperate search for the sword. He closed on a fragment of his broken blade. It was shorter than his forearm, with a jagged break at one end and the sharp tip at the other. He lashed it at Yanagisawa's head.

Yanagisawa let go of Sano's neck to protect his own face. He snatched at the blade fragment. Sano stabbed at Yanagisawa's throat. Yanagisawa caught the jagged end before the tip cut him. Scuffling frantically, he and Sano rolled atop the shogun, each with both hands locked tight around the blade between their bodies. Sano felt its edge slit his right glove while they each hung on and tried to drive the tip through the other. Their legs kicked and scrambled. The blade sank into Sano's palm. Pain flared. Warm blood spilled.

If he let go, he was dead.

He and Yanagisawa lay on their sides, across the shogun, face-to-face. Sano pushed. Yanagisawa pushed. They gasped and grunted, breathing each other's breath. Yanagisawa's bared-teeth grimace was a mirror of Sano's own. Their bodies were as inseparably close as if they were lovers. Yanagisawa thrust. The tip grazed Sano's stomach, cut through his robes, and pricked his skin. His muscles contracted as he thrust at Yanagisawa. He saw, at the edge of his vision, that Yoshisato had Masahiro pinned facedown, his knee on Masahiro's back. Masahiro screamed as he struggled. Terrified that his son would be killed, desperate to be free to rescue him, Sano heaved with all his might. He and Yanagisawa roared as the blade sank into flesh. They both stiffened. Yanagisawa's face reflected Sano's surprise. They lay together, unmoving, muscles locked.

Yoshisato and Reiko came running. They looked terrified—they knew someone had been cut but not who. Sano wasn't sure himself. He hurt all over, and the boundary between him and Yanagisawa seemed to have dissolved. Yoshisato and Reiko pulled them apart. Sano couldn't catch his breath. There was blood all over him and Yanagisawa. Reiko and Yoshisato were crying. As Sano lurched to his feet, Masahiro and Akiko rushed over. They and Reiko supported Sano. Akiko hugged his waist. She wept with joy because Sano was unhurt except for his cut hand and other minor injuries; the blood on his stomach wasn't his.

Yanagisawa remained lying on the bed, across the dead shogun. The broken, jagged end of the blade stuck out of his belly. Blood spread around it like the petals of a scarlet flower unfurling. The tip had been driven up under his rib cage. His face was white, ghastly, the mask of death upon it.

Numb with disbelief, Sano squinted, as if in the light of a new day.

AS·HE LOOKED up at Sano standing over him, Yanagisawa was at first too indignant to feel any pain. This wasn't how it was supposed to end!

He tried to sit up, to see how badly he was hurt. The blade shifted. The pain skewered through him. His whole body, the whole world, was made of the agonizing, indescribable, unbearable pain in his midsection. Yanagisawa's mouth opened in a scream, but all that came out was a gurgle. Something was wrong with his lungs. As he gasped for breath, his thudding heart pumped blood from his cut viscera, through his abdomen, and out around the hole from which the blade protruded. His bowels released a warm gush; sweat poured from his skin. Freezing cold, he shivered violently. Yanagisawa knew enough about battle injuries to realize that this one was mortal.

He was dying.

He'd recovered from disasters in the past, but there was no recovering from this one. He'd always had a plan for triumphing over them, but all the plans in the world wouldn't save him now. Death was the one enemy he couldn't defeat.

Sano had delivered him into the hands of that ultimate enemy.

Helpless, trembling with anger, Yanagisawa beheld Sano, his hatred undiminished by the fact that he had only moments left to live. Sano had shattered his dream of ruling Japan and destroyed him. He whispered, "This isn't over." Every word wrung more pain from his innards. "We'll meet again someday." Blood frothed from his nose and mouth. "Next time I'll win."

Sano's image blurred. Darkness encroached on Yanagisawa's vision. His ears filled with a roaring sound like the ocean as the tide of his life force receded. Through it he heard Yoshisato call, "Father!"

Yoshisato knelt beside him, took firm hold of his hand, and kept him from floating out with the tide. The darkness brightened. Yoshisato's tearful face hovered over him. Disbelief startled Yanagisawa. His tough, obstinate son who hated him was crying!

"Father, you're going to be all right," Yoshisato said, clutching Yanagisawa's blood-smeared hand to his heart. "Just stay with me! Please!"

Yanagisawa dimly realized that Yoshisato had blurted the truth about their relationship. But it didn't matter to Yanagisawa that the secret was out and he could no longer claim that Yoshisato was the shogun's son and eligible to inherit the regime. Dying changed a man's priorities, Yanagisawa discovered. Yoshisato cared about him enough to beg him to live! He wanted to tell Yoshisato how happy he was despite the horrible pain. He wanted to say that this joy was worth dying for and how sad he was that it required his death to bring them together. But he hadn't enough breath. Fighting the pain, he lifted his other hand, stroked Yoshisato's cheek, and whispered, "My son."

Yoshisato cried, "No!" His eyes darkened with horror. It wasn't that Yoshisato didn't want to be claimed as his son, Yanagisawa knew. Yoshisato realized that Yanagisawa didn't care if their fraud was exposed, because Yanagisawa knew he was dying.

"Don't die, Father!" Yoshisato pleaded.

Yanagisawa wanted to weep, too, because he and Yoshisato had found their way to each other but soon they would be separated forever. He wanted to rail against the unfairness of fate; he wanted to curse Sano. But his fading spirit cleaved to the samurai code of honor he'd ignored all his life. A samurai had only one death and he shouldn't waste it on unseemly displays of emotion. And Yanagisawa had a better use for his limited time on earth.

He gathered his scarce breath around the vicious pain that sent spasms through his body. "I wish I hadn't waited until you were seventeen before I got to know you," he said in a whisper so faint that Yoshisato leaned close to hear. "I wish we'd always been together." Yanagisawa didn't apologize for everything he'd put Yoshisato through; he knew that given another chance he would do it again, he would use Yoshisato or anybody else to further his ambition of ruling Japan. Dying didn't change a man that much. Instead of wasting his last breath on lies, he said, "You've made me proud. You're the best son I could ever have wanted."

His voice was gone. His lips formed the words he'd never spoken to anyone except in jest or as a means of manipulation. *I love you.*

The roar in his ears drowned out the sound of Yoshisato's voice begging him to hang on. The darkness pulsed with his weakening heartbeat, obliterated the world. The tide was unexpectedly warm and comforting. The last thing Yanagisawa felt was Yoshisato's hand holding his.

41

A NOISE LIKE fireworks roused Taeko from a drugged sleep. Her body was stiff from lying in bed too long, her head ached, and the pillow under it was wet. Her eyes were sore, swollen, and crusted, and her mouth tasted sour. She smelled gunpowder and heard shouting and booms outside as she remembered her quarrel with Masahiro.

It was over between them. He was with his wife.

Taeko began to cry again. More firecrackers exploded. She didn't know what was going on, but she didn't care. All she could think about was Masahiro. He'd betrayed her, and she'd said terrible things to him, and he'd left her even though he knew about the baby. She hated him! And yet she still loved him so much.

She wished Kikuko would die. Maybe then Masahiro would come back to Taeko. Kikuko was young and healthy, but she might catch a disease or have an accident. But that seemed impossible. So did having the baby. Taeko remembered a pregnant servant girl who'd jumped off the Ryōgoku Bridge and drowned. The idea appealed to Taeko. If she were dead, she wouldn't feel this pain anymore, and when Masahiro saw her drowned body, he would be sorry about how he'd treated her. He would realize how much he loved her and he would hurt the way she was hurting now.

But even as she imagined walking to the bridge and climbing over the rail, she knew she couldn't do it. She could kill herself but not the baby she loved so much. Taeko curled up and wept in helpless despair. What was she going to do?

"MAMA, I'M SCARED," Kikuko said.

She and Lady Yanagisawa sat in their chamber in the Mori estate, listening to the gunfire outside. "Don't worry, darling." Lady Yanagisawa stroked Kikuko's long hair. "Everything will be all right."

She kept her voice calm; she mustn't let Kikuko know how afraid she was. Half her fear was for herself and Kikuko. Any moment the enemy could break into the estate. Half was for Yanagisawa. He could be killed during his attack on Edo Castle. Her lips moved in silent prayer. *Please let him be safe!* And under that prayer, like the second voice in a duet, came the usual one: *Please make him love me!*

A cannon boomed. The black smear of blood from the hemorrhage in her eye jittered across her vision as Lady Yanagisawa started. Kikuko wailed. Lady Yanagisawa said, "It's just noise. It can't hurt you."

But her husband's chief retainer had warned her, *The enemy soldiers could rape and torture you and your daughter. You should be prepared.* Lady Yanagisawa glanced at the long, flat black lacquer box on the floor beside her. It contained a knife. Should the enemy come, she must kill Kikuko and herself, to spare them the pain and indignity, to preserve their honor.

"I'll tell you your favorite story," Lady Yanagisawa said. "In a land far away, there was a magic garden. The sky was always blue. The sun shone every day. The trees never lost their leaves because it was always summer."

"And the flowers were all the colors of the rainbow," Kikuko said. She knew the story by heart. Her tense body relaxed.

"And all the animals could talk."

"All the deer, and the birds, and the squirrels, and the rabbits, and the butterflies."

"In the garden, in a little cottage, lived a father, a mother . . ."

"And their beautiful daughter who looked just like me." Kikuko smiled.

"The father was very handsome. The mother was very plain, but he loved her very much. And they loved their little girl." Lady Yanagisawa smiled, too, caught up in the fantasy she'd invented years ago. "The father played the samisen. The mother sang happy songs."

"And the little girl played with her friends, the animals who could talk."

"There were no other people, but they were never lonely, because they had each other."

The sound of someone shrieking and running interrupted the story. Lady Yanagisawa and Kikuko looked up in fright. Lady Yanagisawa felt a cold sensation in her chest, like icicles dripping.

"Wait here." She disentangled herself from Kikuko.

Kikuko clutched at her skirts as she rose. "Mama, don't leave me alone."

"I have to see what's wrong. I'll be right back." Lady Yanagisawa ran down the corridor and stopped at the threshold of the room where Lady Someko knelt with her arms clasped around her stomach, rocking back and forth as she shrieked. Her face was ugly with pain and tear-blotched makeup.

Lady Yanagisawa disliked Lady Someko and rarely spoke to her, but she had to ask. "What's wrong?"

Lady Someko looked up with eyes as glazed as a blind woman's. "Yanagisawa is dead! He's been killed in the war!"

A thump in her chest struck Lady Yanagisawa, as if her heart were wood split by an axe. Her voice burst from her in a whispered plea. "No!"

"It's true," Lady Someko said, hoarse and breathless. "Sano did it. Yanagisawa is gone! I'm free of him!" She laughed exultantly as she wept.

Lady Yanagisawa felt an internal shattering, as if her bones were fracturing, organs rupturing. Yanagisawa was dead. He would never love her. The destruction within her released emotions like gases from decaying meat. Anguish and fury spewed. Reiko's husband had killed her husband. Reiko, whom she envied and hated, must have been involved somehow. Lady Yanagisawa wanted to find Reiko, claw her beautiful face, and strangle her. She wanted to lie down and mourn for Yanagisawa and never get up.

"Mama, Mama!" Kikuko called.

Blind maternal instinct propelled Lady Yanagisawa toward her child. The invisible tie that had bound her to Yanagisawa was severed. Her body was like a Bunraku puppet whose sticks were animated by a one-handed puppeteer. She fell to her knees beside Kikuko. As she sobbed, her eyes gushed tears as thick and salty as blood.

"Mama, why are you crying?" Kikuko anxiously patted her face.

Lady Yanagisawa tried to take comfort from the fact that she still had her daughter, but half a reason for existing wasn't enough. She couldn't bear to live without Yanagisawa. But if she didn't go on living, Kikuko would be alone in a cruel world with nobody to love her. A thought ripened in Lady Yanagisawa's mind, as seductively sweet as a poisonous fruit. Even as it filled her with horror, she knew what she had to do.

"Lie down," she said, "and we'll finish the story." Kikuko obediently laid her head in Lady Yanagisawa's lap. "Let's close our eyes and go on a trip to the magic garden."

Kikuko smiled; her long-lashed eyelids closed. She loved make-believe. "Can I play with the talking rabbits?"

Lady Yanagisawa wept as she said, "Yes." She opened the lacquer box and removed the black-handled knife. Gunfire boomed, distant and sporadic. Lady Yanagisawa gazed through her tears at her daughter's innocent face. Before her resolve could waver, she slashed the knife across Kikuko's smooth white throat.

Blood spurted from the gash, drenching their robes, the floor. Kikuko jerked and stiffened. Her eyes snapped open. She stared up in pain, fright, and confusion at Lady Yanagisawa. Her lips parted. Blood oozed from them as they shaped the silent word, *Mama!*

Horrified by what she'd done, Lady Yanagisawa sobbed and moaned. "You're going to the magic garden, my love." Kikuko choked; she went limp as the life faded from her eyes. "Your father is there waiting for you. I'm coming soon. We'll all be happy together."

Lady Yanagisawa raised the red, dripping knife and slashed her own throat.

* * *

ALONE IN HER bed, Taeko came to a reckoning with reality. The baby would be born in a few months, and she had to plan for its future even though she didn't want to face her own. The knowledge strengthened a will she hadn't known she possessed. She sat up and dried her tears on the sleeve of her robe, surprised to learn that this was what it meant to be grown up—putting her child's needs first.

Taeko dragged herself out of bed, shivering in the cold, and trudged down the corridor. The fireworks sounded far away. Somewhere in the house a woman was shrieking. Taeko wasn't curious enough to find out who or why. She had to apologize to Masahiro and ask him to take her back. She would be his concubine so that she and the baby would have a place to live and he would support them. She would put aside her pride for the baby's sake . . . and because she was still in love with Masahiro and wanted to be with him no matter what the conditions were.

What if Masahiro and Kikuko were making love? She would wait patiently until they were finished, and she would pretend not to care. She would throw herself on his mercy.

She reached the section of the guest quarters where the Yanagisawa family lived. Through an open door she saw the shrieking woman. It was Lady Someko, kneeling and rocking back and forth. Midori and Magistrate Ueda stood outside a nearby room. Midori was leaning over, her hand to her head, as if fainting, while Magistrate Ueda supported her. They saw Taeko.

Midori cried, "Don't look in there!" Magistrate Ueda put out his hand to stop Taeko, but she was determined to go through with her decision. She pushed past him and her mother into the room.

Masahiro wasn't there. Kikuko lay on her back; her eyes gazed up at the ceiling; her mouth was open in an expression of frightened surprise. Her complexion was as white as ice, a shocking contrast to the bright red and pink kimono she wore and the bright red ribbon around her neck. Her head rested on a long, thick, gray and dark red pillow. Taeko frowned, puzzled by the strange sight. Then she saw the ribbon around Kikuko's neck drip thick red droplets into a red puddle that covered the tatami. She smelled the sweet, salty, iron smell, and her stomach flipped. The puddle was blood. So was the red pattern on Kikuko's clothes. The ribbon was a gash across Kikuko's throat. The pillow was a woman wearing a bloodstained gray kimono—Lady Yanagisawa. Her face was white, too, her throat also cut, her eyes blank and filmy. The blood puddle framed her head. Beside her hand lay a knife covered with her blood and her daughter's.

Masahiro's wife is dead.

Taeko couldn't believe it. She hadn't really wanted Masahiro's wife to die. But she had wished it, and her wish had come horribly true. Taeko screamed and screamed and screamed.

42

EDO AT NIGHT rested in an uneasy state of cease-fire. The army, swelled by troops newly arrived from the provinces, occupied the city. The rebel *daimyo* and their armies had retreated into their estates. The rain had stopped, and the fog dissipated, but smoke from bonfires veiled the sky. Soldiers loaded corpses onto oxcarts that rolled through the deserted city toward the temple districts and the crematoriums.

Inside Lord Mori's estate, a sick ward had been set up in the barracks. Physicians ministered to wounded soldiers who lay on beds in rows on the floor. Maids brought tea, gruel, and fresh bandages and removed soiled dressings and basins of blood-tinted water. The atmosphere was thick with heat from charcoal braziers and the smell of medicine.

"I have to get back to the castle." Detective Marume, wearing a bandage wrapped around his left shoulder and back, sat up in his bed. "Sano-*san* is up there alone!"

"You have to rest." Kneeling beside him, her bandaged arm in a sling, Reiko sponged his face. She'd found him lying unconscious outside the palace. "You're badly hurt."

"It's just a flesh wound. Sano-*san* needs me."

"He can take care of himself." But Reiko was worried about Sano, too. Some twelve hours had passed since they'd left Sano at the castle, and they'd had no word of what was happening there.

A physician said to Marume, "Rest or you won't heal. You've lost a lot of blood." He glanced at Reiko. "So have you. Go to bed or infection could set in. You could lose your arm."

Marume reluctantly lay down. Reiko walked on shaky legs to the guest quarters. She feared that even if Sano survived, their marriage wouldn't. She'd realized how much she loved him, but maybe it was too late.

INSIDE THE PALACE reception chamber, Lord Ienobu sat on the dais. Sano, his hand stitched and bandaged, knelt at Ienobu's right. On the floor below them, the Council of Elders sat in a row apart from the Tokugawa branch clan leaders, who included Lord Yoshimune. Sano had briefed them on the extraordinary events in the shogun's bed-chamber. They looked as shocked as Sano still was.

Sano still couldn't believe Yanagisawa was dead. He felt strangely un-balanced, as if a part of him was gone and he hadn't yet adjusted to the missing weight. Although he'd seen Yanagisawa's body carried out of the palace, and he knew Yoshisato had gone to the Mori estate to break the news to Yanagisawa's family, the reality of Yanagisawa's death wouldn't sink in until he'd checked the whole city and made sure his enemy wasn't lurking someplace.

But he couldn't leave the castle yet. Masahiro had taken Reiko and Akiko, the paralyzed Hirata, and the wounded Marume to the Mori es-tate, while Sano stayed behind to deal with the aftermath of the war. A messenger had brought Sano the news that Lady Yanagisawa had killed herself and Kikuko. Heaven only knew when Sano would see his family again or what else would happen. Sano gazed down at the assembly gath-ered to figure out what the government should do.

"Call the meeting to order," Sano said.

"I call the meeting to order," Lord Ienobu said.

The senior elder, a bald, pugnacious man named Ogita, scrutinized Lord Ienobu. "Is his mental condition permanent?"

"It's impossible to tell," Sano said.

"He's otherwise normal?"

"Apparently. His physician has examined him." Sano added, "He can eat and attend to his personal needs and read and write, but he doesn't seem to remember anything at all."

"And he won't do or say anything unless you tell him to."

"That seems to be the case."

Lord Matsudaira, spokesman for the *daimyo*, glared down his long nose at Sano. "For all practical purposes you're in control of the shogun, the regime, and the whole country."

Sano was still shocked by this reversal of his fate.

"This is an untenable situation," Senior Elder Ogita protested. "We can't have a shogun who's unable to think for himself!"

A chagrined silence ensued as everyone recalled the dead shogun, his body hastily cremated because of the measles.

"Lord Ienobu has an extreme case of mental impairment," Lord Matsudaira said. "He shouldn't be shogun." Other *daimyo* nodded. Yoshimune was silent, perhaps chastened by the knowledge that he might have been convicted and put to death for the old shogun's murder if Lady Nobuko hadn't confessed.

Although he'd not asked for the opportunity to rule Japan through the new shogun, Sano was reluctant to let it slip away. Yanagisawa would die of envy. Sano had to remind himself that Yanagisawa was dead. "I could tell Lord Ienobu to step down, and he would do it, but then who would be shogun?"

"I understand Yoshisato has given up his claim to the dictatorship," Lord Matsudaira said.

"That's correct," Sano said. Yoshisato had told him so.

"Lord Ienobu's son is next in line for the succession," Senior Elder Ogita said. "He's only two years old, but a regent could be appointed to rule on his behalf until he comes of age."

"Lord Ienobu wouldn't have wanted to be shunted aside," Sano said. A big responsibility accompanied his stroke of good fortune: It was now his duty to look out for the interests of Lord Ienobu, who was helpless to look after them himself. And it was a chance for Sano to try his hand at ruling Japan as well as to control his own destiny.

Maybe he'd absorbed some ambition from Yanagisawa at the moment he'd taken his life. The thought was disconcerting.

"What he would have wanted in the past is irrelevant. He obviously hasn't any objection now." Senior Elder Ogita eyed the placid, silent Lord Ienobu.

"How would we explain to the world why he was stepping down?" Sano asked.

"We could say he was seriously injured during the battle. Which would be true."

"If his son becomes shogun, the government will be in virtually the same situation as it is now—with a dictator who's unfit to rule. It'll just be someone other than me in charge."

Lord Matsudaira smirked. "Precisely." The other *daimyo*, except for Yoshimune, nodded.

"Who would be the regent?" Sano asked.

Each *daimyo* except Yoshimune volunteered for the job. The elders chimed in to support their favorites. During the loud, heated argument about who was most qualified or deserving, Sano said to Lord Ienobu, "Tell them to stop."

"Stop!" ordered Lord Ienobu.

The argument fizzled. Sano said, "You're already fighting about who'll control the dictatorship. What makes you think it will be one of you?" The men looked startled. "A regime with a child at its head and his clansmen squabbling over control of it—that's a ripe apple for picking. Remember, many of the other *daimyo* revolted today. They could start a full-scale civil war, and if they win, that'll be the end of the Tokugawa regime."

Sano was disturbed to hear another voice in his head, speaking the same words—Yanagisawa's. How long would it be until he stopped hearing that voice? How long until he could speak or act and not wonder if it was what Yanagisawa would have said or done?

"Sano-*san* has a point," Senior Elder Ogita said reluctantly.

"He's just trying to hang on to the power that his influence over Lord Ienobu gives him," Lord Matsudaira said. "If we let him, *he'll* pick the apple!"

The very idea amazed Sano. So did the fact that although he'd once done his best to keep Lord Ienobu from rising to the top of the regime, now he was trying to keep him there. "The regime will be more stable with an adult as shogun, and the other *daimyo* respect Lord Ienobu even if they don't like him."

Outraged and incredulous, Lord Matsudaira said, "He's your puppet!"

"Not a word of what's happened to Lord Ienobu will appear in the official record," Sano improvised. "Only a few people know. We'll swear them to secrecy."

"He never went out much," Senior Elder Ogita admitted. "If he stays out of sight, no one will suspect the reason." The other elders nodded.

"You can't hide him all the time," Lord Matsudaira said. "He'll have to hold audiences."

"I'll make sure he behaves properly," Sano said. "And Manabe will look after him when I'm not with him." Sano and Manabe had made a deal: Manabe would take care of Ienobu, keep quiet about his condition, and not make trouble for Sano; Sano wouldn't punish Manabe for kidnapping Yoshisato and deceiving the old shogun. It went without saying that Ienobu had gotten his comeuppance for those offenses.

"But he'll be even less in charge than the previous shogun was, which is to say not at all! You'll be as good as ruling Japan!"

"I did it while I was chamberlain to the previous shogun," Sano pointed out. "I'll be Lord Ienobu's chamberlain and do it again."

"I won't bow to your authority!"

Yoshimune spoke up. "Give Sano-*san* a chance. So he's a puppeteer—if you don't like how his show is going, then you can cancel it and make Lord Ienobu's son shogun."

There were murmurs of agreement. Yoshimune still had a commanding air about him. Lord Matsudaira, overruled and disgruntled, said to Sano, "All right, here's your first test: How do you propose to handle the men from Yanagisawa's faction?"

Sano turned to Lord Ienobu. "Pardon them all."

"I pardon them all," Lord Ienobu said.

An uproar broke out. Senior Elder Ogita said, "Pardon the enemy? Are you serious? It's never happened in all of history."

"A lot has happened today that's never happened in all of history. Pardon them, put the whole blame on Yanagisawa, and the regime will hold together. Charge them big fines. But if you try to confiscate domains and hand out death sentences, you'll start that civil war you don't want." Sano thought of Yoshisato's plan for a coalition to improve the government. He added, "I don't intend to run Lord Ienobu's government by myself. I welcome your advice. Somebody else might not be so willing to cooperate for the good of Japan."

"I suppose you'll be purging your enemies and putting your relatives and friends in high positions," Lord Matsudaira said.

"My son, Masahiro, will have my old post as chief investigator. I may make some other changes. Anyone who doesn't perform to my satisfaction had better improve or watch out."

"What are you going to do with Lady Nobuko?" Senior Elder Ogita asked. "Don't forget she murdered the shogun."

"It wouldn't do to let the world know," Sano said. "A regime that let its dictator be stabbed by his crazy wife? We'll go down in history as the biggest laughingstock of all time. His official cause of death will be measles. I'll have Lady Nobuko put in a convent and kept quiet."

Everybody seemed willing to let that matter lie. Everybody also seemed willing to give Sano his chance to run the government—rope to hang himself. "Next he'll be pardoning all the criminals in Edo Jail," Lord Matsudaira grumbled.

Not true, but Sano would issue a pardon for Dr. Ito.

Lord Ienobu raised his hand. Sano said, "You may speak."

"I'm hungry. Can I have something to eat?"

As Sano led Lord Ienobu from the chamber and everyone bowed to them, Sano imagined Yanagisawa fuming at him from the netherworld.

AT THE MORI estate, Hirata lay on his back in bed, his eyes half closed, while his wife and children held a vigil around him. He felt no sensation in his body. It was like a carcass connected to his head, swollen with blood and poisons leaking from its damaged organs. He drifted in and out of consciousness, through different dimensions in time and space, as his brain gradually died.

He saw Midori crying and the solemn faces of Taeko, Tatsuo, and Chiyoko. He and Sano rode their horses through Edo, laughing together at some joke. He sat cross-legged outside a mountain temple, meditating. He and General Otani dueled on the battlefield at Sekigahara. They were the only ones still standing; the field was strewn with corpses. They lunged and swung their swords at each other. Cuts in their armor oozed blood from their wounds. General Otani roared, "Damn you for ruining everything! I'll make you pay!"

There was no one to break the spell that had put the ghost inside Hirata. They were both shackled to Hirata's mortally injured body.

Hirata floated in darkness, near the mouth of a cave where strange lights and shadows flickered. The cave was the portal to the netherworld. The sound of Midori crying returned him to his bed. She crawled onto it and wrapped her arms around him. Hirata couldn't feel her except where her face, wet with tears, touched his.

"We can't part like this." Her murmur in his ear was raw with sorrow. "The last words I said to you—" Time inverted. They were in the alley in Nihonbashi. She screamed, "I hate you! I wish you were dead! I never want to see you again!"

Now, as they lay together, Midori wailed, "I wish I could take it back. I didn't mean it. I was so hurt, I wanted to hurt you. I never—"

They stood facing each other at the portal to the netherworld. They were as young as when they'd first met nineteen years ago. Hirata was healthy and strong, Midori fresh and pretty. Her tears gleamed on smooth, rosy cheeks. "I never stopped loving you," she said.

Joy elated Hirata. His wife loved him despite all the wrongs he'd done her. He took her in his arms. She clung to him and whispered, "Please say you forgive me."

On the corpse-strewn battlefield, Hirata and General Otani were so wounded and exhausted, they could barely lift their swords, but they kept fighting. In the room where Midori hugged the paralyzed wreck that he was now, Hirata moved his cracked, gray lips and whispered, ". . . I forgive. Do you?"

"Yes!" Midori wept with relief and gratitude. The shadows and light from the netherworld played across her young, smooth face. "I love you," Hirata said, as young and ardent as on the day they'd married. He stepped free of her embrace. "I have to go." A sense of peace comforted him: Their separation was only temporary. "Tell the children . . ."

"Good-bye for now," he whispered to Taeko, Tatsuo, and Chiyoko.

He saw their tearful smiles and heard them echo his farewell. As he backed away from Midori, she ran after him, arms outstretched, calling his name. The distance between them widened and her figure shrank. "I'll be waiting for all of you," Hirata called.

He collapsed on the Sekigahara battleground. General Otani fell beside him. Darkness obliterated the field, the dead soldiers. The portal to the netherworld beckoned. Hirata crawled through it, dragging General Otani with him. General Otani beat at him with armored fists and shouted, "Damn you to hell for all eternity!"

They were across the threshold. As they melded with the light and shadows, Hirata's last sensation was the ghost disengaging from him, like a chain around his spirit loosening and crumbling away.

MORNING DAWNED COLD and clear, with a wind that chased white clouds across the pale blue sky as the sun rose. Servants outside the castle lugged away dead horses, raked up arrows and bullets, and mopped blood off the streets. Sano rode accompanied by a big retinue of troops from the same army he'd fought against two days ago. The man who controlled the shogun was a target for assassination.

When he reached Kan'ei Temple, Sano left his horse and retinue outside the cemetery. He entered the gold-trimmed, red double gate flanked by pillars. On a stone pedestal surrounded by evergreen trees and snow stood the shogun's funerary urn—a big stone drum with symbolic carvings. A few wooden prayer stakes were planted in the ground around the base amid a few rice cakes, cups of sake, and lit candles. The fact that the shogun had the measles had been kept quiet, and so had the stabbing. The citizens wouldn't learn of his death until they returned to Edo, and in the aftermath of the war, his officials and troops were too busy to visit his grave.

Sano pressed his prayer stake into the hard soil. He bowed his head as he came to the humbling realization that although it was easy to criticize someone else's shortcomings as a dictator, it would be harder to avoid making mistakes now that he was in effect the dictator himself. The shogun had taught him a valuable lesson—how not to rule a nation. How to rule it well was up to Sano.

He heard a step behind him, turned, and saw Lord Yoshimune. "I hope you don't mind my joining you."

"Not at all." Sano was finished, for now.

"I want to thank you," Lord Yoshimune said as they stood side by side at the grave. "So does my cousin Tomoe. If you hadn't discovered that it was Lady Nobuko who stabbed the shogun, we might have been put to death by now."

"All in a day's work."

"I'd like to repay you for saving my life and Tomoe's. Whatever I can do for you, just ask."

Sano recognized that Yoshimune, like any astute politician, wanted to be on the good side of the power behind Lord Ienobu. "Support the new shogun." Lord Yoshimune had already helped him bring the council under his control. "Tell the other *daimyo* to do the same."

"That's little enough. I suppose you'd rather not call in the whole favor until I'm in a position to do more for you." Contemplating the grave, Yoshimune said, "I'll be shogun someday."

"When Lord Ienobu dies, his son will inherit the dictatorship. His son's only two. He could reign for a long time and outlive you."

Yoshimune shrugged, unperturbed. "Anything can happen. The events of the past few days have proved that. Besides, I feel lucky." His grin showed a hint of his old brashness. "When I'm shogun, if you're still around, I'll give you a nice position in my regime." He bowed and departed.

Sano bid the dead shogun a silent, grateful farewell, then went to join his retinue. He had another meeting that promised to be less friendly than this one.

* * *

TAEKO STOOD, HER face puffy and tear-stained, on the
veranda of the guest quarters of the Mori estate. She'd come outside for
a respite from trying to comfort her brother and sister while her mother
and the servants prepared her father's body for the funeral. In the garden where she and Masahiro had quarreled, patterns of sunlight and
cloud shadow moved across the muddy snow. She looked at the opposite
wing of the house and thought of Kikuko dead and all the blood. She'd
wished Masahiro's wife would die, and she felt as guilty as if she herself
had cut Kikuko's throat.

Masahiro came out of the house and stood beside her. Taeko felt
even guiltier. She still loved him and wanted him so much that his very
presence made her tremble. After everything that had happened, she
was still hurt by his betrayal and terrified of what would become of her.
What a selfish person she was!

"Can I talk to you?" Masahiro sounded uncertain and nervous.

She couldn't look at him, didn't deserve to have him with her. Afraid
of what he would say, she nodded.

"I'm sorry about your father."

Fresh tears of grief, shame, and guilt burned down Taeko's chilled
face. She was worrying about her troubles when her father had sacrificed his life! She knew what courtesy required her to say to Masahiro.
She swallowed hard. "I'm sorry about your wife."

But it was only half true. She was sorry that Kikuko had died in such
a horrible way, murdered by her mother, but she wasn't sorry Kikuko
was dead.

"So am I," Masahiro said with a sigh. Taeko stole a glance at him, to
see whether he was heartbroken. But he only looked exhausted. "This
probably isn't a good time . . . so soon after . . . but . . ." He drummed
his fingers on the veranda railing and said gruffly, "I want to explain why
I . . . the other night . . . well, you know."

Taeko gripped her arms under her sleeves, pressing them against the
baby, as the memory of him and Kikuko sickened her stomach.

"I didn't mean to," Masahiro said, "but she was the most beautiful girl I'd ever seen. And she somehow knew the things I wanted. It was so . . . exciting, we did it three times, all different ways. I couldn't help myself."

The news that he'd betrayed her not once but three times, and the awe in his tone, were like stabs to Taeko's heart, and he didn't seem aware that he was hurting her. It was her punishment for wanting Kikuko to die.

"But I didn't love her. I don't think I ever could have. Because it's you I love."

The passion in his voice astonished Taeko. She turned to gape at him. He seized her hands and said, "Please tell me you don't really hate me! Please take me back!"

It didn't matter that he only *thought* he couldn't have loved Kikuko; it didn't matter that her death might be the only reason he wanted to be with Taeko again. Taeko pressed his hands to her face and sobbed, wracked by joy and guilt. Masahiro sniffled as they clung to each other. He stepped back to look at Taeko. His cheeks were wet from their tears. "Will you marry me?"

She was so unworthy of this good fortune. If he only knew about her evil thoughts toward his wife! She had to confess.

He misinterpreted her hesitation. "Oh, you're worried about our parents. But I'll stand up to them this time. I want to be with you, and our baby."

"But—"

"I know, you're not sure you should trust me." He drew a deep breath, let it out, and said, "I'm not going to make any more promises I can't keep. If somebody else like Kikuko comes along . . . well, I'm as weak and selfish as you said. All I can say is, if you marry me, I'll try to be better." Impatient, he said, "Will you?"

Taeko was impressed by his honesty, thrilled by the prospect of being his wife and their baby having a father. "Yes," she whispered. She could live with knowing that Masahiro might hurt her again someday. She would probably hurt him again. They would make up. She would remember Kikuko, and she would try to be better, too.

Masahiro laughed, hugged her, lifted her off her feet, and spun her around until she laughed with him. "As soon as my father comes back, we'll tell everybody."

SANO LEFT HIS retinue in the courtyard of an inn located down the street from the Shark Teahouse. He climbed the stairs to the balcony and knocked on a door. Yoshisato opened it. He wore plain cotton garments and a somber, aloof expression. The sight of him gave Sano a shock. Despite his tattoos, Sano could see Yanagisawa in him more clearly than ever. It was as if Yoshisato had absorbed some of Yanagisawa's persona.

"Come in," Yoshisato said.

Sano recalled Yanagisawa's last words to him: *This isn't over. We'll meet again someday. Next time I'll win.* Maybe they didn't need to meet again in order for Sano to get his comeuppance. It was a son's duty to avenge his father's death. But Yoshisato gave no hint of aggression. Sano entered the room, which was small, sparsely furnished with a bedroll and a charcoal brazier on the tatami floor, but clean. He heard someone moving around in the chamber on the other side of the wooden partition. Yoshisato faced Sano and waited.

"I'm sorry for your loss." Sano didn't offer the excuse that Yanagisawa had attacked first. Nor did he say he was sorry he'd killed Yanagisawa. That would be a lie, and Yoshisato would know and feel insulted.

Yoshisato accepted Sano's qualified but genuine sympathy with a stoic nod. In the awkward silence, Sano looked around the room and noticed a trunk and a knapsack in the corner and Yoshisato's cloak thrown over them. "Where are you going?"

"Back to Osaka."

"To your gang?"

"Yes. My mother is coming with me." Yoshisato slid open the partition. In the adjacent room Lady Someko knelt by a trunk, folding clothes into it. She looked up at Sano, smiled, and bowed. "It'll be a fresh start for her."

"You don't have to leave Edo," Sano said. "Lord Ienobu is going to pardon everyone who fought in the war against him."

"You mean, you're pardoning us." Yoshisato's eyes glinted with amusement; he was among those who knew what had happened to Lord Ienobu. "Don't worry, I won't tell anybody that you're the real shogun. But I am leaving. It's for the best."

"I came to offer you a position in the regime."

"You don't need to buy me off. You've nothing to fear from me—I won't swear out a vendetta against you. Yanagisawa's death was really his own fault." Bitter sorrow twisted Yoshisato's mouth. "He had a grudge against you, and he just couldn't let it go."

Sano was impressed that Yoshisato had the insight to realize it and not simply blame Sano. "I'm not trying to buy you off." Sano was trying to assuage his guilt about hurting Yoshisato, whom he now respected more than ever. "The regime needs talented, capable men like you."

Yoshisato's thin smile said he saw through Sano's ploy. "I'm honored, but no thanks."

"Please consider it," Sano urged. "Your life as a gang boss is bound to be violent and short."

"And my life at court wouldn't be?" Yoshisato uttered a sarcastic laugh that sounded eerily like Yanagisawa's. "I saw what politics did to my father. They brought out the worst in him. I'm not following in his footsteps."

Sano remembered Lord Ienobu saying that Yoshisato had no stomach for politics. It hadn't been true then, but now Yoshisato had made up his mind and wasn't going to change it. And perhaps he was right: Politics and power could destroy, and Yoshisato might have more in common with Yanagisawa than mannerisms. Blood was blood.

"Let me at least do something for you," Sano said.

"All I want is this: Just leave me alone. I promise not to hurt you. Whatever I do, look the other way."

That was a lot for the boss of a criminal gang to ask, but Sano said, "Very well."

WHEN SANO RETURNED to the Mori estate, Akiko ran ahead of him through the guest quarters, exclaiming joyously, "Papa's back!"

More nervous than when he'd faced the assembly at Edo Castle, Sano entered the chamber where Reiko and Masahiro, and Midori and her children knelt by an oblong wooden box wrapped in white cloth and a table that held smoking incense burners. Sano already knew Hirata was dead; he'd heard it from Marume, whom he'd just visited in the sick ward. The others were silent while Sano stood by the coffin, bowed his head, and said a final, unspoken good-bye to his friend. A sense of peace alleviated Sano's grief. Death was better than living trapped with a ghost inside a paralyzed body. Sano and Hirata had already said everything that was necessary. Sano raised his head; his gaze met Reiko's.

Her eyes reflected his uncertainty and discomposure. Sano was hardly aware of walking with her to their chamber; everyone else seemed to recede from them while their surroundings changed as in a theater set moved by hidden stagehands. Sano spoke first rather than let her say what he dreaded hearing—now that the crisis was over, she was going to leave him. As he explained what had happened at Edo Castle, his gaze moved between her impassive face and her bandaged arm, which symbolized all the ways in which he'd brought her pain.·

Why had she defended him against Yanagisawa? Surely not because she cared about him, but because he was her children's father, because of duty toward him, not love.

When he was finished, Reiko spoke in a toneless voice. "You and your honor won."

She seemed dismayed rather than gladdened by his reversal of fortune. She saw his victory as a victory over her. That was how she thought he saw it. But nothing could have been farther from how he really did.

His honor had stood up to every test. By faithfully serving it, he'd gained power beyond imagination. But the spoils of his victory were devalued by what he'd lost—the woman he loved in spite of all their differences, the wife who'd risked her own life to save his. He felt as defeated as if he, not Yanagisawa, had been killed in their fight. The dam that contained his emotions crumbled. Anguish flooded Sano. He wished he had been killed, rather than live without Reiko. All he could do was give her what she wanted, what he owed her after ignoring her wishes for so long.

"I'm moving back to Edo Castle. If you don't want to come with me—if you don't want to be my wife anymore . . ." Sano blinked and swallowed; he was going to cry. But although it devastated him, he would let Reiko go. "I'll give you a divorce. Pick a place you'd like to live, and I'll build you a house there and support you." Sano's heart broke as he thought of the children. He couldn't take Akiko from her mother, and Masahiro surely wanted to be free of his father's demands. "Masahiro and Akiko can live with you. None of you will ever have to see me again."

Reiko stared as if at a tornado whirling toward her. Sano was too distraught to analyze her reaction. Tears ran down his face; sobs heaved his chest. He was as good as shogun, and he must pay the price. "You'll never again have to take second place to my honor."

Honor was all he would have when his family was gone.

"Is that what you think I want?" Reiko cried. Horror was written so clearly on her face that Sano couldn't miss it. "No, that's what *you* want— never to see me again!" She was crying, too. "It was too much to hope for, that you would still love me after I've criticized and blamed you. Why should you, just because I still love you?" Her expression scorned her own hope. "Don't worry—I won't fight you this time." She held her head high, wiped her streaming eyes on her sleeve, and gathered her pride around her like a torn cloak. "I'll go."

"What?" Sano said. "No! That's not what I want!"

Confused and astounded, they stared at each other. Reiko said, "Do you mean—" and Sano said, "I want you with me. Because I love you. I want us to start over." She gasped, smiling through her tears, and nodded. Overjoyed that she still wanted to be with him, astonished that love had survived their ordeals, he felt as if he had the world at his command.

Sano slowly moved toward Reiko; she slowly moved toward him. Her eyes reflected his caution as they came close. After years of avoided contact, they'd forgotten how to be lovers, but their bodies remembered. Reiko's waist fitted into the curve of Sano's arm. His cheek rested against her hair, her cheek on its familiar place against his heart. They

338

were careful not to touch the wound on her arm, his palm. Eyes closed, they wept as they held each other.

It was a line crossed that Sano had thought they would never be able to cross.

As happy as he was that they could make a fresh start, Sano didn't want it founded on the illusion that love erased everything that had kept them apart. He had to be brutally honest with Reiko, with himself. He sniffled, cleared his throat, then said, "I have to tell you: There are people who don't want me controlling the regime. I can't promise you and the children safety or prosperity or peace."

"It doesn't matter," Reiko said with quiet passion. "When I saw you losing the fight with Yanagisawa . . . well, I didn't try to save you from him because I wanted to be free of you. We belong together."

Sano was glad to learn that, but he said, "Before you decide whether you really want to be with me, hear this: If I had it all to do over again, I would do it the same way." Coming close to losing what he held dearest changed a man, but not entirely. Reiko was motionless, quiet, listening. "If you stay with me, I promise to do the best by you and the children that I can. But"—voicing the truth that would never change, he faltered over words whose solemn formality didn't come naturally to him—"I'm just as married to honor as I am to you."

Reiko tilted up her head to look at him. "I wouldn't want you any other way." Her smile was serene with a hint of the mischief he hadn't seen in years. "Before you decide whether you really want me, hear this: If I ever think you're doing something wrong, I will tell you."

Her warning meant more than that she would never be a conventional wife; she would always put their family ahead of honor and duty. A revelation during a life-and-death crisis hadn't changed her entirely, and Sano was glad. He wouldn't want her any other way. He laughed with exhilarated humor. "Fair enough."

They were both laughing now, tearfully, their emotions spent. They both knew that life in the inner circle of the new shogun's court wouldn't be easy, but being together on any terms was better than what had almost happened—losing each other forever.

Akiko rushed into the room, breathless with excitement. "Masahiro and Taeko have something to tell you!"

MASAHIRO AND TAEKO came in, solemn and frightened. Midori trailed them, wringing her hands under her sleeves. Reiko stepped away from Sano, reluctant to leave the newfound warmth of his embrace. Her gaze flew to Masahiro's and Taeko's clasped hands.

"We're getting married," Masahiro announced.

It was so soon after Kikuko's death, but Reiko was glad to see him and Taeko reunited. She wouldn't deny them the mutual comfort of their love. They deserved it, after Masahiro's first brief marriage that had been forced on them, that had ended so disastrously.

"I think that's a wonderful idea," she said.

Masahiro and Taeko smiled, but they knew that Reiko's opinion wasn't the one that counted. They turned anxiously to Sano. His expression was sad, fond, and regretful.

"Please let them!" Midori begged, extending her clasped hands to Sano. Frantic to secure her daughter's happiness, she called in the favor that his family owed hers. "Taeko's father sacrificed his life for you. That ought to make her good enough to marry your son even though she can't bring you a big dowry or important connections!"

"I did what you wanted last time," Masahiro said. "This time I'm going to marry Taeko and nobody else."

This was the first test of Sano's promise to do his best by the children. Reiko held her breath, afraid he didn't understand, wouldn't pass the test. Then he said mildly, "I think it's a wonderful idea, too. In fact, I was going to suggest it." He added with a wry smile, "I'm sure the shogun won't have any objections, either."

Now that he was in control of the shogun and the government, he could afford the risk of letting his son marry for love and foregoing a politically advantageous match. Reiko exhaled and Midori wept with relief. Masahiro and Taeko laughed and jumped up and down.

"The wedding has to be soon," Masahiro said. "Taeko is going to have a baby."

Reiko's breath caught. She and Sano gaped at Masahiro, who looked proud and sheepish, and at Taeko, who blushed, clasped her stomach, and looked at the floor. They turned to Midori and Akiko, who beamed— they'd already been told. Sano and Reiko looked at each other, not really surprised by the news of the pregnancy but astonished to realize they were going to be grandparents.

"She's so young, she won't know what to do with a baby," Midori said, putting her arm around Taeko, "but that's all right." She seemed at peace with Hirata's death and ready to forgive Sano and his family for the sake of her daughter. "I'm going to live with her and Masahiro and help her take care of it. She'll learn."

The thought of a baby evoked the familiar surge of emotions in Reiko, but the tears that fell were tears of joy that diluted her sorrow for the baby she'd lost. She felt Akiko tug her hand, and knew that the vestige of emptiness inside her would soon be filled by her first grandchild.

"I have news, too," Sano said. "Masahiro is the shogun's new chief investigator. Which means he'll not only have a good stipend, but he and his new family can live in our old estate inside Edo Castle."

Everyone expressed delight, including Reiko, but she was alarmed by the thought of her son taking on such an important, responsible position. "But he's so young and inexperienced."

"I can handle it, Mother," Masahiro said, brashly confident. Taeko beheld him with love, pride, and trust.

"He'll have you and me to advise him and Detective Marume as his assistant. He'll learn." Sano looked at Reiko; they smiled as they remembered the hard lessons of the past and looked ahead to the challenges of the future.

"We all did," Sano said. "We all will."

Historical Note

SHOGUN TOKUGAWA TSUNAYOSHI died in February 1709. Some sources say he was stabbed by his wife, who wanted to prevent him from making Chamberlain Yanagisawa's son the heir to the dictatorship. Other sources say this story was mere rumor. The official cause of death was measles. His nephew Ienobu became shogun. Ienobu's reign was uneventful. He died in 1712. His five-year-old son became shogun and died in 1716. Tokugawa Yoshimune became shogun and ruled Japan for twenty-nine years. He went down in history as a great, enlightened reformer. Yanagisawa Yoshiyasu died in 1714 at the age of fifty-six. I took the artistic liberty of moving his death up by five years.

Acknowledgments

WRITING MY NOVELS is a solitary endeavor. Publishing the Sano Ichirō mystery series for eighteen books has required the help of too many people to name. I'll do my best to name and thank some of them here.

My parents, Lena and Raymond Joh, who taught me to love reading and value books. My brother, Larry Joh, for know-how and family leadership. My husband, Marty Rowland, for thirty-three years of laughs.

The late George Alec Effinger, my mentor and extraordinary science fiction author, and the writers' workshop he founded. That workshop is where it all started. To my fellow longtime members—John Webre, Mark McCandless, Marian Moore, Andy Fox, and Fritz Ziegler—thanks for the insightful critiques that helped a fledgling author get off the ground.

My first editor, David Rosenthal, who published my first book and started my career. My current editor, Hope Dellon at St. Martin's Press, who kept it going.

The writers's organizations that gave me a community: SOLA (the Southern Louisiana chapter of Romance Writers of America), Mystery Writers of America, and Sisters in Crime. And the Wordsmiths: special thanks to Elora Fink for starting the group and holding it together, and to Candice Proctor and Steve Harris for many spirited discussions.

Garden District Books in New Orleans, where I did my first-ever bookstore signing. Thank you, Britton Trice, for your continued support.

My readers: If not for you, my series couldn't have lasted twenty years. I hope you've enjoyed the adventures of Sano and company and you won't be too sad that this is the end. Many thanks for your loyalty.

Pam Ahearn, did you think I forgot you? No way! You've been the best agent I could have asked for—always there to advise, encourage, and inspire, and to fight on my side. Your belief in Sano, and in me, is the engine that's been powering the series from behind the scenes all this time. I can't thank you enough. We've been together for twenty-one years, and I wish it could be twenty-one more.